AVOIDANCE

AVOIDANCE

CHRIS DAVIES

Matador
9 Priory Business Park,
Wistow Road, Kibworth Beauchamp,
Leicestershire. LE8 0RX
Tel: 0116 279 2299
Email: books@troubador.co.uk
Web: www.troubador.co.uk/matador
Twitter: @matadorbooks

ISBN 978 1800462 878

British Library Cataloguing in Publication Data.
A catalogue record for this book is available from the British Library.

Printed and bound in Great Britain by 4edge Limited
Typeset in 12pt Adobe Jenson Pro by Troubador Publishing Ltd, Leicester, UK

Matador is an imprint of Troubador Publishing Ltd

Camille Pissarro (1830-1903), Lordship Lane Station, Dulwich, 1871,
oil on canvas, The Courtauld, London (Samuel Courtauld Trust)

For Kathy

AUTHOR'S NOTE

Many of the characters in this novel are based on people who really existed. I have called them by their real names, because their real lives and their fictional lives are inextricably mixed-up in the book. I've taken considerable liberties in telling their stories but – with a couple of well-deserved exceptions – not at the expense of anyone's good reputation I hope.

PROLOGUE

1906

Dearest Brom

Many thanks for the kind words of congratulation on my betrothal to Frances, old chap. I am indeed a very lucky man, I know that. I've got myself a corker of a girl.

Mind you, she does bring rather more than her fair share of in-laws along with her. Now you might point out that she's stuck with our lot in return but I must in all modesty say that we're pretty easy-going by comparison. It's just five of us for Heaven's sake. Poor old Frances copes with a family roughly the size of a small town, most of whom enjoy nothing better than congregating for loud conversations about absent relatives and boasting of their youngsters' sparkling achievements (you will be interested to know that five year old Sidney is currently making excellent progress in Greek, whilst Gerald/ Erskine/ Petal/Tulip/Marigold and all have got into Eton, Balliol and the Guards, composed an opera, spent the summer in Baden Baden, received a commission, won a prize, fallen off a horse, bought a motorcar and been presented to the King and Queen).

I enclose a jolly photo of the get-together at the family mansion on the day our betrothal was made official. Eleven of us in front of the camera: good old Uncle Reg; two young army men; two young women, Frances herself standing below my left shoulder, next to her clever cousin Rose Fell; five aunts in massive hats, one sporting a pair of giant flowers like headlamps on hers, senior aunt Mary Harriette furiously knitting. And yours truly at the back trying to look like there's nowhere else on earth he'd rather be.

Mustn't forget Aunt Gertrude, hidden for an eternity beneath the camera's focusing cloth from where she kept instructing us to smile, which perhaps explains the slightly strained looks on all our faces. Once this ordeal was finally over, we went inside to receive Mrs Pickersgill-Cunliffe's imperious blessing, in the sad absence of Frances's deceased grandfather and father. Nor was Frances's mother, the notorious Nell, able to join us. She, though, is very much still in the land of the living, which for her happens to be America.

Any number of other aunts and uncles and cousins were also unable to join us on the day, but doubtless I shall have the pleasure of meeting every single one in the goodness of time. Those present were more than enough to be going on with and they were all very keen to discover everything they could about the new boy, plying me throughout luncheon with questions about our family, my education, my motoring habits, and my thoughts on certain liturgical and contemporary issues. I did my very best to answer each one in good spirit, even when they raised their eyebrows and said "oh really?", and "well that is quite an unusual perspective on the matter, I must say" in their loud plummy way.

There you are. You set off on a day like this determined to embrace your new family, opening your mind and your heart to people who will become part of your life for ever. You end the day thinking, Good Lord, what have I let myself in for? I can imagine only too well how hard it must have been for Frances when she first came over, trying to make a good impression and earn their approval. I doubt I shall ever quite succeed in doing that myself but you have to try your best, don't you, for your beloved's sake? Because this is her family, and it's what you do.

Ever your loving brother, Basil

P.S. After luncheon in hushed tones, Frances's cousin Rose gave me the bare bones of their grandfather's unfortunate accident. Pretty strange business, by the sound of it.

PART ONE

1871-1885

1

Nell Pickersgill was just ten years old when her family first moved to the country. The children and their mother were surprised to discover just how very close their new home was to the railway. Just the other side of a long high boundary wall, it couldn't be seen but it could certainly be heard. The floors of the house vibrated whenever fast trains went by and all the windows rattled when the slow ones passed. In their first week there, Nell and her brother Ellis managed to convince five year old Mary Harriette that trains went straight through the house each night, under the stairway and down the long corridor. The next evening her nanny found her screaming in her bedroom, terrified of the approaching dark; her first real panic attack.

In one sense their foolish fiction had a basis in truth, because the London-to-Brighton line did actually run through the site of the old Hooley House, sacrificed by the previous owners to progress and a hefty sum from the railway company. For reasons best known to themselves, those owners had chosen to have their new bigger and better house built as near as possible to the site of the original; something Mrs Pickersgill imagined, and sincerely hoped, they must have come to bitterly regret. Her husband assured her that she would soon pay the trains no mind; he had no idea how wrong he was about that.

The Pickersgills came out to Coulsdon in 1860 to escape London's latest scarlet fever outbreak, which had carried off their six year old son Tom. For a while it remained their only home, Mr Pickersgill travelling most days to his work in the City, often briskly walking the two miles to the station. Their new property suited him very well. Set in 40 acres of rich Surrey farmland, it bordered the bigger estate to the east that belonged to his older brother William, his partner in the family bank. John Pickersgill liked to be lord of his own manor, with its farm, its little cottages for the staff, its greenhouses and stables. The trains never bothered him, so regular you could set your watch by them, he liked to say. They drowned out the rest of the world whenever he tended his beloved rare plants, or retreated to his study to mind his own business.

Nonetheless, as time went on, Mr Pickersgill increasingly felt the urge to escape. His wife Helen carried on producing children at Hooley House at the rate of one per annum, and it was no joy for him to share his home with them all, waking him in the night with their screaming, leaving the nursery during the day, running and shouting through the corridors, bursting in on him, expecting him to get their names right every time. He was not an uncaring father, but it was normal for a man to find children more congenial when you could have proper conversations with them, at times of your own choosing.

Helen didn't object when he announced after a few years that he'd bought another house in London. Hooley became the home where the smaller children were kept and where Mr Pickersgill came for respite from town, before returning there for respite from the smaller children. His wife was always happy to join in him in London during those few months in the year when she wasn't about to have another baby. And as time went on, the older children were allowed to spend time there too, it being the best place for girls to find husbands of good standing. If the family was to keep moving up in the world, it could not afford to languish in the country.

John Pickersgill had recently moved up in the world himself, in receipt at last of a long-expected legacy. It was something his young wife had managed to charm out of his fearsome aunt Cunliffe when they were first married. Pleased by the dear girl's warm admiration for her side of the family, the aunt bequeathed them an extensive property in Yorkshire – on the one strict condition that John, despite already having Cunliffe as his middle name, must do what his parents should have done long ago and include it in his surname as well. He was only too happy to oblige. In fact, he liked the sound of his new name so much that he decided to announce his retirement from the bank and stand for parliament.

When William learnt of the legacy, he proclaimed himself shocked and disappointed to discover that his younger brother had shown so little regard for precedence. John assured him it had certainly not been any of his doing, and he'd never really expected it to come to anything. Contested wills, lost in Chancery, *Bleak House* and all that.

"A bolt out of the blue," John innocently explained to his brother, who agreed that they should not let this unfortunate issue come between them.

Despite his determined efforts, John Cunliffe Pickersgill-Cunliffe began to find it increasingly hard to keep the various elements of his life on track. He lived in fear of the bank suddenly losing its way, especially as relations with his brother continued to be frosty; his wife was pregnant again, although he had presumed her well past such things; his attempt to enter parliament had ended in farce when he won the seat and then humiliatingly lost it to his opponent who'd challenged the result in court; and most recently, his eldest daughter Nell had taken it into her head to accept an offer of marriage from a burly, brooding lieutenant in the Royal Navy by the name of Charlie Hodgkinson, a man quite without prospects.

Mr and Mrs Pickersgill-Cunliffe were obviously far from delighted by this news, but thought it wiser not to forbid an engagement which – having been settled without their knowledge or consent – did not actually constitute an engagement at all. They bided their time, counting on their daughter's impulsive and romantic nature to bring the issue to a painless conclusion soon enough. When her lieutenant sailed off to join the Mediterranean Fleet in late 1871, where he was due to remain for the next two years at least, they warmly encouraged her to lead the normal life of a well-heeled young lady in London society, which Nell was perfectly content to do. But unfortunately she had no intention of jeopardising her sacred ties to Charlie, regardless of any frivolous flirtations she might find herself enjoying in the meantime unless they proved irresistible which, to her parents' growing despair, none did. They could only hope that her betrothed might manage to blot his copybook in some dreadful way whilst in Malta; he seemed the type.

2

alta was hardly the worst of postings for a young officer if he happened to have cash to burn, which poor Charlie definitely did not. When off duty, he spent his daylight hours squeezed into his tiny cabin, whittling model ships and writing to his Nell, and the evenings in the wardroom bar. He was already a seasoned drinker by the time he joined the *Lord Clyde*, and in Malta his drinking rapidly developed beyond the reach of his meagre finances. Such habits tended to sow the seeds of eventual disaster for young officers, but these were not issues to speak of in the bar.

The ship and its crew floated inoffensively in the harbour into 1872, with just the prospect of a few weeks' patrolling the Mediterranean to keep them on their toes. Time passed painlessly enough in the meantime, but the promised joys of Malta had delivered precious little so far, until it was announced that the officers of the *Lord Clyde* were to host an afternoon dance on board at the start of February.

The official aim was to foster good relations with local society and encourage the crew to take some pride in their ship. The possibility of fostering good relations with the local ladies occupied rather more of the officers' attention than the tiresome business of transforming their warship into a ballroom. When the day arrived Captain Bythesea, never keen on such diversions, stood mournfully at the top of the steps, greeting guests whose expectant smiles wilted the moment they stepped down and looked around them.

Charlie stood nearby, quietly watching out for some sweet girl to dance with, only to find himself confronted by a group of fellow officers from the *Lord Warden*, the fleet's flagship and the *Clyde's* more distinguished and seaworthy sister ship. They grinned at the drab decorations and surveyed the still empty dance floor. The youngest of them, a sub-lieutenant by the name of George King-Hall, looked around in exaggerated horror and asked where all the ladies had gone. Charlie assured them that there were certainly many on the way, and promised to find them a few if they didn't know how to do that for themselves. They set off laughing and Charlie was left seething.

He'd abandoned any hope of finding a partner for the first dance when he suddenly became aware of a sparky young face looking up at him. Its owner was small, quick and self-assured, and had come out of nowhere.

"How do Captain!" she said, flashing a winning smile. "Annie. Dance with me?"

"Lieutenant Charles Hodg-," he began, but she'd already charged off towards the main deck. She laughed as he caught up with her, panting and grinning, but the hilarity quickly vanished when they saw the dancers all around them tripping and stumbling, frowning and cursing, the air turning blue.

Annie dug her fingers into Charlie's arm and asked what was going on. He shook his head in despair. "They made a mess of it," he explained. "When they oiled the deck for the dance."

Annie looked at him like he was mad. "And now it's gone sticky," he added helpfully.

"So it has," she muttered, amidst the rising hubbub of grumbling dancers and deep-throated heckles from the watching sailors. "Come on, don't give up!" she called, and they struggled through to the end of the first dance, their shoes clinging to the deck so that it was almost impossible to move in time with the steady thump of the band.

Charlie led her off the dance floor, thanked her stiffly for her company, and offered to return her to her chaperone. She nodded vaguely back at him.

"I came with my sister Lizzie. We're each other's chaperone you might say." She waved towards a small group of women standing and chatting on the other side of the deck and they all waved gaily back, apart from one who just fluttered her fingers and sent a quiet intimate smile in their direction.

"Your sister?" Charlie perked up suddenly. "The lady in green?"

"Yes," said Annie. "The beautiful one."

"And her husband is not with us today?" he asked casually.

"Oh no! Professor Camilleri's no longer with us at all, poor man," she said, her attention already drifting across the ship in search of more interesting possibilities. With a friendly pat on his arm and "such a laugh, eh Charlie?", she shot off to join those still determined to enjoy themselves. He glanced back across the deck, but her sister had disappeared as well.

Over the next few dances the less reserved guests worked out a kind of high stepping and uninhibited style that, in a blur of décolletage, short skirts and flashing legs, brought the afternoon back to life. Charlie eventually caught sight of Annie again, sharing a joke with her sister. With a little mutter of encouragement to himself, he set off towards them but immediately found his way blocked by Commander May, the navigation officer, demanding his attention regarding a matter of some urgency. "Do you think it wise that this nonsense carries on any longer, Mr Hodgkinson?" he asked, gesturing dismissively at the dance floor.

"No sir," Charlie agreed, without hesitation. "Not wise at all."

"Certainly not," said Mr May. "We must not allow our guests to leave with a bad opinion of us."

"Definitely not, sir," said Charlie, his blossoming hopes for the afternoon dashed in an instant.

The band started up again, and a number of the more impetuous types returned to the dance floor, calling out to one another and laughing. The Commander surveyed the scene for a moment more, and strode off to shout something into the bandleader's ear. After the present dance ended, the leader called out "Final dance gentlemen! *Polka schnell* – give it all you've got!", which drew an approving cheer from those still keen to carry on. Annie was last seen wandering to the back of the dance floor in the company of the wretched King-Hall boy, but Charlie's attention was now entirely on her sister, who had rejoined her group of laughing ladies, all of them clearly bent on ending the afternoon in as congenial a way as possible. He wished he could join them.

Many other guests were making their escape by now. The Captain reappeared and was trying his best to send them off in a dignified manner, but few seemed keen to hang around even for that. Charlie presumed there would be repercussions from this afternoon's work.

His thoughts were interrupted by a cracking sound and a small cry from one of the dancers. He turned to see Annie's sister in a heap with one of her shoes in pieces beside her. Her friends helped back to her feet and she limped off the dance floor, grimacing as she tried to squeeze her foot back into her broken shoe. Charlie hurried over to retrieve her lost heel and followed after, catching up as Captain Bythesea was solicitously asking whether there was someone who might see her safely home. With a glance towards Charlie, she explained that she was quite alone, her sister having left already feeling unwell, but that was not a problem at all. Bythesea said he was sure that Lieutenant Hodgkinson would be pleased to assist her back to land, find her driver and make sure that she got safely home.

Charlie, hardly believing his good fortune, helped her very attentively down onto a launch. Once back on shore, it turned out that she didn't actually have a carriage of her own, and a cab was soon found. As he offered her his arm to help her up, she asked him if he could possibly spare just a few minutes to accompany her on the journey home, and it seemed that he could. As the cab moved off, he enquired after her sister, and hoped that she was not too unwell.

"Oh no!" she laughed. "She's in good hands I'm sure."

"I am relieved to hear that, Mrs Camilleri," said Charlie, blushing.

She touched him lightly on the hand and threw him a knowing little smile. "We don't need this formality, do we?" she said. "You can call me Lizzie."

"I'm Charlie," he said.

"I know," she said.

She winced slightly as the cab bounced on over the cobbles; he reached out to steady her, and she looked straight back into his eyes. She told him her ankle seemed to be swelling fast, but did not hurt too much, and with an artless grin apologised for the trouble she had caused. He said that it was he who should apologise on behalf of his shipmates for the accident that had befallen her, and said he would be honoured if she would allow him to repair her broken shoe himself, and have it dispatched to her as soon he possibly could.

"Oh no!" she cried, and Charlie looked briefly crestfallen. Then, in a lower voice, "It would be so much nicer if you could bring it to me in person, if you wouldn't mind terribly."

Charlie could think of nothing he would rather do, and said so.

It was a short enough distance to her home, a quaint old house in a little street close to the Upper Barracca Gardens.

He helped her down from her carriage, and gave her his arm as she hobbled up the steps to her front door. She told him she'd be going nowhere for several days, and he would certainly find her at home. A maid opened the door and looked on, not particularly amazed, as Lizzie removed her broken shoe, handed it to Charlie with a final charming smile, and slipped inside the house.

Charlie was able to fulfil his promise to Lizzie Camilleri a lot sooner than he had dared hope, only a couple of days after sending a whole package of Valentine's Day treats to Nell. He found himself knocking at Mrs Camilleri's door at the ordained time, heart thumping, discreetly wrapped shoe in hand, reassuring himself that he would probably not stay long on this occasion, and need have no cause to feel guilt. The door was opened by Annie, who grinned cheerfully at the sight of him.

"Welcome, Charlie!" she said, taking his hat. "Lizzie's looking forward to seeing you."

She was seated on a wide low chair, her left leg resting on a stool, quite ravishing in a little red jacket and a black dress out of whose large billowing skirt peeked one pink slipper. She apologised for not getting up, and invited him to sit down on a chair close to her. They paused whilst Annie poured Charlie a cup of tea, and then demurely withdrew. Charlie asked Lizzie how her ankle was getting along, and she told him it was on the mend, but still a little bit sore, and lightly waved the whole thing away.

"And tell me Charlie, how is everything on board your magnificent ship?" she asked.

"Excellent," he lied. "Everyone is very busy."

"But you've been allowed leave to come and see me," she said. "I am so fortunate."

Charlie lifted up the bag containing her shoe, and then didn't quite know what to do with it. "As promised, I have – "

" – extremely good of you," she said, without moving to take it. "I mean, to have brought it yourself."

Charlie slowly let the bag back down onto the floor. "My pleasure," he said, looking around the room for some clue as to what to say next. "So, um, have you lived in Malta long, Lizzie?"

"All my life," she said. Her father, an English naval captain, had married her Maltese mother and settled down in Valetta nearly thirty years previously. After they decided to leave for England, Lizzie stayed on, having accepted an offer of marriage from Mr Camilleri, a professor of medicine, a dear gentleman but by no means young any more, whose house this had been. That was twelve years ago, the last nine of which she had lived here as a widow, with a small income, and free as the air. Annie had returned from England to live with her there just a couple of years previously, and they had made a very pleasant life together.

How nice, Charlie said, hoping she wouldn't ask him about his own circumstances. "And what about you?" she asked, smiling easily. "Do tell me about your adventures at sea, Charlie."

"Oh I'm sure you wouldn't want to hear about all that sort of stuff," he said, relieved.

"Well I'm sure I would," she said, laughing. "I love the stories sailors tell."

But at that moment he heard the front door bang shut, and glimpsed Annie disappearing up the street. There was a moment's thoughtful silence, and then Lizzie shifted position and frowned. "Charlie, I am so sorry to ask, but would you be kind enough to move my footstool? My maid is off duty today." With what seemed like a bit of an effort, she raised her leg slightly as he knelt down before her, and gently pulled the stool towards him. Her calf briefly brushed the edge of his large hand as it settled back onto the stool.

"One more thing, if you wouldn't terribly mind," she said.

Still kneeling before her, he earnestly assured her that he would be happy to be of service in any way at all.

"It would help ease the discomfort in my poor ankle very much," she explained, "if you could bear to gently *stroke* it for a short while."

He nodded vigorously, struck dumb.

"You're too kind," she said, and lay her foot onto Charlie's knee. He stared down at it in amazement and began to touch the tender skin around her ankle as lightly as his rough sailor's fingers would allow. He looked up at her. "Is that all right?" he croaked.

"Oh yes," she told him, with an encouraging smile. "Good man, Charlie."

H.M.S. LORD CLYDE – The Illustrated London News. April 1872

The misadventure to this fine ironclad war-ship, on the 14th March, was happily not attended by such disastrous results as might have been feared. The *Lord Clyde*, which forms part of the Mediterranean Squadron, had been sent from Malta to the aid of an English steamer, the *Raby Castle*, aground on the island of Pantellaria. The island is situated between the Tunisian peninsula of the African coast and the south-western shore of Sicily. By some means the *Clyde* herself had got aground. A report of the accident was sent to Malta, and Rear-Admiral Key, in the *Lord Warden*, with a few tugs and lighters, went off immediately to help the *Lord Clyde*. She was eventually got afloat, but was found to have lost her rudder and stern-post, and to have sustained damage in her screw and other machinery. The *Lord Warden* towed her to Malta for the repairs needed.

The buildings of Valetta were golden in the sun and, spread out below them, the tall masts of the British Mediterranean Fleet swayed peacefully over the blue waters of the harbour. A small skiff containing a large bearded oarsman and his two laughing passengers wound its way between the ships, pausing for a few moments at each one in turn.

"This must be George's!" Annie shouted, as they glided into the shadow of an ironclad three-master.

Charlie nodded. "Certainly is," he said. "Perhaps you should climb up and pay him a visit."

She stuck out her tongue and grabbed another champagne bottle from the picnic basket. Lizzie, seated in the back of the boat next to her, gave Charlie an encouraging smile as he rowed them vigorously away from the *Warden*, the sight of which he had come to detest. The *Lord Clyde* was nowhere to be seen on the water, because it was currently propped up in dry dock; out of sight and in disgrace, its viability under assessment, the prognosis not good.

"You know, Charlie, George thinks it was rotten luck, what happened out there," Annie told him. "Not your fault at all. He reckons your boat is the worst one in the Royal Navy. Couldn't sail straight if it was on rails, he says. Isn't that right Charlie?"

"Hush, silly girl," her sister said.

Charlie grunted. "What happened wasn't the ship's fault," he said. "And it wasn't the fault of anyone on it. Just the bloody Navy expecting the impossible, as usual. But no doubt some of us will have to pay the price."

"Not you, surely!" Lizzie cried.

"Don't know," he muttered. "Maybe." Lizzie feared that their little outing was not going as well as she'd hoped; she really shouldn't have let her sister come along. She gave Charlie a long, slow, meaningful look, to let him know that she'd make it up to him later. His face flushed and he returned her look with added intensity.

Annie had no time for their nods and winks. "So Charlie, I trust your lovely fiancée is well. Your Nellie. She must worry about you."

"Oh Annie!" moaned her sister.

"Well it's not a secret, is it? Come on Charlie, tell us all about her. She's an heiress, isn't she?"

"I'm very sorry about my horrible little sister," Lizzie said, and squeezed Charlie's knee. "You know what she's like."

Charlie said nothing as he rowed them over to a quieter patch of water. He shipped his oars and let the skiff float there for a while. "Who can say what the future will bring," he answered eventually, holding his glass out for Annie to refill.

"I bet Nellie can," said Annie.

"That's quite enough," said her sister, firmly. "We're trying to help Charlie recover from his terrible ordeal. The *Clyde* nearly sank. He could've drowned."

"It was George's ship that saved them of course," Annie said proudly. "Though he did say that Charlie was by far the most solid officer on the *Clyde*."

"Did he indeed? Good of him to say so," Charlie said. "I was simply doing my duty."

"You're such an Englishman Charlie!" cried Annie, applauding. "Oh Lizzie, don't you want to marry him yourself? I do think you should. You can't let that Nellie have him."

Charlie gave Lizzie one of his yearning looks, and she feared he was about to seize the moment to embarrass them all dreadfully. She glared furiously at her sister, an unmistakable warning of serious trouble if she did not stop this nonsense immediately.

Annie was having too much fun, and had no intention of doing any such thing. With a beaming smile, she began to extemporise. "Do you realise, Charlie, that this is exactly where, thirty years ago, our father proposed to our mother? Right here! He rowed her out to show her *his* ship, into the middle of Grand Harbour in a little boat exactly like yours. He went down onto one knee, terrifying our mother, and asked

16

this shy young Maltese girl if she would consider marrying a rough English sailor. She burst into tears of joy, and cried YES! and all the sailors in the harbour threw their hats in the air and cheered!"

Lizzie looked at her sister in amazement. Her constant teasing of Charlie was one thing, but this ridiculous story of their parents – more or less complete fabrication – was simply too much. She was about to suggest to Charlie they tip Annie into the harbour when it struck her that his shoulders had slumped and his attention seemed to be drifting.

"Are you all right, poor boy?" she asked, reaching out to touch his brow. "Maybe we should go back now? I can row if you like."

He shook his head, and held out his glass for more champagne. Lizzie frowned. "Is that wise?" She stroked his cheek. "You don't look too good, you know."

"I'm fine," he muttered.

Charlie stretched himself out on their sitting room floor the moment they brought him in. His eyes closed and he plunged instantly into a deep dark sleep.

"He's drunk," said Annie.

"I'm not so sure," said Lizzie, hoping her sister was right but beginning to suspect otherwise.

They didn't know what to do with him, because he was too big to drag upstairs. They put a pillow under his head and covered him with a blanket, and he lay lifeless as a fallen oak tree until morning came. The maid couldn't hold back a little scream when she found him, though he was no stranger there. Lizzie ran downstairs and saw Charlie trying to raise himself off the floor, lost and confused.

"I know what this is," Lizzie began, having seen much the same expression in her late husband's eyes, one awful morning many years ago.

"It's nothing," Charlie muttered. This was how he always felt when he first awoke.

"I am rather afraid," she said softly, looking up at Annie who had arrived by now, "that he might have the Maltese Fever." Annie stared back at her sister, knowing what she'd had gone through all those years ago when the poor Professor came down with the Fever, and never came up again. So no time was wasted in getting Charlie out of the house and over to the military hospital at the Harbour, where Lizzie's worst fears were confirmed and Charlie's happy bachelor days in Valetta were brought to a sudden and miserable close.

The prognosis for Charlie was both good and bad: he would probably not die, but could expect the Maltese Fever, being undulant, to come and go as it pleased for the rest of his life. You'll be fine for months or even years on end, not giving it a thought, the doctor told him, when with no warning at all it will come back and leave you feeling like death and bleak as blazes for a day or two. Lizzie knew the risks, and did not come near him again until the day one month later when he boarded a ship back to England. She had written him many kind and caring letters during those weeks, with all the latest gossip from her sister who sent him lots of kisses. He also received a brief note from Sub-Lieutenant George King-Hall, expressing his condolences on yet more rotten luck. Brought down many a good man, he wrote, has that wretched fever.

Lizzie promised to meet Charlie at the quayside when it was time for him to leave, and he spent the night rehearsing what he would say to her to make sure she would hold him always in her heart. She greeted him warmly, touched his cheek one last time with a gloved hand, and told him to remember his Maltese widow fondly if he must remember her at all.

"It's Nellie who should have this, not I," she said finally, slipping a silver anchor brooch, that he had once bought for her at considerable expense, back into his hand. He looked at her with his yearning eyes and tried to protest, but she gave him one last fond smile, turned and walked away.

The long journey back to England gave Charlie plenty of time to feel sorry for himself. During the first few days at sea, in his still feverish dreams he found himself constantly trying to choose between two women, each of whom he cared for with all his heart: a conundrum that entirely ignored the fact that one of these women had never been a choice that was his to make, whilst the other was the choice he had made long ago and could certainly not afford to unmake now.

As his ship ploughed on towards the cold grey waters of the English Channel, the blue clear Mediterranean and all that went with it a thousand miles behind him now, Charlie's heart began to lighten. He thought increasingly of the future almost within his grasp: appointment to a smart new ship, a decent chance to prove his worth, then marriage to Nell and settling down together in a lovely little cottage by the Solent.

3

"We must talk frankly about your future plans, Nell," her father said, lining his cue ball up on hers. "Now that your intended will soon be back amongst us."

"In what respect Papa?" she asked. With a neat plick! he sent the red ball into a pocket.

"You are a grown woman now Nell. I think it's about time you understand certain ... realities ... of what lies ahead, for you both."

He replaced the red ball, and studied his options. Nell watched him, praying he was not embarking on the kind of conversation one could only, ever, have with a mother.

"Nell, do you actually know what I do for a living?" he asked, delicately striking his cue ball, nudging the red ball back into the pocket.

"Well of course Papa. You're a banker."

"But what do you understand by that?" he asked. "I mean to say, do you happen to know what being a banker involves?" Once more, he replaced the red ball.

"You look after people's money, you keep it safe for them," she ventured bravely.

He looked at her with wry amusement. "Well indeed I do," he said. "But not really by locking it up for them. Do you think that would get me all that I need if I am to pay for everything

20

we have, for our houses and carriages and horses and servants, for the cost of all you girls?"

Presumably not.

"No, indeed." He thwacked his cue ball forcefully, so that it jumped off the table.

"My turn," said Nell. She wasted no time in taking her first shot, and fluked a cannon.

"Well done," said her father, impatient to return to the matter in hand. "So, I am sure you know the origins of the bank."

"John Pickersgill and Co was started by great grandfather and then grandfather joined and it became John Pickersgill and Son singular and then when great-grandfather died grandfather took over and then you and Uncle William joined and it became John Pickersgill and Sons plural and when he died you took over, although you became Pickersgill-Cunliffe but Uncle is still just Pickersgill," she recited without taking breath, then skilfully nicked her father's cue ball into the pocket. "And now you have retired, or have you not, because you are still going to work much of the time aren't you?"

"Some of the time," he agreed. "Take your next shot, please."

Nell turned her attention to the red ball, which she sank twice in succession, to her father's growing irritation. "So," he said, with gravity, "perhaps I should explain the ins and outs of our business."

Nell saw a lecture coming on, and deliberately messed up her next shot in order to get her father back to the table, but he was not about to be so easily distracted.

"Our business was founded on large financial investment in crops of great value. Sugar from the West Indies, and the humble cotton plant which, as you know well, is imported from America," he explained. "You do know that, do you not?"

She was quite sure she did.

"Since Uncle William and I took control of Pickersgill and Sons, our interests expanded in many directions. Timber, shipping, railways, land. Although obviously we do not actually *trade* in any of those things ourselves." He looked at her, for some response.

"Obviously not," she agreed.

"By no means. Over many years, we have gained an unparalleled reputation for understanding the market, so that we may guide and enable the finances of those who themselves wish to trade in such commodities between England and the Americas, back and forth."

Nell nodded keenly, hoping some climax was in sight.

"Whilst you need not concern yourself with the details of all this, it is most important that you are aware not only of the high regard in which our company is held but also of the inevitably precarious nature of all business endeavour."

She promised him that she was beginning to understand it all very well now, and it was very interesting.

"I haven't got to where I am going yet," he snapped. He felt far from clear himself about where that might be. "Wait," he said, and tried to focus more calmly on his next shot, unaware of his daughter's silent eye-rolling behind him.

"My point is," he announced, striking Nell's cue ball by mistake, "that however good we are at our jobs – and we are extremely good – however good we are – things may sometimes go wrong – large sums of money can be made by one moment of brilliance – and equally suddenly can be lost through no fault of ours whatsoever. Through a change in the weather several thousands of miles away. Through a betrayal of trust, a broken contract, a falling out between nations, an unforeseen invention, the vagaries of fashion." He stood back from the table and lowered his voice. "For example, your grandfather was actually forced by our own Government to give up vital business assets in Trinidad. By law."

"Why would they want to do that?" Nell asked, indignant.

"Politics," said her father. "Politics. He nearly lost everything at the time. It became impossible to run his plantations, without those assets."

Nell had no idea what such a thing as an asset might be, and no desire to find out. But her father was not finished.

"I refer of course to the men and women who worked the plantations," he explained. "Indentured labourers, strictly speaking. Men and women who required costly housing, feeding and instruction, for which they were sometimes far from grateful I might add. Having them removed from us like that might well have destroyed the family business, but your grandfather was a determined man. He eventually managed to secure compensation from the Government. Reasonably generous, as it turned out." He paused, in order to find his way again, and added with great solemnity, "But it could so easily have ended otherwise."

Nell tried to look equally solemn.

"I can see that I am alarming you," he observed, quite inaccurately, given that she perceived no connection between his words and her life. "That is, I'm afraid, my intention."

"Sorry?" she said, after the meaningful pause had gone on long enough.

"We cannot, Nell, make the mistake of taking our own continued prosperity for granted. It may not always be ... granted."

"Are you saying," she asked, catching his drift, finally, "that *we* shall be poor one day?"

"No, not that exactly," he said. "But there could come a time when we have to be – more careful perhaps I should say – less expansive in how we live than we have been in the past."

"No longer live here, or the London house?" she asked, suddenly appalled at the thought.

"Well Nell, you are planning to have your own home before too long, are you not?" he pointed out. And then, having so fortuitously stumbled on the real matter at hand, continued "the thing is Nell – "

Nell hated sentences that began like that. The thing seldom turned out to be a nice one.

" – the thing is, you must not make unrealistic assumptions about your marriage settlement. That is all I am saying."

"ALL?" she screamed. "What exactly *are* you trying to say Papa?"

This was the very last kind of conversation he would have chosen to have with Nell, if it had been left up to him. It had certainly not been his idea to talk about his financial affairs with her, even if it was a necessary tactic. He had always avoided talking to his children about business. He wished his daughters to marry well, and his sons to distinguish themselves in fields far removed from business and trade: the military perhaps, or gentlemen farmers, men of independent means, respectable and comfortable in the best society.

"Your mother is keen that you should embark upon marriage with Lieutenant Hodgkinson under no illusions," he said, aware that he was rather weaselling out of this. "We are *both* keen, I should say, that you understand, *should* you continue on this path, which you are under *no* obligation to do I might add, we are most keen that you understand that there will *not* be unlimited funds available to support you in what at this stage, I must say, seems to be a somewhat unwarranted venture. Given Charlie's prospects at this moment."

He spoke those last words to a disappearing Nell as she strode out the door, slamming it behind her to provide a reasonably satisfying punctuation to these hateful sentiments. End of match.

from Mary Harriette's Diary

August 15th 1872

Poor Nell has been in a dreadful state of excitement all today in expectation of Mr Hodgkinson's advent. About half
past 5 he arrived; Nell hoped to have him all to herself whilst
we were at tea, but Alice had been peeping over the stairs
and witnessed the meeting. He looks much better than we
expected, but his hair and beard are quite golden instead of
dark brown and red. His hair is very thin at present and looks
more like the down on a chicken's back than anything. Just
now he is talking to Papa in the dining room, I only hope he
won't be captured for billiards afterwards.

August 17th

This afternoon I have been sitting in the orchard with Mr
Hodgkinson and Nell, but they took little notice of me. After
tea was ready this afternoon I came to fetch them from the
library and caught them tenderly embracing; Mr Hodgkinson
got so red when he saw me. Nell proudly showed me the
charming little brooch, shaped like an anchor, that Charlie
had brought all the way back from Malta for her, and had just
given her.

August 30th

I dined with Papa and Mamma yesterday and they talked in
a most depressing way about Nell's prospects and gave me
solemn warnings not to do likewise.

December 4th

I had a long letter this morning from Nell. She has discovered
that Charlie is in debt and they are debating whether they
ought to tell Papa, but she cannot make out the rights of the

story as they are all so mysterious. However, Charlie is going there on Friday and hopes matters will be set right.

February 5th 1873

I played billiards with Papa for an hour after lunch while he smoked. Mother is coming home today we hope; Papa wasn't very well yesterday so perhaps it was just as well she didn't come last evening. Even this morning he was cross with Nell for forgetting he could not eat sausages.

February 14th

This morning of course there were lots of valentines for everyone except me; I never have any.

February 17th

Charlie arrived on Saturday. He and Nell both went up together to the seventh heaven whence they have not yet returned. He has managed to gain an appointment to the naval base at Sheerness, which pleases Nell very much.

July 8th

Last night Papa brought me a lovely gold locket, he is so good to me. He told Mother that as I am not pretty, not such a favourite as the others and as my godmothers don't often give me things, he must make up the deficiency.

August 22nd

I had a long letter from my dear Mother this morning warning me against falling in love with the wrong person, or marrying anyone without loving them because they were rich. I wish she hadn't told me that last, for I always meant to marry the first eligible gentleman I could get and I shouldn't like to if Mother disapproved so strongly.

September 22nd

Ellis came home Saturday evening and very glad we are for a sad misfortune has fallen on us. This morning Papa set off as usual for town and as he was crossing the railway line to where he gets in he ran against a train which knocked him down. They sent him at once by his own desire up to Guy's Hospital where he now is. Ellis and Mother have gone to him and Dr Holman also I am glad to say. They are afraid that one of his legs may have to come off.

***

The clock was running down for Papa. It was 12 days since his terrible accident, and on this Saturday evening the older children were at Hooley House having tea with Auntie, who was living with them for the time being. As they had every day, the older ones – Nell, Mary Harriette and Evelyn – discussed the latest bulletins, the fact that their father's chances of recovery were very remote, and wished for a peaceful and timely ending.

"I fear for dear Mother's health, the longer this awful business goes on," said Mary Harriette, and the others murmured regretful assent.

"Poor Papa," said Nell, "there is clearly no further help for him in this life."

Maggie, the youngest present, cried out in shock. She and Gertrude had been permitted only that day to join the older ones for tea, and both were appalled by the fatalistic turn that conversation had taken over recent days.

Ellis arrived at that moment, a little late, checking the time on the gold hunter watch that his father had already passed on to him. Mary Harriette felt a fierce urge to tear it from his hand, and scream at him to wait just a little longer surely to God, but said nothing. He looked askance at the younger girls' presence, but carried on regardless with his latest bulletin.

"There is little improvement," he said, importantly. He informed them that their father now recognised people only a few minutes at a time. "There is talk of removing the other leg," he added, "as an inevitability, even though that might very well prove to be more than he can take any more."

"Then why – " asked Gertrude, horrified.

" – because not to do so would be irresponsible," Ellis explained. "There is no choice."

Nell put her arm around a quietly sobbing Gertrude, whilst the maid brought in cake and left, rapidly.

"As you know," Ellis announced, "Father signed his will yesterday, which was a source of great contentment to him."

"What does that mean?" Gertrude asked, alarmed.

"It means that his affairs are now in order," explained Ellis. "That is a blessing."

"Is Father really going to die soon?" asked Maggie, indifferent to the slice of cake she was handed.

"Well he might well, yes dear," said Auntie. "We must be brave and accept God's will."

After a few more minutes of struggling unhappily with their tea, Auntie shepherded the two younger ones off to the nursery, leaving the others to talk more freely.

"What do you think it will mean for us all, Ellis, should Father sadly die?" asked Mary Harriette.

He frowned. "Mother says that the houses will certainly have to be sold very quickly, as they are part of Father's estate." This prospect had been speculated on every evening since the accident. "But Father was fully confident when signing the will that our lives will go on as before and that we will all receive our due settlement from his estate. Our circumstances shall certainly not change for the worse."

"What will happen to Father's business interests?" asked Evelyn.

Nell answered. "I think Father had retired, hadn't he? And

now everything is in the control of Uncle William. None of us will be involved in the business, will we Ellis?"

He concurred.

"But I presume you will take responsibility for the family interests?" asked Nell, disingenuously.

"I shall of course," he said, looking at Nell suspiciously. "That goes without saying."

"Hmmm," said Nell, and Mary Harriette threw a conspiratorial glance at Evelyn. All three sisters knew perfectly well who would really be in charge. And if Ellis hadn't yet grasped the fact, he soon would: this house was in the hands of the women, Mamma and her lieutenants; the men were mere decoration now.

Ellis was not so easily undermined. "But I suppose," he said, as if the thought had just struck him, "there is bound to be considerable significance in this for all of you."

The smiles froze on their faces.

"I mean, with respect to our Mother," he said. "Auntie is a highly valued member of the household, of course, but it'll be you girls to whom Mother must turn for support in the long run."

"The long run," echoed Evelyn. "What are you saying?"

"It is only reasonable to expect," he said, "that a mother can depend upon her daughters, especially as she grows older, for the remainder of her life. Nothing less, I would imagine."

A longer silence.

"Wouldn't you agree?" he said.

Nell cast her eyes downwards, discounting herself from the scene, whilst Mary Harriette and Evelyn looked at him in horror, suddenly and without warning confronted with the prospect of enforced spinsterhood. It is far from easy, when you are as young as they still were, to accept the reality of your whole life, all your hopes and foolish dreams, being settled in a single moment.

"Well, I daresay we shall see about that," said Mary Harriette eventually.

Evelyn nodded vigorously. Nell, six years older and fully committed to the prospect of escape, remained silent. She knew, and her sisters didn't doubt, that she hadn't the slightest intention of being deflected from marriage to Charlie, and freedom.

Auntie returned. "Time for prayers," she said.

DEATH OF PROMINENT BANKER. *The Morning Post.* October 1873
Yesterday an enquiry was held at Guy's Hospital into the circumstances attending the death of Mr John Cunliffe Pickersgill-Cunliffe, who had been knocked down by an express train on a level crossing at Caterham Junction, on the London, Brighton and South Coast Railway.

There were two trains passing at the time of the accident – an unscheduled excursion train on its way up to London and a passenger express going down to Hastings. It was the latter train that struck the victim.

Driver Frank Constable had time to see Mr Pickersgill-Cunliffe, an umbrella under his left arm and a newspaper in his right hand, emerge from behind the signal box at the end of the platform and start across the level crossing to the opposite platform. The victim appeared to be looking at the ground, unaware of the Hastings train approaching on the far line, and walked straight into it. Driver Constable believed that Pickersgill-Cunliffe ricocheted off the driving wheel of his engine, but subsequently it was understood to be the step of the engine that hit him, smashing his legs and throwing him into the air.

He seemed not to have been paying attention, or possibly he was distracted, or possibly – it was ventured – had no care for his own safety. In any event, it is believed that he was crossing the line not to catch a train, but in order to sit and read his newspaper on the down platform, where the station's only bench is to be found.

Mr Pickersgill-Cunliffe had been going back and forth across the tracks at Caterham Junction – like every regular passenger – for many years, and would presumably have known that the Hastings express came through at this time every day. It can only be presumed that he had been momentarily blinded to the imminence of that train on the far line by the unexpected arrival of the first on the near. At any rate, his mind entirely failed to alert him to the rushing express that was upon him. Mr Pickersgill-Cunliffe later had no recollection of what happened, the force of the event appears to have overwhelmed his mental functions.

It took a further mile for Mr Constable to stop the Hastings express, which was estimated to be travelling at 40 miles per hour, or even somewhat more.

Mr Pickersgill-Cunliffe's clarity of mind immediately following the accident was remarkable. After the train had passed, "witness found gentleman on the ground, his clothes very much torn". He was, witness explained, perfectly sensible, and in reply to the question whether he should be taken to the hospital, said yes. He further said, "My left leg is broken, if not my right; I shall be sure to lose it, if not my life." He insisted on being taken by train to London Bridge, and had his own doctor summoned to attend him at Guy's Hospital. The deceased was 54 years of age, and had retired from his role as the head of a large international banking firm just a few years previously.

The jury, after a brief deliberation, returned the following verdict "That the deceased died from injuries received on the railway at Caterham Junction." They appended to their verdict a recommendation that steps should be taken to prevent persons cross over the railway at this place, in consequence of the great number of trains constantly passing and repassing.

4

Around two in the morning, the Commander of the Sheerness Dockyard, Captain Cork, was awoken by Chief Petty Officer McLaren to be informed that Lieutenant Hodgkinson, currently the Officer of the Watch, had not been seen or heard from since shortly after midnight. A small search party consisting of the Captain himself accompanied by Executive Officer Andrews and Chief Petty Officer McLaren was immediately convened. After they had checked various key locations across the Dockyard and behind the Barracks, calling out continuously for the Lieutenant, he was finally discovered in his own quarters, slumped in an armchair, loudly snoring, his uniform in disarray, and smelling strongly of alcohol.

On being robustly challenged by CPO McClaren, who had to shake his shoulders firmly in order to awaken him, Hodgkinson suddenly sat upright, stared wildly all about him, and attempted to repulse McClaren in a brief struggle, before being firmly subdued and held in place by force.

Captain Cork then asked Lieutenant Hodgkinson if he was conscious of the fact that he had been apprehended asleep in a dishevelled and drunken state whilst Officer of the Watch, and that this obviously constituted a major dereliction of his duty.

The Captain and Executive Officer both recalled that Hodgkinson, on hearing this and apparently in a state of

32

some confusion, shouted "The **** it is!" and "Get the **** out of my room you bunch of *******s!", or words to that effect. McLaren was once more obliged to subdue Lieutenant Hodgkinson until he regained composure sufficiently to account for his actions. Hodgkinson, after a period of agitated reflection, finally claimed that he was by no means drunk but rather, shortly after the start of the middle watch, had been taken by a severe recurrence of the Maltese fever, the chief symptom of which was a sudden overwhelming desire for sleep. The Lieutenant explained that on realising what was happening to him he had, as previously advised by his doctor, returned immediately to his quarters to take a restorative glass of brandy, but unfortunately this failed to forestall the urge to sleep. He was confident that he had actually been asleep only very briefly before being discovered.

The Executive Officer informed Hodgkinson that his proffered excuse was duly noted, and may be cited in any future Court Martial. Captain Cork informed Hodgkinson that he should consider himself confined to his quarters until further notice. Chief Petty Officer McLaren would place a guard outside his door to ensure that this was the case. The Captain also expressed his opinion that the Lieutenant should prepare himself for an inevitable and ignominious conclusion to his naval career as the consequence of this most distasteful episode.

Charlie slept until 10 the next morning, when Executive Officer Andrews, accompanied by a scowling officer of the guard, burst into his bedroom and, with little ceremony, loudly informed him that he was to vacate his quarters, and leave Sheerness for good by midday.

"May I know what action is to be taken against me?" Charlie asked, feeling the horror of the night before in his throat as soon as he tried to speak.

"You may not," snapped Andrews. "That is still to be determined. All that I can tell you is that you are no longer welcome here. Your future will be decided by others." And off he marched, together with his fearsome companion. Charlie slid out of bed, and began a slow painful process of shaving, dressing and making himself presentable. He had had frequent reasons for low spirits during his career so far, but nothing quite so bleak as this moment. He had no idea what to do next, nor how he could bear to relate what had happened to him to those who most needed to know. At least he was escaping this miserable apology for a posting a good deal sooner than he'd expected. He was sorry, though, that he was going to leave without getting to say goodbye to his pals there, with whom he'd spent some pretty lively evenings.

Throughout his naval career, Charlie had usually been considered a good-natured fellow by his brother officers, dependable in a crisis but not the kind to show his shipmates up. Given the lack of urgency and stimulation that pervaded most working days at Sheerness, the gatherings in the mess had proved, on a few occasions at least, to be the best thing about his time there. Just as he was wondering whether he should try to leave some kind of farewell message for his pals, he heard his name being called outside. He opened the door and looked out uneasily, expecting to find a guard coming to take him away, but instead saw a fellow Lieutenant, Walter Graham, standing there.

"How're you doin', old chap?" Walter asked, concerned.

"Not so good, Walt," he muttered.

"Listen, old fellow. We've all heard what's been going on, and it sounds damned harsh. Very damned harsh. And you with the fever again I understand?"

Charlie grunted. "I believe so," he said, avoiding his friend's kindly gaze.

"All that on top of a fine old time in the mess, I must say, Charlie boy. You must feel like death."

Charlie nodded, and wondered whether he should admit the truth. "Listen," he began. "It wasn't really – "

"Don't matter what it was, anyway, old fellow," Walter interrupted. "What's done is done, could've happened to any one of us, just sorry that it had to be you." He reached and clasped Charlie's arm for a moment. "Simply wanted you to know we're all very sorry. All the chaps in the mess. Really sorry. Going to miss you there."

The two men stared at each other in a regretful kind of way for a few moments more, then Walter gave Charlie an odd embarrassed half salute, span on his heels and marched off, arms swinging.

Everyone knew what had happened by that evening. The news travelled at the start of the day via formal report from Captain Cork to the Admiralty in London, seeking advice on the best way forward, and making it clear that he intended to send Charlie away from Sheerness that morning. From there garbled reports of the events of the previous night spread at extraordinary speed to Charlie's father, from him to Charlie's sister, from her to his fiancée in one direction and to his mother in the other, and along the way to everyone else who might possibly be interested, all before Charlie's train had even left Sheerness. When he arrived in London, he really had no idea of where he would go or who he should see. He could not face the prospect of returning home to Havant to his mother just yet, or the prospect of explaining himself to Nell.

But his father was a different matter. Much as the thought of the old Captain's inevitable disappointment tortured him, he knew that his father's unfailing kindness would ease his own agony, and perhaps he might actually be able to find some way of keeping him in the Navy, for instance by drawing yet again on the kind patronage of his old shipmate Admiral Farquhar, who also happened to be Charlie's godfather.

Because if those efforts failed, Charlie knew that he must immediately give Nell her freedom, and begin his life again entirely from scratch, which was a reality he could not begin to contemplate just then.

Once in London, Charlie made straight for the City, and the lane off Fenchurch Street where his father kept a tiny flat – just around the corner from the Worshipful Company of Ironmongers whose Master he was, an honour bestowed in recognition of a life-time's service in the Royal Navy. Charlie had once imagined such a future for himself, but that vision had steadily faded away over the course of the previous twelve months, and then the previous twenty-four hours knocked all ambition on the head once and for all. The caretaker let Charlie into his father's quarters, to wait uncomfortably for his return. He dozed in an armchair until his father returned and woke him with a gentle squeeze to his shoulder.

"What is there in which a person of Mr Hodgkinson's talent is likely to succeed?" Helen Pickersgill-Cunliffe archly inquired a week or two later, of her oldest daughter who had just returned from a fraught few days with Charlie and his family.

"What is there *what*?" Nell moaned. "Are you mocking him?"

"I certainly am," said her mother. "Your fiancé is, without the slightest doubt, the most hapless man I have ever known. Unless you have discovered some as yet unrecognised talent on his part."

"It's so unfair," said Nell, trying to instil a positive spirit into what was clearly not intended to be a pleasant chat. "The most dreadful bad luck for poor Charlie. He did nothing very wrong."

"Certainly nothing to do with luck of any kind. Wilful stupidity I would say, or simply a bout of insanity, I suppose, if you want to be generous."

"Who knows the truth of it, Mamma," Nell said, quietly.

"I think that when it's been decided that a person is to be in trouble, then everything has to be made to seem black and white. Give a dog a bad name – "

"– and he may as well jump overboard," said her mother, keenly. "Indeed."

Nell pressed on regardless. "Charlie didn't think he was asleep at *all* when they found him."

Her mother sighed. She couldn't abide any of this. Her life had turned unrelievedly grim by the time the old year ended. Most dreadful of all, her daughter Maggie had died at the end of November, only a few weeks after her husband. Caught a cold, wouldn't shake it off, got weaker and weaker, died. Not quite thirteen. Over the previous twenty odd years of her marriage and motherhood, Helen had already lost two children – a baby girl who had lasted barely a month, and dear Thomas who'd died of the fever – and she had prayed every night not ever to see another child die; but it turned out that God had other plans for her.

Trying to care about the problems of Nell and her wretched fiancé was an increasingly intolerable effort after all that. But now she had no choice: this latest disaster threatened far more than Nell's future; it was a stain upon the reputation of the whole family. God knows what her husband would have said about it. He would have put an end to any further talk of marriage, that was for sure. But everything was different now, and all Helen asked was that Nell and Charlie did nothing wild or stupid for as long as it took to make a wedding possible, and presented her with no further reasons for withholding her permission. Nell had stuck with Charlie through it all and, appalled as she was by the foolishness of her daughter in doing so, Helen wanted nothing so much as to get this particular daughter off her hands.

"So it appears no ship was willing to take Charlie, despite all his father's valiant efforts," Mrs Pickersgill-Cunliffe said, getting to the matter in hand. "Not even the Admiral could get the Navy to change its mind?"

"We'd been hopeful, but in the end it was not to be," said Nell.

"And now he must resign the Navy," said her mother.

"He's already resigned. Well, retired actually. On a Lieutenant's pension," Nell added. "So that's very good. And there's to be no court martial, that's all finished with now that he's retired."

Not so hapless after all, thought her mother.

"But," Nell continued, "I think we have a plan."

Her mother sighed.

"There's this ex-army gentleman called Captain Buxton who heard of Charlie's plight and is keen to meet him. To meet both of us, to make a proposal apparently. An exciting venture, that will suit Charlie's many talents, actually, very well."

"And where would this be?" asked her mother.

"Brighton," said Nell.

"What do you mean, *Brighton*? There can no venture in *Brighton*."

"No no," Nell said, flustered. "I mean the meeting with the gentleman will be in Brighton. The venture is in America. Somewhere that rice is grown. No, not rice, cotton. Somewhere that cotton is grown. Captain Buxton made his fortune there and he wants Charlie to take his place."

Mrs Pickersgill-Cunliffe snorted, but the voice inside her head threw a small prayer of thanks upwards to Heaven. She stared at Nell without speaking for a few moments, torn between scorn and self-interest. "And Mr Hodgkinson's Navy pension will pay for all this, will it?" she asked, eventually.

Nell took a deep breath. "Well I thought it might be a good way of investing my inheritance from Papa – everyone says there will be considerable profits to be made. I am sure Papa would have approved." Another long silence. "Don't you think?"

"I think Papa would have known to take considerable care before deciding on the wisdom of any investment," said her mother, swatting aside this flimsy effort at securing her approval. "I think you should be very careful before agreeing to anything. You must take Mary Harriette along with you to meet this man."

"Oh no!" cried Nell. "Why on earth – "

"Because she is far more sensible than Charlie. Or you, for that matter." Nell flushed, fighting down the urge to argue. "But," she continued, balancing her distaste for her future son-in-law against a deeper pragmatism, "I do not entirely think it wrong of you to consider such possibilities, Nell. You must have realistic plans for the future, if you are to prosper in your marriage –"

"– then you do accept that we are to marry?!" Nell cried out, excited.

"– if you are to prosper in your marriage, *if* that should ever take place. Although it seems to me that every day brings fresh reasons why that would be the worst thing you could possibly do with your life."

Without pausing for a reply, Helen Pickersgill-Cunliffe afforded her daughter a blistering reminder, as if she needed reminding, of Charlie's well documented problems with money, drink and luck. "Things go wrong for your Lieutenant," she said. "And then he manages to make them go even worse." She found herself heading in a direction that she had not intended, but a wave of indignation carried her onwards. "Can you truly believe that things will work out any better in the future, given all we know of this young man? *And*," she added, by way of clinching the case, "how could you possibly consider exposing your future children to the vagaries of his bad fortune, and complete lack of self-control?"

Nell began to panic. It was hardly the first time her mother had spoken like this, but it was the nastiest. Wisdom said restraint, but emotion said otherwise.

"It is too late for that, Mamma, far too late!"

It was her mother's turn to feel alarmed. "What on earth are you saying Nell?" Silence. "Is there something you must tell me?"

"Charlie and I are, to all intents and purposes, already married," Nell cried, going for bust and then, seeing her mother's jaw begin to tighten and grind dangerously, retreated fast. "No, no, Mamma! I only mean to say, in terms of the … reciprocal intensity of our affections … our sense of ease with another. That our lives belong together, that's all I am saying. I love him Mamma, that's all."

Mrs Pickersgill-Cunliffe ignored her daughter's tearful appeal, and forced herself to concentrate on the thing that would bring her something approaching tranquillity in the long-run. And that thing unquestionably involved Nell leaving her in peace for ever; America would do very nicely.

"Well," she said, "perhaps it could be for the best."

Nell tried to subdue her amazement and any indication of triumph, and nodded back with all the humility she could muster.

"But you must understand, Nell, that this will come with very tight strings attached. Do you understand what I am saying, Nell? Do you? When you do receive your money it will be under the most severe conditions. You must not be allowed to fritter it away on the first hare-brained enterprise your husband comes up with. You must keep me fully informed of what this gentleman from Brighton is proposing, and I will only give you my final judgement on the matter when I have had sufficient time for the most careful consideration."

Nell nodded keenly, and was prepared to go through anything, whatever it entailed. She would do what her mother demanded, and then when she was married she would do what she liked, although she could not begin to imagine how the coming months might actually turn out for her and Charlie.

But fortunately her mother had had enough of conversation, informing her daughter abruptly that she was now going to take her afternoon rest. Nell backed out of the room with an uncharacteristic bow of her head, and hurried off to tell Mary Harriette the good news.

Outside, just beyond the high boundary wall, a south coast express rushed past and onwards through Caterham Junction at speed, its wailing whistle destroying any hope Mrs Pickersgill-Cunliffe may have had of losing herself in sleep.

Mary Harriette's Diary.

June 1874

I spent yesterday with Nell and Charlie at Brighton, and Charlie saw Captain Buxton. The interview was very satisfactory and he is only waiting for Mother's consent to give his final decision. Captain Buxton wants them to be married and come out immediately but they haven't asked Mother about that part yet. I do wish they could, it would be so much better for Charlie. He says I must go too and take care of them and then she will be quite happy and there is a nice scheme afoot that I shall marry Mr Dawkins, Charlie's future partner in South Carolina, which they all agree would be a very good plan. The prospect of making his fortune in America has returned Charlie to his old good spirits, which worryingly seemed to have deserted him for ever.

Capt. Buxton is constantly attentive to me so of course I like him, though he is perhaps a little too silky.

***

Despite what Nell had hinted to her mother all those months ago, the wedding night could truly be counted as their first time proper. But it was certainly not their first shared physical intimacy, if one counts explorations across the boundaries of fondling into something more transgressive, first tentatively and then less so. There were never any circumstances where they could be sure of not being interrupted for long enough to attempt more than that, although Charlie was not beyond proposing this and Nell was not beyond encouraging him. Once, when Nell herself hinted at such a thing as the wedding approached, he told her in a strangled voice that they could hold on now that the time was so close, and they consoled themselves with another bout of exploratory fondling that went more than far enough as it was.

This was no more than she had been urged to do by her married friends, on an evening soon after the date of the wedding was finally confirmed, at a boisterous gathering to induct her into the society of wives. There was complete agreement on the importance of being good and ready, so to speak, for the demands and pleasures of the marriage bed, when the special night finally arrived. There were differing views on how to achieve this, from reading certain kinds of informative literature that they would discreetly lend her, pampering herself with oils and ointments, and having as much harmless fun with her fiancé as he would allow in the meantime. Her friends' testimony revealed wide variation in the extent to which husbands expected their wives to participate in the act of love, and some were shocked to discover from others what they had been missing.

Nell was determined not to let that ever happen to her, but it didn't take long to find that she had nothing to fear in this respect. It was clear, and had been almost from the start, that they had and likely would always have a turbulent relationship but here, over the nights and days that followed the wedding, they discovered a compatibility that might carry them through the hardest of future times. When Nell finally surfaced for air two or three days later, she wrote her mother a loving letter thanking her for her kindness, and relating how their wedding night had been devoted first to their private Bible reading, then to Charlie reading to her from his own Bible.

Her mother did not believe that story for a moment, but it was the simple truth. On the night, both Nell and Charlie had found themselves unexpectedly hesitant as they stood looking at one another for the first time across a bed, each hoping the other would make the first move. Charlie finally broke the silence by clearing his throat and solemnly suggesting they read their Bibles for a while. Nell immediately agreed.

As a diversionary tactic it was extremely effective. For a couple of minutes each read in silence, sitting up in the bed beside one another, not touching. Then Nell put her Bible down and asked Charlie to read out loud to her. She moved up against him and he found her hand resting on his thigh. In a few moments more, the rumble of his deep voice reading the scriptures gave way to the sound of his Bible crashing to the floor, and Nell's laughter.

5

When the newly-weds finally arrived in Montmorenci in early spring 1875, after a journey from England so long and uncomfortable that Nell resolved never to travel anywhere ever again, she was devastated by the state of the house that had supposedly been prepared for them. Broken windows, dirty and derelict, tubs lying about, everything open to the elements and every passing stranger. But Charlie reminded her that it was theirs to do with as they wished, and they'd soon make a palace out of it. They had money to spend, which they spent like big city folk, ordering new furniture, new wallpaper, rugs, a dresser for the wedding gifts of china and glass that eventually caught up with them, a big new bed and things for the baby that might possibly be coming along already.

They immediately made friends with Mr Dawkins, their new partner and close neighbour, with whom they owned a double portion, 12 of the 30 hectares of land that Buxton had amassed during his time there, with other candidates currently being assessed back in England to take over the remaining three portions. Dawkins had himself been there for a few months, trying to prepare their shared land for sowing now that spring was approaching. Charlie soon found that Dawkins was no wiser than he was when it came to most things to do with the enterprise and every evening, in each other's house, they would sit together and talk through the day past and the days to come, share a beer or a glass of whisky, and agree that the whole business of cotton farming was rather a mystery, but they were definitely up to it. The poorest darkie farmers, Dawkins reminded Charlie, seemed to be able to grow the stuff and sell it, apparently, so they were not going to find it too hard.

In those first days, Nell and Charlie would take a break from cleaning floors and painting walls to wander together around Montmorenci, to get a feel for the place, and make the acquaintance of some its inhabitants too. The town did not strike them as particularly delightful, or even worthy of the name town, consisting of single storey buildings on the main street containing a variety of small businesses, big houses behind big trees further out of town, then smaller houses like their own, and further still occasional cabins, fields, horses. A single road went through it, with small tracks going off to farms and houses in the distance.

There were a few stores, for domestic and farm provisions, a post office, a tidy wooden Baptist church, a courthouse and jail, and the railroad. It didn't amount to much and it didn't seem particularly friendly. The local white farmers certainly didn't seem interested, when Charlie first went calling and tried to introduce himself. They would look at him suspiciously as he walked up their tracks and hailed them, and turn hostile as soon as he opened his mouth.

"You a northerner mister?" asked one, hardly turning to look at him from his work.

"No sir," said Charlie. "I'm from England."

"Another carpetbagger," said the farmer.

Charlie had no idea what he was talking about. "No, I don't think so," he said uncertainly. "My name is Lieutenant Hodgkinson, and I used to be in the British Navy."

The farmer grunted and continued cleaning horse tackle.

"My wife and I have taken over a farm over the other side of town," said Charlie. "Trying to get to know the neighbours, you know."

"Is that so," said the farmer.

The negroes that Charlie tried to meet seemed even less willing to communicate when he approached them. He had hailed some on the road, as they passed by with loaded horse-drawn carts, but they just kept moving. Looked at him, nodded, said nothing, kept moving. He had tried calling at a couple of their cabins, but nobody responded to his banging on the doors. "Hello in there!" he'd shout, into the darkness. "I know you're in there!" He was only looking to hire some help, but nobody ever answered.

"Good news," Dawkins announced one evening, excited. "I've met a gentleman in town who came down from the north a few years back to set up as a lawyer, and he seems to know what's what. He said that it was not surprising at all that we've not made much progress with the locals, because the politics of it all is still hot and troubled here, what with all the new laws after Abolition. He told me that outsiders like himself, and like us too, can never expect to be well liked down here."

Dawkins looked uneasily at Charlie, to see if he was following, then continued, "and as for the blacks, or better call them negroes he says, we should try to speak to them respectfully."

"Sorry?" asked Charlie.

"Well he reckons they've learnt not to trust any white man," he said. "And he says we ought to show them respect."

"Respect!" he said, "Who is this man eh? Do we need him to tell us how to treat the hired help?"

Dawkins blanched, but said that he most definitely thought that they did, and maybe Charlie could come along tomorrow and meet the gentleman, Sam Cross, because in case Charlie had forgotten, they hadn't managed to find anyone willing to be the hired help as yet.

Charlie told Nell about all this, and said he had no intention of meeting this Cross chap, but she told him he must.

Charlie's instinct was sound enough when it came to choosing the right side to be on, and he suspected that an outsider like Sam Cross wasn't someone he wanted as an ally in these parts. He did go along with Dawkins the next morning, and listened as attentively as he could whilst Cross talked about the kind of change that he and his associates wanted to bring about, helping the freedmen to better their lives, get themselves educated, employed, housed, elected onto local councils and all that. It was a big movement, he said, many good folk come down from the north and a number of southern Republicans too, all committed to making the Reconstruction mean something – to truly heal the divisions of that terrible war.

"I don't know much about all that," said Charlie, firmly. "Doesn't concern me at all."

Oh but it should, Cross insisted. Such an important job – made a man proud to be part of such a great change, he said pointedly, but Charlie said nothing.

"You must understand," said Cross, rising to the challenge, "that this is no longer the South of slavery and secession – that South is dead. Ours is the South of union and freedom."

Charlie shrugged, and Cross sighed quietly.

"Anyway. How about I introduce you to some of the freedmen families round here?" Cross suggested. "I daresay many of them would be happy to take work with you, and help you make a success of your farms."

Dawkins' face lit up and he glanced encouragingly at his partner, but Charlie kept his mouth shut. The more Sam Cross talked, the more Charlie was sure that this was not the kind of friend he needed. He wanted nothing more than to be accepted by the local farmers, the chaps whose town it truly was, and get on with his life. He didn't come all this way to get involved in American problems; none of his business.

"You know," Cross said cautiously. "I kind of think that things might have gone a lot better here for your Captain Buxton if he'd been more willing to listen my counsel."

Charlie reddened. "Captain Buxton seems to have done quite well for himself, as far as I can tell," he said. "He accrued a considerable fortune during his time here I believe."

"Is that so?" asked Cross. "I did not realise that." He stared at Charlie, and then tapped the table to acknowledge the end of the conversation. "Very well, then – I wish you good luck Mr Hodgkinson."

"Lieutenant Hodgkinson," said Charlie.

"Very sorry," said Cross. "Be that as it may, you will always be welcome here. Drop in for a talk any time you feel like."

Charlie made a curt farewell and left the office, followed by an anxious Dawkins who paused long enough to shake Sam Cross's hand and mutter an apology. "You come back, okay?" Cross said.

As they went out onto the street, Charlie spotted one of the farmers he'd previously approached, now riding by right in front of them. "Damn that Sam Cross," Charlie announced loudly to Dawkins, waving his hand dismissively. "We don't need help from the likes of him." The farmer spun his head around and Charlie nodded pleasantly. The farmer nodded back.

Nell's moods went up and down all the time, as they always had, and during the first months she was particularly susceptible to the hormonal challenges of early pregnancy, and then the crushing disappointment of a miscarriage. But the summer was coming and there was work to be done. Throughout her life she never had been and never would be one to give up, but she wasn't beyond proclaiming sometimes that she'd had enough and wanted to go home, and Charlie was not beyond telling her what he thought of that, and things would get out of hand for a while.

The sound of their sudden rows would occasionally float all the way over to Dawkins in the next house, as he sat alone and peaceful on his porch enjoying the still evening air. Not even the sudden silences of reconciliation encouraged him to contemplate finding a wife for himself, even when Nell made heavy hints. She never seriously entertained the idea of bringing her sister over for him, but she was certainly keen to find someone who might serve their respective needs for female company. It wasn't long before she had arranged a party in the hope of finding him a nice local girl, inviting people they'd finally begun to know in town, local farmers, their wives, sisters and children. In the event Dawkins simply failed to turn up but, rough and ready as the party was, there was a good friendly atmosphere that augured well for their future acceptance in the town. Dawkins later sent his apologies, and Charlie reminded Nell that he was not particularly popular around here anyway, having thrown in his lot with the abolitionists, Republicans, northerners and, who knows, freedmen as well. He was a decent man, they agreed, but there was no future in making yourself an outcast, and it had certainly been easier that he'd stayed away on this occasion.

It was not that Nell and Charlie thought of themselves as anti-negro, if they ever thought about such a thing at all: they claimed to be perfectly happy with the maid whom they eventually managed to hire, and with her father whom they sometimes employed to work their fields, but they were also utterly blind to the history of injustice etched into the Black faces they passed every day. They found it considerably easier to sympathise with their white neighbours' unyielding devotion to the Confederacy, their bitterness over what had been taken from them, and their anger at those who'd come south to become rich at their expense. Everything had worked just fine before the war, just fine for everyone, their neighbours insisted, whatever anyone tells you; Nell nodded sympathetically, and pronounced it all a crying shame.

When Captain Buxton came over in May, to see how they were progressing and to bring the new recruit, he was uneasy to discover how ardently Nell was expressing her own newly acquired hatred for northerners. No abolitionist himself, Buxton knew that outsiders such as them should keep their heads down; be friendly, don't express an opinion. Nobody likes an outsider who takes sides. He also wondered whether it had been wise of her to put up a sign saying "Private" on the gate, but Nell soon set him straight on that. Anyone was welcome in her house, she explained, but only on her say-so.

Buxton didn't stay long on this visit, as he was to come back again in September to conclude his involvement there, to his great regret. His charm, confidence and enthusiasm had convinced his newest recruit, himself about to marry, of the wisdom of investing now whilst the prices were still affordable, and the new chap was confident of bringing in another couple with whom he might partner. Then Buxton straightway made tracks. It had been an uncontroversial visit, because the sowing was now completed and, for all that Charlie, Nell and Dawkins could tell, a decent crop was on its way. Their optimism survived no more than another month or two, though, and then soon shrivelled like the cotton plants they inspected with rapidly dying hope each morning.

For Nell, the humid sub-tropical heat of South Carolina felt increasingly unbearable during August but apparently, as they were told many times, weather-wise this had been a good year for growing cotton. Plenty of sun, rain, but no drought and no flooded fields. So they imagined, the three of them, that the fault must have been all theirs: they'd chosen the wrong seeds, planted them the wrong way, tended them not enough or too much. Whatever it had been, their fields looked increasingly pitiful as September approached. Occasional flashes of white, as the first flowers unfurled, some of them pollinating and turning pink by the second day, but most of them curling up and dying; some bolls appearing, but too few and too small, and when they did open there was little of the white fluffy brilliance they'd expected to see filling the fields.

Dawkins had hired a new farm-hand, Nathaniel Jones, more farm manager really, and on the last day of August they all went out into the fields with him to assess the prospects for the crop. Nathaniel had worked in cotton fields as a boy, since before the war, and on and off since then, had a wealth of experience, even though he had sworn never to go near cotton fields again. He was softly spoken and thought carefully before he expressed an opinion, but he'd already seen enough of the dying cotton plants to know what the problem was.

"Your earth is exhausted, mostly. If you look after your fields over the winter, a few of them, you might make some of it good enough for growing a little cotton next year, but nothing's going to happen this year." He pulled off a boll for a cotton plant, and held it up to them. "See," he said. "Hardlock."

Nell looked at Charlie, not sure if she had heard correctly. "Well yes," she said, "it certainly feels that way."

"No, ma'am," said Nathaniel. "I'm saying this boll has hard *lock*. Look, try for yourself. Won't open. Even the cotton you've got you can't have, 'cos it's locked inside these bolls, and they won't open. Hardly worth trying."

"Are you saying that there's no hope for our crop? At all?" Nell asked. She looked at an appalled and speechless Charlie, who just stood there, tears forming in his eyes. Dawkins, at least, seemed to have accepted the verdict already. He shook Nathaniel's hand, and thanked him for his expertise and forthright words.

The sun was already high in the sky, the temperature and humidity were rising fast, and Nell felt sick. Which might have been good news, for all she knew, but then Charlie said he too had felt sick that morning, although *that* might have been because of all the drink he had drunk last night to make himself feel better. Or they might both have some kind of illness, because everything felt sticky and dirty right now, even the clothes from England that she was still wearing, all wrong for this place anyway. Walking back home, with an unusable cotton boll in her fingers, she thought of her faded fantasy of making lovely cool dresses from her own cotton to wear in the South Carolina sunshine. None of it would matter, though, if the sickness was for the good reason, and it seemed increasingly that that might be the case with every ghastly morning that passed over the following weeks. By mid-September she knew for sure that she was pregnant again.

Their new friends the local farmers, previously taciturn on the subject of Captain Buxton and the whole cotton project, admitted they weren't in the least surprised when Charlie and Nell told them how badly things were going. The farmers explained that at the best of times this part of South Carolina had never been ideally suited to cotton, and once the railroad came and opened up more suitable territory, the big plantations around there had disappeared fast. Add to that the fact that in his relatively short time in Montmorenci, Captain Buxton had had little success himself, and the little he had grown had only succeeded in ruining the soil further. They reckoned he had set up in the first place by getting his hands on Reconstruction money, and they didn't think too much of that, especially seeing as how he'd squandered it. They'd said nothing; just watched and waited for the inevitable. It wasn't their place to tell folks how to live their lives.

But now that things were in the open, they advised Charlie and Nell as best they could. If you had more money than sense, they said, you could spend it on feeding your soil, but it probably wouldn't make much difference. Better you get the Captain to return the investment. Then you could stay and farm your own smallholding, grow vegetables, beans, potatoes, whatever. Till your own fields, grow enough to feed yourselves and maybe also a small cash crop, see how things pan out.

Buxton was shocked, on his return in late September, to discover how unpopular he'd become during his absence. Mr Dawkins was fairly temperate, recognising that part of the problem was probably his own ignorance of cotton farming, but Charlie and Nell wasted no time in telling the Captain what they thought of him, calling him a charlatan and a thief, and demanding their money back. It was somewhat distressing for the four new recruits who'd come along with him, hopeful and wide-eyed, only to hear that they'd spent their savings on a pile of worthless dust.

Buxton was flabbergasted and disappointed, and for a while he stood his ground. "All the land I promised you is here, it's had cotton grown on it before, by me and many others in the past, it may not be perfect but you paid low for it, you know that, otherwise you wouldn't be here," he told them, firm but calm. "I have been straight with you all along. And here I am, still looking after your interests, not running away with your money."

So pay us back, they insisted, over and over again, until in the end he agreed. "One thing," he said to Charlie, as they signed contracts of sale back to him for a large portion of the land, leaving Charlie and Nell the house and less than half the land they had initially bought. "You stop slandering and libelling me, or there'll be trouble for you."

"What do you mean?" said Charlie, as if he didn't know.

Buxton pulled a few torn and crumpled handbills from his bag. "What do I mean? *These*," he said, "that you've put all around town. Not to mention the letters you've sent to all sorts back home I have no doubt. Saying I'm a trickster, rogue and thief. I'm not joking boy – you'd better stop that fast."

The four new recruits immediately packed their bags and set off back to England, where a variety of welcomes awaited them, depending on the seriousness of the failures they'd left behind. Charlie and Nell set about planning their second attempt at farming, keeping their indignation on the boil for the next few months, to the extent that Nell wrote her own furious letter home correcting in no uncertain terms her mother's unhelpful suggestion that perhaps Captain Buxton had not done anything so terribly dishonest in the first place.

Day-by-day, their life in Montmorenci settled into a meandering kind of existence, not entirely unproductive but with little scope for improvement either. This was their life now. They worked their land as best they could on their own. Their money ran down, but there was always enough coming in from Nell's inheritance to keep them in bare necessities. They came near to giving up entirely after little Austin died, not three months old. Nell decided that if she had any more children they would have to live in England because South Carolina wasn't a place where a frail English baby could ever hope to thrive. But there they remained, despite everything. There were times when they argued furiously, and Charlie would disappear into town sometimes and returned with whisky and more debt, but they also laughed and made love as often as they cried and fought, until Nell was pregnant again and sick for weeks on end.

They never actually fell out with their neighbours, and joined in local social events regularly enough, dances and open air parties, family events. Nell's friendly manner and good humour always made her welcome but Charlie never truly gained the confidence of the local farmers. They eventually lost interest in giving advice, suspecting the English couple of not taking their farming seriously, of not needing to, and never entirely trusted them, because they were Britishers, and friends with Dawkins.

That was true enough: Dawkins was their one true friend there. He never judged them; they shared their struggles and helped one another, even though no longer working as partners. He battled on with his cotton, and did better the second time around, greatly helped by Nathaniel. Things went downhill the third year, and his cotton failed so badly then that by the autumn of '77, not long before Charlie and Nell's son Tom was born, Dawkins announced that he planned to leave in the spring to go north. He told them this when they came over to his house one evening, and they all – Nathaniel included – sat down together and drank home-made beer. There was a bang on the door, Dawkins said that Sam Cross was joining them too, and the party was complete.

Charlie and Nell walked home in silence for a while. "Mr Cross doesn't seem such a bad chap," Nell said, after a while. "He's good company for Dawkins."

"It seems so," he said, non-committal.

"And I like Nathaniel too. But is it wise, do you think, to make such a friend of his negro?" she asked.

"It most certainly is not, not around here," Charlie said. "I think Dawkins might have been taking a grave risk."

"Oh I hope not," said Nell.

He raised his eyebrows, and gave her a long meaningful look. "Not the only risk he's taking, I'd say."

Nell didn't understand.

"I really cannot talk to you of this, Nell. But in the Navy you hear of certain things from time to time." Nell said she had not the faintest idea what he was talking about. "Men with

… other men," Charlie said, uncomfortably. She continued to look blank. "Sam Cross, woman! Not the first time I've caught sight of him there. I'll wager he'll be there in the morning too."

"Oh," said Nell slowly. "Oh I see. I think." She had heard of such things, vaguely. A nephew of hers who'd got into trouble at Eton, no-one would say exactly how, but her sister Evelyn had tried to tell her about what went on in ancient Greece apparently, or had it been the Romans? Anyway, love between men. She hadn't wanted to hear more at the time, and now she wished she had.

"Are you sure?" she asked. "How can you tell?"

Charlie shook his head. "Because it don't look right," he said.

"I'm not sure what I think about anything anymore," she told him. She found it hard to explain to him, but she'd begun to feel differently about many things as her time in South Carolina went on. Life was harsher here, and her view of the world had lost its sharper edges. "I care for Mr Dawkins. And Nathaniel. And Mr Cross seems nice too. They're not bad folk."

"Maybe so," said Charlie. "But people round here would never countenance that kind of thing, if they even suspected it to be the case. They'd be hanged three times over."

"No!" said Nell, appalled. "Mr Dawkins is the kindest person we know."

Charlie nodded. "We mustn't ever speak of this, not to anyone," he said. "I should never have mentioned it," although he did mention it again, in one of the letters he occasionally wrote to George King-Hall, whom he'd made into a kind of confessor. George's response was gratifyingly full of dire warnings against the wages of sin.

The mood in Montmorenci was much altered by the time Nell and Charlie finally left. Reconstruction had come to an end, and scores were being settled. They retreated into their farm more and more, and survived there until the middle of 1878, achieving little and making futile plans. They no longer felt they could ever belong in Montmorenci and their new son Tom deserved a better life than this. Sam Cross told them about a good little farm for sale at a fair price in Warrenton, a small friendly town in Virginia. Friendlier than Montmorenci, that's for sure, he said with a wry grin. They wrote to both their respective families requesting a loan to buy the new farm, having succeeded in selling the Montmorenci farm for virtually nothing.

Mr Dawkins had left not long before they did. Charlie and Nell stood by their gate, watching him slowly drive away in his heavily loaded trap, pulled by his old horse, together with Sam Cross and Nathaniel Jones, the three of them heading north for another new start.

from Mary Harriette's Diary: Warrenton, Virginia, U.S.A. 1879

June 3rd

I have got through the voyage and the journey and am now settled down. I can't quite realize it yet, though I hear little Tom shouting upstairs and Nell is working at the machine in the same room, while Charlie is out in his garden. It was a long voyage, 13 days, only three fine days the whole time, but I was not often sick.

Nell was delighted to see me; she is now an enormous woman, but very well and most energetic: she gets through quantities of work of all kinds and seems to me much improved. She tells me that Charlie is not so better as we hoped, indeed he has had a slight attack of delirium tremens; I am so grieved. I do hope he will keep all right while I am here, for if not I must go straight home.

June 20th

My visit here does not promise to be replete with interest much as I enjoy it: day after day passes, each like the former and busy as we always seem to be, nothing occurs worth recording. After breakfast Nell and I usually get the beans and peas and prepare them for dinner which occupies a long while; after which I try to get through a letter and then work till dinner time. In the afternoon it is too hot for anything but sitting in the shade, but I, not feeling it badly, can always work or read. Sometimes we pay a call on some neighbour later on in the day. Tea is at 6 o'clock and after that we all sit out till 10 p.m. talking and pleasant it is when Charlie and Nell do not squabble, which is a meaningless though disagreeable employment, as a more devoted couple never lived.

June 27th

I have had a trying time this week: on Sunday came the news that Ellis was *very* ill with vilio-intermittent fever, and Mother was very anxious over him. Charlie did his best to comfort me, so I tried not to talk about it, for I felt wretched and only longed to be home, doing my part.

Today is frightfully hot; Charlie has a bilious attack and Nell is poorly; I alone am jolly and not hot so I sit out and write. Tom also does not seem to suffer. Except that I am in a constant bath of perspiration and get tired with nothing, I do not know it is hot: the sun is very powerful and Charlie has got me an enormous hat and I enjoy myself beneath the vast expanse of shade.

July 1st

I looked anxiously for letters but none came till last evening. There were two from Evelyn and one from Mother which I opened first for I *knew* what I should find in it. Sure enough, it was to tell me that our precious old Ellis has been taken away from us, falling asleep, they said, like a tired child at 10.30 on June 18th. Mother feels it a "second widowhood" she writes for he was her friend as well as son, but she "gives him willingly back".

July 28th

Charlie has been unwell for several days with his liver, and today he has a swelled face from a wisdom-tooth; it is his birthday and I may well wish him "many happier returns of it". Nell had a panic this morning that she was going to be laid up, but the symptoms have subsided, a fortnight hence will be early enough to think of it. All yesterday afternoon Nell and Charlie quarrelled and though I shut my room I could hear it all; it was terrible, and Charlie uses such bad words: if it be an average married state, I think I can almost accept old maidenhood with gratitude. The clergyman and his wife called one day but nothing else has happened this week.

August 17th

We are in the uncomfortable state of waiting: Nell has had her nurse to sleep here every day this week, and daily expects she may be laid up, and Charlie is so excited and impatient about it that he can settle to nothing and makes us all feel on the go. He is now working up for another liver attack, and for the last two days has been what Nell calls "on the ramp", so that I do not think she has been able to sit still for one hour at a stretch, he is always routing her out. I am beginning to get frightened again and spend as much time as possible in writing and reading that Charlie may not talk to me.

August 28th

I do not believe Nell will be ill till next month, though she has almost daily alarms. Charlie got over his liver attack more quickly this time, but first he got a lot of whisky and made himself worse with that, and I have in consequence got to a pitch in my dislike of him and long more than ever to get out of his house. He leads Nell an awful life poor girl! and at times I can hardly be civil to him, I hate him so, for it.

September 22nd

We had a terrible time on Saturday. Charlie's attack reached a climax; he would drink a lot of some horrid wine he had got and went quite off his head, much worse than usual and when Nell tried to give him his soothing mixture, said she was trying to poison him, and got very wild. After that he went into a fit of hysterics, and Nell got nervous and having administered the dose, got him to bed and sent for the doctor. Poor Nell! what a life for her!

Charlie slept well and rose all right the next morning. Nell was equally recovered, being of a most elastic temperament, fortunately for her, poor dear. I do not think I shall recover till I am safe away.

September 28th

Nell continued very well till Friday 26th when after the usual routine of needlework, scraping radishes and taking a walk with me till 5.30 she was taken ill at 6 o'clock. Nurse and doctor were both with her by 8 o'clock and at 8.55 a little girl was born. Charlie worked himself into a wild state and went into hysterics, he has not the least notion of self-control, and I believe thought it a display of affection, instead of selfishness. Next morning I telegraphed and wrote to Mother, and Charlie took the letters into town so we had a peaceful morning, but Nell is wonderfully well and she is accustomed to his worryings. I am glad to say that he got so tired that he went to bed before 8 o'clock and slept soundly till morning. Everything is all right at present, and I pray, may so continue.

I can go home happily now that I have held my niece in my arms. Such a dear plump thing, little Frances Helen.

6

C harlie knew he was in peril when it came time for dreaming. He had been five days without alcohol, and was heading straight for a fresh bout of the DTs. He had been through the whole business before, and knew how bad it had to get before it was over, but he was determined to stick with it this time. The pain that his drunkenness caused his wife and three children, the shame from that, the disgust he felt for his own behaviour, these things were no longer tolerable. He didn't want to die suddenly, although he knew from years of severe warnings that it might already be too late. But if that must happen soon he wanted, at least, to leave his family thinking well of him. No More Drink. Ever.

Most previous attempts to stop the drinking had ended the same way, with a desperate grab for the bottle before the blue horrors destroyed him: nightmares, crawling hallucinations, a sense of impending doom, and then the tremors, sweating, heart beating out of control, the pressure inside. He knew very well what was coming and was mentally prepared for it, resolute to plough on through. He knew that a day or two before the DTs began was when the bad dreams would start, coming from whatever terrible place they inhabited, until he could no longer hold them off. He hardly dreamed at all when drinking heavily, which was a good enough reason to keep drinking heavily, but now he had made the choice, in the full knowledge of what was going to happen next, to let the dreams and whatever followed come on and do their worst, and go all the way with it.

Their Tuesday evening together as a family had been calm and sweet; Nell was pleased with him and told him so. They enjoyed their tea together, and afterwards he carefully thanked Savannah and little Betsy for their trouble. He hugged young Tom, nine years old now and a plucky lad, then kissed his perfect pair of girls, five-year-old Frances and Virginia, four. Held them all extra-long, like he was going away somewhere bad and wanted to remember them, and then nodded to Nancy to take them to their beds. Nell suggested the two of them walk around their fields for a while, it being a beautiful late spring evening, the light not quite beginning to fade. She could tell he was scared, trying to keep it to himself. They went to see the pig, they talked to the horse, and they looked at the first seedlings coming through and were pleased with the way things were going, and even had a good word for George White, who was turning into a good worker, though still with much to learn.

They kept walking for a while, up the track and into town. Nell held his hand and Charlie didn't stop her. He felt safe in her company then, the two of them invisible and private in the fading light. As it got dark Nell asked if they should go back now, while Charlie wanted to carry on just a bit longer, to maybe tire himself out some more so he could sleep sound and still, or just to keep one step ahead of sleep for an hour or two more. But Nell gently steered him back around towards the house, and they made their way to bed.

The big dream is underway for Charlie now. It is taking place on board a large warship, the *Lord Clyde* until King-Hall explains that it's the old *Euryalus* in fact. They are on a side deck, all sorts of people he knows and doesn't know passing by, music, laughing, girls galore. Charlie is telling one of them how the Captain had his head blown off! The girl laughs but an imperious old lady chastises them for lack of respect and the girl runs away in tears. Charlie sees a young man in Midshipman's uniform weeping on the far side of the deck and wonders if it's himself, and then sees that it's poor dead Boyes.

Charlie goes into a cabin and meets a woman who says she's Lizzie but he's not sure until he wraps his arms around her. She tells him they must leave the ship fast and they run to the deck and straight over the side, him and Lizzie and another girl. They scramble and slide all the way down the side of the ship and then they're all in a skiff together. It's Portsmouth Dockyard and not Naples, the clouds grey and ominous in the distance, though Charlie no longer knows his way around, it's not quite right, but he keeps rowing. The two women sit opposite him while he rows and then he finds himself between them, loving each in turn but unsure which girl is which. The other one says "She's your Maltese widow, ain't she Charlie!" He thinks, I must get out of this before my wife catches us.

Things start exploding all around them, they are under attack, gunfire and cannonballs flying, screaming, the women are screaming and Charlie can feel his heart beating so hard it must burst and kill him before he can get them to safety. He tries with all his strength to help them up the steep sheer slippery harbour wall, clinging to chains, moving from one ledge to another, some too high to reach, trying to pull both women up behind him but near the top Lizzie starts to slide down out of his grasp, clutching at his hand saying she has the fever and must surely die and she's gone. She plummets straight out of sight into the dark, the dark water out of sight far below, and Charlie finds himself falling as well and cries out as he goes down and down crying Oh My Poor Widow! Oh my God!

Cries so loud he wakes himself, and sees a horrified Nell leaning over him, stroking his face, trying to calm him while he stares blindly into her face, shouting.

Nell had been panicked at first by the state he'd been in, but she'd seen worse when the DTs came on, or the Maltese fever returned for a while, or like as not both at once. The first two or three times she'd been terrified, but she'd got used to it over the years and would either calm him down or, if she couldn't and he seemed like he might lose control, leave him to fight through it on his own. This had been going on eight or nine years now, the drunkenness getting so bad sometimes that it seemed that he would die if he didn't stop drinking, and might die if he did. She didn't want him to die, however much she despised him sometimes. He was her husband, and she could not conceive of surviving there or anywhere without a husband. He was Charlie, and when he was *her* Charlie, she loved him more than anything, more than her own children.

That morning's nightmare had not been so different when it woke her and she tried to bring him out of it, clutching his wrist to pull him bodily out of wherever he was, and pressing her hand down on his forehead. That was when he started shouting, hard to make it out, but she could tell he was terrified. She heard the words "Oh God!", and she was sure she heard "widow" too. It seemed like he was trying to tell her something she needed to know, the way he was staring at her so intensely. As he came back into the waking world, she urgently tried to discover what he'd been saying before it vanished.

"What are you talking about, Charlie?" she asked, almost hissing. "Tell me what happened."

He looked at her uncomprehendingly, the world completely strange to him. She shook him. "Come on Charlie, wake yourself, wake yourself," she cried.

"I ... " he faltered. "I thought I ... was going to die."

"You're fine, Charlie. Whatever it was, you're safe now. You won't die! You're here with me, and you're okay." She stroked him. "What were you trying to tell me?"

Then Charlie remembered; he remembered losing hold of Lizzie, he remembered shouting something, the feeling of terror as he shouted, he could still hear the sound of his own voice in his head, but not the words. They were gone. They had been about Lizzie, that much at least he remembered.

"I don't know Nellie," he said. "I don't recall any of it."

"You said Oh God for sure," she said, "but something else before that. I wish you could remember – it sounded so important to you."

"I don't know," he moaned. "I thought I was bound to die."

She knew she would get nothing more from him now, and left him to more sleep. She hoped that he might just spend the rest of the day that way but a couple of hours later he appeared downstairs and announced that he felt much recovered now, and was going out riding, to clear his head. He also needed to see a couple of people with whom he had business to conclude. He would return some time in the afternoon. He went outside, and told George to get his horse ready.

"He didn't look so good this morning," said George, watching Charlie ride away up the lane. "Drank a good deal last night?"

"Not last night, not at all," said Savannah. "After their dinner he came over real serious and told me and Betsy how excellently we'd smoked the ham, and the biscuits were the best he'd ever tasted. Stone cold sober."

"Seen the light, again."

"Won't end well of course," she said, and both laughed. There wasn't often much to laugh about, when you had Charlie for a master. Slavery had been abolished twenty years by now, but some masters still liked to act like plantation bosses. Charlie didn't actually try to beat any of his servants even if sometimes it looked like he might. He could get boiling angry when he had a mind to, when he'd drunk a bottle or two, and they had got used to being dismissed on a regular basis, for nothing more than a dish not being to his liking. Then the mistress would give them a nod which they knew well by now, just go out quietly and come back later, carry on as if nothing has happened. They carried on, they had nowhere else to go.

Tom also was wary of Charlie. He loved his father, was utterly loyal to him, and knew you just had to give him the air to breathe, like his mother told him, if you didn't want to cause trouble. Leave him to breathe his own air, he'll soon get better. Tom could judge how things stood, from the sound of his father's voice and the crash of his footsteps, and he would get out the way until it was all okay again. If he ever got a slap from his father it was because he taken too much of his air. He didn't blame his father, even when he was afraid of him.

Frances couldn't get it though, however often her mother tried to tell her. She couldn't manage to stand back far enough from trouble when it brewed, and always ended up in tears, which never proved to be much of a safety curtain and annoyed her father even more. Her sister Virginia cried too when he shouted at her, but instinctively knew how to keep small and stay clear of the line of fire, which Frances thought very unfair. To Virginia, her father was a larger-than-life character in the secret stories and games she incessantly muttered to herself. She was fascinated by him, you could tell from the way she steadily observed him from her distant corners, in all his different moods.

The children watched him go this morning and, in the case of the two older ones at least, felt the relief of his departure, tinged as always with worry for the mood he'd be in when he returned.

As he rode off up the lane away from his house, he really did begin to feel better, and wondered if he might not be already over the worst. It could be, he told himself, that on this occasion he had, after so many failures, discovered the inner strength to prevail over the cursed drink before it could drag him back inside its dark cave. He believed in himself, for the first time in a very long while, in his own strength of mind. The spring was in full bloom under a brilliant sun and he speeded up, suddenly turning away from town at a canter and heading on a whim towards Borrows Run a few miles away to the south of the town.

Once there, he had a mind to relax a little by the stream. He lay on the bank in the shade of a tree and listened to the water, while his horse stood patiently by and chewed some grass. Charlie closed his eyes, and thought back over his dream of Lizzie. He seldom managed to summon her image back into his waking life now, but from time to time she would appear to him without warning or reason in his dreams, briefly very close to him and then lost again, leaving him longing for her return through the whole day. But this time it had all gone crazy, she'd suddenly died and so had he, and he realised it was a warning that he must heed – a warning from the edge of the grave, that death can strike you anytime it chooses, can destroy you and those you love without warning. You have to change your ways now Charlie, he vowed to himself there by the stream, you have to live your life honest, straight and clean, and don't throw yourself down into the darkness.

He awoke to the sound of someone close by calling his name. "Hodgkinson! Charlie Hodgkinson! Wake up man! What're you doing hiding out here?"

Charlie opened his eyes and tried to find where he was, and what might be going on. A big man was standing just over him, the sun blindingly behind him. Charlie propped himself up on one elbow and shaded his eyes. "Oh. It's you Russ," he said.

Russell Westmore was a local miller, and his father J.B. the leading merchant of seeds, feed and farming equipment in Warrenton. Charlie owed both of them considerable sums of money, and a small amount to his farmer brother as well.

"You swore you'd come into town and settle your debts today Charlie," Westmore said. "First thing this morning, you said. I've been waiting, we've all been waiting, all morning."

Charlie cursed silently, and looked up at Russ, searching for an excuse.

"Ted said he saw you riding out this way, so I came out to find you. And here you were, sleeping peaceful as a baby. Come on man, can you not stand up?" Westmore was showing his frustration. Charlie wondered if he meant to hit him, and struggled to his feet, trying to appear conciliatory without looking craven. "No need to get heated," he said. "I hadn't forgotten." Westmore cursed him, in some disgust. He was peaceful enough as a rule, but lying he could not abide. He grabbed Charlie by the collar.

"This will not go well for you Charlie," he hissed into his face.

"I'm sorry! Sorry! I've really not been well. Had a very bad night. Needed to clear my head before I came to you." He shook himself out of Westmore's grip and stood back.

"Yes?" Westmore growled. "And clear now is it?" No reply. "You're not getting away with this any more Charlie. Got to settle it today. Last chance."

Charlie sighed, knowing perfectly well that there wasn't the slightest hope of him settling anything today. He looked down at the ground for a moment, and considered his options. Straight and clean's your only way now, Charlie.

"Listen Russ," he said. "I'm going to be honest with you."

Westmore sighed theatrically, as if he had heard this before.

"You will get your money, you most certainly will. But I was lying when I said you could have it by today, that's the honest truth of it. I lied to you." Westmore nodded at him to continue, scowling. "You know me Russ, and I shan't lie to you anymore, not about any of it. I've had more than my fair share of difficulties, and like a fool I turn to drink, and a drunk always lies, you know that."

Charlie stopped for a moment to collect his thoughts, and figure out how honest he really needed to be if he was to get through this in one piece. Quite honest, he decided.

"You know when I started playing poker with you boys, that's when it really went wrong, when I lost control. I'd lose, I'd get drunk, and then I'd gamble some more, thinking this was the day my luck would turn." He paused again. "But it didn't," he continued. "Of course it didn't, and by then it was too late, and shame drove me deeper into the drink."

"Okay, Charlie," Westmore said. "I know all this. What do you propose to do about it all?"

"I've given up the drinking for always now Russ, I really have. That has to be first, otherwise none of the other stuff means anything. I will never drink alcohol again as long as I live, I swear."

Westmore shrugged. "Drink as much as you like Charlie. Don't care what happens to you, so long as you pay us what you owe."

"Yes, yes," agreed Charlie. "I'm going to return home and tell my wife everything. Come clean with her about everything, Russ – the gambling, the drinking, the debts. She's got her own money and I've never asked for it till now. When I tell her, she'll help me sort it out, I'm certain of that." Charlie offered Westmore him a big encouraging smile, which was not returned.

"You do just that, Charlie," he said. "And then you come into town tomorrow morning, first thing, and you bring your old lady with you, and then I might start to believe all this shit you're giving me."

Westmore rode off without another word, leaving Charlie trembling with relief at what he had just pulled off, and also with dread at what he had to do next.

He returned home, and spent the rest of the day carrying out a few minor repairs to the stable, letting young Tom help him by hammering on the occasional nail. The girls came by at some stage, but their brother said that he and Papa were busy and they wandered off again, looking for useful things to put in the little baskets they carried with them everywhere. Then Savannah came out and told them it was time for their evening meal, and Charlie told Tom that he and Mamma weren't eating with them tonight, and sent him on his way with a kindly pat on his head.

Although Nell was shocked to learn of his encounter with Russ Westmore, it came as little surprise to hear about this latest crisis of debt. She had known for years about the trouble he got into, borrowing money from one acquaintance to pay off a long-delayed debt to another, generously buying drinks for himself and the others whose company made his own drinking seem less desperate. The gambling with the Westmore bunch surprised her, but it wasn't the first time he'd got into that kind of trouble either. Sometimes Mary Harriette would write and ask if Charlie had mended his ways, probably at the behest of their mother, and she found it hard to say that he had with any conviction. During those times when she wanted desperately to return to England and leave this place and Charlie for ever, she encouraged their pious concern for her welfare. But mostly she preferred to stay far away from the disapproval and interference in England and struggle on here in Virginia; picking peas and beans and beets, sweating and weary, deprived of all the comforts she had known throughout her previous life, but still able to hold her troubled and troublesome man close, and still free to manage her own life as she wished.

So, to Charlie's considerable amazement and relief, she readily agreed to come with him to meet J.B. and his boys the next morning, to thrash out terms for paying back what was owed them from her secret supply of cash, the money she had promised her mother never to reveal to Charlie under any circumstances. There would be tough terms for Charlie to fulfil as well, but that could all come later.

Meanwhile, she asked him if he'd managed to remember any more of the terrible dream that morning. He said he had not, no, nothing, to his great regret. She told him that she was sure she had heard the words "my dear widow" or some such. She needed to know. He rocked from side to side on his chair for half a minute or so, and then said he had no idea, and doubted that was what she had heard. But maybe, he conceded, such words might have burst from him when he thought he was dying. Really? she asked. Makes sense he said. It surprises me not at all, he intoned, that my final thought on dying would be of you.

Oh Charlie, she said.

Yes, though I doubt very much these were the exact words, he added, mightily relieved to have steered his way through those particular jagged rocks.

They ate a light supper, and chatted pleasantly enough, avoiding serious issues; Nell shared some interesting speculation about the pastor and the postmaster's wife, and Charlie listened and tried to make responsive noises. He was feeling increasingly dizzy, and found it hard to pay attention to what she was saying. As the evening drew on, he also began to feel extraordinarily tired and limp. Savannah came and turned up the lamps as the sky became suddenly black, and a tremendous downpour crashed down onto the house and surrounding countryside.

"I hope the stable door is shut," said Nell, looking out the window. "Can't tell from here."

Charlie looked at her, a little perplexed, started to stand but then gave up and fell back into his chair. "Sorry," he mumbled. "Too late. Must go to bed." His voice was deep with tiredness. She helped him up again and he leaned into her, clearly exhausted by his efforts of recent days.

"Wake me if you feel bad," she said to him, gently, as she lay down beside him.

Charlie was already asleep.

Nell found herself, sometime in the very early hours, trying to break out of the liminal state between waking and dreaming, trying to make sense of the dreadful noises going on inside her head, or outside it. Gradually, as she woke up, she understood that the noises were two quite separate phenomena: the renewed clattering of rain on the roof, and the heart-stopping, rasping sound of her husband struggling to catch his breath right beside her. Her first thought was that he was dreaming again of dying, and that she must softly wake him and bring him again out of his torment. But this time he did not respond to her touch, he did not stir, the struggle to breathe would not diminish, and it came to her that this was the sound a man makes when he's actually dying. This was the sound of Charlie dying.

She threw herself out of the bed, ran screaming to the door for help, for light, for the doctor to be called, for her husband to be saved, and then in near darkness managed to wet a cloth and began to bathe his head and invisible face. Savannah came in with a lamp, and said that George had already gone for the doctor. Nell knelt beside Charlie, whispered reassurance and encouragements that he could not hear, told him over and over that she loved him, and continued to bathe his head and stroke his face. In the course of a very few minutes more, his breathing became rapidly more stertorous, intermittent, and unachievable, and then stopped. Silence in the room, torrential rain outside.

Doctor Ward arrived soon after Charlie died, and immediately confirmed what Nell knew well enough already. He made a cursory inspection of Charlie's face, head and hands, and determined that the cause was apoplexy. "Cerebral haemorrhage. Blood on the brain, brought on by self-abuse, which is to say an excess of alcohol, that he had been warned of far too many times." If Nell was looking to the doctor for warmth or comfort, he wasn't in the mood to offer it. He had been soaked by the rain, it was two in the morning, and frankly he felt revulsion at the sight of this ruined life, and all the ruined lives that it left behind.

"He must be buried at once," he announced. "As soon as can be arranged. I will contact the undertaker at break of day."

Nell wanted him to explain why there had to be such a rush, it made no sense to her, but he clearly wasn't prepared to say more and she wondered if he'd decided that Charlie had done this on purpose. She was too distraught to press the case further, and also feared what he might choose to say to her if she forced him. The children were sobbing in their room, aware that something terrible was happening, and that life would never be all right again, and she went to see them, leaving the doctor without another word.

The rain was too relentless the next morning for the children to follow the coffin to the graveyard, so it was only Nell that came after it, hardly able to see where she was going but determined to show the world how proud of her poor brave boy she was and always would be. At the graveyard, she made the undertakers remove the lid of the coffin for a moment before it was lowered into the grave, so that she could lean down to kiss Charlie's face, and drop in the old anchor brooch and a scrap of paper with a short inscription. The words read: To my Charlie with love for ever, from your poor widow.

PART TWO
1895-1903

7

From the moment Nell and Charlie had left England for South Carolina in 1875, there had never been a time when lengthy letters full of gossip, heartache, news of every kind, had not been going back and forwards across the Atlantic, crossing each other's path, overlapping and out of sequence. In earlier times, emigrants to the Americas were usually never heard from again once they left the old country, but in this modern age distance counted for little when ships could make the journey in a week, and the telegraph was almost instantaneous. Telegrams cost a fortune, though, and were normally reserved for travel news, births, deaths and weddings, all communicated in the tersest possible terms.

Apart, that is, from Nell's second wedding in 1890, five years after poor Charlie died. She had preferred to announce this particular piece of news in a letter that wouldn't arrive until well after the event, having postponed as long as she could the uncomfortable task of explaining how she had, quite out of the blue, decided to marry the nephew of the man she had originally expected to marry; not something well suited to telegraphese. Her family had thought they could no longer be surprised by anything Nell threw at them from across the ocean; she would always be their Nell, of course, but it was increasingly hard to know what had come over her during her years away.

Her mother was distressed above all by the sinful fact that Nell had married one man whilst loving another; a sin she herself found painful to contemplate. Most objections were less theological, or less personal: Nell had only known the man for three weeks when she married him, THREE WEEKS!, he was *much* younger than her (if he did but know it), which in itself was improper, and a travelling shoe salesman, which was simply out of the question. At least the first Dent had been a Captain, even if no-one had any idea of what precisely. Whatever the true story, which could not be fathomed from the melodramatic outpourings of Nell's letters, one not entirely unvoiced thought floated constantly below the surface of acceptable conversation: she had married out of carnal desire, and would have probably taken any man she could lay her hands on if truth be told. Having long ago demonstrated her preference for personal gratification over good sense in cleaving like a foolish limpet to poor Charlie, Nell had once again allowed her baser instincts to overcome her better judgement; all the more appalling for being of an age now when all that should surely be safely behind her.

The whole shameful story could be endured only if the full facts remained on the other side of the ocean; Nell's suggestion of making a trip to England with her new husband was, of course, out of the question. Nobody, beyond the closest family, was to know exactly what had taken place, or how, and Nell's siblings were agreed that any comments on the matter to outsiders should be brightly uninformative at most. Regrettably, though, their mother thought otherwise, and grimly shared the whole story with Aunt Fanny, who was not really a member of the inner cabinet, and was bound to leak it to anyone who might be interested.

Nell wrote a few weeks after her initial announcement to say that she had now fallen in love with her husband, that they were happy, and would not after all be making a visit home; but she failed to provide a satisfactory explanation of how she'd come to marry this Dent rather than the other one. Perhaps she simply could not bring herself to say the obvious fact that she had simply needed a man in her life and, given the sudden unavailability of Captain Dent, his somewhat disreputable nephew Manny just had to do. She'd spent nearly five years since Charlie had died barely managing to get by on her own; not alone, of course, but on her own. She knew well enough from her years with Charlie that a man did not have to be perfect to provide what she needed from a husband.

Occasional physical pleasure went without saying of course, but most important was the appearance of solidity and authority that only a husband can provide; someone able to go out and do the things on her behalf she was not permitted to do for herself. It didn't even matter if he wasn't much good at doing those things, so long she was able to get on with her life without having constantly to overcome the insurmountable obstacle of not being a man.

Mrs Pickersgill-Cunliffe was firmly of the opinion that the chief beauty of marriage was that, once the knot was sealed, the problems of the wife belonged exclusively to the husband, and vice versa. That was really the whole point of the thing. Nell had made her bed and now must lie in it come what may, and whatever did come should be nobody's business but hers. But as time went by the more Nell began to hint that her marriage was not going well and, worryingly, that things were going quite badly between her children and their stepfather, the more the others insisted that what was happening in America was still very much the business of her family in England. The well-being of the children was what concerned everyone most when Nell married Manny, and it was soon impossible to ignore the question of when and how to bring them to England, and away from the influence of a man so obviously unsuited to the role of step-father.

Mrs Pickersgill-Cunliffe tended to believe that the likelihood of children being in danger, though a matter of serious concern were it ever shown to be true, had probably been exaggerated. She suspected that Nell simply wanted to be rid of her offspring, of the cost or bother of educating them, and made her husband take the blame for her own failures as a mother. She doubted the veracity of Nell's occasional dramatic revelations about life in Graceham, their home in Maryland, and Manny's behaviour there. Was he hitting them, or worse? And what could be worse than hitting them? She could not imagine.

"Oh mother," said Ethel. "If only you knew the truth of what goes on in some families."

"Not," said her mother, unmoved, "in a family such as ours."

But if it did mother, her daughters asked. What if it actually did?

The facts of the matter should be ascertained, once and for all, and Ethel was the one elected to go there and get to the bottom of it. She had, as it happened, been invited to join a party led by the wife of the Bishop of Rochester that was undertaking an ambitious tour of churches and Christian communities right across America. It would be a simple matter to tie this in with some time spent with Nell and her family.

After a dreadful crossing over on the S.S. *Majestic*, telegraphing home on arrival the single word 'orange', code for "rough at first, sick almost all through", Ethel went for her first visit to Graceham after a few days in New York. Everyone was pleased to see her and even Manny seemed welcoming and friendly. Ethel's energetic nature helped to create a more cheerful mood than expected, considering the picture of tension and conflict painted by Nell's most recent letters. She stayed for little over a week before setting off on the first stage of her American tour, and apart from a couple of occasions when Nell whispered to her that Manny was being difficult about the children but she could say no more just then, things didn't seem so bad there. Each day would end with whole family all together, scattered into different corners of their living room, too cold to escape outside, reading, knitting, whispering, playing checkers, cheating at checkers, loudly protesting, teasing one another. Manny would slump in his armchair and sleep off the beer he'd drank with his supper and for as long as that lasted things would stay calm enough. Ethel would sit beside Nell and talk pleasantly of trivialities.

She returned to Graceham in January, still far from convinced that there was really any need to rescue the children, to take one or all of them back with her to England, but was determined to confront the issue with Nell before it was too late.

Manny was not there when she returned. He was travelling in Pennsylvania and North Virginia hoping to make some sales, and home felt unusually relaxed. She took them all to Baltimore to have photographs taken of the children to show the people back home, including one of them all together: Nell in the centre, doing her best to look matriarchal; Virginia to Nell's left trying to appear older than she was; Tom, standing slightly askew behind her with his jacket unbuttoned, sporting a slightly rakish air; Frances, standing next to him, brave and bright, a slight smile on her lips. They had made an effort to dress up for the occasion, although Tom's effort was perhaps not all it might have been.

The photographer disappeared behind the camera under his hood, assuring them that this would be a lovely family portrait, but the story it told was not exactly that: there was no husband in sight and Nell, all in black, looked more like a widow than a wife. Ethel wondered how wise it would be to let Manny see it and, from the way Nell looked at it, she must have felt the same although she did thank Ethel very much.

It was a whole week before Manny reappeared, tired and disappointed with his trip, and looking for trouble. This time he did not greet Ethel with any warmth, and it shocked her how quickly the atmosphere in the house began to creak with the tension of his presence. He very soon got sight of the photograph, because Nell thought it would be best to show it to him before he found it for himself. All hell broke loose around the dinner table as he waved it around, shouting at everyone, Ethel included, demanding to know why they'd done this without him. But angry as he was at being left out of the family group, what really made him mad was how *pleased* Frances seemed in the picture; you could see it in her sly smile. Ethel watched him closely as he glared back and forth between Frances in the photo and Frances in the flesh. Suddenly he reached out to her, as if to stroke her cheek but grabbed the back of her head instead and held it hard, staring at her like a crazy thing. "Who do you think you are, little girl?" he said, pulling her face close towards his, everyone else holding their breath. "*Fucking princess.*"

Ethel could bear it no longer. "Stop that Manny!" she shouted. "Let her go!"

Nell looked on appalled, Tom cast a dark crooked grin at Virginia, who was creeping forward to put herself between Manny and her aunt. Manny spun around to his sister-in-law, fist clenched for violence but just managing to hold it back, though not the words that exploded out of him. "Mind your damned business!" he spat. "You've overstayed your welcome woman. Get out, just get outta here."

Ethel resolved that night to book her passage home and, over the next two days whenever she and Nell had a moment alone together, plotted Frances's removal to England.

"How do you bear it Nell?" Ethel asked.

"Sometimes it's all right," Nell said. "It's not bad a lot of the time. Just too many of us in a small house, the kids are getting too big."

Ethel wasn't going to be so easily deflected. "Come now Nell," she said. "You can't even trust your husband with your children."

"He's mostly harmless Ethel. He doesn't mean anything by it," Nell said.

"I think he might," said Ethel, "I honestly do." Nell glared back at her, and then gave up being brave. "Am I going to have to let my children go, Ethel? Lost to me forever in England. I don't think I could bear that," she said.

"Well," said Ethel. "I'm going to take Frances back with me now. Her at least, am I not Nell?"

Nell moaned that *he* wouldn't let her go, that nothing makes him so angry as the family back in England deciding what's best for everyone, and she really didn't know what to do for the best. Ethel hugged her sister, who started to sob vigorously. Then equally suddenly she stopped, pulled herself together, nodded resolutely and agreed. "Yes of course she must go with you. Best for everyone."

They told Manny next day that this was what was going to happen and another huge row exploded, so furiously that for a while Ethel was certain she had entirely lost the chance of rescuing Frances. Nothing was said about the issue the next day, on Nell's advice leaving it be while he calmed down, but the day after that Manny came at Frances with a coach whip, actually hitting her, and then was so shaken by the reaction, everyone screaming at him, that he backed off and finally agreed to let her leave. But, after winding himself up for a few more hours, he told her she would never be welcome in his home again.

Just a week later, in a turmoil of relief and rejection, Frances found herself waving an aching goodbye to her family, those she loved best, them waving as bravely as they could back at her, as she and Ethel set off by train to Baltimore, and from there on to New York where the *Majestic* was preparing itself for another trip across the wild Atlantic.

8

The voyage took almost two days longer than normal, the *Majestic* battling freezing temperatures and mountainous seas all the way across the Atlantic. There were times when passengers were not allowed out on the decks at all, and on one occasion a group of cardsharps and their unsuspecting victims were drenched by a wave that had swept right across her decks and into the smoke room. As the voyage finally made its way up the coast of England to Liverpool, Captain Parsell took his regular tour of the Promenade Deck to charm the wealthier passengers and leave them with a positive recollection of the voyage. "Well now, Miss Cunliffe," he said, when he saw Aunt Ethel. "Another rough old crossing!"

Ethel told him that she had felt completely safe in his hands throughout, although the sea had indeed made her very sick.

"Did I ever tell you the story of a certain elderly lady who used to travel on this very liner, Miss Cunliffe?" Ethel looked at him with as much enthusiasm as she could muster for a story he'd told her twice on the way over. "'Captain,' this lady says to me, 'I've crossed the Atlantic numerous times before in all kinds of weather, and don't ever recall feeling so ill. Why is that, do you think?' And I just says to her 'Bad memory!'"

"Bad memory!" he repeated, still chuckling. "Well there we are," he said, and smiled benignly at Frances. "And might I be introduced to your young companion?"

"This is my niece. Miss Hodgkinson," said Ethel. "Coming to England for the first time."

"Well I hope you have a delightful visit," said the Captain.

Frances looked down, and muttered.

"I'm sorry, Miss Hodgkinson?"

"I'm not *visiting*," she insisted, anguished at having to talk to the man at all, but needing to make this point. "Wonderful, wonderful," said the Captain. "Such a pleasure to have the company of you both." He shook Ethel's hand, gave her young niece an ill-judged pat on the head, and carried on his way. Frances scowled. She hated the attentions of old men.

At the start of the voyage her aunt had taken her to the ship's surgeon, Dr O'Loughlin, to get something for the inevitable seasickness. The doctor assured Ethel that he remembered her very well from the outward voyage, and warmly told Frances how delighted he was to meet her. Whilst he chatted to her aunt, and gave her a brand new and much improved seasickness tonic, Frances sat to one side and studied the many photos of elegant ladies on the walls of the room. O'Loughlin, turning to her, explained that these were portraits of celebrated passengers, all of them his close friends, that he'd had the pleasure of treating in the course of his many previous Atlantic crossings. He brought his chair right up in front of her, came forward and stared into her face with professional intensity. He leaned in and raised first one and then the other of her eyelids, peering for several seconds into her eyes whilst gripping her wrist to take her pulse. Frances flinched from his awful warm breath, squirmed under his touch, and failed to suppress a small shiver of revulsion.

"I must now inspect your tongue," the doctor announced. Frances stared back at him, keeping her mouth firmly shut. Ethel watched with growing alarm.

"The tongue," O'Loughlin explained, "tells us all we need to know about the state of a patient's health, so if you would please open wide … " He cupped her chin in his hand, as if to make her open her jaw, and her eyes narrowed in resistance. Then, without warning, she suddenly did open wide and, furiously glaring, stuck her tongue right out at him.

He jumped back, and muttered that everything seemed to be entirely in order. Ethel took this as the moment to bring the consultation to an immediate conclusion. "Thank you so much," she chirruped, and pulled her niece out of his office without waiting for a response. They clattered away up the deck, Frances's cheeks flushing at her own audacity.

Ethel retired to her bed once the weather worsened, and very little more was seen of her. Frances, who experienced hardly a moment of queasiness, happily wandered the ship on her own, through saloons, libraries, promenades and restaurants. Her appetite unaffected and virtually the only passenger braving the grand dining room on some occasions, she permitted the bored and flirtatious young waiters to try out their most exotic dishes on her: Blue Point oysters, Egg à L'Argentuil, Striped Bass in Sauce Diplomate, Parisienne Potatoes and Calf's Brains à L'Italienne. Each time she survived one of these they let her loose on the pastries. Such indulgences were quite unfamiliar to her, and she wondered if this was how her new life in England might be; but was then immediately mortified to think of what her siblings back in Maryland would be eating that day.

The wild ocean behind them at last, Ethel telegraphed the Hermitage from Queenstown Harbour with the news that she and Frances would arrive in Liverpool the next morning, and should make it home by dinner time. The telegram brought immense excitement and rejoicing to aunts, uncle and grandmother, as they hadn't even known for sure whether she had actually managed to extract Frances from the clutches of Manny Dent.

The two women left Liverpool on the London express at 4 pm, with just enough daylight to glimpse the northwest of England under dirty snow. Frances pressed her face to the window, but could see little of the beloved homeland constantly rhapsodised by her mother. Miserable snow-covered trees, houses, factories, stations. In the first part of the journey they mostly dozed or stared blankly into the darkness outside, but travelling out from London Bridge towards Kent, a compartment to themselves, Ethel thought the time had come to prepare her niece for their arrival at the Hermitage.

"There's really nothing to be nervous about, dear," she said, in her brisk, kindly way.

Frances nodded, but with little conviction. She wanted the journey both to be over and continue for ever.

"You will be completely safe in your new home," Ethel assured her, smiling kindly. She patted her niece's nervously twisting hands. "There now," she said.

After a minute or two, Frances said "Will everyone be there? How should I greet them all, how will I remember who everyone is?"

Ethel knew well enough what her family could be like at such times. "Oh, don't worry about that," she said. "Just let them hold and kiss you. You won't get a word in."

The road from Higham Station was strange that night to both of them, newly contoured by several days of snow. The brougham rumbled and slithered over rutted tracks as it struggled up the steep hill from the station to the church. Once out of the village and into open country, they suddenly were able to see all the way down to the estuary, the fields and distant water brilliant and gleaming in the moonlight. They travelled on without speaking for a short while more until Ethel said "Look Frances!" and they saw the warm lights of a huge house standing proud behind a high wall. "Here we are," she said, as they turned in through the gates.

The welcoming party – Mary Harriette, Evelyn, Gertrude, Kay, Milicent, Herbert, Mother – had spent the day waiting for news, calculating and recalculating arrival times with each new telegram. They passed the long hours as best they could: Gertrude, Kay and Herbert tried billiard tricks, Evelyn visited her elderly ladies, Mother kept herself occupied in her own room, Mary Harriette wrote letters and knitted. Then a final message came from Ethel setting back their arrival at Higham Station until after 10 pm. They all sat together in the Library and started to think seriously about what it would mean to have this unknown girl in their lives. The romance of bringing her over to England was, they suddenly realised, about to become a reality. She would certainly need a good deal of loving help if she was to learn how to become an accomplished young English lady. They doubted that Nell would have managed to instil all the necessary talents into her, out there on her isolated American farms.

Evelyn proposed they make a list then and there of all the things Frances needed to know, and learn how to do.

"Wonderful!" Mary Harriette said, excited at the prospect. "We shall start immediately. Just call out the first things that come to mind." She grabbed a pen and paper from the desk by which she was sitting.

"Deportment," said Gertrude.

"Golf," said Milicent.

"Swimming," said Evelyn.

"Arithmetic," said Kay.

"Sewing," said Mary Harriette.

"French," said Milicent.

"German," said Mary Harriette.

"Shakespeare," said Evelyn, and everyone nodded.

"Should we not simply get her a tutor first of all?" called a dubious Herbert, who had settled in a far corner with *Punch*. "Or send her straight off to school."

"Well, I think we might be capable of doing a great deal ourselves," said Mary Harriette, "considering of course that both myself and Evelyn have long taught Sunday school."

"Right, yes," said Herbert. It struck him that he actually had no idea how his sisters spent their time.

"Music," said Gertrude.

"Managing a family budget," continued Mary Harriette.

"The economy of the kitchen," added Evelyn.

"British manners," said Milicent. "And speaking the Queen's English."

Total agreement.

"We cannot presume that she will have had an adequate education in the basics of Anglican theology," said Mary Harriette with a solemnity that briefly silenced everyone apart from Herbert, who sighed.

"I'm sure Nell will have done her best in that respect," said Kay.

"Well I am not," declared Mary Harriette. "At any rate, we have a good number of printed sermons by the distinguished clerics of our own family, with which a well-educated young lady might at least be acquainted I should think." Herbert threw Gertrude a quiet grin.

"Or novels," said Milicent.

"They have novels in America, you know," said Gertrude. "*Uncle Tom's Cabin*, *Little Women*. Jolly good ones."

"*Huckleberry Finn*," added Herbert.

"British novels," Milicent corrected.

"Scott? Or George Eliot, perhaps," said Mary Harriette.

"Steady on. The poor girl's only 15," said Herbert.

At this moment, the travellers expected any moment, their mother came down and joined them, and asked them what they had been talking about. She immediately referred them to what Mr Ruskin had to say on the matter.

"I have been rereading *Sesame and Lilies* this evening," she said, "with specific respect to this very question of a young woman's education. Especially the nature of the home as the Place of Peace." At that very moment and before their mother could develop this thought, they heard the sound of the carriage drawing up, and they all rushed outside into the cold wintry air to greet the travellers.

Frances alighted first, followed by Ethel in high spirits. Hugs, approving inspections at arms' length, further hugging: the Frances that most were seeing for the first time turned out to be a slight dark girl with nice eyes, dressed in blue and wearing a little felt hat and a grey cloak, all carried over by Ethel in the hope of coming back with Frances. They cooed with delight as she carefully greeted each one of them by name in her soft American drawl.

The travellers were hustled inside, and everyone sat around watching whilst they ate their supper. Ethel related the full drama of the dreadful voyage, making the most of the danger the ship had been in, whilst Frances worked her way through cold mutton, tomatoes, bread and cheese, Bakewell tart.

"You must be fatigued, dear," said Mary Harriette.

"I'm very well, thank you," said Frances, looking around at all these family members she hardly knew. "It makes me so happy to see you all."

"We must seem terribly strange to you," said Kay kindly.

"Oh no!" said Frances. "Mother has told me so many lovely things about each one of you."

Much approval all around.

"So you will stay with us a while longer?" asked Herbert, tactlessly teasing.

Frances looked alarmed.

"I only – " he began and then, glares from all around, gave up. "Have some cream on your tart," Mary Harriette suggested, taking a big dollop for herself.

Once done with the eating, the travellers were escorted straight upstairs, and Frances was whisked off to bed, where she lay awake for a while, buzzing with too many emotions, until she suddenly found herself confronted by a shining white English morning and a cosy fire crackling in the grate, as a special once-in-a-lifetime treat.

After breakfast, Aunt Mary helped Frances unpack her trunk, looked over the clothes she'd brought with her and then immediately took her to Gravesend to buy some necessities: Sunday hat, coat and gloves, and some evening slippers. Frances was thrilled of course, though had to go to bed soon after tea, as she was beginning a cold, which gave the grown-ups ample opportunity to discuss her, and Nell, and Nell's dreadful husband.

They found Frances completely delightful but, of course, quite fragile, in terms of her spirit certainly and perhaps her constitution as well, which was only to be expected. Ethel confirmed how volatile the situation was in Graceham, and that Brother-in-Law had decreed that Frances was never to enter his house again. It made them all quite disgusted with him, and rather confused about Nell, whom they did love without reservation, but whose behaviour with respect to Mr Dent was hard to fathom. Whilst they would never consider questioning the authority of a husband, they could not help observing that it was Nell's money that had paid for everything, including the house in which Frances was now no longer welcome. And her departure from Graceham was far from being the end of that particular problem.

"It's all right Aunt Mary," Frances said. "I can do this myself."

"Very good dear, I'm sure you can," Mary Harriette said, with absolutely no intention of taking the hint. "But I'll just stay here to see if I can be of any use."

Frances breathed hard, and then picked up the first of her embarrassingly threadbare frocks, trying to take charge of the mending process before Aunt Mary found more to repair than strictly necessary. Mary Harriette made a great effort to leave her to it, smiling encouragingly, and kept her counsel for as long as she could. Grimly, Frances started sewing up rips in the first frock at some speed, until she felt her aunt leaning in and looking rather closely at her work.

"I don't suppose," Mary Harriette said, "that you ever read the book I sent you years ago on this very subject?" Frances stared at her blankly. "The little book I myself wrote."

Oh Lord, thought Frances.

"Sarah Best's Work Basket."

"Ah yes," Frances said, frowning. "I think I did."

"Well be that as it may," said Aunt Mary, unconvinced, "it was just a modest thing, I know. But it did try to tell a simple but important lesson about life, which I daresay you were too young to understand at the time."

Frances desperately wanted her aunt to think well of her. "I guess I might now, Aunt Mary."

"You *believe* that you might," Mary Harriette said, to an uncomprehending Frances. One thing at a time. "The lesson of the book is about how we live best if we do the simple things in life well, with patience and care. Simple things such as sewing an old frock."

Frances blushed, to think of the clothes she had brought with her.

"If you can take pride in doing the smallest of tasks for the *Lord*, you need never be downcast." Mary Harriette warmed to her task. "In everything, Frances, even mending a skirt, He cares for us and for our labour. If we do the work for Him who died for us, it can never be wrong."

Frances looked at her clumsy stitching and knew that she would have to undo it and start again. She desperately did not want to offend Aunt Mary, not to mention the Lord Himself.

"Do you understand now, Frances?" Mary Harriette asked kindly.

"Yes I do, I do," Frances said, solemnly starting to unpick her first efforts.

"Very good," said Mary Harriette, sensing that the piety might be getting out of hand. The dear girl, so keen to please, she thought, and for what good? Her old frocks would all be sent for burning or given to the poor as soon as her grandmother saw them.

9

Abigail Adams volunteered three evenings a week at the Girls' Friendly Society hostel, which lay in the shadow of Rochester Cathedral. She was a small, pale and fairly anxious young woman, younger than most of the friendless girls she was trying to help and, despite her enthusiasm for education and deep wish to be of value, not really up to the task of teaching troubled young women. The Pickersgill-Cunliffe sisters liked to refer to them as Ethel's rough girls, and this had proved to be uncomfortably accurate as far as poor Abby was concerned, given the kind of things they got up to when they'd had enough of her reading instruction. Just slight teasing, and holding her back when she tried to stop them throwing the Bible out of the window; it was so easy to make her cry. Ethel caught them at it one evening and as soon as she'd told the smirking girls what she thought of them, offered to walk Abigail home.

"Your help is greatly appreciated," she told Abigail, as she led her at a brisk pace through the darkened streets of Rochester. "But I think we need to consider how best you might devote yourself to our cause in ways you might find more, ah, appropriate?"

Abigail nodded. "I always thought I could do well as a teacher," she said. "I thought that if I just kept trying – "

" – yes indeed," said Ethel. She stopped and took Abigail's hand, an idea suddenly taking shape in her endlessly buzzing mind. "But might I suggest a rather gentler path to learning the pedagogue's trade, dear?"

Abigail nodded tearfully.

"I have this niece, you see," Ethel said.

The following Monday morning, exactly on time, Abigail arrived at the Hermitage to start her new job, having walked up in the rain over the fields from Higham Station. It was no small indication of how much she wanted to make a success of this, of anything really, that she did not immediately turn tail and run when she passed through the gate and looked up at the big house, with its high ivy-covered walls and windows, gardens everywhere and a conservatory so big you could fit the whole of her own home into it. Faint with anxiety, she rang the bell and was eventually admitted to the hall, to wait nervously until Ethel appeared and showed her up to the schoolroom: along past the main staircase, through a narrow door and down a long back corridor, through another narrow door and up a small spiral staircase, and finally back down another long corridor. "It's so much quicker to get there this way," she explained, unnecessarily. Abigail understood well enough; she was an employee, she wouldn't have expected to go any other way but the back way.

Ethel threw the door open to reveal an earnest-looking Frances waiting at her desk, a clean exercise book, fresh pencils, eraser, pen and ink neatly arranged before her. "Here she is!" Ethel announced, neither of them quite sure which one of them she was referring to.

For the next few hours, through careful enquiry and easy tests, Abigail did her best to chart the highs and lows of Frances's educational history. It was by no means a straightforward picture for, despite some shocking gaps, Frances was more or less as well-educated as most girls of her age and class: her handwriting was quite nice and her punctuation seemed by no means hopeless; she knew the important parts of speech but had no idea of what it meant to parse a clause; she had heard of a few memorable figures from history: King Arthur, Queen Boadicea, Robin Hood, Guy Fawkes and Sir Francis Drake, and her favourite book was *Rob Roy*. She could do sums in her head but claimed never to have encountered long division. Nearly all that she did know seemed to have been taught her by her mother, including a few words of French. The Classics were a closed book to her and so, disappointingly, was any knowledge of world geography. She had very little awareness of the events of her own time, in terms of wars, politics, prime ministers and the like. She had been taught, many times, about the American War of Independence at school, and strongly disapproved, but to Abigail's amazement she knew nothing of the Civil War, not that something so recent could be considered history as such, anyway.

Despite her own chronic trepidation, Abigail quickly relaxed in the company of her new charge, and by the end of their first morning Frances thoroughly approved of her new tutor; she liked the patient way she listened to her, and the fact that she was young and shy. She was sorry when their first morning together came to an end.

So was Abigail, because she knew that her own morning was not over until she had been interviewed by Ethel's daunting elder sister, Miss Pickersgill-Cunliffe. It was just a formality, Ethel explained, she's a dear thing really; Abigail had glimpsed her a few times down at the Girls' Friendly Society, and that had not been her impression at all. Trembling slightly, to her own annoyance, she knocked on the door of the library and was summoned in.

"Bonjour, Miss Adams," said Mary Harriette, in a sturdy English accent. "Asseyez vous, s'il vous plait. Puis-je vous demander quel âge vous avez?"

"Merci, madame," Abigail replied, in a very small voice. "J'ai dix-neuf ans."

"Sehr gut," said Mary Harriette. "Sagen sie mir, bitte, waren sie je im Ausland gegangen?"

"Um," said Abigail, in an agony of blushing. "Nie, es tut mir leid zu sagen." Then, apologetically, "I have never left England."

"I see," said Mary Harriette. She threw her a few questions about this and that, her studies in school and adult evening classes, her opinion of certain authors, and whether arithmetic was a proper field of study for a young woman, which they both agreed it was, and Abigail told her that history was her greatest love. Having rapidly established that Miss Adams possessed more than ample knowledge of all the things a modern young lady might need to be acquainted with, Mary Harriette moved on to the topic of Frances herself.

"In your opinion, do you think she will be a good pupil?" she asked.

"Oh yes," said Abigail. "She wants to be, I am sure. I will enjoy teaching her."

"But you will be prepared to show firmness when that is called for?" Mary Harriette asked, representing her mother's very specific instruction. "'Whom the Lord loves he reproves,' you know."

Yes, she knew. They made a big point of that at the Girls' Friendly Society, and it hadn't helped.

Mary Harriette sat silently for some seconds, nodded to herself and then told Abigail how glad she was that she had been available at such short notice. She stressed the fact that this would be merely a stopgap arrangement until an appropriate school could be found for Frances. Miss Adams's task, therefore, was simply to ensure that Frances would make a respectable showing of herself when that time came. There was certainly no intention of trying to turn her into a bluestocking; heaven forbid. Abigail blanched slightly, aware that both in appearance and her deepest desires, a bluestocking was what she herself would always be.

Mary Harriette reached out to shake Abigail's hand as she rose to leave.

"Without going into detail, you must be aware that my niece has not had the easiest of childhoods," she said, softening, "so we must balance firmness with kindness at all times. My niece is easily upset, it seems."

From 9.30 to 12.30 each morning tutor and pupil worked through three different lessons, meticulously timed by Abigail to allow for instruction, exercises, correction and revision. She also did her best to ensure some variety in what was an inescapably dreary curriculum, so that the morning always involved at least some arithmetic, dictation, and conversational French or German, sometimes with a little story from history or the Bible or Shakespeare to keep things light. At 11 every morning there would be five minutes' relaxation over a glass of milk and a slice of cake or a biscuit. The morning would end with Miss Adams proposing one or two tasks that Frances might work at on her own during the afternoons.

Frances approached her lessons with Miss Adams in a good spirit, but by the end of the fourth day she was feeling overwhelmed by the relentless schedule, which was a good deal more intense than anything she had ever experienced before. Neither did all this work entirely shield her from her aunts' interest in her education. Aunt Mary continued to insist on daily sewing lessons and Bible study, and when Aunt Kay proposed a quick burst of mental arithmetic at tea-time after an afternoon working on her own in the schoolroom, Frances said she didn't feel well, refused a slice of cake, which she did not mean to do at all, and ran out of the room. She cheered up by dinner time to everyone's relief.

She was moody again the next evening, although this was not the direct result of studying too hard. She had just read through a newly arrived letter from her mother and, in the quiet time between tea and dinner, seated by a blazing fire, was suddenly overwhelmed by the realisation of how her life had changed. "I'm so selfish!" she wailed, "I've got everything I could possibly want here and they hardly have enough to eat and keep them warm at night and I never give them a thought, not a thought!"

Ethel had a brief word with Abigail as she arrived the following Monday morning, to alert her to the recent evidence of Frances's fragilities. "Perhaps," she said, "you could consider lightening your plans for today's work in some way. If you think that might be possible. Or appropriate, in your judgement."

Abigail assured her that it definitely was; she was only too delighted to abandon the schedule for today. "I wonder," she asked, "if I may borrow a volume of some kind from your library?"

When she entered the schoolroom, she found Frances seated as usual at her desk, staring glumly at an extremely old schoolbook.

"It's horrible," she muttered. "My grandmother gave it to me. She said there is none better."

Abigail looked over her shoulder. "Good heavens yes!" she said. "The Young Ladies' English Grammar. Must be a hundred years old!"

"It's horrible and it's stupid," said Frances, scowling. "Look at this: *The firft perfon fpeaks of himfelf as I fingular.* What on earth does that mean?"

Abigail turned over the pages with her. "Or this! *A VERB is a word which fignifies to be, to do, to fuffer.* That's what you're doing right now Frances, you're fuffering!"

Frances looked alarmed.

"That's just old-fashioned ways of printing words," said Abigail. "It's easy enough to read once you get used to it. This is an excellent book, if you want to understand grammar."

"Well I don't," Frances muttered.

"Excellent, because that's not what we're going to do today," said Abigail. She sat down beside Frances, took a large leather-bound volume out of her bag, and laid it on the desk in front of them both. "Chapter 1: I am Born", she began. She glanced at Frances, who was earnestly listening, read the opening paragraph, and saw she already had her full attention. So she read on all the way through the first chapter, and then paused. "Do you know this book, Frances?" She shook her head. "It's *David Copperfield* by Charles Dickens. You've heard of him I am sure."

She had. She remembered Nell reading to them about a boy who asked for more gruel, and about Christmas ghosts, and about a brave man who got guillotined, which used to make her mother cry.

"Such a great man. He lived very near to here, you know, in Higham. Gads Hill. He died there!" said Abigail enthusiastically. "Don't you love the description of Peggotty with 'cheeks and arms so red that I wondered the birds didn't peck her in preference to apples'?"

Frances nodded approvingly.

"Isn't that perfect?!" Abigail said, pointing excitedly at the page. "And here! He's recalls the smells 'of soap, pickles, pepper, candles, and coffee, all at one whiff'. All at one whiff! Dickens says we can all remember things like that from when we very little."

"Dickens says?" asked Frances, genuinely confused. "I thought that was what David Copperfield said."

"Well," said Abigail, "Dickens makes David Copperfield say it, I suppose you could say."

"He makes him say it?" Frances repeated.

"Anyway," continued Abigail. "The point is that we can all remember things from our earliest years, if we really try. Are there things you remember like that Frances?"

Frances closed her eyes, and tried to concentrate hard. She stared out of the window for a while, looking up the road towards Higham. "Our horse," she said suddenly. "His big face, he had such a big face. Big nose and big teeth. Nancy said that he frightened me once when I was in my pram and made me scream."

"Excellent!" said Abigail, not sure if this did constitute an authentic first memory. "Who was Nancy?"

"She looked after the three of us, she was with us all the time when we were little, our nanny but we called her Nancy. She was pretty and told us lovely stories when we were little. Like Brer Rabbit and the Tar Baby, and how Brer Rabbit didn't mind being thrown in the briar patch because that's where he lived anyway." Frances explained. "I really loved her but she had to leave when my mother got married again."

"How sad," Abigail said. Frances said it's okay now, it was a long time ago. Abigail waited for a moment or two. "What was your house like when you were little?" she asked. "Was it nice?"

"I think so," said Frances uncertainly. "It was a farm. Down a long stony track. We had a field and a muddy pond which my sister fell into and Nancy had to pull her out. It wasn't very deep. It smelt horrid sometimes." Abigail nodded encouragingly, thrilled to have at last generated a real response from one of her pupils, and read little David Copperfield's visit to Mr Peggotty's magical house in Yarmouth.

When it was time to go, Abigail told her she probably wouldn't be coming for the next few days, and asked Frances if she'd like to do some writing of her own while she was away. "You can tell me about things you remember especially well about growing up in America," she suggested, very carefully, not wanting to stretch Frances's enthusiasm too far. "Whatever comes to your mind. Just tell me about what's important to you."

The next day Abigail sent a letter to Mary Harriette apologising for the fact that, on account of a very bad cold, it would wisest if she stayed at home for the rest of the week.

Among the various other activities laid on for her, Frances worked hard at her special writing assignment, and couldn't wait to show Miss Adams, whose absence she felt keenly.

Abigail finally reappeared at the end of luncheon just over a week later, a great relief as Frances had just been reproved by her grandmother for being fractious and grumbling yet again; Frances had burst into tears and everyone was having a heavy time of it. Abigail was encouraged to take Frances straight up to the schoolroom and out of the way.

Once Frances had calmed down, which she usually did very rapidly, Abigail asked her what she had done during her absence. Frances answered that she had done all her schoolwork as instructed, and her aunts had inspected it every day. She believed that they were very pleased with her progress.

"I also wrote this," she then said, with a conspiratorial look, handing her a piece of paper. "It's the thing you asked me to do."

Abigail clapped her hands in delight. "Did you show this to your aunts too?" she asked.

"No I didn't," said Frances. "It's just for you. It's not schoolwork." Abigail had already started reading it.

Memories of America by Frances Helen Hodgkinson

My favourite memory of when I was little is this story that Nancy used to tell us.

"There was once a woman who wanted to have a daughter more than anything in the world. But she was childless. She was very unhappy because she wanted to share her life with a daughter. One day she was gathering yams in the field and she pulled out one that was perfect and she said, If only this fine yam were a daughter, how happy I would be.

103

"To her amazement the yam answered. If I were to be your daughter, would you promise never to scold me for having been a yam once? The woman promised, and suddenly the yam turned into a beautiful wellmade girl. The woman was overjoyed and was very kind to the girl, who she called Adzanumy. Adzanumy was always useful to her mother. She made bread, she gathered yams and sold them at market.

"But one day she was away too long and her mother got impatient and angry and said Where can Adzanumy be? She does not deserve such a beautiful name, after all she is only a yam.

"A bird singing nearby heard what the mother had said and flew away to the tree that Adzanumy was sitting under and sang a song to tell the girl what her mother had said. Adzanumy went home weeping and her mother asked her what the matter was. The girl sang this song. Oh Mother! Dear Mother! You have scolded me for being a yam. You said I did not deserve my name. Oh Mother! Dear Mother!

"Her mother was very frightened and promised Adzanumy she had never said that. You are my daughter, my dear daughter Adzanumy, she said. But it was too late. Adzanumy hurried back to the yam field and when she got there she changed back into a yam, still singing her song. And when her mother got there she found the yam on the ground and nothing she could do would give her daughter back to her.

The End"

Other things I remember are when Virginia fell in our pond and came out covered in mud. Papa was terribly angry with Nancy and threatened to dismiss her when he saw how muddy Virginia was but it was not Nancy's fault because Tom and I were there when she fell in and we were really to blame to be honest.

Papa died when I was only five. By then there was my older brother Tom and my sister Virginia, who is a year younger than me. For a while we'd had a little brother called Cyril but he died when he was just 2 which was awful. We all cried for days including Mother.

Mother was most sad for a long time when Papa died. She said that her life had ended on the day he died, and I remember being afraid she would die too. She said she loved him more than anyone, and I did too though I was quite frightened of him. He was tall, with a big beard. He sometimes got very angry when he was not well. He died when he was forty years old.

Mother used to tell us what a brave sailor Papa had been. After he died, she used to tell us about the brave things he had done in the Navy, fighting pirates and saving the Admiral's life. We asked Mother to tell us that story over and over, and she did, because she used to like talking a lot about Papa after he had died.

But then she got married again to Manny Dent who is my stepfather. Manny gets drunk which is worst of all, although Mother says he cannot help it, and what about your father. But our father never did what Manny does. I cannot believe that anyone could be as horrid as Manny. The worst when he is drunk is he pulls you onto his knee, and tells us to call him Papa. But we will not. And then when you try to get away from him, he starts to shout and if you shout back he hits you. I screamed at him and he pushed me away, and told me to leave the house and never come back. He whispers in your ear and says awful things when mother is not around.

When Mother found out about the things he whispers she got furious with him, and decided it would be better if I came to England.

At first Abigail grinned approvingly at Frances a couple of times, but began to look rather more serious as she went on. She read it all through twice without saying anything.

"Oh Frances," she said quietly, when she finally finished.

"Don't you like it?" Frances asked anxiously.

"Well yes! No!" said Abigail. This was coming out all wrong. "You've done wonderfully well Frances, really. To write this. But I'm so sorry –" Abigail was appalled at what she had unleashed; she'd had no idea. But then she saw that Frances was looking pleased, though why she could not imagine.

"You said to tell you about me," she said. "So I did. That's right isn't it?"

Abigail took her hand, and told her it was completely right. "Do your aunts know? About all the difficulties? With Mr Dent."

Frances nodded, a little uncertainly. "I think they might," she said. "My aunts discuss things about me all the time, but not when I'm there of course so I've no idea what they say."

"Of course not," said Abigail, who feared she might be hearing more than she ought to. She judged it would be unwise in her position to encourage Frances to tell her any more, and she should definitely not raise such matters with the aunts herself. So she left it there, and just gave Frances a small intimate your-secret's-safe-with-me look; the less said the better.

Then she clapped her hands brightly and asked Frances whether she wanted to carry on with *David Copperfield*, and Frances cried out a delighted "oh yes!". But as Abigail opened the book to find the start of the next chapter, she glimpsed the name Murdstone, remembered what was coming next, and decided that there was no great merit in reading about bullying step-fathers just now. She paused a moment.

"On reflection," she said eventually, "I think we really ought to carry on with your equations now." When she left at the end of the morning, she took *David Copperfield* with her, just in case.

As far as Frances was concerned, it was no great loss. She was never going to make her own way through a book as long as that.

Supremely practised as she was in forbearance, which nobody could doubt, Mrs Pickersgill-Cunliffe found it increasingly hard as she grew old to tolerate children, especially when they acted childishly. She had for some time expressed severe reservations as to whether the Hermitage could in fact accommodate her grandchild at all, should she be rescued from America; the house was nowhere near as spacious as people presumed. But the fact that the girl was nearly sixteen and therefore on the threshold of womanhood had finally convinced her grandmother to allow her to come. Mrs Cunliffe was far from happy to discover, once Frances had arrived, that she was beyond question still very much a child in many ways, all of which her grandmother found irksome. So on serious and prayerful reflection, it probably would be best if they sent her to boarding school sooner rather than later, she explained to Mary Harriette who, though she definitely did not feel that way, knew well enough when an argument was lost before it had even begun.

Mary Harriette was talking with Gertrude and Evelyn in the library, about the progress she had made in selecting a suitable school, when Frances came bursting in from her dancing class and realised from their sudden silence that she was once more the subject of discussion. She demanded to know what they were saying about her. Mary Harriette explained, with as much lightness of spirit as she could muster, that they were merely exploring the possibility of her perhaps going away to school after Easter. She had written to a very nice lady called Miss White, who ran an excellent school in Brighton, to explore the possibility.

"Without telling me?" Frances shouted. "When were you going to tell *me?*"

Mary Harriette, flustered and upset to find that the last thing she had wanted to happen had just happened, reached out towards Frances with tears in her eyes. "Oh my dear child," she cried. "Of course, of course, as soon as things were clear. I was just trying to see —"

" — why do I have to go away again? I am doing very well with Miss Adams, so why must I go away?" she shouted, and ran out of the room once more. Gertrude told Mary Harriette that she sympathised entirely with Frances, and she should indeed have consulted her before trying to organise everything as she always did. Evelyn looked on silently, as her two sisters had a short outburst of heated words and tears, followed by boot heels clattering up corridors, doors banging in the distance, and a cry from Mother upstairs, demanding to know what exactly was going on.

Any attempt at a firm decision was deferred until Gertrude and Evelyn were able to talk things over with Frances. Mary Harriette then invited her into the library, after she'd had a day or two more to reflect on the plan, to see how she felt now about going away to school. Everything had in fact been agreed with Miss White by now and a deposit paid over, but Mary Harriette wanted her to feel it was her own decision. To her considerable surprise and relief, it emerged that Frances, liking the sound of Brighton very much and warming to the notion of being with girls her own age, was firmly in favour.

During Abigail Adams's final weeks as Frances's tutor, she took care not to stray from the agreed curriculum any further, and Frances laboured away at those things that might be expected of her at Miss White's. They worked happily together at tasks neither found particularly interesting or enjoyable, but which had to be done, because they had to be. As a reward for her positive attitude, Frances was allowed to go with Miss Adams to her home in Rochester on their last Friday together, before carrying on to her dance class. Despite discomfort from a gold band that had just been installed across her teeth, Frances was thrilled by this treat. She felt immediately at home in the nice little house where Miss Adams – Abigail, *Abby* – lived with her parents, who kindly joined them for some cold veal pie and carrots, and then left them alone to chat.

"Do you have any thought of what you might do with your life, eventually, Frances? When you've finished with school?" Abigail asked.

"I don't know at all," Frances said. "I suppose I shall get married one day. But I'm not sure that I want to, though I can't imagine what else I might do."

"Something," said Abigail, firmly. "You should do *something* Frances. That's the thing." She leaned forward and spoke more quietly than ever, her eyes sparkling. "I have a confession to make. I told a wicked lie to your Aunt Mary."

Frances's eyes widened.

"You know when I was away for over a week with a cold? I didn't have a cold at all!" She flushed. "I was in Oxford, being considered for admission as a student of the University. Oxford! Can you believe it?"

"You?" Frances said in surprise. The only thing she knew about Oxford was that it was where uncles went.

Abigail explained that nowadays there were colleges for women at Oxford, and so she'd written to the lady in charge of one of them, Miss Wordsworth, and she kindly invited her to come for an interview.

"I think she thought I was perhaps too young or not strong enough, but we talked and talked and she told me she liked my enthusiasm and decided I could take the entrance examination later in the week. I was terribly nervous, but it wasn't as difficult as I'd feared, and I thought I had not done badly.

"But when I left and came home, I thought, oh it's hopeless, they shall never want me and I am definitely not up to this, and what a ridiculous girl I am! And it was so very beautiful there, and all I ever wanted was to go and be there all the time, and I was certain then that I would never do that. I was really sad, and came home and thought my life was over. And I spent the whole weekend in bed, not daring to get up and see if the mail had arrived.

"And on Monday it did arrive, just an old envelope and in it a letter written by Miss Wordsworth herself! Do you want to see it?" she asked Frances, jumped up excitedly and ran out of the room, returning instantly and out of breath clutching a crumpled note in her hand, which she read out to Frances.

"Dear Miss Adams, thank you for coming to the College last week. I enjoyed our conversation very much. I am delighted to tell you that, as a consequence of a strong performance on the women students' entrance examination, we would be pleased to admit you as a student at Lady Margaret Hall at the start of Michaelmas Term 1896, and in addition propose to offer you a scholarship to cover the full costs of your tuition. Please would you be so kind as to inform me if you do indeed intend to take up this offer by return of post. Yours most faithfully, Elizabeth Wordsworth (Miss)."

Frances looked at the beaming Miss Adams, and smiled in amazement to see her so happy. "What will you do there all the time?" she asked, perplexed. "Is it like school?" she asked.

"Not really," said Abigail. "Or yes, maybe. Like a school where you learn very clever and difficult things!"

"It sounds awfully hard," said Frances uneasily.

"Oh yes," said Abigail beaming. "*Dreadfully* hard!"

Abigail accompanied Frances through Rochester to her dance lesson, on what was turning out to be a warm and sunny spring day. They walked through the streets arm-in-arm like sisters, and promised to stay in touch through all the years to come. As they approached the river, they suddenly heard a racket of shouting and jeering, and three young ladies in full bicycle gear came pedalling towards them up the High Street, laughing and calling to one another, taking no notice at all of the abuse and derision from onlookers. Abigail and Frances stood and waved approvingly at them as they went by, and the ladies waved back, handsome and sturdy on their beautiful black bicycles.

"Now *that's* what I'd like to do," said Frances decisively, followed by a sad sigh. "I suppose my grandmother would never allow it."

"Well then," said Abigail, "Oxford's the place for you! Miss Wordsworth told me that the women at my college have their own bicycling club, and go out into the countryside every Sunday."

Frances looked uneasy. "I'm not sure if I'm cut out for being at university," she said.

Abigail smiled and said she wasn't sure if *she* was cut out for bicycling, but when Frances came to stay with her in Oxford, as she absolutely must one day, she would be pleased to give it a try. "Oh yes please!" said Frances.

The next day was Saturday. Abigail came in for a final morning's work, to make sure everything that had been started was now finished. Aunt Mary joined them to make a list of all the subjects that had been covered so that she could inform Miss White. She congratulated Abigail on her efforts, and Frances on her achievements, and then took Abigail downstairs to her study to hand her a cheque, personally made out to her by Mrs Pickersgill Cunliffe.

Frances was waiting by the front door. She ran over to give Abigail a long hug; then Mary Harriette shook her by the hand and wished her well. As the door closed behind the departing Abigail, Frances turned to Mary Harriette. "Oh Aunt Mary," she said. "My teeth hurt horribly."

"My poor girl," she said. "What can we do to cheer you up?"

"I want to learn to ride a bike," Frances said, without hesitation. "Can I, please Aunt Mary?"

10

Education at Miss White's school in Brighton did not come cheap. Mary Harriette claimed to have cut quite a decent deal with her, on account of friendly family connections, but the cost was nonetheless 25 guineas per term. Nell was of course expected to cough up for this, which struck everyone but her as entirely reasonable. It necessitated the quarterly transfer back to England of a solid portion of the payment that went out to her quarterly from England. Judging from a spate of letters on the matter, she was far from happy about this, and she was not the only one. "*How* fucking much?" Manny had spluttered when she told him. Without a moment's further thought, he announced that, as the head of the family, he must now insist that Frances return to Graceham immediately. Nell jumped up from her seat at the kitchen table at this, her eyes flaming, fist clenched. "Thin ice, Manny," she hissed. "Thin ice."

"Well," he muttered, backing off. "Be that as it may. But the other two aren't going anywhere, I can tell you that." At the familiar sound of a row next door, Tom looked up from the corner of the living room where he was trying to complete his schoolwork and silently raised his eyebrows at Virginia, who responded with a long, slow, weary groan.

Nell never really imagined that things would improve with Frances gone, but her departure did bring slight respite from months of tension at home, and for some time this eased the grief of losing a daughter, with whom she had once imagined being so much closer than she had ever been with her own mother.

But as the weeks went by, there was little time for that grief because Manny now began to focus his attention entirely on Virginia. Now it was Virginia alone who would find herself pulled back off balance down into his lap, told to give her papa a kiss, his arms steel around her belly, trying to struggle like it was just a game, saying let me go Manny LET ME GO, relaxing all her muscles and sliding down out of his grasp before he had time to pinch his nails into the flesh of her arm and hold her there. I will never, she reminded him. I've told you. Never.

If he fought back or shouted at her, it was the signal for one of them, Tom or her to shout as loud as they could for Nell, wherever she was about the house, busying herself and doing her best not to know what was going on. He would quickly stop when she finally paid attention, and slump sulking back into his chair, and Tom would wonder, does every man when he grows old have to drink, shout and feel sorry for himself? He often wanted to kill Manny, and told his mother as much but she took little notice and said she often felt that way herself, and that's families for you. But Manny, when not yet too far gone, could see the look in Tom's eyes and took note also of the fact that, at 17, the lad was on the way to becoming a threat to him, and began to suggest that it would better for all of them if Tom moved out, took an apprenticeship or something.

Manny finally managed to catch Virginia on her own in early summer when the others were all working far out in the fields, and she had gone to the barn for some twine and he'd followed her in so fast and quietly she didn't know he was there before he was right behind her locking an arm around her waist, smacking one hand hard over her mouth, hissing "no-one'll hear you shout now girl" right inside her ear, "so just relax. Not gonna hurt you." He breathed his hateful hot breath into her ear, and told her no-one need ever know, he was going to make a woman of her right now and one day she'd thank him.

But she struggled with a violence that surprised them both, freed an arm and desperately tried to reach behind her and grab him as hard as she could where it would really hurt, like Tom had told her to. She fought like a crazy thing and screamed so loud that she certainly could be heard now; it was Tom who was listening out for her because he'd suddenly realised that Manny wasn't anywhere to be seen, and he came running straight into the barn before Manny could regain control or do any more harm, and walloped him so hard over the back of his head that he dropped a shrieking Virginia right onto the earth and Tom pulled her up and out of the barn leaving Manny on his knees gasping and they went straight to find Nell.

That's how Tom described it, anyway.

Virginia had refused to talk about it at all, and although Nell didn't entirely trust in the truth of Tom's version, it's what she told the family back home in another series of anguished letters, whose purpose was to ensure that Virginia's name was now added to the exodus, and maybe Tom's as well (pushing her luck) given the fact that the bad blood between him and his step-father had reached boiling point. Helen was as sceptical as ever about Nell's stories, and it did not really help matters when a letter was received from Manny himself, offering a radically different perspective on events.

"You know," she said to Mary Harriette, "I do still wonder if Mr Dent has not been badly misrepresented in all of this."

This, in a nutshell, was the American Question. Mary Harriette looked at her in amazement. "I see here a man who has been sorely tested," her mother continued, "whose wife does not respect him, and who has taught her children the same."

"Deservedly," said Mary Harriette, with feeling.

"Surely," continued her mother, "we should afford him the forgiveness for which he pleads, should we not? He says that his actions were mere foolishness, committed under the influence of alcohol, and have been grossly exaggerated. Nothing, he assures me, truly untoward ever occurred." Mary Harriette was about to protest, but her mother continued undaunted, waving a just-let-me-finish finger in her face. "I consider that this may well be the case."

It dawned on Mary Harriette that the thing her mother most dreaded was the possibility of Nell leaving her husband and returning to England. "I don't follow," she said. "What is it you believe she truly wishes for?"

"The impossible," snapped her mother. "Her children to go and her children to stay. Her husband to go and her husband to stay."

"Life has not been easy for her."

"Indeed," said her mother. "One thing is beyond doubt – a passage must be booked for Virginia as soon as possible." She paused for effect. "Given all that we know, it would be sinful to do nothing to avert further sin, however slim the likelihood of that may be."

Mary Harriette quietly thanked the Lord for moderating her mother's intransigence.

"But her brother must remain in America. We are not a hostel," Mrs Pickersgill Cunliffe said, with unmistakable finality.

11

"How'd you manage to do this then?" the young man in overalls asked the undergraduate, as he crouched down to inspect the damage.

"Had a tumble riding over a little bridge out near Aynho," said the undergraduate. "What do you reckon?"

"The forks are quite a mess," he said. "But I can fix 'em. Cost you a fair bit though, have to do some delicate brazing. Good ten bob's worth here I'd say."

Basil sighed. He didn't have anything like that right now. "Just want to be able to ride it again. Whatever it takes, doesn't have to look good."

"I'll see what I can do," said the young man, not returning Basil's encouraging grin. "Suppose I could get you rolling again for five bob or so. Might last you a while." He stared thoughtfully at Basil's old bike, and turned to him with a sudden show of warmth. "On the other hand," he said, "I can build you a brand new bicycle that wouldn't smash up so easily the next time you ride into a bridge. Three guineas, all in."

More than the allowance his father could afford to give him for the whole year. Before he could bring himself to explain the hopelessness of this proposal, Basil glimpsed two young ladies in cycling clothes looking at them through the garden gate. Basil gave a friendly wave and the smaller one, a pale little thing, jumped back momentarily, took a deep breath and then addressed him firmly. "Mr Morris?" she asked. "We wish to hire two of your bicycles, if we may."

Basil pointed at Morris. "He's your man," he said and stood back out of the way, adding that he didn't mind waiting, not one bit.

He watched Morris look the two young ladies up and down quite intently for several moments. "Well I have something that would suit *you*," Morris said to the taller of the two, "but not so sure about you," he told the smaller one.

"Oh dear," cried the taller one. "That will never do! We must both have a bike!"

What's that accent? Basil wondered. Very slight American twang perhaps? He wasn't so sure, Americans weren't particularly common in Rochdale, or Oxford colleges for that matter.

The smaller one peered into his little workshop for a moment. "What about that one?" she asked, pointing into the darkness.

"Child's bike," said Morris. "Guess I could set it up for you to ride, though, if that's what you really want."

"Oh Abby!" said the other girl. "Surely not?"

Abigail assured her that this would do just fine. It wasn't as if she intended to go riding far, on that or any bike.

Definitely American, Basil decided. American and rather nice. Lovely eyes. He tried to think of some ways that he might be able to offer his help and bicycling expertise to these charming angels. Well, more accurately, to one rather tense little bluestocking, and one rather charming angel. But before he could come up with anything sufficiently gallant yet insouciant, Morris had turned to him with a decidedly hostile glare and said, "Look, no need to hang around, it'll take me some time to deal with these two ladies. You come back in a couple of days and pick up your old bike when I've sorted it out, all right?"

"What about this idea to build me a new one?" Basil offered.

"If you can't afford ten bob," said Morris, "I don't really imagine you'll manage three guineas. Cheerio." He turned his back on Basil and started to busy himself with the young ladies.

As he went reluctantly out the gate, Basil took a final glimpse back at the American girl and felt his heart swell. *Coup de Foudre!* Bursting with energy and resolve, he charged off back across the bridge that separated the city and its university from the lesser universe of East Oxford, to borrow another bicycle so that he might scour the streets of Oxford and bump into her again somehow, but instead he bumped into some pals on their way to play football in the Parks. They said he could join them, and he'd never say no to that.

He kept watching out for the American girl with lovely eyes during the days that followed, until he was struck by another thunderbolt – love at first sight through a shop window for only the second motorcycle he had ever seen.

The year was 1899.

12

1901

I t was a dank December evening in Kennington Park. Frances sat alone and bereft on a park bench, trying to imagine what might happen next.

The park was a designated place of recreation right in the heart of one of the most overcrowded parts of south London, an essential breathing space in the fetid air of Southwark, Lambeth and Newington, open to all for their good health, delight and silent reflection. It wasn't very grand and had rather a melancholy character, despite its pathways, trees, flower beds, fountain, bandstand and neat little café.

Frances, severely and sombrely dressed all in grey, was making ample use of the opportunity for silent reflection, miserably considering her current prospects beneath the wintry plane trees. She had begun her time at the Bishop of Southwark's Greyladies College, also known as the Women Workers for God, only one month before, and she was beginning to wonder now, in the lonely desolation of this bleak Sunday afternoon in Kennington, whether she should not simply admit defeat and, just this once more, beg her grandmother and aunts to let her give up and try something else.

But seeing as how this is precisely what she had done last year, even before the end of her one month's probation as a nurse in Eastbourne, and seeing as how this year she had been sacked from the job she took next, looking after elderly widows in the north of England, and seeing as how she refused to even consider the job of matron at the Ramsgate branch of the Metropolitan Association for Befriending Young Servants, which struck her as a ridiculous proposal and everyone knew it, and seeing as how she could not possibly conceive of what she might do now other than this, she was obviously going to have to struggle on. All in all, reason enough to be sitting here in this dreary park quietly sniffling the afternoon away.

The first weeks at the Greyladies College had promised better things, despite the disappointment of meeting her house-mates for the first time, and the ghastly uniform she had to wear. But on her second day she was welcomed into the living room of the Bishop's sister, Miss Yeatman, lady head of the College, to meet Ursula Bethell, who was to shepherd her through her Greylady probation. Miss Yeatman assured Frances that she would receive from Miss Bethell the most serious of introductions to the ways and practices of the College, but when Ursula came rushing in a few minutes later, flushed and a little out of breath, she greeted Frances with a radiant smile and clasped her hands warmly, and Frances beamed straight back at her in relief.

"Come on," Ursula cried gaily, as soon as they'd broken free from Miss Yeatman, and led her straight across the road into the Park. They walked the paths and chatted, before sitting down to talk seriously. They queried each other's odd accents, and discovered that they both had come to England at the difficult age of fifteen, five years apart, one from America and the other from New Zealand. Also, they discovered that they were both effectively parentless, their fathers having died in the very same year and their mothers having, each in her own way, badly let them down. To Frances it felt like a deep bond.

"Mine did come over to England for a while, at the start of the year," she said, "so I suppose I can't say I've lost her. But I didn't like her turning up without warning and expecting to be my mother again, considering how she sent me away in the first place." Ursula was unembarrassed by such honest expression of painful feelings, and nodded her complete understanding.

"Many people can give you maternal love, Frances, if you let them," she said, taking hold of Frances's hand for a moment. There was a brief uncertain moment of silence, as if Ursula was about to say more, then she rose from the bench and they walked again.

"I know we shall be the closest of friends," she said, accompanying Frances back to her room in Lorrimore Square. "Tomorrow we can go about together and I'll show you some of the parish work you might do. A mothers' meeting in the morning and later on visit the girls' club up in Union Street. I want you to get an idea of the things that are worth doing around here. Not everything is." She frowned and would have gone further, but resisted. "And I will do my best to tell you what you need to know, in order to be a good Greylady." She gave Frances a little hug and a half kiss on the cheek, her pointy nose getting slightly in the way, and then she was gone. Frances went inside, in time for evening prayers followed by a simple supper and the rest of the evening in her room, writing letters, to Aunt Mary, Ethel, Virginia and her grandmother.

Over the midday meal next day, Ursula asked Frances if she wanted to chat about the College rules. Frances had done her best to learn them verbatim before coming, and started to recite them to Ursula.

"A worker," she said, "must have herself well in hand. She must be healthy-minded and sensible with regard to food, rest and recreation. And un-something hopeful."

"Unfailingly, I believe," Ursula suggested.

Frances nodded, and continued, "She shouldn't expect to be praised for the things she does."

"No indeed," said Ursula. "Although it might be nice sometimes."

"I'm used to it," Frances said. "I wasn't spoiled for praise in my last two jobs, but then I seldom knew what I was doing much of the time." That made Ursula laugh out loud, drawing little looks of pained surprise from other Greyladies in the room.

"What else?" Ursula asked, in a lower voice.

Frances looked down at her beginners' pamphlet, and read straight from it: "'She must not try to draw those amongst whom she works to herself personally'. Is that really so?" she asked.

"It's difficult," said Ursula. "It's telling us we shouldn't get too close to the people we care for. But it isn't always possible to keep your distance. And it isn't always best either."

Frances loved the company of Ursula and thanked her good fortune in having her for a guide and friend. She admired the look of her, taller than she was, thin, almost gaunt, a bony face not beautiful exactly, but magnetic on account of her deep eyes, as if she was always thinking something clever. And she admired her manner, a little remote at times but always courteous and kind, capable of sudden warmth and humour at any moment. Frances was proud that Ursula seemed to like her and value her company, talking with her openly about the problems of working with the poor and dispossessed, people who were frequently far from easy to love or even like. Despite the fairly minor age difference, Ursula struck Frances as being

122

infinitely wiser about the world than she would ever be, and she loved having someone to look up to who treated her as an equal.

In their second week together, Ursula took her to the Boys' Brigade group that she helped run in Southwark, as she wanted to show Frances the work that mattered most to her. Working with boys was not normally part of the Greyladies mission, but the opportunity had arisen and she took it gladly because she was determined to start her own boys' club back in New Zealand. She confessed she was thinking of doing that more and more these days.

Frances soon saw how good she was with these boys, teaching them about Christian values but respectful of their resistance: how can you love your neighbour, one said, when he's trying to steal the little you've got? Yes, she said, but not everyone's like that are they? So they all tried hard to think of acts of kindness they'd experienced, until Ursula admitted defeat and it was time for bread and jam. Afterwards, as they walked back down to Kennington, Frances told Ursula how much she'd enjoyed listening to them talk, and how she'd loved watching Ursula with them. Ursula said that was nice of her, but the truth was that she didn't know what to do most of the time, and it was presumptuous of her to think she could change their lives. She was not qualified in any way, she could neither teach nor originate anything, she said. Her strength of feeling shocked Frances.

"You're so good with them," she said, trying to keep pace with Ursula as she marched up Newington Butts. "They trust you."

"I'm so sorry," Ursula said, smiling as best she could. "My terrible mood will soon pass. I think too deeply about these things, too much alone with my own thoughts no doubt."

The next afternoon Frances spent several hours at the girls' club in Union Street, where Ursula left her to lead a group of girls in embroidery and dress making on her own. The mood was cheerful, and she began to believe that this was something she could actually do. She was elated, and afterwards Ursula praised her ability to cope on her own, and to appear relaxed and confident with the girls whilst doing so. That was the secret of it all, she said. You won't be needing me for much longer. A while yet, I hope, Frances had said, suddenly anxious. Oh yes of course, Ursula said.

As they left the tram just by St Mary's Church to go their separate ways for the evening, a pleasant looking woman of indeterminate age rushed up to Ursula and greeted her with a delighted smile. They hugged for a moment, and Ursula introduced Frances.

"A new Greygirl!" said the woman. "Very pleased to meet you."

"This is Hannah," said Ursula. "Renowned star of the varieties."

"Miss Lily Harley, Charming Chanter!" she said, blushing, at the same time shaking her head at the nonsense of that. "That was long ago."

Frances shook her hand warmly. "I'm very proud to make your acquaintance Miss Harley," she said.

"Do call me Lily," said Hannah, beaming at Frances. "We shall meet again – I must run – little boy's waiting for his tea. Just popped out to buy him a small treat." She showed them the sad little package in her hand, and then grasped Ursula's arm for a moment. "Do come and see me soon, Ursula, if you can," she said, hurrying off, and Ursula called after her that she certainly would.

At breakfast the next day, Miriam, one of the other younger Greyladies in Frances's house, came across to her at breakfast and told her that it had been decided that she should partner with her for the time being. Apparently Ursula was feeling very poorly all of a sudden, and Miss Yeatman had told her to take a proper rest. Frances felt a small cold wind blow through her heart.

She didn't see Ursula again until the week after next. The days went by and Frances settled to her work, and found a tolerable routine taking shape. Miriam was as earnest and pious as she had seemed from a distance, and in her company Frances began to trust in her own capacities. She found these hard London girls less frightening than she had feared – they were as foreign to her as she was to them but not in the ways that mattered most: she knew what it meant to have a difficult time growing up, and how that stayed with you. She discovered that she could talk to them quite easily; much more so than Miriam however many years she'd been trying.

But she badly missed the special light that Ursula's way of seeing things, and talking about things, cast over everything. She missed the way Ursula made her feel special herself, and prayed that it would not end like this, before it had really begun. It was on that particularly damp Sunday afternoon in early December when from her window, to her delight and relief, she saw Ursula stepping up to the house in Lorrimore Square. She rushed down to the hallway, threw her arms around her friend, and hoped she was feeling better now. Ursula said she was getting along quite well, thanked Frances so much for her very kind note, and suggested they might walk one more time in the Park again. On the way Frances told her about what she had done during the two weeks, working alongside Miriam and so on, and Ursula said that she had no doubt already that she would prove to be a first-rate Greylady.

And then, as soon as they had settled down on a bench in a quiet corner of the park, Ursula took a deep breath, looked at her seriously, and Frances knew that bad news was on its way.

"Frances. I have to tell you that I shall be leaving the Greyladies rather sooner than I had intended. Over the next few days in fact." Frances let out a moan and then, seeing Ursula look alarmed, immediately apologised.

"Oh no, I'm the one who should be sorry," Ursula quickly said. "For leaving before I have finished my work with you."

She took hold of Frances's hand.

"I cannot say more," she said. "I really can't." It occurred to Frances that the problem must be her. She was too demanding, or too young and naïve, didn't really understand the important things that Ursula wanted to talk about. It was awful enough to think that her arrival might have led to Ursula's departure, but even more awful was the knowledge that Ursula had found her interesting at first and then, once she had got to know her, had realised she wasn't after all.

"I truly do not mind if you would rather not look after me any more," she said, shaky voiced. "I'll be fine with Miriam now. You don't have to worry about me."

Ursula badly wanted to tell her that she did indeed worry about her, very much, and that she was the one thing that had tempted her to remain with the Greyladies a while longer, that her strong maternal feelings for her were unchanged. She could not talk frankly about why she had to leave, not without making Frances herself lose faith in the College before she had even started. She should not have her see the tiresome untidy feckless old Greyladies for what they really were, how everything there was wretchedly unorganised, no two bits of work running together, just mistaken effort and ignorant wasting of forces. The more she thought about it – and she could not stop thinking about it – the harder it was to bear. She could stay not a day longer.

So without any word of explanation at all, just a brief clumsy hug and a whispered apology, Ursula rose up and stumbled away, leaving Frances alone on a bench, stunned and miserable beneath the wintry plane trees of Kennington Gardens, feeling sorry for herself, no idea what to do next.

She sat there for such a long while, in fact, that she drew the attention of a watcher, someone who knew what sadness looked like. The watcher stood quietly in the shadow of a nearby tree for some minutes, waiting until she resolved at last to approach Frances, very carefully, so as not to cause alarm.

"Hello dear," said Hannah, as gently as she could. Frances jumped. "It's all right! Do you remember me?"

Frances stared blankly at her, and then sighed with relief. "Lily!" she said. "I'm *so* pleased to see you."

"I hope you don't mind me asking," said Hannah, "but is there anything wrong at all?"

"Oh no," she said, then hesitated. "It's nothing really."

Hannah smiled and invited her home for a cup of tea, an invitation which, given all she had been through this day, she gladly accepted; she needed to be cared for. Once in Hannah's room, though, she was confronted with the reality of difference between their private worlds. This kindly woman lived a life that was desperately hard, and was quite clearly a great deal more fragile and in need of care than Frances would ever be. She had hardly any possessions, the sink was full of unwashed crockery and, from the mess and bedding squeezed into the corner, it was clear she wasn't the only one trying to fit into this tiny room. On a small table by the window was an old sewing machine, with half-finished blouses piled all around.

Frances wondered how anyone could live there at all. She couldn't put a name to whatever it was at the heart of that uniquely terrible mess of smells there, but Hannah could: Hayward's pickle factory – you get used to it, she assured her. There was much more than that, not just the burning vinegar and sharp spices but also constant waves of boiled cabbage and flannels from downstairs, the stench from the slaughterhouse at the back, passing clouds of alcohol and tobacco from pubs on the Kennington Road, rotting fish and meat from the shops on the corner, and sewage. And it all seemed to come together in this very room, all at one whiff.

Hannah talked rapturously to Frances of her days dancing and singing on stage as Lily Harley. She'd made a good living, was admired, had a nice home and her own housemaid on a much smarter road far away from the smell and filth. She'd left her husband by then, a leading vaudevillian himself until he turned to drink and eventually drank himself to death. Her own voice had deserted her one day when singing on stage and her career came to a sudden and unforgiving end, then all she had after that was sewing and whatever else might turn up from time to time. Her and the two kids: Sydney, a kind and thoughtful boy planning to go into the merchant Navy; Charles, a bright little thing, a wild boy, who spent his time out on the streets doing heaven knows what, often managing to bring home extra pennies from his little jobs, sweeping up, making cheap toys, performing for an organ grinder. He was the true star of the family, dancing and singing and making people laugh wherever, on the street outside the pub, in the Park doing somersaults, and sometimes now even being paid to go on the stage from time to time, clog dancing. He was certain to be famous, she told Frances, and rich; he'd promised to look after her for the rest of her life.

Frances felt so sad for her. She wondered if Hannah really believed such fantasies. She resolved on her own initiative to befriend her, in the knowledge that this was what Ursula must have been doing also, and would surely have wished her to do. During the months that followed she went around to Methley Street quite regularly to see how Hannah was getting on, and spend an hour or so with her. Frances feared that there was little she could do to help but all Hannah wished from her anyway was friendliness, especially when her boys had not appeared for days on end. Although it was really against the rules for her to make visits on her own, Frances was relieved as time went on to discover that the senior Greyladies were flexible about the rules they themselves had devised – so different from when she'd been a nurse, ordered about every minute of the day and night, and criticised the whole time. So long as you tried your best and did so with humility, your efforts to improve the lives of the needy women in the parish received approval, regardless of whether or not there was any strong basis for supposing that they did much good.

After a few months, she found that Hannah and her boys had moved out of Methley Street and disappeared completely. They'll turn up again sooner or later, her landlady assured her, don't you worry.

1902

It was nearly three years since Frances and Abigail had met in person, although they corresponded regularly, and Frances was shaken to see what had become of her friend in that time. Abigail had become shockingly thin. Slight of build and hardly five foot in height, she had always seemed far younger than her years, but now she had the look of an aged child and on this unusually warm day, even inside a humid Kennington Gardens tea-room, continued to wear her overcoat.

"You look so well!" Abigail said, cheerfully. Frances, looking particularly well-fed following a recent visit home, was uncomfortably aware of the contrast between her own blooming state of health and Abigail's skeletal appearance.

"And you!" Frances replied, brightly. Abigail smiled pleasantly and said she felt well, yes, and asked Frances how she was enjoying life as a Greylady, and if she intended to make her life there.

Frances made a face. Not forever, she knew that much. And what about you? she asked.

"I do hope I can remain in Oxford," Abigail said.

Since passing her final exams with distinction two years previously, she had been able to stay on in the College in return for advising new students and helping to run the College library. She had hopes of being appointed to a tutorship before too long. "But Miss Wordsworth is concerned about my constitution. She called me in, and told me that I might need to think about taking some time away from the College." Her eyes were welling with tears. "In order to rest completely, so that my health might recover." She looked desperately at Frances, who opened her mouth as if about to speak, but Abigail carried on without pausing.

"But my health is excellent, it really is." The tears were now streaming down her face. "And the College is my home now. It's the only place I can bear to be – I hate to leave it ever. I don't need to leave it ever." She began to breathe quickly.

"Miss Wordsworth has insisted that I go back to Rochester and stay with my parents over the summer. And so I must." Frances reached out and touched her hand, and Abigail looked anxiously back at her, wheezing slightly. She could not bear to repeat what Miss Wordsworth actually said to her, in her kindly blunt way: that she needed to spend some time away from her books, and have her mother put some meat back on those poor bones.

"Well at least that has brought you here," Frances said. "What shall we do now? Would you like a tour of the parish?"

Abigail closed her eyes, and fought down the urge to flee this place and all the people milling around the Park. "Can we go somewhere quiet?" she asked, and so they went back to Frances's room, just five minutes away. She was calmer by the time they had settled into the old armchairs, the room so warm and stuffy she could even be persuaded to take her coat off at last. For a while, at Abigail's insistence, Frances chatted about her work, about the poor people of Kennington and their struggles, and the frustrations of being in London during the summer.

"Sometimes I wish I could just get on a bicycle and ride out to the countryside," she said, smiling at the memory of their shared adventure in Oxford all those years ago. "Do you cycle at all these days, Abby?"

She shook her head and looked down at the floor, blushing unhappily, unable to reply.

"Abby?" Frances asked. "What's wrong? What did I say?" Frances looked her straight and openly in the eye. This much she had learnt from Ursula: have the courage to make people talk, and accept whatever it is they need to say. The more the better. "You can tell me, Abigail," she said, and Abigail did. She told Frances that the whole nightmare really began that day three years before, when they had hired bikes for their ride around Oxford together.

Mr Morris had made a great show of trying to find suitable bikes for them. He had been particularly attentive to Abigail, talking to her almost like she was a child, which she had not liked, any more than she had liked the way he held the seat of the bike steady for her when she mounted the bike. But she imagined that was just the kind of thing a bicycle man had to do for his customers. She had glanced at Frances when he'd done this, but Frances was too busy looking over her own bike, and the other man had gone already so there had been no-one to see what had or had not happened in that brief moment.

He told them to leave the bikes by the college lodge when they'd finished with them. He would pick them up the next day, all part of the service. They paid him and wobbled off up the Cowley Road and over towards the Marston Road, avoiding Magdalen Bridge with its buses, horses, and people everywhere. They turned down lanes that ran through the farms and alongside the river all the way up to the ferry. Once over the river they went on to Wolvercote and then back into the City as far as St. Giles, where they entertained themselves by weaving through the trees and some sheep loitering there, before turning back to Abigail's college. Not a very long ride, in the end, but neither of them was a seasoned cyclist, and there had been quite a lot of stopping to adjust things, admire things, avoid dogs and find their right way. But despite Abigail's initial unease, the outing had been a great success and by the time they returned she was blooming with the satisfaction of having cycled safely over all these testing tracks and roads, easily as much as Frances who had been the keenest for this long-promised adventure.

And then, just two weeks later on a Saturday afternoon, she had a message from the college porter that a gentleman was at the lodge, saying he had a bicycle for her. She went down, mystified, to find Mr Morris waiting just outside the gate with his hands resting on the handlebars of a pretty little bicycle.

"Oh good afternoon, Miss Adams," he said, very politely. "I hope you don't mind my impertinence. I just came on the off-chance, in case you might be interested in owning this little beauty ..." He proffered her the bike, with a proud grin.

She told him that it looked delightful, but she was really not in the market for her own bicycle or able to afford such a thing at present. But so kind of him to think of her.

"I did indeed, Miss Adams," he said, undaunted. "I thought of you the moment I saw it. It was in a bit of a state when it came into my shop a few days ago but, as I say, I thought of you and so I put a bit of elbow grease into it, smartened it up a bit, and wondered if you would be interested – it's turned out quite well, I must say."

Once again, she told him, she was sorry to say that it was out of the question at present for her to contemplate buying a bicycle.

"Oh no," he said. "I'm not making myself clear. I just wondered if you'd like to try it out, and see what you think of it, and if it suits you, well it's yours. If you want."

She told him she couldn't possibly accept such a gift.

"A loan then," he said, grinning. "You can think of it as an extended loan." He nodded towards her encouragingly and the longer she stared at the bike, the more she did begin to feel some slight tremblings of longing for it. All the same, she could not.

"I tell you what, Miss Adams. Might I suggest a gentle trial ride of a few miles – just far enough to see whether you like the feel of it? I shall of course accompany you in order to ensure your own safety." She said nothing, uncomfortable with his pressure, but already a little in love with the bike and the thought of the solitary freedoms it would afford. "If you don't find it to your liking we'll leave it at that, and if you do like it, well I am sure we can come to an arrangement you'll be happy with."

So on a bright late spring morning a few days later, Abigail Adams and Will Morris set off through Oxford, out past the railway station and away from the city. Morris had not offered any assistance when she mounted the bike, to her relief, and kept a safe distance from her on the road, leading the way through the city streets, and then deliberately slowing down along Botley Road waving her to go past and off the leash, so to speak. She whistled past him, a broad smile on her face and her hair blowing behind her. He must have known he'd got her then.

Morris took the lead again as they turned up towards Wytham and along a farm track running through woods. She began to find it quite hard to keep up with him but then, just as she was about to call to him to slow down, he had pulled up and was suggesting they might take a break.

"I took the liberty, Miss Adams, of bringing some simple refreshments for just this moment. Shall we go and sit by that tree?" She could see nothing but trees, and the one he had in mind turned out to be quite some way in from the farm track, surrounded by soft grass. He produced a little blanket for her to sit on, and an assortment of treats: ham, cheese, bread, fruit cake, pears and lemonade. She was more than a little taken aback by the extent of his preparations but, still glowing from the joy of her ride and fully determined to accept his loan of the bicycle until she could buy it off him, resolved to go along with his little picnic in a good spirit. Anyway, she was ravenous.

"He violated me, Frances. There in the wood, with no warning. He suddenly threw himself over me, telling me I was the sweetest little child, and a little devil too. He threw his body all over me and there was nothing I could do. He forced his way under my clothing and I couldn't stop him, I screamed at him to stop and he covered my mouth and warned me not to be an awful little tease.

"I didn't know what he meant to do, I didn't know what was happening and I don't know how long it lasted but it hurt horribly and he was gasping and grunting and saying I was his little girl. I felt his hands everywhere and he violated me with his fingers Frances. His long, hard, filthy fingers."

She stopped dead, sobbing, and looked straight at Frances in an agony of recollection.

"I've never told anyone, not anyone but you Frances," she said. Frances had waited all this while without a word, just nodding and listening, but now Abigail seemed to have run out of words.

"What happened Abby? Could you escape?" she asked.

Abigail gave a bitter kind of laugh. "He lay down beside me when he was finished, and smiled at me, and called me his sweetheart. I could hardly breathe and I waited as long as I dared in order to collect myself. Then I got up off the ground slowly and arranged my clothes, as if everything was normal. He smiled at me. I said something about my lovely bicycle and walked over towards the track again. He followed me, watching me closely to see what I would do. Then he came right up close again and took my arm.

"I tried to scream at him to leave me alone, but I could hardly make a sound and he squeezed my arm really hard to stop me trying so I tried the hardest I could and I sort of howled and immediately a man shouted 'what's up?' quite close by it seemed, and at that Morris let me go, grabbed his bike and was gone, and I was left alone crying and moaning, too weak to stand any more, sitting on the grass by my horrible little bicycle.

"And just a few moments later an elderly farmer came running and panting up the track. He asked me if I was all right and said he'd seen a man cycle past, and was he the reason I'd been shouting? I just nodded, and tried to catch my breath. How are you going to get home, girlie? he asked. I couldn't imagine how to answer.

"He was so kind, such a kind old man. He picked up my bike and we went and got his horse and cart, and I asked him if he would just take me to the railway station and he said gladly. And when we got there I had to tell him I had no money with me but he said that was of no account to him, the good man, so I told him to keep my bike. He said of course not, and I said I *never* wanted to come near it again and he gladly took it then.

"I went to the ladies' room at the station and tried to make myself look respectable. Then I made my way as invisible as I could be back to my room and stayed there, shut away right up there in the eaves of the College. For ever."

After she had left, Frances hoped that it helped Abigail to tell her story. She felt it must have done, and she was sure that Ursula would have been proud of her for listening so well. There were things in her own life that she would never tell anyone, because they would overwhelm her if she tried to put them into words. She hoped it would not be like that for Abigail, she really did.

1903

Hannah Chaplin was losing grip. Thoughts she could neither resist nor comprehend were leaking through her skull, and telling her to do things that she would never do, and would not remember having done later. She had felt out of sorts for several days but had still managed to maintain some kind of normality when little Charles – Charlie – was around, although sometimes she could feel him looking at her as if there was something wrong. She desperately needed to find Sydney, and had gone out looking for him, walking around the streets of Kennington asking people where he was, and not believing them when they didn't know. But now she was back in their current tiny room in Pownall Terrace, sitting by the window as usual, trying to make sense of the long-dead faces that floated in front of her from time to time.

The door suddenly flew open and standing there was Charlie, staring at her. She stared back at him, without a word or even a smile for this boy she loved so much. "Mother!" he shouted, and then ran over to her, dropped to his knees and hugged her. She stroked his head and asked him what was wrong. "You're not well," he said. When he arrived home just now he'd been greeted by the little girl from next door telling him his mother had gone insane; going around all day, knocking on doors and handing out lumps of coal as birthday presents for the children; walking in and out of people's houses.

"What've you been doing?" he pleaded. "What's wrong?"

"They're trying to keep Sydney from me," she murmured.

"He's away at sea Mother, he's not in London," he said.

"You know that. Please don't talk like this." She stroked his head, not listening.

"We need the doctor, Mother," he said, jumping up. She told him not to go, terrified to be left alone again. Charlie ran down the stairs to find that the landlady had already called the parish doctor. When he arrived, an unfriendly and grumpy old man, the landlady told him what had happened and he struggled slowly up the stairs to the top of the house to see for himself. A brief look at Hannah was all he needed.

"Insane," he confirmed, writing out a paper. "Take her to the Infirmary." He announced that she was suffering from malnutrition, gave Charlie the piece of paper to show the doctors there, and then left without another word. The landlady tried to reassure Charlie as the two of them helped Hannah get ready, telling him she'd be fed and looked after at last. A small crowd of neighbours and children gathered around the front gate to watch enthralled as Charlie led her away like a lost child.

As they began to make their way up the Kennington Road, two almost identical ladies came arm-in-arm towards them, laughing and blind to their presence. Charlie resolved to drag his mother straight between them, force his way through without slowing down, but one of them – dressed in a long grey dress buttoned to the neck – suddenly recognised Hannah. "Lily!" she cried out, reaching out towards her. "Are you all right?" Charlie screwed up his face. "No she ain't," he growled, and pushed on, no intention of stopping to talk.

"Please wait!" she called after them. "Can't we help?"

"No you can't," he called without looking back. He didn't know who these women were, but the one in grey looked official like a nun, and there was no way he was going to end up in the workhouse again.

That was the first time Frances had actually seen Lily's little boy, although she'd often looked for him in the little urchins and chancers who wheedled her as she passed and half-heartedly tried to sell her something. He seemed as scrawny and puny as all of them, but there was something unusually assured in the way he took control of the pavement. She watched him hurry his poor distracted mother away, and turned to her sister in great agitation.

"I know her, Virginia," she said, almost in a whisper. "We must do something."

"Must we?" Virginia asked, seeing bother ahead.

Frances grabbed her sister's elbow and took off up the road after them. "I just want to know where he's taking her," she said. "She's a friend of mine."

"A *friend?*" her sister repeated. Frances ignored this, and did her best to speed her sister along when little Charlie and his mother, now a good fifty yards ahead, suddenly veered off to the right down the far side of a big church and out of sight. Frances and Virginia followed after them and found themselves in a small overgrown garden at the back of the church, with no apparent way onward until, half-hidden beneath an overgrown and painful hawthorn bush, they found a small gate that opened onto a dank path behind a row of houses.

Charlie must have known a way through the houses to the road beyond, but Frances couldn't see where it was. She looked desperately into the gloom, then suddenly pointed and shouted "There! Daylight!", and they were off again, into a tiny dark alleyway that went between and under two tall adjoining houses. They tottered nervously through, swerving past a dog suddenly awakened by all the unusual traffic, stumbling over logs and buckets filled with reeking remains until they reached the open air. Looking all around for some clue as where to go next, Frances stared blankly for a moment at the building looming over the nearby houses, just a quarter of a mile to the north. Then she realised where they had landed up.

"Along here," she said breathlessly, and they swung into another crumbling terrace, which curved out of sight at the far end. "The hospital's at the end of this. *That's* where they're going!" For just a brief moment as they came around the bend they glimpsed what must have been little Charlie and Hannah at the far end of the street, turning the corner near to the Lambeth Infirmary gates.

They weren't to be seen by the time the two sisters arrived at the hospital entrance, and Virginia stopped dead. "Frances! Just wait will you? What on earth are we going to do if we do find them?" she asked, not at all pleased to have been press-ganged into this crazy goose chase.

"What do you mean?" cried Frances, who did not have a plan as such, just a determination not to turn her back on poor Lily.

"We're not needed now, are we?" continued Virginia, with some authority. "Now that we've managed to chase this boy and his poor mother halfway around London – despite which he has managed to get her safely to hospital – I would imagine we might wisely go home now and leave them to it. Wouldn't you say?"

Frances looked back at her and tried to think what would be for the best, not particularly appreciative of the telling-off from her younger sister even if she might, as usual, be in the right.

"Certainly not," she said, turning around and leading the way into the hospital.

They were made to wait inside the main entrance by a slow-moving and obtuse charge-hand, who said that people came by all the time and it wasn't his job to tell people where people had or had not gone. But Frances's uniform earned her some grudging consideration, and in the end he went off to make enquiries, returning eventually to say that the doctor would come and speak with them shortly. After nearly thirty minutes more, during which Virginia came very close to leaving, a young doctor came down the corridor, smiling pleasantly and apologising for having taken so long.

"Hello," he said. "I'm Dr Quarry. I gather you are acquainted with Mrs Chaplin?"

Frances, hoping that this would not get back to Miss Yeatman in exactly this form, explained that she had been caring for Lily, Hannah, for quite some time in her capacity as one of the Bishop of Southwark's Greyladies, of whom the doctor might perhaps have heard (he hadn't). She'd caught sight of her son bringing her to the hospital under what appeared to be most difficult circumstances and was most concerned for this poor lady's welfare.

The doctor listened to Frances very attentively. "It's good she has people who care for her," he said. "She is very sick, I'm afraid. A danger to herself, and perhaps to others, I would say."

Frances gasped. "Surely not!" she said. "She's so gentle."

The doctor nodded. "Well sadly, for various reasons which we can possibly never know, she has currently lost her mind, and is no longer the person she was." As evidence, he showed them the form that he had just signed, *Order for the Reception of a Pauper Lunatic.* "Such a state is far from uncommon in these parts, the lives these poor people must endure. As I am sure you know well enough yourself, Miss ..." Frances introduced herself, and her sister, and the doctor expressed his pleasure at meeting them both, with hardly a glance Virginia's way. Then he apologised for needing to return to his patients, but assured Frances that he would be pleased to furnish further information about poor Mrs Chaplin's condition at any time.

"That would be most kind," she said. "And what about her son? We didn't see him leave – is he still here?"

"I believe not," said the doctor. "He gave a very clear account of his mother's condition, leading up to the crisis today. He assured me that he would be well looked after by his aunt while his mother is in hospital, so I sent him on his way to her. I could see that he is an unusually responsible young man." Frances said she was glad to hear it, and thanked the doctor very much indeed for all he was doing for Mrs Chaplin, and assured him she would return in a few days. Virginia watched Frances with growing interest.

Young Charlie, meanwhile, was long gone. He had been relieved to have talked his way out of the doctor's interest in the first place, only too aware of the danger of being judged too young to fend for himself and finding himself shut up in the workhouse once more. And then, just when he thought he had got away with it, he had seen the two women, the nun and her friend, waiting for him by the main entrance. He spun into a side corridor, around several corners, down some dead ends and back again, until he came across an orderly pushing a trolley full of bundles of dirty and bloody sheets through a large service door. He caught up with the man, held the door open for him in his most cocky way, and then before anything further was said had dashed out through the back entrance of the hospital, and down another long alley that he knew well, that took you around the back of the workhouse and out onto Newington Butts.

After a few weeks of observation, Hannah was committed to the Cane Hill Asylum, in Coulsdon, where she had been kept before, and where this time she stayed for eight months. Frances visited Hannah on a number of occasions during her weeks in Lambeth, and also managed to find time to become increasingly friendly with, and then engaged to, Dr Marcus Quarry, who to his surprise and her delight swept her off her feet. Her aunts and grandmother were also delighted, despite their disappointment at the couple's obvious indifference to basic proprieties when first making each other's acquaintance.

PART THREE
1903 - 1906

13

Basil did not come from a wealthy family. His father was a vicar, his father's father a carpenter. There was no habit or expectation of wealth in the family. Life for him at Oxford University at the turn of the century had been seriously constrained compared with what some of his fellow students could afford. That didn't bother him very much for the first couple of years, as it cost him nothing to play cricket and football and rugby and row for the college, beyond the occasional price of a beer afterwards. His had his old bicycle, which Mr Morris had repaired very cleverly, and it met all his needs, including his journey once a week to visit a girl who lived nearly 20 miles from Oxford. He was bursting with energy, loved to go as far as his legs could take him, and counted his bike as his greatest possession. What could be better than that? Something with a motor, perhaps?

He'd had a brief ride on a very primitive motor tricycle way back in 1897 but it had failed to impress; almost impossible to start up and, once started, so slow and ungainly it hardly seemed worth the effort. He was no more convinced when, on one very wet day a couple of years later, he and some friends witnessed the end of a smart looking French motor bicycle in the centre of Oxford. They'd watched expectantly as its sodden mud-soaked rider tried to make a sharp left turn at Carfax, the top-heavy Werner slipping away from under him without a moment's warning and crashing to the ground. They'd shouted loud encouragement as its owner scrabbled desperately away from his wrecked machine, which was bursting into flames. It burned furiously for quite some time, in front of the appreciative and increasingly vocal audience that rapidly gathered to watch its final moments.

But it wasn't long before a cycle dealer in the centre of Oxford created a sensation by exhibiting the stunning looking Singer motor tricycle in the window, available immediately to whoever could afford the £75 asking price. This vehicle was enamelled in black, picked out in green and gold, and had an engine that lived inside the front wheel, with eight wide highly polished aluminium spokes either side of it. The general opinion was that it was considerably more than handsome, and the students clustered around the shop daily, wondering how they'd find the money to buy one.

After a week of this, Basil could hold back no more and asked the dealer if he might be able to take a trial ride. The dealer, to his amazement, was only too pleased to oblige and they arranged to meet at a spot outside town early in the morning, before much other traffic was about. The test was not an unqualified success. On his first try Basil very nearly managed to drive straight into a ditch, just being saved by the dealer who was running desperately alongside. Once he'd worked out how to stay upright and go straight, Basil very quickly found it unbearably uncomfortable to ride. This road, like most roads, was made up of stones held together with earth and gravel, flattened by a heavy roller, a way of binding it all together that never lasted very long under the iron tyres of carts, the heavy shoes of horses, and the disintegrating effects of rain and frost, always sooner or later ending up as a mess of bumps and holes. The tricycle, which had very little suspension, bounced and crashed over these bumps and holes, until it felt to Basil like his teeth were being shaken out of his gums, and his eyes out of their sockets. Only much later did he come to understand that the faster you went over such a surface, the less it hurt.

His best chances of finding a machine worth taking seriously came from cadging rides with the richer undergraduates in his college and their equally rich friends from other colleges, most of whom had far more money than sense. These young aristocratic types were in regular trouble with the Proctors for their incessant larking about and nuisance-making. It was in their genes: sounding hunting horns in the middle of the night, climbing up the side of buildings after riotous Bullingdon parties, chucking flower pots and hot potatoes out of their windows, soaking passers-by in the streets below with soda syphons and being too fuddled to speak their names when caught. Motor cars and motor cycles drastically extended the scope of their misbehaviour, to the anguish of the university authorities who correctly suspected the better-off undergraduates of spending their days at horse races and their nights with women of dubious character and ill repute. One such student, to the admiration of his friends, was fined £5 and gated for the remainder of term for taking an actress to Henley in his car, which managed to break down on the way back, forcing its owner and the actress to shelter overnight in a country inn.

In the months that followed, Basil began to make himself indispensable to his new friends, who liked to buy the very latest and most expensive machines they could find and ride them with terrifying recklessness, without the faintest idea of what made them work or why they kept breaking down. You didn't need to know much about motor cycles to know more than these rich boys knew and, whilst he didn't know that much himself, he did know that the answer to any problem was right in front of you if you cared to look at it hard enough. He loved to discover why a motor cycle had been put together the way it was; he loved to take it apart, put it back together again, and ride it until he understood everything about it. His new friends were always happy to have him around just in case, and even let him tag along occasionally on one of their drinking, dining and plate-smashing nights. He didn't manage much revision in the final weeks before his final exams; he just hoped it wouldn't matter.

He left Oxford in the summer of 1901 and, to his family's surprise and his great embarrassment, with quite a poor degree. He had no real idea of what he might do next other than be ordained, his father's dearest wish but by no means his own as yet, and quite possibly never. He'd had a wonderful time at university, full of diversion and laughter. Now a wondrous new world of progress and machines awaited him, a world which made complete sense to him but he just couldn't see the way into it for someone with a degree in theology. So he took a job in a preparatory school far away down in Devon, to pass the time earning money, in reasonable comfort at least, until the direction for his future made itself better known to him.

1902

Life in Devon proved to be more than bearable and in some ways a man like him could easily become accustomed to the pleasures of sport, decent food, a congenial social life and a steady income. But as his first winter there set in and hardened, he became increasingly despondent to realise that, both spiritually and literally, he was going nowhere. The work was not hard, but the school was hidden a long way down deep dark lanes, and he still only had his ageing push-bike for transport in a very hilly county. As soon as spring came and the roads became more or less passable again, he could barely tolerate the limited horizons imposed on him by geography and lack of funds, and set off to a cycle shop in Barnstable, determined at least to splash out on a more modern, lighter push-bike. As soon as he walked into the workshop, though, he was transported to a higher plane of desire by the rich blue fumes and staccato bark of a Werner motorcycle struggling to get started.

Seeing Basil, and the ecstasy in his eyes, the wheezing dealer took a welcome break from trying to pedal the machine into life, and set to work fanning the flames of Basil's motorcycle love. They engaged in technical talk for hours, the agent clutching Basil's arm and doing his best to blind him with the latest science of motor cycle design, and Basil trying to look like he knew what the man was talking about. Eventually they talked money: all this for just £45! Hard as it was to walk away, Basil resisted and said he would think about it overnight.

And he did think about it, all night long. There was a process to go through first, because he knew he should not succumb to this too easily even if it was perfectly obvious what would happen in the end. Before actually committing himself to an expense that would take him a year at least to repay, he went to visit the other cycle dealer in town to see what he had to offer. He was immediately given the exceptional opportunity to buy a brand new Ormonde, apparently the world's best motorcycle, at a knockdown price. Still Basil held off. He had already discovered that neither dealer had in fact sold a single motorcycle until now and they were sure to be getting desperate.

He spent the next few days pushing each dealer to their furthest limit until the one selling the Ormonde appeared to crack and let Basil have the bike at rock bottom, in return for him agreeing to garage the machine in the shop window from time to time. Each of them was reasonably confident that he had pulled off a good deal. The dealer even undertook to engage an experienced mechanic to pedal alongside Basil on all his early outings, which quickly proved to be both embarrassing and pointless.

Two central facts of Basil's life were established that day: 1) debt was to be his constant companion, 2) the possession of a motorcycle, any motorcycle, made him complete. Now after years of feverishly dreaming of all kinds of exotic machine, he actually had one to call his own. It soon turned out, of course, that the Ormonde was not the answer to his motorcycling dreams and nor, when an Excelsior replaced it a few months later, would that be for long. Every bike he would come to possess would be better than the last and worse than the next; but it was never one machine or another that made motorcycling wonderful for him, so much as the part he would play in the evolution of the whole species.

1903

"Have you often fallen off sir?"

"I might have, once or twice," said Basil.

"We saw you sir, when you came back here once, your face was all mashed up. We knew you'd fallen pretty hard."

"What happened sir? Sir? Tell us about it sir. Please sir."

He was surrounded by eleven over-excited youngsters, stretched out on picnic rugs at the far side of the school playing fields, the remains of an impromptu feast scattered around them. It was a warm afternoon in July, the school year was nearly over, and Basil had arranged a special leaving party for the senior boys.

"Scottish sheep. Shifty little beggars. Going flat out down the Ord of Caithness on the old Excelsior. The roads were truly terrible around there and this part was particularly steep. Probably reaching speeds of 60 or 70 mph downhill, which is of course not legal but no-one else there to see. I'd come around a corner, just hanging on, and before I had a moment to think about it, saw that what I had assumed to be the surface of the road was in fact a bunch of sheep, snoozing away directly in front of me. I slammed on the brakes as hard as I could and must've swerved hard off the road. Before I knew what was happening I'd done a parabola over the handlebars and taken to the air, minus the Ormonde. Don't know what happened after that, I was completely out for some time. When I finally regained consciousness I found myself lying on my face surrounded by a tall forest of scraggy heather and a couple of curious sheep. No idea where I was or what had happened.

"In some pain, I got back on my feet, and gradually remembered. I was some thirty yards off the road, all on my own. No sign of the Ormonde anywhere. Finally found it some seventy yards further down the hill, admirably camouflaged in heather. I dragged it out, kicked it straight, mounted and rode on. It wouldn't fire properly but with some hard pedalling I got as far as Pitlochry and had no choice but to stick it and myself on the train. I think I was more damaged than the bike to be honest, so I suppose that's the occasion you horrible boys remember with such pleasure."

"Why weren't you killed sir?"

They already knew the answer perfectly well, because they'd got it out of him many times before.

"Very good question, Peploe, very good question."

His audience held its collective breath.

"People ask about the dangers of motorcycling and I suppose you could say there are many, but I have covered many miles by now on some very weird and perilous mounts I admit, without ever injuring myself seriously. Or anybody else for that matter.

"How can that be? you ask. Well. A motorcyclist tumbles like a baby or a drunken man when he comes off. If he is thrown he is thrown like greased lightning. There is no time to stiffen the muscles and create the resistance which leads to a bad fracture on impact. On that occasion in Scotland I went over the handlebars like a sack of flour, so escaped with a few cuts and bruises.

"The finest escape from the jaws of death that I ever witnessed was achieved by a sporting parson at a hill-climbing event not far from here. The hill was easy enough, and the cleric was riding a big twin-cylinder Zenith. He streaked over the crest of the hill at a mile a minute, and then steered into a rut. His machine went over and as he was flung clear, he curled his body up into a ball, with his head tucked well into his stomach. He bowled along the road for yards like a tennis ball, but took all the shock on his shoulders and sit-upon, so that he was not a penny the worse."

"*Really* sir? Did he really roll along the road sir?"

"Would I lie to you Napier? Have I ever told any of you anything but the bald unvarnished truth?"

The boys grinned back. "Never sir, no sir."

"No sir, indeed. Never in ten million years would I exaggerate. Or even slightly embellish the truth, as you all know perfectly well. Now will you all please get a move on and finish up the delicious food." He pushed the remaining boiled eggs, pickled onion and cherry cake towards them.

"I'm not saying that you can't get badly hurt or killed on a motorcycle," he continued. "But motorcyclists are mostly well-designed to come out alive. Our quick wits, swift steering, ready brakes, and narrow dimensions usually wriggle us out of the clutches of imminent death. And a bit of danger makes you feel alive, doesn't it boys?"

"Yes sir. That's why we're going into the Navy, isn't it sir?"

"Life on a warship can be pretty dangerous, sir."

"Just look what happened to Nelson, sir."

Basil realised that this was going further than he intended.

"Well I have no doubt you boys will have a fine time in the Navy, that's for sure." They grinned proudly. "And maybe you will find yourselves in the middle of a war one day, and I'm sure you'll do your country proud if you do." Loud cheers. "But let's hope that the dangers you encounter are nothing worse than the occasional hurricane out at sea, or maybe the odd ravenous mermaid in some faraway port."

He looked at their flushed faces, this bunch of thirteen year olds in their last days as children. Once the summer was over they were all due to start as cadets at Dartmouth, spending the next few years with 300 other children on the *Britannia,* in the bunks and decks where their predecessors had lived, and some of them died, back in its days as a battleship.

"No-one should ever consider themselves immune from danger," he said. "However brave and reckless they are."

They all tried to look like they took this seriously.

"Anyway," he said, clapping his hands encouragingly. "It's time to get your whites on for the masters match. And I must warn you boys, we shall slaughter you."

General disagreement and traditional insults against the uselessness of the teaching staff as cricketers.

"Are you going to bowl against us sir?"

"Of course I am, Cruttwell. No doubt that thought terrifies you somewhat?"

Basil's cricketing prowess was legendary, and especially the pace of his bowling.

"I shall knock each ball for six," Cruttwell announced, which was the idea of course. There was a general understanding among the masters to take it easy on the leavers, although not all of them managed to contain himself on occasions, one once almost crushing a particularly tiny batsman when he fell heavily onto him in a race to run him out. But the boys knew that they could count on Basil.

As they worked their way through the remains of the picnic, Montague-Pink pulled a magazine from his bag. "Sir?" he asked keenly. "Would you be so kind as to sign this for me?"

It was the current issue of *The Motor Cycle*, which contained the latest contribution from none other than Mr B. H. Davies B.A., a two-page guide to everything the keen rider needed to know about motor cycle touring. He had already published an account of a trip around Devon he'd recently made with his sister, earning him seven shillings and six pence per thousand words, and the same for a short piece on hill-climbing in the Cotswolds. He had now begun negotiations to raise the payment to ten shillings per thousand and although the editor was still holding out, the warm response from readers to this latest piece would soon clinch the deal. Basil looked at Montague-Pink for a moment, wondering whether he should agree to this request, which clearly crossed far over the important line between schoolmaster and human being. Suddenly five other boys pulled exactly the same magazine out of their bags. "Please sir, please sir," they said.

He sighed and picked up the proffered pen. "Just under here, would you sir?" asked Peploe, pointing to the photo of him standing by his 2¾ horsepower Excelsior, alongside a stone wall at a crossroads somewhere in Devon, looking relaxed and confident.

"Sir?" another boy, Spurgin, piped up as he came up to have his copy signed. "Is it true sir?"

Basil looked blankly at the boy.

"Is it true that you're leaving the school too, sir?"

"Yes sir, is it true, sir?" asked several others, all at once.

"I bet he's going to be a motor cycle racer," said Crutwell, blushing at his own impudence.

Basil raised his hands, to hush all this talk. For a moment he said nothing, but he knew that, in so many respects, all his efforts to preserve just a few vestiges of teacherly mystery had now come to absolutely nothing.

"I am definitely not," he began, "about to become a motor cycle racer, which isn't really a job at all as you well know. Not yet at least."

There was a murmur of disappointment. He took a deep breath, and looked down at the grass, wondering why he was finding this hard to say.

"I am going to be become a priest," he announced, to shocked gasps. "I am going to be ordained, as has always been my intention ever since I first went to university."

The boys looked at him in a mixture of incomprehension and disappointment.

"Will you have to give up your motorcycling, then, sir?" asked the boy whose copy of *The Motor Cycle* Basil was now signing.

Basil laughed. "Most certainly not, Ouchterlony."

"And you'll keep writing for *The Motor Cycle* sir, won't you?"

"No, I think not, that might not be considered quite proper for a priest, don't you think? They've given my job to a chap from Greek mythology. You may remember that I taught you all about him – he was tied to a burning wheel for all eternity. Do you recall?"

"Yes sir, I know sir! Ixion sir."

"Very good Peploe. But do say it right, boy. It's Ix-*eye*-on. Like that. Ix-*eye*-on."

"But Ixion must be dead, sir."

"Tied to a wheel for eternity, Crutwell. He should have some pretty good stories to tell by now."

14

November 18th 1903

Dear Ursula,

I am writing this in St Mary's. I don't know if it's correct or allowed to write in church, but it's completely silent and empty right now, and I really need to write down all the things I must tell you.

I received your letter this morning and read it many times. I am happy to know you haven't forgotten about me because I certainly haven't forgotten about you. I missed you a lot after you'd gone because you made me believe that I would love my life at Greyladies, but after you left it all became ordinary, not bad just ordinary.

And now you are on your way back to England! To be honest I had not actually known that you had left but now I understand. New Zealand is so very far away. I can imagine how hard it must have been to think of us here whilst you were over there & unwell for so long. I am sorry to hear about how bad the pneumonia was. How awful that must have been. You seemed so sad when you left — was pneumonia the cause of that? I was quite worried about you, but I am very pleased to hear you're all right now.

It would be nice to see you & talk to you because you were always so good at listening & making sense of things for me. So I'm trying to talk to you now in case it's the only chance I get and I know that you understand better than anyone how bad it feels to lose people you care for. I lost you of course but since then I've kept on losing people and so I wonder if it's me, if there is something wrong with me, which is silly I know but I really do wonder.

After you went I saw Hannah often and we became good friends. I so much needed someone to talk with after you'd left & I visited her often because she made me welcome & I liked it that she loved you too. You'd said you'd be like a mother to me & I thought Hannah might be the same because she is above all such a loving mother herself. But you will know already of course that she was in far greater need than I. After a few months she disappeared for a long time, and when she came back she seemed changed, she couldn't seem to concentrate on what she was saying or what I said to her. You would have known what to do but I didn't & though I kept an eye on her when I could, one day she broke down completely & lost her mind, and was sent to the asylum.

So that's how I lost her. But at the same time I found someone else, which seemed like a blessing, although it did not turn out that way I'm afraid. It's so hard to tell it now.

The person I met was a doctor at the Infirmary, who tended to Hannah for a while, and was very thoughtful to me. Marcus. He was most concerned about her, and that brought us close. Quite out of blue I had met this man & found I liked him, and he said he liked me very much, and everything in my life changed. I felt sad for poor Hannah when she was sent away, but Marcus made me understand that you can only do what you can do & shouldn't worry overmuch about what you cannot do.

I knew I was ready to get married. I'd decided that I was ready to have a family and look after them for ever and not spend the rest of my life trying to help people I hardly knew. In the summer my grandmother invited him to stay at Northwood Hall for a few days, and everyone liked him when they met him & before he left my grandmother spoke to him in private & soon after he proposed to me. I accepted immediately. It all felt so easy & straightforward & I felt happier than I had ever felt because my days as a Greylady would soon be over.

Now it all seems so long ago but it was just last year in fact.

Then Abigail died.

I think I might have told you about Abby, but I might not. She had been my tutor when I arrived in England, and then my friend. She was very clever, so she went to Oxford to be a bluestocking. She was much too clever for me really. I went & stayed with her in Oxford, in her room which was full of books and she had charts of history on her desk, I don't know what for, but it was all her work & she was so proud of it. She meant to stay there for ever & maybe she would have. But something terrible, terrible, happened and she lost heart. She came to visit me here and by then she was wasting away. I worried she had a wasting illness, consumption or an ulcerated stomach or something of that nature, but she had just given up. Everything. She never went anywhere, did nothing, did not hardly eat. She just wanted to be quiet and on her own, in her room at the college. Which is because of the terrible thing that happened to her, I am completely certain.

When she came to see me she was on her way to stay with her parents and get well again, so that she could return to Oxford. But she never did. She wrote me a couple of short letters and told me she would soon be better. Then last September her mother sent me notice of her death. I went to her funeral. She had just stopped living, all her strength had just drained away and she had got too weak to live. It happened in September, and it felt so terrible, but Marcus said that these things happen and life goes on. He said it's very sad old girl but these things happen you know.

So I told him. He took me down to Brighton for the day, because he could see I was not feeling happy and he wanted to cheer me up, and he knew I liked it there. But we ended up arguing horribly about what happened to Abby. You see she had been made ill by a terrible thing a man did her some years ago. He had taken her into the woods and attacked her, and after that she cut herself off from the world and got so terribly thin. I tried to tell Marcus about it, and he didn't understand which I suppose was my fault really because I couldn't say exactly what the man did, except to tell him that he had violated her. He said it probably wasn't like that really, and anyway that wouldn't have killed her. She just got ill, people get ill and die you know. It's sad but they do. And I burst into tears & told him he didn't understand at all.

He asked me whether the man was much older than Abigail and I said he was quite young, her age I'd say. Marcus asked me if Abigail was used to being in the company of young men and I said certainly not and then he said well that's it, isn't it? She was naïve and he was probably inexperienced and it was more than likely just a misunderstanding. She'd gone into the woods with him, hadn't she? And he'd imagined she was game for it, and in a way she was partly to blame for what happened. He was sorry to say it, but that's the real world. Men and women.

I told him I knew the real world well enough, and that wasn't it at all. The man had violated her & ruined her life. And Marcus wouldn't have it and I wouldn't have what he said, and we sat there on the stony beach, the grey sea bashing onto the stones in front of us and the wind blowing, and I said take me home.

159

I wanted to stay in love with him but in the days after I didn't even like him. We carried on being engaged & made sure not to speak about Abigail again but I think we should have done. A few weeks later, just before Christmas, Marcus came to stay at Northwood Hall again and my aunts were still nice to him, and everyone was talking about a wedding in the spring. Aunt Mary showed me the announcement of the engagement that she was going to include in the Family News, but I wasn't as pleased as she had expected.

Then the next afternoon something really silly happened. We were all gathered in the drawing room for afternoon tea, and Marcus came in late, several minutes after everyone else. He didn't even apologise or say anything, just sat down and grabbed a plate. I looked around to see if anyone would say anything, and noticed that Aunt Mary was staring at his feet, just staring at them like they were on fire or something.

He'd come down to tea in his carpet slippers and

"Excuse me, miss. I am so sorry to disturb you," said the young curate. "Is everything all right?"

Frances jumped up in alarm, pieces of writing paper falling all around her.

"Please don't worry, no need to move away," the curate continued, coming forward to help her pick up the papers. "I just wanted to let you know that Evensong will begin in a few minutes. You are very welcome to stay, of course."

Frances was shocked to realise how long she must have been there, scribbling. She grabbed her bits of paper, apologised for writing in church, and said she would go rightaway. The curate said it certainly wasn't a problem.

"You're a Greylady, aren't you?" he asked. "I have heard so many good things about your order."

"We are not nuns," Frances said.

"No, of course, but I know you do much good work around here."

"Thank you," she said, taking her things from him.

"I'm new here," said the curate. Frances nodded absently. The curate looked at her.

"Have we met before?" he asked. "I'm sure we've met before."

"I don't believe so," Frances said. The curate looked at her, shaking his head, hoping she might solve the mystery. He put out his hand and said "Basil Davies" and she just nodded at him, still clutching her crumpled pages, thanked him for his kind help, and took her leave.

"American," Basil muttered, frowning with the effort of recollection.

"My God!" he said under his breath as the memory dawned. But by then she was hurrying off, clearly not in the mood for a conversation. He noticed, once she had disappeared, that she had left behind an envelope on the floor, addressed to Miss Frances Hodgkinson, Greyladies College, Kennington, with a letter inside. The next day Basil took it around to the College in the hope of returning it to its owner in person. The porter went off to find her, only to discover that the young lady was not available after all, so Basil regretfully left the letter with the porter and went on his way.

15

Over a year went by after their fleeting encounter in St. Mary's Church before Basil and Frances actually spoke, despite living just a couple of streets away from one another, and indeed crossing each other's path in those very streets more than once. Frances lowered her eyes whenever she saw Basil approaching, and he would let her go by without a word, wishing he didn't. They did finally manage to exchange nods at the summer fête in the park, Basil looking her way several times, but nothing more as she was in the company of other Greyladies. He showed more confidence a few weeks later at a harvest festival party, walking right up to her, and saying very nice to see you again Miss Hodgkinson. The fact that he knew her name made her blush, and she said something silly like "yes Father" before someone came up to speak to him and she hurried away again. Several more weeks went by until, shortly before Christmas, she decided to attend evensong at St Mary's. He stood chatting to parishioners at the church door as they left after the service. This time she did not run away but went up to shake his hand and tell him how much she'd enjoyed his sermon. He threw her a beaming smile and warmly clasped her hand with both of his, earning a raised eyebrow from one of the ladies waiting behind for their turn.

On her return to Kennington after Christmas and the New Year with her aunts in Northwood, she went back to St

Mary's for another evensong on the off-chance, but found the vicar himself leading the service, no sign of Basil. She wanted to ask the vicar where his curate had gone, and whether he was ever coming back, but instead just suffered through the service and left without a word, feeling unaccountably angry, at the vicar for not being Basil, and at Basil for not being there. She went back to the Greyladies house, furious with herself for minding at all, and resolved not to go near St Mary's again.

Nothing relieved the February gloom, and Frances made little effort to hide her disenchantment with life, London and the Greyladies. She thought often of the way Ursula suddenly walked out and never came back. She began to dream of leaving like that. But then the Greyladies burglary took place.

The first Frances knew of it was when she wandered into the dining room for breakfast to find the cook, the parlour maid, and a few of the older Greyladies, including Miss Yeatman, looking at her as if she'd done something terrible. Frances faltered uneasily, and then Miss Yeatman dramatically announced that the house had been BURGLED during the night. Were they actually blaming *her* for that? Yes, it seems they were.

"Frances dear," Miss Yeatman said, holding up the little Provident Fund cashbox, flipping its lid open and displaying its utter emptiness to her. "I thought we had agreed that this was to be locked in the safe every night without fail. I think this was agreed, Frances, when you so kindly undertook to take responsibility for the fund?"

Before Frances could answer, the cook suddenly pointed towards the dresser and let out an agonised cry. "Oh Miss Yeatman! The silver spoon!" she wailed. "Our silver spoon is gone."

It wasn't just the silver spoon that was lost, but a good deal of clutter whose disappearance that morning had brought cheer to the parlour maid at least: bone china flowers in bone china flower pots, a wooden cross and a pewter crucifix, chipped pottery vases whose dried flowers had been emptied onto the floor, miniature pictures of the Holy Land in ivory frames and a big picture of Jesus turning water into wine in a wooden frame that one of older Greyladies had shakily decorated by hand, a photograph of the Bishop of Rochester in a silvery frame, a tiny Bible and prayer-book set in a tiny leather case, a stopped clock that was nonetheless correct twice every day, two antimacassars, a letter opener, a toast rack, and irreparable damage to a large fern and its plant pot that one of the clumsy oafs must have kicked over as he came in through the window, even then not managing to wake a single Greylady.

Eventually a large policeman arrived at the house in response to Miss Yeatman's urgent messages.

"Do you have any notion, Constable," she asked, sweeping her hand around the room, "who might have done all this?"

He began to chuckle at the thought that the available evidence might enable the apprehension of any specific thief or thieves amongst a local population which, as far as he was concerned, was made up almost entirely of thieves.

"Have I said something amusing, Constable?" asked Miss Yeatman, flushing.

"We shall do our best, madam, of course. Not much to go on is there?" he said, solemnly inspecting the soil spread over the carpet from the pot plant for a footprint. "Unless we catch the villain red-handed when he tries to offload your silver spoon." He quickly smothered any unwarranted optimism. "And that's not going to happen."

"Is it likely," continued Miss Yeatman, voicing the fears of all the Greyladies who had by now assembled in the dining room to receive the wisdom of the police force, "that the villains might return tonight for more loot?"

The constable thought about this for a few moments. "In all honesty madam, it sounds to me like they took all they could ever want and a bit more besides. I suspect you won't be hearing from these boys again."

"But might you leave an officer on guard outside our house for a few nights, at least, Constable?" she asked. The constable looked at her open-mouthed. "Would you be so kind as to ask your commanding officer at least?"

"I shall do my best madam," he said. "But I hold out extremely little hope for that."

Little hope was all they were left with after the policeman's visit, and the most hopeless of them all was undoubtedly Frances. She sobbed so loudly in the drawing room that she was sent upstairs to sob in her bedroom, but the distant sound of her sobbing turned out to be no less irritating and she was sent to the park for some fresh air and a very long walk, assured that she need not concern herself with her normal duties for the rest of the day. She walked around the park one time, feeling that the last thing she could bear to do would be to sit alone on a wretched bench ever again, and hurried straight out.

She wandered north up towards St Mary's, without any particular intention to go inside, but nonetheless did just that. As ever, the middle of the afternoon, the place was quite dark and cold; she hesitated to sit down and just walked slowly down the nave until she glimpsed movement. Basil, in his long curate's cassock, emerged from behind the altar with a screwdriver in his hand and paused in front of the big cross to see who was standing there.

"Miss Hodgkinson!" he called. "How nice to see you! Can I help in any way?"

She didn't mean to disturb him.

"Such a cold afternoon," he said. "Perhaps I could persuade you to join me for a cup of tea in the parish office?"

The office was warm and cosy, boasting a little coal stove with a kettle bubbling quietly on top. He made a pot of tea and produced the remains of a small fruit cake. He smiled very nicely as he handed her the larger piece, and she felt a kind of after-sob come over her which she didn't quite manage to hold back. He gave her a gentle look of enquiry, which was all she needed to launch into the saga of the stolen money. She told him how useless the whole thing had made her feel.

"For all we know," he said, choosing his words carefully, "the money that was stolen might be used to feed a starving family. It might. Even the worst things can turn out to be for the best."

"Do you really think so?" Frances asked.

"Well, you never know," he said, with an encouraging smile. "But wherever the money went, none of this was your fault. And that's not the problem anyway. It's the disapproval that hurts, isn't it?"

"Yes! Yes!" she cried. "Exactly! That's worse than anything. When I disappoint people. I simply cannot bear it."

"We all hate it when people think badly of us. When they stop thinking *well* of us."

"Exactly Father! That's it exactly!" she cried.

"Never mind," he said and then, in a low conspiratorial voice, "it brought you here so that I could share my last piece of cake with you. The Lord moves in mysterious ways."

He asked her a few questions about life as a Greylady, and she expressed more enthusiasm for the work than she felt, but that wasn't really the point. The point was that neither was in a hurry to stop talking.

Basil wrote her a note that very evening, assuring her that he was always available, if she needed to talk more, about anything on her mind. She replied, thanking him for his kindness, apologising for not having thanked him sooner, and promised to contact him if the need arose. Just two days later he wrote to her wondering if she would be interested in joining him at a small concert of sacred music taking place at the Cathedral the following Saturday afternoon.

The concert wasn't an unqualified success, and neither was their conversation at first. Nonetheless, whilst accompanying her back to the Greyladies house afterwards, Basil finally summoned the nerve to ask whether she might possibly be willing to do him a tremendous favour. Frances looked at him anxiously, and he hurriedly explained that he simply wondered when she could assist him with a lady parishioner whose problems concerned him greatly, and regarding whom the understanding of a Greylady would be most welcome. Perhaps she'd accompany him on a visit to the lady's home? "Unfortunately the poor wretch has recently moved beyond the bounds of this parish somewhat – Whitechapel – something of a journey to get there," he explained. Frances thought that should not be a problem.

"I tend to make such journeys by motorcycle," he continued, more tentatively. "Would you be willing to venture such a trip with me, on my machine? You are highly likely to get there and back in one piece." She agreed that this sounded a sensible plan, and she wouldn't mind giving it a try, although she could not imagine that Miss Yeatman would approve.

"Perhaps we should not burden Miss Yeatman with such a request in the first instance," he suggested, and she thought that was a good idea too.

Basil kept his machine in a lock-up garage behind the rectory, about half a mile from Lorrimore Square. It would be wise, they had agreed, not to meet too close either to his church or the Greyladies house, to avoid misapprehension. She thought about this for a few moments, and wondered if it might not be simplest if he collected her from the Elephant and Castle electric railway station. Perfect, he said, and suggested she wait for him just inside the side exit. As soon as I arrive, he said, out you come and off we go. Absolutely no need for subterfuge. It would be sensible, though, he added, to make sure you're very well covered up against the weather.

The clatterings and whirring of Basil's motorcycle were barely audible against the roar of London and its traffic, but it was hard to ignore the gleaming brass and shiny blue steel of the little three-wheeler and its courageous crew crossing London Bridge. Basil, in full-length gabardine, peaked cap, goggles and big leather gloves, controlled everything from his seat in the centre of the vehicle, one hand clutching the brass knob of a large horizontal wooden steering wheel and the other busy working the throttle, concentrating intently. Frances, under a colossal windblown hat held down by a bright yellow silk scarf, was perched ahead of him on her seat between the two front wheels, meeting everything that London had to throw at them face-on.

The pick-up plan had gone smoothly. Frances had arrived late at the underground station but Basil nonetheless contrived to turn up just half-a-minute after she arrived, having actually gone around twice already to avoid any suggestion of waiting impatiently. "Perfect timing!" Frances said, as she stepped delicately on-board, feeling rather as if she was climbing into a boat.

Although terrified at first to find herself sitting unprotected at the very front of this flimsy machine bobbling through the waves of London traffic, she soon abandoned herself to the confident ease with which Basil steered them forward and held his ground in the midst of it all. When they got to Whitechapel the poor parishioner they had hoped to visit could not be found and hadn't been seen for days, presumed to have most unwisely returned to live again with her drunken and worthless husband. Rather than curtail their afternoon together, Basil proposed a somewhat longer and rather more interesting journey home, through the City, around St Paul's, along The Strand and up The Mall to Buckingham Palace, down to Parliament Square and along the Embankment as far as Lambeth Bridge, where they would cross the river and then make their way down to the southern tip of Kennington Park, the end of the voyage. Frances, equally keen not to curtail the outing, gave her enthusiastic approval and prayed that they didn't encounter Aunt Ethel as they crossed the bridge.

The only moment of drama came when the motorcycle's wheels lost grip crossing the greasy and treacherous tramlines by the Oval cricket ground, and they found themselves slithering towards a madly swaying three-horse bus that was almost upon them. At the very last moment, Basil managed to jerk his machine out of the way as the bus thundered past. Amazed that they hadn't turned over, he pulled over to check the condition of his wide-eyed and gasping passenger, but she breathlessly assured him that she was fine, and gave a crazy little laugh of excitement.

Following this, Frances began to attend evensongs at St Mary's on a regular basis, even though it was not strictly the preferred church for Greyladies. More than two weeks went by after their outing to Whitechapel before they could find a moment alone again, but she had received a lovely note from Basil the morning after, thanking her for so kindly giving up her time in what on that occasion had proved to be a lost cause, but hoping that she would nonetheless risk doing so again should a similar situation arise. Her reply, warmly in the affirmative, was with him within the hour.

Before that could happen, Frances received a short note on Lambeth Infirmary notepaper, signed simply MQ, written with great circumspection to let her know that poor Hannah Chaplin was back in the Cane Hill Asylum, at Coulsdon, now sadly more insane than ever after a brief period back out in the wild. She replied very politely, thanking Dr Quarry for his kind consideration and wishing him well. Then she wrote to Basil, rather more urgently, to wonder if he might just possibly be willing to carry her on his motor cycle to visit a kind lady she knew who was incarcerated in hospital. It was not very far, in a place called Coulsdon. He replied immediately, telling her that he had carefully checked the Profile Road Book for the journey, and could assure her that on that part of the Brighton Road they would encounter no hills so steep that she would have to get off and push. He made her laugh.

They went on a bright early spring day in April. Frances had travelled one stop along the line from Kennington to Stockwell, where this time she found Basil already waiting for her. It was only a fifteen mile trip to Coulsdon, and they were there in less than an hour.

Hannah was delighted to see Frances, and seemed in good form on that particular day. She was especially excited by the appearance of a tall handsome man, and swore that she should have married a vicar, and then she would have lived the life she deserved. She talked incessantly about her own past on the stage, and of her plans to revive her career very soon. Basil looked around the room at the playbills she'd put on display, and his eyes suddenly stopped in front of a poster for a touring production of *Sherlock Holmes*. "Billy!" he cried in amazement. "That little lad was brilliant – I saw him play in Rochdale! A tiny dynamo, I've never seen anyone so agile. You couldn't take your eyes off him when he was on stage."

"That's my boy Charlie!!" Hannah screamed, almost melting with pride. "That's *my* boy."

"Good heavens," said Basil. "A future music hall star, without a shred of doubt."

Frances smiled in delight, and grinned at Hannah. "You always said he'd go far. That's what you always said."

"And she never believed me!" Hannah said, "but it's true enough vicar, isn't it?"

As far as Hannah was concerned, the visit had been a considerable success.

Basil and Frances ate their lunch in the asylum garden, sitting on a bench together, eating brisket sandwiches and pickled onions that Basil had brought. He asked Frances about Hannah, and she came dangerously near to explaining about Dr Quarry, which she was not yet ready to do. And then, to make matters worse, Basil couldn't resist bringing up the subject of his very first sight of her, in Oxford all those years before.

"I don't blame you for not remembering," he said, with a diffident grin, "but I must tell you that you made quite an impression on me at the time."

"That's very nice of you," she said. "When do you say this was, exactly?"

"'99. At the workshop of Mr Morris," he said.

"Mr Morris?" she asked, shocked. "Is he a friend of yours?"

"Good Lord no! But at the time you confused me for him. You had come along with your little friend, to borrow bicycles. Do you remember?"

"I remember going there well enough, yes," she said, her face darkening.

"Mr Morris sent me away. But I didn't want to leave, because of the impression you'd made on me," he continued, feeling that this story, which he had hoped would charm her and do something to take things between them some way further forward, was not working out quite how he'd intended. There was a long silence.

"Have I said something wrong?" he asked at last.

"Not wrong exactly, although I wish you would not have referred to poor Abigail as you did," she said, very quietly.

"I'm so sorry," he said, baffled. "What did I say?"

"You referred to her as *little*. My *little* friend. It's demeaning to talk of someone so brave and clever like that," she said, with the tears she had so desperately wanted to resist now oozing out of her eyes. "Even more so, given that she is no longer with us." Basil blanched.

"I'm so very sorry," he said, touching her hand as gently as he could. She pulled it away.

"No," she said. "This brings back to me things that are too painful to talk about. I'm very sorry." They sat together in miserable silence, Basil bizarrely finding himself longing for a pickled onion, Frances acutely aware of the onions he had already eaten.

He asked her if she would like to tell him about what happened to her friend. "No," she said, again. "I can't talk about any of that now."

"Well I hope you might one day," he said. "I really do. I can see it is all very painful, and I'm mortified to have made things worse. I very much want you to think of me as someone you can trust."

In fact, she desperately wanted to tell him everything, because she did already trust him, more than any man she had known. But she dared not risk it. What if he reacted the way Marcus had done? What if he turned out to be the same as him, casually dismissing Abigail's torment as just a young girl's ignorance of the world? That would be the end of everything, and she could not and would not contemplate such a prospect. There were so many things in her life, she realised, that she would very much like to tell him, but never would.

"Do you want to go home now?" he asked her, again touching her hand, permitted this time to leave it there.

"Not yet," she said. "Let's just sit here together, do you mind?"

They sat there for another half-hour, making occasional conversation about the garden they were in, about Hannah and her boy, and the troubled lives of the poor of their parish. Frances let him hold her hand throughout. When they finally stood up to go, Basil began to hope that he may not have ruined everything between them after all, and turned to face her with a significant look on his face, as if he meant to kiss her there and then.

"I appreciate your companionship Basil, very much," Frances said, evading the moment and, above all, the appalling prospect of a first kiss that tasted of pickled onions.

She regained her composure on the return journey, and her good spirits too. As they swept through the Surrey countryside in the gentle spring sunshine, the trees and hedgerows bursting all around them, Frances thrust her face forward into the breeze, and became the figurehead of a galleon cutting through wild green waves of springtime, the warm air blowing all sadness away. She hardly noticed the dust that was covering her from head to foot – it was glorious to be driven along like this, and not for a moment did she doubt Basil's ability to bring her safely home. She couldn't see him from where she sat, but she could feel his presence behind her, very powerfully.

Basil was away from London quite often throughout April and over Easter, but just before Frances was to go away herself for a couple of weeks they managed to spend an afternoon walking together over to St Paul's. They took their time, talking all the way there and all the way back. He told her about the many things he managed to do in his spare time, and she said she couldn't ever imagine doing so much, and such clever things too. He said not clever at all, he was just doing what he needed to do. She told him how lonely she had been, here in London, and he told her he too was often lonely, however busy he managed to be.

16

Frances had always been very happy to have a break from her Greylady responsibilities and return to the comforts of the family home. On this occasion, though, she found herself longing to be back in Kennington almost as soon as she got to the current grand family home, on the western edge of London, and spent the whole stay in a state of nervous anticipation that she didn't quite manage to hide from her aunts' attentive eyes. She burst into the house with a bright energy, demanding to hear what outings were planned, what cousins were coming, and what shopping trips might be possible, dying to tell everyone about something special that was taking shape in her life, but very certain of the need to keep it to herself for now.

Everyone could see that Frances was far more animated than usual, and the aunts keenly guessed the reason why. No-one had seen her like that since the episode of the louche doctor. Suspicions of something being up, or about to be up, were intensified towards the end of her two-week stay when she summoned the courage to ask Mary Harriette for an advance on her allowance, explaining that she desperately needed a new outfit. Summer clothes. Mary Harriette asked if these would really be of much use, given the requirement to wear her uniform at all times when in London.

"Oh Aunt Mary!" she cried, ready for a fight. "I cannot

tell you how much I hate walking through the streets in those awful clothes."

Aunt Mary appeared suitably shocked.

"Through the streets?" she cried. "Surely it goes without saying that you must always go out as a Greylady when you *do* go out?"

Frances tried to explain that sometimes, as a 25 year old woman, when she had time off from her responsibilities, she might wish to go out to a concert or a museum with her cousin Rose for instance, and no, on such occasions most certainly not as a Greylady. Her aunt stared at her appraisingly.

"Well dear," she said brightly, "I think we should first of all see if any of the younger aunts have anything that might be suitable for you." Frances had been expecting this. "Those girls buy so many things that they hardly wear more than once. They'll always be happy to pass something lovely on to you."

Frances waited.

"And I'm sure we could splash out on a smart new hat for you," Mary Harriette conceded. "Just the thing for meeting the occasional cousin."

"That's very kind of you," Frances muttered.

Mary Harriette didn't want to be unkind, but it was a matter of great principle these days that lines must be drawn in terms of expenditure, and her mother's constant scrutiny of the accounts would permit no crossing of those lines with respect to the most basic principle of all: each according to his, or her, own station. And anyway, the girl was hiding something.

Frances hurried off disappointed but not much surprised to the kitchen, and there made a prodigious pile of chocolate caramels, which had been on her mind since her arrival, even if that didn't leave her much time for the work she had to do for tomorrow's meeting of *The Family News* editorial board.

Mary Harriette's devotion to spending substantial parts of every day writing in her secret diary was well known to all, and indeed constituted for some an unaccountable source of irritation. The habit sometimes proved invaluable, though, in settling disputes and solving mysteries, whereby Mary Harriette would be carelessly asked if she could remember this or that, and she would disappear for a while, to return with the answer without being required to explain how she knew. The day finally arrived when her brother Herbert, doubtless prompted by their mother who had a principled objection to her children having secrets of any kind, asked Mary Harriette if she might be interested in extending her presumed talents as family chronicler to the production of a properly printed newsletter, such as was becoming quite popular these days, he believed. The idea appealed to her very much and she required little persuasion, even if nothing would ever deflect her from making her nightly private diary entries.

The Family News was formally initiated one misty autumn afternoon in the Northwood Hall library, launched with some ceremony and a generous donation from Herbert. Mary Harriette was of course appointed its Editor which, as she herself pointed out, was entirely right and proper given that only someone as bossy as her could ever hope to manage an editorial team of wayward sisters and the occasional niece.

It was clear that this was to be far more than a mere newsletter, but rather a professionally printed periodical distributed quarterly to all the various tribes of the extended family, who could purchase a costly bound version annually if they chose to, which many did. Contributions from family members soon started to flow in, covering an array of interesting topics: *A Motor Trip to Swanage, Canon Dale as a Preacher, The Superiority of Eastbourne Shops, In the Hills of Ceylon, The Agricultural Motor Cultivator: Its Social and Economic Aspect, Recollections of the Boer War, A Few Facts about the Richardson Family, First Impressions – Tracheotomy, The Story of an Unsuccessful Wolf Hunt* and *Gruyere, the Land of Cheeses*, for instance.

Actual news from family members – *Family Items* – filled the first page or two of each issue: announcements of weddings, births, christenings, and deaths; news of appointments, commissions, postings, prizes, expeditions, accidents, changes of plan, changes of address. All submissions to the journal were subjected to ferocious editing and revision to make sure that they satisfied the key aims of the journal: to amuse, inform and not let the side down; no shocking revelations, no unpleasantness of any kind.

Frances had been press-ganged onto the editorial board by Aunt Mary because it would do her good somehow. But it was in every possible respect not Frances's sort of thing at all. She'd felt out of her depth from the start, not having much idea who all these family members actually were and which ones precisely were to be admired, pitied or mocked, and deeply uncomfortable about having to rewrite anything they submitted. She dreaded the editorial meetings, which could sometimes prove quarrelsome, and hated having her own efforts discussed by everyone.

The task Aunt Mary had allocated to her for the present meeting had been to cut as much as she could from a lengthy and fervid death notice of a lady who'd insisted on being called Aunt Emily, despite not being any aunt of theirs. The problem was that this particular issue of the journal had to report a number of other deaths that were a good deal closer to home: Mrs Pickersgill-Cunliffe's sister Aunt Clara, who had left a gap quite impossible to fill; cousin Laura Richardson, whose family name carried considerable weight in the journal and far beyond; an old nurse called Nurse who had been a stalwart of the various family homes and a profound believer in the family that lived in them. It was out of the question that any one of these should be asked to sacrifice richly merited obituary space to this Aunt Emily, who was rather odd by the sound of her anyway.

To everyone's surprise, Frances had easily solved this little problem by simply chopping out most of the original. She read out the little that remained to considerable approval.

> Emily Gracilla, an intense lover of children and flowers, has left us aged 81 years. She may be described as one whose whole life was laid out for God and for others. She said once 'I made a hole long ago and buried all my likes and dislikes in it.' It was true, and she never dug them up again. She is the last of her family.

"You've captured the gist of it jolly well, Frances, whatever that was," Mary Harriette said, smiling approvingly. "You are clearly beginning to learn the ruthless arts of editing, dear!" Frances blushed. She had not intended to be ruthless; she'd just chosen the bits she liked the best. But the praise was nice.

It was agreed that a piece by her sister about her experiences in teacher training college was one of the highlights of the new issue, though for the life of her Frances could not see why. There was even more enthusiasm for *An Exciting Moment on a Tobacco Plantation*, a striking description of a revolt by Chinese coolies in Malaya, in which a yelling mob had tried to kill the author and his assistant.

"Oh my God how *disgusting*," said Milicent as she read it through. "Listen to this!"

> Suddenly the stillness was broken by a slight shuffling sound from the far end of the huge shed. I got up leisurely and glanced down, when to my horror I saw Mr H holding on to one of the benches at the side of the shed, nearly smothered in coolies. My heart seemed to stand still, but then with a yell that broke the hideous

silence I dashed to the rescue. My shout was now taken up by the hitherto silent coolies with their terrible cry of "Pah, pah" ("kill, kill"). Quickly I reached H's side, and with hands and feet attacked the yelling mob, only to be soon overpowered and dragged down. Never shall I forget the look of those distorted faces and the horrid yellow smell of their naked bodies as they trampled me under foot; the despair of that moment is indescribable.

"Oh heavens!" Frances cried. "Did he survive?"

The others looked at her despairingly. "Yes dear," said Kay. "He's the one telling the tale, so I imagine he did." Frances laughed at her own silliness and was informed that, whilst Mr H had a few ribs broken, the author himself amazingly escaped more or less unhurt. "Happy ending," said Milicent.

The longest and, from the Pickersgill-Cunliffe family perspective, the major highlight was the final instalment in the inspirational history of the Reverend Thomas Pelham Dale, one of their mother's many ecclesiastical siblings, who had the distinction of having spent time in Holloway Prison.

"He was imprisoned," explained Mary Harriette unhelpfully, "for being a contumacious priest."

She smiled benevolently at Frances's sigh of incomprehension, and spent a futile couple of minutes trying to make sense for her of Anglo-Catholicism, Ritualism and her uncle's insistence when conducting services on waving incense, wearing elaborate vestments, ringing bells and making the sign of the cross – practices which were outlawed in the Church of England, strictly speaking.

"He was sent to prison for wearing the wrong costume in church?" cried Frances, urgently needing to know what kind of vestments, exactly, got a vicar sent to prison.

"Yes indeed," Mary Harriette continued, solemnly. "It caused your grandmother tremendous pain to see her brother treated like that."

"Is he still in prison?" Frances asked, very quietly, dreading to hear the answer.

"No dear, it was just for a few weeks. Long enough, all things considered. But many years ago now." She was impressed that her niece seemed so moved by the story.

Frances breathed again and changed the subject by hurrying around with a tin of the chocolate caramels she had made the previous day, now melting in the heat of this exceptionally warm day in May.

Unusually, Frances did not feel at all sad when the time came for her leave again. She felt like running for joy as she walked away down the long driveway.

"Did you notice," said Aunt Kay after she'd gone, "the spring in her step?"

"Most definitely," said Mary Harriette, more convinced than ever that something was up. "No tears of parting, you will have noticed."

Frances arrived back at the Greyladies house by lunch-time on the first day of June, and rushed to her room to see if there was a message of some kind from Basil. This, she knew, was an entirely irrational hope, given that they had both agreed before she went away that it would be wisest not to risk sending any kind of note, however harmless, that might be read in error by an inquisitive old Greylady. There had, of course, been absolutely no question of writing to her at Northwood Hall, where her grandmother monitored all the correspondence that came to the house, and had no scruples about opening anything unexpected, suspicious or of possible interest.

Nonetheless, Frances was sure there'd be something waiting for her in Kennington, and gasped with delight on finding a sepia postcard of the old harbour at Douglas, Isle of Man, delivered that very morning, with just the following words:

Some delightful circuits around this lovely peaceful island. Back to work on the evening of the first. Yrs Ixion.

Frances hurried along to St Mary's that evening to witness a bleary-eyed Basil conduct the service. They were able to talk briefly afterwards on the way out, enough time to say hello and how nice to see you again and exchange highly charged looks. It was not easy to find a moment when they could be alone together.

Basil invited her to tea at the Rectory the next day. The housekeeper looked after them very well, but never left them alone for long, so the conversation stayed mainly light and harmless. Basil told her about his visit to the Isle of Man with his motorcycling chums and committee men, to lay down plans and rules for holding races there. It's a lovely island, he told her, you'd like it very much. She was sure she would. But it's hard old sea journey, I can tell you, he said. All night being thrown around on the wild Irish sea, and then the long slow journey by train back down from Liverpool. That wouldn't bother me at all, she said.

You look wonderfully well, he said. So do you, she said, and they looked at each in silence, foolishly grinning, until the housekeeper came back in again. Then he became serious, and told her he had to return home to Rochdale soon, because his father wished to talk to him about something important. He'd be away for several days at least. She looked disappointed and said Maybe you could write me a letter, while you're away. If you've a moment free from all your motorcycle writing. Oh! he said, I will find time.

And he did write, about his mother's ill health and his father's worries over his clerical pension. About how he was concerned for them, because they had decided to leave Rochdale. He told her about riding out into the beautiful raw Pennine hills, and how sad it would be to leave all that. He wanted to take her there, and she wrote back straightaway to say how very much she would like that. She hoped he might be returning soon. He wrote back immediately to reassure her that he most certainly was, and to suggest an outing together. Perhaps they could go to London Zoo early the next week; they'd be able to talk properly. She counted the days, and the hours, until that happened, and tried to imagine what he might want to say.

Basil took her along a special route to get there, stopping in the square where her mother had been born, and then to look at Portland Place where her family had its London home until her grandfather's tragic accident. Aunt Mary had often talked about the wonderful times she and Nell had enjoyed in London as young ladies and Frances thought how hard it must have been for her mother to leave that dazzling life for a struggling farm in South Carolina. But she understood. Her mother had been in love with her father, and that was what they chose to do. Just the two of them, alone in a hostile world.

"You know," Basil said later, as they watched the orangutans swing around in their cage. "Charles Darwin used to come here for hours on end, to watch Jenny the orangutan. Apparently it was Jenny who finally convinced him that we are descended from the apes, because of the way she rolled around in a tantrum, just like a small child."

Frances looked uneasily back at Basil. "Are we really though?" she asked.

"Oh yes," he said, enthusiastically. "I believe so. It all makes sense to me. I think evolution must have been God's idea. It's such a wonderful idea."

Frances nodded at him with the smallest flicker of impatience, to suggest he might get on with the main point of the day, whatever that was. She was in an agony of expectation and uncertainty.

"My dear girl," he said, slowly and very seriously. "I must tell you first of all that I shall be leaving St Mary's quite soon."

Oh.

"My father has asked me to join him at his new church, as his curate," he explained.

"Where is that to be?" she asked, faintly.

"Esh," he said. "In County Durham."

"Is that very far from here?" she said, looking blankly at an orangutan, who was looking back at them both in his vague, solitary way.

"Very far," he said.

"How soon will you have to leave?" she asked, very quietly now, tears forming.

"A couple of months," he said. She crumpled slightly. He put his arm around her.

"How will I ever get on without you?" she whispered.

"I don't want you to ever get on without me," he said.

"You don't?"

"No."

She turned and looked at him, and through her tears saw him take a deep breath, and assume an earnest solemn face.

"Frances," he said.

"Yes?" she said.

They floated back through the frenzied afternoon traffic at Elephant and Castle like angels, ethereal, with a secret knowledge that the mortals around them could not imagine. Everything was different now; between just the two of them, and between the two of them and the rest of the world. They agreed that it would be best to stop acting as if they had something to hide. They were just two friends out for a drive. Or, two parish workers coming back from parish work. It didn't matter, they had nothing to be ashamed of. Basil drove calmly past St Mary's and the Rectory, turned left towards the Square and pulled up right outside the Greyladies house. Frances sat immobile for a moment, waiting to hear the engine stop and receive the tap on her shoulder from her captain that told her it was safe now to disembark.

"Are you sure this is all right?" Basil asked, one more time. Frances nodded happily as she took off her gloves and goggles. She stashed them in the wooden box over the rear wheels and, flushed with the rapture of their hours together, told him that everything was wonderful. Basil looked at Frances adoringly, and was about to say the same when the front door of the Greyladies house was flung open, and a loud voice called her name. Frances felt her soaring heart crash to the ground.

Basil spun around to see a plumper version of Frances staring furiously at the two of them. "It's all right," Frances whispered, relieved. "It's only my sister."

"Pudgie!" she cried loudly, as if delighted by this lovely surprise.

Virginia's eyes flared at Frances with a warning of retribution to come, and then walked slowly down to the steps towards them.

"May I introduce the Curate of St Mary's Newington?" said Frances with a slight squeak.

"How do you do, Father," Virginia said, glaring at Frances for a few moments more before turning to inspect Basil.

"I won't offer you my hand," he replied with an easy smile, holding up a pair of oily palms. "Miss Hodgkinson number 2, I take it?"

"We've been visiting parishioners," said Frances, as naturally as she could. "Have you been here very long Vee?"

"A couple of hours I imagine," Virginia said.

"Oh my God, I'm so sorry!" Frances cried in shock. She froze for a moment, and then moaned as it all came back to her.

"You completely forgot, didn't you?" said her sister. Frances couldn't argue with this.

Virginia turned to Basil. "I'm to be interviewed for my first teaching post tomorrow morning. At the school of St John the Divine," she explained. "We thought it would be such fun if I came to live here in Kennington too." She swung back to Frances, a further wave of irritation sweeping through her. "Such fun. So can you put me up tonight after all, or are you too busy?"

"No, no, yes, yes of course," babbled Frances. "I've been so looking forward to you coming." Another pause, then Virginia gave a frosty nod to Basil and, turning to her sister, very firmly said "shall we go inside then?" like she was addressing a class of inattentive eight year olds.

"Well," Frances said as brightly as she could, reaching out to touch Basil's oily hand and then stopping herself. "Goodbye for now Father." She couldn't quite resist bowing her head just slightly towards him.

"Miss Hodgkinson number one," he said, bowing back politely. "Very many thanks for your company today." He watched until Frances and her sister disappeared inside the house, and then turned his attentions back to his machine, gingerly touching the brass fuel igniter, which had a tendency to burst into flames whenever the vehicle came to a rest after too long in London traffic.

"At the ZOO!?" shrieked Virginia.

Frances flapped her hands in panic. "Shush," she pleaded. "People can hear everything in this house."

"And you said yes?" Virginia asked, in a stage whisper.

Frances nodded wildly. "Yes I did!" she cried.

"Best not shout," said Virginia, tapping her on the nose.

Frances paused to catch her breath, and looked uneasily at her sister. "So?" she said finally. "Well?" She was trembling.

"You want him, don't you," Virginia said, a touch lasciviously, making her sister blink and flush. "Anyone can see that. Of course you should marry him, stupid!"

Frances yelped with delight, and hugged Virginia. "You mustn't tell Aunt Mary," she whispered into her sister's hair. Virginia wriggled slightly and they disengaged. "You mustn't tell anyone," Frances continued. "This is just between us for now. I can't let anything go wrong."

"Yes, well …" Virginia said, raising her hand in caution. "The aunts already think you might be up to something."

Frances asked her what on earth she meant.

"Well actually," said Virginia. "Aunt Mary asked me to see if I could find out what's going on here, if you must know."

"You came here to *spy* on me?" said Frances.

"No!" she cried. "Of course not! But I did mean to make you tell me. And now I know."

"What on earth made them think I was *up* to something anyway?"

Virginia didn't really want to explain that it had been her uncharacteristic cheerfulness that had everyone wondering about her. It was a major topic of conversation the previous weekend. "No idea," she said. "Can I have a cup of tea now?"

While making the tea Frances began to chatter on about Basil and, once started, clearly found it impossible to stop. Eventually Virginia raised her hands in surrender. "Yes all right, I believe you, he's the best man that ever lived. Mind you, the last one wasn't bad either."

"Vee!"

Virginia shrugged. "Frances, you can do what you want now. It's your life after all."

Frances looked dubious.

"All right," said Virginia. "Not entirely true. They do rather hold all the cards, I agree. Especially you-know-who."

"Dearest Granny," whispered Frances.

"Indeed," said Virginia. "But they can't wait to marry us off, really. You know that. Dearest Granny most of all. Just need to make sure the chap in question doesn't suddenly do something they don't approve of." Which, she said pointedly, is not always as easy as one might think, isn't that right?

"You know," said Frances, "it wasn't the slippers really. Not as far as I was concerned."

"Really?" said Virginia. "Well you never can tell."

She sat in silent thought for a couple of minutes, then suddenly leant forward and clapped her hands. "I'm going to tell Aunt Mary about you and your curate as soon as possible," she announced.

Frances began to protest.

"No, honestly," said Virginia. "I just need to find the right moment to do it, which isn't always easy because you have to get her on one of her good days. But she's a loyal old thing, and if we play our cards right she'll protect you from the Gorgon."

"VEE!" said Frances, grinning delightedly.

The next afternoon the two sisters and Basil had a happy time in the Kennington Gardens tea-room, celebrating Virginia's appointment that morning as assistant mistress at St John the Divine, and discussing what she should say to Aunt Mary, and when she should say it. Basil told them about a long trip he was making in a few days' time, on behalf of a leading manufacturer, to prove that the ordinary man could now expect to motorcycle safely and happily for as long and as far as he wanted. After that he'd be ready for anything, he said.

17

"So why exactly should I be reading this?" said Mary Harriette, looking with slight distaste at an article headed "1,279 Miles in Six Days", illustrated with photographs of the author, on page 5 of the latest edition of *The Motor Cycle*.

Virginia smiled patiently. "Just have a quick look at it. The first few paragraphs," she said.

Mary Harriette read carefully for a couple of minutes. "Very interesting," she said, without conviction. "Does it have something to do with one of your cousins?" she asked.

"Oh no," Virginia said. "Far closer to home than that."

Mary Harriette pondered a moment, and then it dawned on her. "You mean Frances!" she said. "Of course! Good work!" She looked back at the article, and at the pictures. "And this mysterious motorcycle man is …?"

"Yes," said Virginia.

"Hmm," said Aunt Mary. She proceeded to read all the way through the article, slowly and very attentively.

"He writes quite well," she said, grudgingly, "although I obviously don't have the faintest idea of what he's on about. And it all sounds rather exhausting." She studied his photograph. "He seems sturdy enough," she said. She slowly looked up at Virginia, and asked "Is it serious?"

"Oh yes indeed," said Virginia, nodding enthusiastically.

"I see," said Mary Harriette. "And what exactly does he do? When not riding around England in the rain?"

"He's a priest," she said, but Mary Harriette was not about to be impressed.

"Ah," she said. "A poor parson."

"A very clever one," said Virginia, disappointed at the failure of her revelation.

"Clever enough to find a nice heiress," said Mary Harriette.

"She's hardly an heiress," said Virginia. "Any more than am I."

"And you've met him, I take it?" Aunt Mary asked, after a few moments' silence.

"Yes I have," Virginia said. "He's funny and very well-mannered."

"You approve."

"I do, Aunt Mary. I haven't seen her like that for a long time. I don't think ever, really. She's blossomed. He's perfect for her."

Aunt Mary nodded. Blossoming, yes, lucky girl.

"And what do you propose should happen now?" she asked. Virginia bit her lip, and looked wide-eyed at her aunt.

"It's up to you of course Aunt Mary. Frances desperately hopes you will help us put this on a proper footing. When the time is right."

"So she means to marry him, for sure?" Mary Harriette asked.

"Yes obviously!" said Virginia, highly shocked at the suggestion of anything other than that.

"Good," said Mary Harriette. She was pleased to be asked, and even more pleased to have this secret to manage. She particularly liked the idea of keeping her mother in the dark for once.

A cold bright winter's day in Oxford. The mood inside the house was unusually lively, the nearest thing to good cheer that 12 Bradmore Road had seen since poor Aunt Clara passed away. The black drapes had finally been removed, expensive hot-house flowers now decorated the living room, and the housekeeper was rushing around, letting in as much light as possible, and discussing the luncheon menu with Milicent. Uncle Reg, composer of the well-known hymn "Oh Jesu, Thou art standing," shuffled in and immediately back out of the living room, pointedly taken aback by the preparations.

He paused at the door and looked back into the room. "I must go over to Binsey Church, I'm afraid," he said. "I shall return in time for luncheon."

"When does John's train get in?" Frances asked, as soon as he'd gone.

"He should be here within the half-hour," said Milicent.

Frances was very fond of her cousin John, her Uncle Herbert's son, granted the full John Cunliffe Pickersgill Cunliffe in memory of his late grandfather. A Lieutenant in the Worcestershire Regiment based in Ceylon, he was back in England for a few weeks following the recent death of his father. John was a dedicated hunter of big game and an all-round adventurer. He loved to send vivid reports of his kills and other exploits to *The Family News* including, only a few months previously, *From Columbo to Kandy and back by Motor Cycle*, recounting how he survived heart-stopping mountain hairpin bends, vicious attacks by pariah dogs and being chased by an enraged cow. He was, as it turned out, most keen to meet the well-known motorcycling journalist Ixion, who had been invited in his honour, Aunt Milicent told him.

John turned up earlier than expected as always, and was greeted very warmly by everyone. He had only arrived back in England a few days earlier, and looked surprisingly mature for a young man of 21. He hadn't been able to return in time for his father's funeral, and he received extra hugs and sympathy on account of that great sadness. There was a whole hour to wait before the renowned motorcyclist's arrival, which the four of them filled with a torrent of family gossip.

To John's delight, Basil arrived on the very Triumph motor cycle that he'd used for his famous six-day 200 miles-per-day ride around England earlier that year. Frances knew the distant bark of its engine immediately, and couldn't entirely suppress a twitch of her head in the direction of the window a moment before the others were even aware of its approach; Milicent noticed and smiled quietly. They all hurried out the front door and down the steep steps to the driveway as Basil rolled to a halt, put one foot down on the ground and lifted his goggles. Frances hadn't seen him for several weeks now that he was up in Northumberland but, turning a deep red, forced herself to hold back and watch in silence.

The ladies soon went back inside, leaving the men to talk motorcycles. John started straight in asking Basil questions about the Triumph, and Basil cheerfully interrogated him about his epic Ceylon journey. They got on very well, which was fortunate because John had begun to suspect that the luncheon might not, after all, have been primarily arranged in order for the two of them to meet. He'd divined some murky plan or other and certainly wouldn't put it past his aunts to be cooking something up for his shy little cousin Frances, if her blushes were anything to go by. That was fine, it didn't bother him at all, because a chap had to let the ladies do what the ladies had to do.

Luncheon went on a good long time. The talk ranged over motoring, life in the army, the behaviour of the natives in Ceylon, and quite a lengthy disquisition from Uncle Reginald on the complexities of hymn writing. As the time went on, John's suspicions were fully confirmed by the cautious little looks he caught passing between his anxious cousin and the tall witty priest. Over coffee afterwards, Milicent decided it was time to move things forward.

"You are aware, Reverend Davies, that my niece Frances here is a dedicated parish worker down in London?" she said. "In your experience, do such volunteer workers tend to provide useful assistance to the clergy?"

It was Basil's turn to blush. "Yes of course, most valuable," he said eagerly. He turned to Frances. "I very much admire the kind of work you do, Miss Hodgkinson."

Frances didn't know how to reply, and just stared hard at the table cloth.

"Marvellous," said Uncle Reg, ringing the bell for the housekeeper. "I propose we take a walk in the Parks quite soon, before the daylight goes. Such a lovely day. And then Frances can tell us all about her experiences as a Greylady."

The party eventually set off up Bradmore Road, Uncle Herbert pointing out the homes of various distinguished academics along the way. "To your right," he said, "is where poor Walter Pater lived at one time and, just ahead of us in Norham Gardens, is the home of the distinguished Regius Professor of Medicine, Dr Osler, newly arrived from Baltimore. I recently had the pleasure of talking with him, and a more charming man you could not hope to meet." Baltimore is where my mother lives! Frances said to Basil, who was already accompanying her. Oh really? he said as if he didn't know. Yes, she said. Her and her husband Manny. He wants to be a doctor too. What an interesting coincidence, said Basil. But he is not such a charming man, Frances muttered, and Heaven help anyone *he* treats.

They continued to the entrance to the University Parks, and walked all the way around and down to the river, cold and still in the pale December sunlight. John said such a pity they couldn't go punting, and Milicent said they would die of cold if they tried. They walked on around the park, Basil and Frances ahead on their own now, and chatting away as if they'd known each other for ages. As they reached the gate nearest the river, Basil took them along a little path that went behind the gardens of Lady Margaret Hall. Just follow me, he said.

As he had hoped, they found a nice old punt, tied up there as it had always been, against the bank in the little tree-covered tributary that ran into the college grounds. He climbed down into it and reached a hand out towards Frances. She grasped it straightaway, and stepped lightly down from the bank to join him, just as the others arrived. The two of them stood there together for a moment, grinning, whilst everyone applauded but insisted that it really was *not* the moment to go out on the river.

It was almost dark by the time they walked back; a wistful Oxford evening with the winter mist making the houses glowingly warm and inviting. Frances and Basil were some way ahead of the rest of their small group, talking privately. As they came back into Bradmore Road another young couple – a tallish woman, with a young man also in a clerical collar – walked out of the big house on the corner and headed towards them. As the two couples were about to pass each other by, the tallish woman suddenly stopped dead in the middle of the pavement, lifted her arms up high, and cried out "Frances! Is it really you?"

Frances gasped. "Ursula?" she said, almost inaudible.

Careful not to outstay his welcome, Basil departed for his lodgings shortly after they all returned to no. 12, amidst warm handshakes and the clear understanding that an important acquaintance had now been properly established. Frances was the last to say goodbye, waving him off for much longer than all the others. Then, as Ursula had begged her to do, she hurried the short way along the road to no. 18. She was warmly greeted at the door by Professor Mayhew, who showed her into the living room and started to introduce her to his large family, until Ursula took her away and they went into the study to talk uninterrupted.

"I've so hoped to see you," Ursula said, taking hold of her hand, "but the time has never seemed right. It's a miracle that it happened by chance like this."

"I don't understand," said Frances. "What are you doing here?"

She'd lodged with the Mayhew family for many years when she'd been at school in Oxford, and they were like a second family to her, Ursula explained. She'd been staying there for several weeks in fact, since arriving finally back in England. "Maybe it is not so odd that we should meet like this after all," she said. "The world that you and I come from is quite small really."

They looked at each other without speaking for some moments.

"And the man you were with," asked Ursula. "He's someone special to you, isn't he?"

Frances nodded, damp-eyed with the emotion of the day.

"Will you be married?" Ursula asked.

Frances nodded vigorously. "Yes," she said. "We shall." Ursula hugged her, and told her how happy she was for her.

"And is your family pleased with your choice?" she asked.

"Well, they've only just met him," Frances explained. "I can't afford to be impatient and nor can Basil, so we must take our time though I do hate to."

"I know it will all come good," said Ursula. Frances smiled, and they hugged more.

"And you?" Frances asked, gesturing towards the living room. "Might you also be hoping to marry soon by any chance?"

Ursula stared at the floor for a moment. "I've thought for a very long time that I might one day. I have been so very fond of the older boy here," she said, "for many, many years." She shook her head very slightly. "But too many years, in the end, I think."

She squeezed Frances's hand. "It isn't truly what I want," she said, "and it's a considerable happiness really, to know that."

They talked about the Greyladies for a while, and Ursula had no hesitation now in urging Frances to get away from them as soon as she could. Don't even wait until you're ready to marry, leave now, she said; they suffocate you, and Frances said they certainly do.

"Will you come to my wedding?" she asked. Ursula smiled, and said she would have loved to, but she had decided once more to leave England, and go back to New Zealand to make a proper life for herself there. Buy a cottage, make a garden, write poems, and be whoever it is she really had to be.

"Poems?" asked Frances. Ursula promised to send her some, one day, if she felt that they deserved to be read. They sat holding hands for a few minutes more, not saying very much, until Ursula accompanied Frances back to no. 12. They kissed goodbye at the gate, then Ursula hurried away into the December night and out of sight forever.

Family Items – April 1906

- A letter from Mrs Dent informs us that Mr Dent must now be known as Dr Dent. His medical practice in Baltimore, for which Mrs Dent is Head Nurse, Receptionist and Chief Clerk all the one time, appears to be thriving.

- The name of Miss Frances Hodgkinson must be added to the sick list. She is now recovering from a slight attack of rheumatic fever, which has caused her many weeks of severe suffering and which will incapacitate her from work as a Greylady for months.

- Mr J.C. Pickersgill-Cunliffe has returned to his regiment in Ceylon after a short visit to his mother at Hindhead.

- Miss Rose M. Fell, who has been working under the Sisters of St Thomas ye Martyr, Oxford, has accepted a post for instructing mothers and inspecting babies in the East End of London.
- Miss Frances Hodgkinson has lately become engaged to the Rev. Basil H. Davies, who is Curate to his father at Esh, near Durham.

PART FOUR

1910-1913

18

Rose Fell and her sister Faith came bursting in through the front door of Ethel's flat, apologising for their lateness and laughing at the same time. Ethel was pleased to see her nieces, especially Rose for whom she felt a particular affinity. Norah, her housekeeper, put her head around the kitchen door and asked the girls if they were ready for a special Sunday feast.

"Hello Norah!" Rose and Faith shouted as one.

"They look ravenous dear," warned Ethel.

Faith rushed over to the window, as she always did when she arrived, and looked out over the garden of Lambeth Palace, and the towers of Westminster in the distance. "This view never fails to amaze me, Aunt Ethel," she said.

"The best in London," said Norah, bringing in the first course, lentil soup. That was followed by broiled slips, as delicate as fillets of sole, then lamb chops and mashed potato, and finally pancakes with fresh lemon, and a dainty potato savoury cooked with cheese. The whole lot, Ethel announced proudly, had cost just one shilling and sixpence, announcing the price of each item as they ate it.

"You're a marvel, Aunt Ethel," said Rose admiringly.

"When the maid goes out marketing," said Ethel, "we send her out with not a penny more than the amount we mean to spend!"

The girls told their aunt and her companion about their adventures that weekend, after Rose had finished her Saturday rounds and Faith had completed the day's work at her art school. They went to *The Taming of the Shrew* in a packed theatre and would never have found a decent seat if Faith hadn't shoved a way through for them, telling anyone that objected that she couldn't help it, she was being pushed from behind. They got two seats right in the middle of the front row.

"Mind you," said Rose, "I can't say I enjoyed it very much. Such a man's play really, wouldn't you say? It was hilarious how the men around us were loving it. 'There you are, Violet' said one. 'Votes for Women indeed! You can forget all about that for a start' but their girls didn't mind telling them just what they could do with such talk."

After lunch Ethel regaled them with tales of her recent activities, a speech given in Sheerness on Wednesday, a lecture to the women of Maidstone prison on Thursday, visits to homes in Folkstone on Friday and then to Canterbury yesterday for a Rescue Work committee chaired by the Archbishop's wife, with Ethel herself as organising secretary. Everything done with just one thing in mind, to persuade girls onto the straight and narrow, and to keep them there. Faith asked her if she was ever overwhelmed by all the different things she had to do, and Ethel said *never*, it was the great interest of her life; and Norah said, but sometimes she should just take an hour or two off, and that is why your visit is such a blessing, dears.

Ethel had something important to ask Rose, and came straight out with it, in her typical way: would she consider attending Frances for the birth of her first child which, as she probably knew thanks to the constantly buzzing family network, was due in late June? Apparently Frances's sister Virginia had originally offered, but she had to withdraw the offer because her fiancé had point-blank refused his consent, and that was that. Frances was quite clear about the fact that *no*-one could be more suitable than her admirable and adored cousin Rose, both for her professional skills in the matter, and her down-to-earth good humour. Might that be remotely possible, do you think Rose?

Well of course it would. "I will write to her immediately," she said, "and tell her how proud I will be to assist."

They carried on, all four of them, talking and loudly playing duets on the harmonium that cheerfully shattered the Sunday silence of the flats, until late in the afternoon, when Faith left to catch up with lost sleep and Rose went to church for the third and final time that day, before dropping in on the girls' club for a while, on her way home.

She got back to her rooms on the Holloway Road too late for supper, so just had two ha'penny cakes made of shortbread with a kind of almond paste on top, and an Ivelcon square that Aunt Ethel had given her when she left, with the directions that it would make a whole glass full of delicious clear soup: just add boiling water from the geyser, give a quick stir with the end of a tooth brush, and you have a lovely supper for almost nothing.

Nell always had faith that things would work out well for her in the end, and was prepared to go through any number of hardships along the way, but she could no longer pretend that she had any prospect of happiness so long as she remained with her husband.

There would never be a place for Manny in the realm of happy endings. After entering the medical business through the back-door of a highly suspect medical training, he had become a general practitioner to the poor and gullible of Baltimore. His interest in his patient's health, never notably strong, began to wane rapidly after the first year or two. He increasingly concentrated his attention on his own medicinal needs, serviced by endless free samples of narcotics from drug companies. His interest in his wife also markedly waned during this time; he was seldom even aware of her presence in the house by the time each evening came.

Her friends in Baltimore all told her to get out and stay out, they insisted, your life's not over yet. She wrote to Mary Harriette for her advice, to Evelyn, Gertrude and Ethel, and to her mother. Mary Harriette said to think carefully before doing anything, her other sisters said leave him immediately, and her mother said you must stay with your husband until death parts the two of you, of course. To the question of where she might go, the answer came equally clearly from her son and his wife: live with us in the fine house we are having built in Piney Point, down by the Chesapeake Bay.

Attractive as she found the prospect of living out her days with her adored Tom and his family, she didn't think that moment had yet arrived. Besides, she could never quite shake off the idea, much encouraged by her sisters whether they meant it or not, that she might return home for good. Whether or not she would actually choose to stay, she resolved to give it a try: her two daughters were busy having babies, her mother was reportedly coming to the end of her days, and Nell herself was over 60. Just two days before the end of 1911 she announced to an entirely indifferent Manny that she was going away for a very long time, maybe for ever. She packed a few precious possessions – bits of jewellery, a few photographs of her children as babies, a small secret packet of letters that had belonged to Charlie, tied up tight in a ribbon and never opened by her – and boarded a ship in which to brave the winter storms of the Atlantic again. The man at the White Star Line had assured her that transatlantic liners had improved immeasurably since her previous trip. The world was changing fast, he said, and for the better in nearly every possible way.

When Basil set off for Northwood to meet his mother-in-law for the first time, on a freezing cold February day, it would be fair to say that he did so without much enthusiasm, given all the different things weighing on him. But Nell was expected that evening, and Mary Harriette had firmly hinted that it would be more than acceptable if he could come over to join the welcome party. And while he was there, she'd added, he might also be able to find a few minutes in which to give her the benefit of his journalistic expertise with respect to the *Family News*; she'd been thinking about how to bring it more up-to-date. He promised to give that some thought in advance.

Basil got to Northwood in time for dinner, but Nell hadn't managed to arrive yet. "Typical of her," said Mary Harriette. Basil admitted that he really knew very little about what his mother-in-law was like. It was not as if Frances was been particularly forthcoming on the subject.

"She looks quite a lot like you in her photographs," he said to Mary Harriette, as they sat together after dinner. "Is she though?"

"Not really," she said. "We were very close when we were young, but our lives took very different directions. She is the person I talk to most openly I suppose. We're always writing to one another, writing down all our thoughts and dramas as they happen, always another letter on the go. For nearly forty years now."

"Good Lord," said Basil. "Well, I'm greatly looking forward to meeting her," he said.

"You'll like her. She's good fun." Mary Harriette said. "She used to be, at any rate, and she certainly has a warm heart, and not much bothered about appearances, which I admire. But not very much of a good Christian I think, whatever she pretends. God doesn't interest her very much."

Basil laughed. "And I don't suppose she'll be much

interested in motorcycles either?" he asked. "We're going to have find something else to talk about."

"Grandchildren and gardening, I suggest. And food of course."

They both stared into the blazing library fire, Mary Harriette doing her trance knitting, and Basil lighting his pipe again.

"So," said Mary Harriette. "The *Family News*, then."

"Yes," said Basil. "Exactly. I've been thinking a good deal about this, Aunt Mary. I do hope I can be of some use."

"Well as you know, I was hoping you could help me make the journal feel a little more *modern*." Basil said he wasn't entirely sure if he was your man for modern really. Oh but you are, she said, out of all us.

"Well, I'll do my best," he assured her, and pulled out some scribbled notes he'd dashed off that morning, well aware of the danger of suggesting anything too radical. "I believe you said among other things that you wanted to get the younger members of the family more interested in reading the Journal. So I thought, well young people, as you know, are in more of a hurry than old ones, they're more used to doing things rapidly. How about having more short pieces of humorous writing, and maybe even some cartoons if you can find someone to do that. The occasional light short story perhaps, a romance or a spy story, or some swashbuckling tales? Catch them young."

Mary Harriette listened in silence, impassive. She nodded for him to continue.

"And perhaps some features *about* the younger family members, short profiles of some of them, with photographs of them actually doing things," Basil continued, warming to the subject. "School sports, riding horses, playing golf, having fun at dances. You know, young people having fun."

Silence. "What do you think?" he asked.

Aunt Mary smiled sweetly. "Well, yes, we might wish to consider something like that. At a later date, perhaps," she said. Oh well, thought Basil.

"Actually," she continued, "I was hoping you might be interested in something rather more substantial." Basil tried to speak, but she held up her hand. "A whole new regular feature in the Journal, in fact, with *you* as its editor."

"I really don't – "

" – in which the wonders and perils of progress are examined intelligently, do you see?" She looked fiercely at Basil. "*You* can see the importance of the new, I know you can, and you're marvellous at explaining such things to people. It's what you do."

"Well," he said, in desperation, "what I *do* is look after a very demanding parish. And try my best to explain the Bible to people."

"I'm not suggesting you should write it all yourself," she continued, undeterred. "We'll invite submissions, and you put them together with some interesting and controversial thoughts of your own. We could call it, I don't know – *Modern Wonders* – what do you think of that?"

There was an extended moment of silence, during which he closed his eyes and rocked back and forward. "Hmm," he said at last, warming to the idea despite himself, "it may possibly be something worth thinking about, I agree. Though definitely not *Modern Wonders*, if you don't mind."

"You're probably right," said Aunt Mary, beaming. "I'm sure you can come up with something better than that. But don't take too long. Time waits for no man."

Nell eventually arrived at Northwood Hall the next morning, having missed two trains the previous evening, causing considerable inconvenience all round. Basil greeted her warmly and called her Mater, which she liked very much. When he got home he told Frances how much he'd enjoyed meeting her, and she was relieved to hear it, even if she did not entirely want her husband and her mother to become too much great friends, and start talking about her behind her back.

"And how did the discussion about the journal go, with Aunt Mary?" she asked.

"Oh," he said. "She wasn't in the slightest bit interested in my clever ideas. But she was kind enough to tell me what I was going to do instead."

19

At the kind behest of the Editor of *The Family News*, I am proud to say that I have taken on the responsibility for a new feature in the Journal, which will aim to examine, extol and, if necessary, question the wonders of the Modern World, and the offerings of Progress.

You may have heard of Mr Marinetti's remarkable *Manifesto of Futurism*, and if you have actually read it, I presume you have either hidden away in your library by now, resolved to withdraw from the modern world, or you have followed its injunctions and burnt all your books. I admit that some of its grand assertions did at first sight make my heart pump faster: "We affirm that the world's magnificence has been enriched by a new beauty: the beauty of speed" and "We want to hymn the man at the wheel, who hurls the lance of his spirit across the Earth, along the circle of its orbit." Others, mind you, simply made my blood boil: "We will destroy the museums, libraries, academies of every kind ..." Hold on, chum! He calls all this "the futile worship of the past" and proclaims that "we the young and strong Futurists" want no part of it! Nor us of you, I can assure him.

Evolution not revolution, I think we can all agree. I must make my own position clear on this: I think that the products of Progress, the many that have come our way over the last decade or two, represent for the most part a wondrous new stage of evolution for all of mankind. Safe, fast, comfortable ocean travel for even the poorest passenger, so that the world can be everybody's oyster now; railways that run frequently and reliably both above and under the ground; the electric light and the telephone so that we can talk with distant friends late into the night, and read the newspaper at the same time; the humble geyser and soup tablet, so that the young nurse or apprentice can make their own evening meal in the tiniest of one-room flats; the airship that shows us the earth as we were never able to understand it before. Such things make us masters of a world through which we used to struggle so wearily, and I happily celebrate each one of them.

Of all of recent improvements, the most admirable and, I would argue, the most beautiful instance is also the most simple:- the safety bicycle. Not, of course, that I am decrying the glorious Ordinary, upon whose lofty wheel certain enthusiasts and eccentrics still wobble their way to a broken collar-bone with my utmost respect. But the safety bicycle has changed the world in ways that few other innovations have ever done, and given freedom to every soul blessed with a modicum of determination to go wherever they wish whenever they wish, without need for chauffeur, horse or petroleum. The safety bicycle is both faster than Shank's Pony, quieter than the motorcycle (my own favoured steed for many years I must admit, but then I am a little mad), and somewhat less temperamental than its four-legged predecessor.

The modern bicycle exemplifies the notion of Progress especially well for two quite distinct reasons, I believe: first, because it is itself such a wonderful product of *technological* progress: the perfect design of its frame, the air in its tyres and the springs in its saddle, the strength of its steel, the brilliance with which it translates physical exertion into speed and joy; secondly, because all these things have themselves also brought about many kinds of *social* Progress. A young man may court a girl in a distant village, to the betterment of human evolution; a young woman may join together with her friends and break the bonds of tradition and convention; men may travel effortlessly to the coal mine or the factory and arrive fresh for a day's work; a policeman may chase a burglar (but the burglar may pedal faster) and a midwife may answer the midnight call at a moment's notice. In these latter respects, the bicycle is therefore not merely a product of Progress but is also, in many respects, its Vehicle.

As it has so admirably shown over the last eight years, this Journal cares equally for the achievements of History and Progress: past, present and future. Our Manifesto is not, we hope, too controversial: we simply say: *let us keep our minds open to the accelerating pace of change in the modern world.* In this section, with the help of our readers, we will examine both admiringly and sceptically the latest manifestations of Progress that have come to our notice, and reflect upon any changes to our ways of life that they might appear to carry with them. Please let us hear your observations and opinions on these matters – and if you will, address these specifically to the Journal's new column, *Vehicles of Progress.*

Basil had mulled over Aunt Mary's proposal on and off for several weeks. He didn't believe he could actually cope with yet another demand on his time and one that was bound to take him away from the writing he had constantly to do for money. But he couldn't really see a way out of it and, he had to admit, her idea did have some appeal for him. It might allow him to go a bit deeper into things than he normally could afford to do.

He did not manage to complete his introduction to the new column, with its somewhat improved title, until nearly the end of March, by which time it was unfortunately just too late for inclusion in the April 1912 issue. Mary Harriette wrote to say that she liked it very much, although she thought it wise at this early stage to refer to it as an "occasional" feature, and see if it "takes". She told him the column would now be published in the July issue, under the nom-de-plume *Hermes* if Basil did not mind. It embarrassed him a little, but she seemed pleased with it so he didn't argue.

The delay in publication proved fortuitous, given that Basil's enthusiastic comment about modern ocean travel would otherwise have been published on more or less the very day that the *Titanic* hit an iceberg and took nearly 1500 passengers and crew to the bottom of the ocean.

The tragedy made quite an impact at his own breakfast table. A few days after the ship had sunk, Basil and Frances read with dismay the lurid details of the tragedy as described in the *Daily Mail*, tales of self-sacrifice, heartbreak and unfeasible survival.

"Oh my Lord oh my Lord," Frances suddenly cried out, staring at the names of the drowned.

"You recognise someone?"

"Yes I do! I do!" she cried, more excited than sad. "Look! Dr William O'Loughlin, the *Titanic's* chief surgeon! I knew him! I met him when I first came over to England with Aunt Ethel. I'm certain he was on the *Majestic* then."

She showed Basil what the *Daily Mail* had to say about the poor doctor. A modest hero, apparently, with a kind word for everyone, and had gone down with the ship without fuss.

"We went to his surgery," Frances said. "He gave us medicine. How strange to think he's at the bottom of the sea now."

"Sounds like a good man," Basil said. "Why were you there? Were you ill?"

She closed her eyes, and tried to place herself back on that big ship.

"The seas were very rough all the way across – I spent most of the voyage walking round the ship on my own. Aunt Ethel had a terrible time and I hardly saw her, but I loved it."

"And was he a nice man, this doctor?" Basil asked. "According to this, everyone loved him."

Frances shook her head. It was so long ago. "He must have been, I suppose," she said. "How sad that he should die like that."

Nell, who was staying with them by now, finally came down for breakfast, and Basil showed her the dramatic front page of the *Daily Mail*.

"Oh Lord!" she cried, with drama. "And to think that I could have been on that ship!"

"What on earth do you mean, Mother?" Frances asked, not hiding her irritation.

"When I was first thinking about coming over, the man at the White Star office told me I could travel over on the *Titanic*. If I didn't mind delaying my journey a few weeks."

"Well of course you couldn't have been on it, Mother," said Frances. "It never reached America. But if it had got there there's no earthly reason why it needed to have sunk on the way back."

Nell snorted. "They said it was unsinkable and then it sunk. Anyway, you know what I mean. I'm just saying I could have been on it. It makes you think."

Her daughter scowled and began to tidy up the breakfast.

"I do know what you mean, Mater," said Basil. "We're all just a hair's-breadth and a heartbeat away from the big dramas of life. Thank God when we pass them by unscathed."

Frances left the dining-room with a dismissive snort, directed at both of them.

The next day Basil travelled down to Brooklands to watch a full programme of motor cycle racing. The last event of the day was a race in which the riders charged pell-mell around the banked track for exactly an hour on all sorts of different machines at all sorts of different speeds; chaotic and highly exciting. Going faster than most was Arthur Moorhouse, a modest and popular chap riding a large Indian motorcycle, which he'd only managed to get started at the very last moment.

The crowd at the side of the track noticed, on his seventh lap and leading the race by a long distance by now, that

Moorhouse's rear wheel was beginning to wobble in its forks. Many spectators waved and shouted at him to slow down. Possibly inspired by what he took to be their encouragement, he roared past faster than ever, headed up the Members' Banking hanging on for dear life, and swept down towards the Railway Straight. At that moment the wheel came out entirely, and Moorhouse went headlong into a telegraph pole. The machine burst into flames, and he was killed outright; all that the spectators could see of it was the smoke that rose from behind the hill a split second later. They all cried out in anguish. He was the first ever motorcycle fatality at the Brooklands races.

"It would be wise, obviously," wrote Mary Harriette after a decent amount of time had passed, "to modify your first piece on Progress in certain respects." Basil took the opportunity to pen an additional paragraph in which he reflected on that aspect of Progress which might be seen as man's misguided belief in his capacity to vanquish God and nature, and included himself in that number for the blithe way in which he had trusted in the unsinkability of the newest ships. At the same time, though, he continued, we should not see this as a rejection of Progress so much as a reminder to be humble and learn from the mistakes we are bound to make on the road to a better future. Whether Captain of the *Titanic*, a motorist racing around a track, or an aeronaut flying too near to the sun, we must never believe that our courage makes us invulnerable. But that courage is also the thing which makes us great, he said in conclusion, and Mary Harriette liked that very much.

20

Rose arrived in Oxford on a beautiful autumn evening, the very last of the year, all fired up for her secret mission. Aunt Kay was looking after things at the Bradmore Road house throughout October, and was only too happy to have the company of her spirited niece for a couple of days. Rose had explained that she was going to see the Sisters of St Thomas the Martyr, with whom she'd worked once and of whom – oh the lies she told! – she was still very fond. The next morning, Oxford was shrouded in thick fog, its streets damp and bitterly cold; as soon as she set off on the mission, Rose felt a strong urge to change direction and visit those dreadful old nuns instead. But she'd coped with far more threatening challenges than this in her time, and certainly wasn't going to back out now.

She and Frances had cooked up their plan during the intense days in July that Rose had most recently spent with her, this time through the birth of baby number three. During their long hours together, Frances had finally told her Abigail's story, all of it, and Rose could not contain her outrage, and swore to take some kind of action on behalf of the poor dead girl. She wanted to know what Abigail had looked like, but although Frances had no photo and couldn't really describe her, she was confident it would not matter very much. Rose was much the same size as Abby, which is to say small and thin like a schoolgirl, with roughly the same complexion and mousey hair, although with a ready wry smile all of her own. But with a pair of severe steel-rimmed spectacles and a floppy black hat she was sure she would pass for her at first glance at least. How long ago was it, did you say? Rose asked. Oh, more than twelve years, Frances said after a few moments' counting. Well then, said Rose. I'm sure it'll work.

Hidden inside her aunt's big warm overcoat, she hurried up to 48 High Street only to find no bicycle shop when she got there, just a confectioner's. She went in and asked the gentleman behind the counter where Mr Morris's shop had gone. He looked amazed.

"He moved four years ago. He does a lot more than bikes now, Miss. He's not far away – just take the left turn into Holywell Street, and you'll find the Morris Garage a few hundred yards up," he said, pointing up the road. "You can't miss it, there'll be motor cars parked all along the road outside."

Rose easily found the place, a good deal grander than she'd imagined, and marched in through the main entrance. A salesman approached her. "Mr Morris?" she asked, and he shook his head.

"No Miss," he said, very pleasantly. "I'm afraid not. He's a very busy man. Can I help you? Do you wish to hire a motorcar?"

"No," she said. "No. I wish to speak to Mr Morris. It's quite important."

"In respect of what, may I ask?" said the salesman.

"It's personal," said Rose.

"Well I'm afraid Mr Morris is not here at present, and I'm sure that if he was he would say that he does not meet anyone without a prior appointment." He smiled again, but not so pleasantly.

"I think you will find," said Rose, "that Mr Morris would not wish me to be sent away. I shall wait for him, I'm in no hurry."

The salesman looked uneasy. "I will see if I can discover his whereabouts, Miss. What name shall I say?"

"Abigail," she said. "Miss Abigail Adams."

He was gone some minutes, and while he was away Rose went across the showroom to inspect a shiny new two-seater car standing there, much smaller than the grand ones outside. It was a strange looking little machine, with a protruding round nose and a canvas roof that looked like a badly fitting hat. Despite herself, Rose found it charming, and could imagine herself driving such a thing.

Then, through the door at the back of the show-room she glimpsed the salesman down the end of a corridor, pointing her out to a rather cross looking man who disappeared as soon as she looked his way. The salesman came back and told her that Mr Morris would see her now, and asked her to follow him to his office. By the time they got there, Morris was sitting behind his desk, and he did not look friendly.

"Thank you Mr Potts," he said, and Potts left, shutting the door behind him. Morris turned to Rose, and stared at her in silence, just looking her over.

"I don't know you," he said, at last. "What do you want?"

"You don't remember the name Abigail Adams, Mr Morris?" said Rose.

"I do not," he said. "Are you her?"

"Yes," she said, looking down at the ground, regretting this line of approach.

"I think not," he said. There was another long moment of silence. "Once more, what do you want?"

Rose lifted her head, and stared into his eyes. "Then you do remember her," she whispered.

He said nothing, and Rose reached into the bag she carried over her shoulder. Morris looked alarmed for a moment, but relaxed when she brought out her purse. She opened it, carefully removed a £5 note, and held it up for him to see. Then she crumpled it into a ball and threw it at him. It bounced off the desk and onto the floor. Morris didn't move.

"That's payment for the bicycle you gave Miss Adams," Rose said. "The day you took her into the woods."

Morris began to growl and rise from his chair.

"Don't worry," continued Rose. "She won't be bothering you. She never recovered from what you did to her and it was her dying wish that you should know that. Now she owes you nothing."

"Get out," said Morris after a long moment, "before I call a policeman. I have no idea what you're talking about, and I presume you're off your head."

"You have every idea what I'm talking about," said Rose. "I know that."

"GET OUT!!" he roared, and Rose could hear voices coming down the corridor.

"YOU'RE DISGUSTING!!!" Rose shouted back, for everyone to hear, as the door flew open and a large mechanic in greasy overalls came towards her. She turned to leave and the mechanic lunged for her.

"Let the little bitch go!" Morris shouted; Rose pulled herself free and pushed her way through the door. She charged down the corridor, past a horrified Mr Potts, and back out into the muddy street, gasping for breath, trembling and wild-eyed. She didn't hang about to see if anyone was following, and hurried away from the garage, past St Cross Church and its fog-covered graveyard, towards the Parks as fast as she could go.

She returned to Bradmore Road in time for luncheon.

"How were the Sisters of St Thomas?" Aunt Kay asked.

"Oh," said Rose, smiling and settled in her mind now. "When I got to the Convent, I couldn't – well, it wasn't a good time apparently. So I went round the shops instead, and then had a long walk in the Parks and along by the river."

"In this fog?" asked Kay, incredulous.

"The silence was strange and beautiful," said Rose. "I walked, and I thought about how the world is, and I prayed for the souls of those no longer with us."

Vehicle of Progress, by Hermes

Among a great number of exciting and advanced new cars on show at the 1912 Olympia motor car show – without a doubt the biggest show ever – there was a relatively unremarked new light car announced by a small but ambitious manufacturer in Oxford. Until now, Will Morris has been known for repairing and building bicycles (as well as riding them very quickly), manufacturing and selling motor cycles and, most recently, hiring out motor cars from his new and very smart premises in Holywell, just across the road from Magdalen College.

But now he has done something that might one day, I suspect, prove to be highly remarkable: in his *Morris Oxford*, he has produced the motor car that the British motorist had been waiting for ever since Mr Ford launched his Model T on the other side of the Atlantic. Mr Morris is selling a small low price vehicle that will be in the reach of those of us who wish to drive along the same roads that until now have been the domain of far wealthier folk. It looks like it will be just what the ordinary man, the clerk or the school master, needs in order to take the wife and babies out, for twirls around the nearest countryside on a Saturday afternoon.

The *Morris Oxford*, currently no more than a two-seater but big enough to squeeze in said wife and babies, will sell for £165 and be available next spring. At the motor car show, so I am told, 400 of the little beasts were ordered right away. I suspect that these orders mark the beginning of an important new phenomenon in motoring for all, and I am willing to predict – having had my own very satisfactory dealings with Mr Morris over the years – that the landscape of motoring might be changed for ever by his funny bulbous little vehicle.

21

Nell had spent the first of her two years back in England leading a sad and dreary existence, in the opinion of her sisters. Apart from her first round of visits to Frances and Virginia, she lived alone in a series of rented rooms in Northwood, within easy reach of the Hall but not actually residing there. Everyone including Nell thought that that would be best, given the lack of an available bedroom and any sign of encouragement from her mother. As far as anyone could tell, Nell made poor use of all the time she had to herself: she took no newspaper, cultivated no acquaintance, read nothing but stories, knitted a few things but nothing much, never went to church. The highlight of most days was to take a drive with Mary Harriette, by car if the horse wasn't feeling well, finishing up at the Hall for tea. Mostly Mary Harriette welcomed her company, but there were times when the emptiness of her sister's existence made her melancholy, or just irritated her. Nell had little of interest to say about anything, and Mary Harriette loved talking about interesting things whenever she could.

Their mother was certainly not desperate for Nell's company. Since her stroke she lived in her bedroom now, and received visitors in the afternoon. Sometimes she liked to talk a great deal, sometimes not at all but if visiting her you would have to stay for as long as you could even if she slept, in case she suddenly awoke and wondered where you'd gone. But Nell's visits to her were few and far between, and never lasted long. Which was a little disappointing, really, given that one of the reasons that Nell had come to England, after all, was to rekindle some warmth between them whilst there was still time. In the event, there was more than enough time, but nothing like enough warmth.

Nell's situation improved in the second year, when she readily agreed to stay with Basil and Frances for an indefinite period, this time as a paying guest. It had been Frances's suggestion, which was nice although Nell was never entirely sure how much it was for the desperately needed cash, and how much for her company. Basil had had considerable reservations about the plan at first, but could hardly object to any scheme that improved their finances, and quite often found Nell to be decent company. Nell wasn't always sure what to make of Basil: he could be flippant and deeply serious all in the same moment. From time to time, late in the evening when an exhausted Frances had gone to bed, she and her son-in-law would chat about things – their childhoods, life in America, life in the Church. He would talk to her about his parishioners and their problems, and ask her what she'd advise.

Frances did not easily show it, but she mostly liked having Nell there. She avoided talking about the past and the many ways in which she had felt that her mother had let her down. She just wanted to be able to care about Nell in all the ways that normal and decent people cared about their parents. If she was willing to play her part in that, then so was Frances, and as Nell's time with them continued, she did actually begin to find herself worrying about her mother's welfare, in the present and for the future as she grew older, which was clearly happening quite fast now.

The past was always dangerous territory, as Basil realised one evening after Nell had been there for a few months and everything had seemed to be going smoothly. The three of them had enjoyed a pleasant dinner together, and in the course of their conversation Nell happened to mention Coulsdon.

"We went there once, long ago," Basil said.

"What, to Hooley House?" Nell asked, amazed.

"No," said Frances. "We visited a friend of mine who was in hospital there."

Hooley House was so lovely, Nell said, although the railway ran much too close for her mother's liking.

"Was that where your father died?" Basil asked. "I don't really know what happened."

"Well no-one ever really understood what happened," said Nell. "But no, it wasn't there exactly. It happened at the station up the road. Caterham Junction. Such a terrible time."

"Was my father there, or was he away at sea?" Frances asked.

"He was back from the sea by then," said Nell. "He helped a lot. He always tried very hard to please Mother." She hesitated. "But it was awful really. She wouldn't allow him to come to the funeral."

"She *what?*" cried Frances

"You know what Granny can be like," her mother made a face. "I expect she thought that Papa would have wanted only his children there. I don't know. It was hard though, for Charlie. It did upset him."

Frances looked at her in silence for a few moments, suddenly feeling overwhelmed with questions she'd never before managed to ask.

"I don't understand," she said. "Did Granny not like Father? Why didn't she like him?"

"I'm sure she did," said Nell, reddening. "Though I don't think either Papa or Mamma approved of us getting married while your father was still a fairly junior officer on a tiny salary. Captain Hodgkinson thought the same."

"Really?" asked Frances. "I know so little about all this. I just know the stories you used to tell us about him. But that's all those were I suppose. Just stories." She paused and then said, "I wished I knew more *real* things about him."

There was a long silence. "He was handsome and strong, and full of life," said Nell, at last. "He would've gone on to captain his own ship in time, everyone said so."

"So why on earth didn't he?" Frances demanded to know. "Why did he suddenly leave the Navy? Why did you both go off to America?"

"To make our fortune!" said her mother. "People did that a lot in those days."

"And so how did he get ill?" Frances asked again, more insistently. "What was wrong with him?"

"He had the Maltese Fever. We were all very concerned," she said, beginning to feel that this conversation was turning into an interrogation. She looked at Frances pleadingly. "It makes me quite sad to think of all this, dear."

"Me too, Mother," said Frances, her face flushing.

"It sounds like he was a jolly admirable chap," said Basil, helpfully.

"I loved him, for his faults as much as his strengths, I think," Nell said, trying to bring the conversation to a close with a faraway look.

"And what about Manny?" Frances asked, in a quietly menacing way, that made Basil's blood freeze. "Do you love him for his faults too?"

Nell glared at her daughter, and gave a little warning nod, suggesting that maybe this was not somewhere she really wanted to go right then. Frances stared back, eyes flaming, and then thought better of it.

"Well, I'm terribly tired all of a sudden," she said. "I shall go to my bed I think."

Nell smiled sweetly, and reached out a hand to her.

221

"Perhaps we should find a time to talk about all this," she said, nearly whispering. "If that's what you'd like."

Frances nodded. "Yes of course," she said, and left the room.

In April Mary Harriette came for her annual visit with Frances and her family, and was surrounded immediately by the children who had already learned to expect gifts from her, too young to be disappointed by their overwhelmingly improving nature. Frances managed to suppress her mounting irritation at trying to cope with children, a mother and an aunt vying for her attention and the children's approval, and a husband whose chronic exhaustion was becoming daily more evident as he struggled against the constant demands of home and of work, which were almost inseparable in that house.

After a few days of this Basil announced that he and Frances would be going away for the night, if Nell and Mary Harriette did not terribly mind taking charge in their absence. They were going to Birmingham, to see a football match and celebrate their wedding anniversary, spending the night in an inexpensive little hotel. The two of them set off to Birmingham by train just before lunch-time, and as the train pulled out of the station both leaned the heads back against the seat tops and closed their eyes for most of the journey.

The match was between Aston Villa and Sunderland, and would determine which team ended up first division champions. Amazingly for a mid-week match, nearly sixty thousand supporters turned up, amongst which there was Frances and just a handful of other women. She was no football enthusiast but that day she fully embraced the license to open her mouth wide and scream as loud as she liked. Basil, a devoted Sunderland supporter, also shouted continuously throughout the match and was delighted with the 1-1 draw, enabling his team to become champions the following Saturday.

After the match they returned to the hotel for a light dinner, which they ate in a hurry, like an adulterous couple. "It's our wedding anniversary," Basil explained to the waiter, whose smirk suggested that he'd heard that one before. Frances flushed deep red but didn't really mind. "Very nice dinner, darling," she whispered.

The lady who shared their lift was clearly shocked by Frances's unsteady gait and poorly contained giggles and even worse, when she loudly cleared her throat to remind them that they were not alone, Basil snorted. They all got off at the same floor and as she was closing her door behind her, the lady was further distressed to hear the words "Will you not come to bed now Father?" followed by the sound of poorly stifled laughter from the other end of the corridor. She thought seriously of going straight back downstairs to report them to the manager but was too tired, which was fortunate because the manager certainly didn't give a damn what his guests got up to.

It was not long before silence reigned in the corridor, and only the sound of rapid urgent breathing could be heard inside Frances and Basil's room. So rapid, in fact, that Frances began to fear it would all be over far too soon. "Basil! slow down!" she whispered in his ear, aware that his movements were getting frantic.

But then he suddenly made an anguished noise, pulled back from her and struggled to his knees, clutching his chest.

"What is it, darling?" Frances called in panic, ready to rush out in her nightdress if necessary, for a doctor or an ambulance.

He looked at her with bulging eyes for a few moments, but his breathing slowly calmed down and he raised a hand for her to wait a moment. "No, no dear," he gasped. "I think it's all right. It's all right."

He had often told Frances that he thought he might die early from a heart attack, and the two of them often made plans about who would care for the children should either one of them or both be carried off early. But whatever had caused the pain that evening, at such a critical moment, it wasn't going to kill him; probably not a heart attack and rather more likely the meat pie he'd devoured with a pint of ale over supper. He was left feeling fragile and not a little scared, whilst Frances was left feeling profoundly relieved to know that her husband was not dying, at least.

He saw the doctor a few days later, at Frances's insistence, despite his fear of what he might discover. For the first two days after their return to Northampton the atmosphere at home was cross and cheerless: Nell had a wretched cold, Basil and Frances were tense and tired from their trip, and Mary Harriette couldn't resist asking what else might they have expected from standing in a crowd of several thousand coughing men. But Basil returned from the doctor beaming, delighted to announce that it appeared he was suffering from chronic stress and had been signed off from his work for a few months, so thank Heavens he had just appointed his new curate Percy Bischoff, an excellent fellow and a fine motorcyclist too. By the end of Mary Harriette's visit, Basil and Frances were preparing to leave for Weston-Super-Mare and a good long rest. The babies were to be planted out during their absence, Nell would take rooms again in Northwood for a while, and Percy would take charge of the parish.

22

Before Basil left for his rest cure, he asked Percy Bischoff if he could possibly do him one further favour. He owed his aunt another short piece on modern transport, Progress, something of that kind, for this family journal that she edits, which was most definitely not what he, Basil, should be trying to do right now if he wanted to recover quickly. Do you think at all that you could throw something entertaining together, Percy, from your own experiences as a motorcyclist? He showed him what he'd already written for the *Vehicles of Progress* column and told him not to worry, do whatever you like along those lines. You mean something about motorcycling? Percy asked. Anything you like, said Basil. Whatever you come up with is bound to be interesting.

Life being what it was, and Percy being what he was, it took him considerably longer than he'd intended to give any serious thought to the task; so long, in fact, that he entirely missed the deadline for the July issue. To be fair, writing was not his strong point, as demonstrated by his rather vapid sermons, but every now and then he would attempt a new opening sentence in the hope of a good idea jumping out of it, and was then mortified to contemplate how weak his own efforts were, compared to his boss's outpourings. So eventually he decided to have a word with Beatrice.

Beatrice Langdon was Percy's fiancée. She lived in Clapham,

where he had previously been a curate. They'd been engaged for a good while now but she was an independent woman and for the foreseeable future preferred the state of betrothal to that of marriage. Quite possibly until the day that she, and women in general, were finally granted the vote. Percy was a strong supporter of women's suffrage; he wouldn't have lasted long with Beatrice if he was not. In 1911, in one of his first races at Brooklands, he had demonstrated his commitment by christening his Triumph "The Suffragette", and tied purple, white and green streamers to its handlebars. Disappointingly he failed to put on a show of racing equal to that of solidarity, but a few months later he and Beatrice together won a gold medal there. He was in the side-car shouting out notes on every turn and pothole while she did the actual riding; quite a combination. She was the first woman to win a motor cycle race at Brooklands.

Now, on this last Saturday in July, Beatrice had come to Northampton to spend the day with him, mainly to get out of London before the place was completely swamped by Mrs Fawcett's suffragist ladies, arriving at the end of their mass pilgrimage from all corners of the nation. It was painful to admit this, but the wholesome earnest footsore suffragists seemed to be winning the struggle now, despite never daring to get arrested or face the groping hands of the police as the more militant suffragettes had done for so long. The suffragists just went on long walks and politely asked if they might possibly be granted the vote. She was seething by the time she arrived at Euston Station, passing a constant stream of these women all along the way. They all looked so happy, so heroic. Some had walked the whole way from the Lake District for heaven's sake, and now had the wind-bronzed look of real adventurers, their expensive coats and boots proudly showing the depredations of weeks spent tramping, sleeping out, running from Saturday night drunks, and coping without their maids. Festooned in glory, as if their little jaunt was going to change the mind of a single man in Parliament.

Percy had occasionally complained to Beatrice about having to write the article for Basil, but she hadn't paid much attention. What's so hard about writing about motorcycles? Now he came out right with it and appealed to her for help, told her how hard he was finding it. The article didn't need to be very long, and didn't need to be entirely about vehicles either. Just about what makes Progress happen, something clever and interesting along those lines. Racing at Brooklands maybe? Being a woman in a man's world, that kind of thing?

For crying out loud, Percy, she said. I'll think about it and let you know. Promise? he pleaded. I promise to think about it, she assured him, and squidged his cheeks quite fondly. Now let's go somewhere nice for a ride.

Less than a week later an envelope arrived in Northampton with Beatrice's fiercely typed article. He scanned it quickly, and it definitely seemed to meet the broad requirements. He had the slight suspicion that it might not be quite what was wanted, but for the life of him would never contemplate changing it himself. So he stuffed it into a fresh envelope, with a cover note explaining to Miss Pickersgill-Cunliffe that he and his fiancée had written this on Rev. Davies's behalf and if it wasn't quite the thing, she may feel free to amend it in whatever way she prefers. With Best wishes, Revd. P. Bischoff, Curate and Acting Vicar, St Sepulchre's, Northtn.

Militant Action as the Vehicle of Progress

In 1909, a courageous Australian-born suffragette by the name of Muriel Matters took flight from Hendon Airfield in a balloon emblazoned with 'Votes for Women' on one side, and 'Women's Freedom League' on the other. She intended to fly over Westminster during the State Opening of Parliament, and shower the King and MPs with hundreds of pamphlets from the skies. Sadly for the magnificent Miss Matters, adverse wind conditions and a poorly functioning motor saw to it that she never reached her target, and instead she was carried out over Wormwood Scrubs, Kensington and Tooting, before finally being blown west of London to Coulsdon, where she came to land after an hour and a half in the air. Despite the failure to achieve the flight's primary goal, her brave venture earned considerable fame for herself and the movement, all around the world.

Opinions differ as to whether this flight actually achieved anything, but in that it can be viewed as an imaginative use of a vehicle in the hopes of bringing about much needed progress, by which we mean the right of women to the vote, it unquestionably deserves to be celebrated in this column. Of course, balloon flights will not themselves achieve women's suffrage, any more than motorcycles, motorcars, caravans, trains, aeroplanes, boats, bicycles or horses. The vehicle that is essential for this blessed goal will prove in the long run to have been something quite particular: militant action.

Unquestionably the most dramatic instance of such action in support of women's suffrage occurred only a very few weeks ago, when Miss Emily Davison sacrificed her life for the cause under the hooves of the King's Horse. For many people in this country, what that brave lady did was an unforgivable outrage. For many others, as the magnificent funeral procession through London demonstrated, her action showed that only by breaking the bounds of good behaviour will we make the world take notice of our cause. Miss Davison's act will be remembered long after the noble pilgrimage of the good ladies of the NUWSS.

In the first article for this column, "Hermes" asserted a preference for evolution over revolution, and that is indeed a desirable goal for humanity: to advance naturally and without conflict towards improvement, physically, intellectually, morally, economically, politically. On reflection though, the evidence of history does not really suggest that this will be the case. It appears that Man's endless need to achieve his ambitions can only be fulfilled by more forceful methods, such as building factories that darken the skies, enchaining slaves and carrying them over to the New World to pick his cotton, or going to war with his rivals and killing thousands in the process. Whilst Woman has never before in history wished to adopt such a ruthless path to improving the human condition or her own circumstances, the fact remains that as long as Man prefers revolution to evolution, militant action to gentle persuasion, then so now must Woman.

"Absolutely NOT," said Mary Harriette without the need for further reflection. "It is the most biased thing that has ever been submitted to the *F.N.* We could not possibly consider publishing it."

"To be fair," said Evelyn, "we have rather ignored the whole suffrage issue over the years."

"And for good reason!" cried her sister. "If, at least, she had offset her blathering with serious consideration of other points of view, I might have felt different. No mention, for instance, of Mrs Humphrey Ward's excellent work at the Women's Anti-Suffrage League."

"And I do think she might have known where Coulsdon is," said Evelyn.

Mary Harriette wrote to Reverend Bischoff and Miss Langdon, explaining that she was regretfully unable to publish their very interesting piece on this occasion, and resolved to discuss this unfortunate incident with Basil when he was fully recovered.

The Family News. November 1913

Vehicles of Progress by The Treasurer
Speaking as someone who is constantly delighted by progress of every kind – in the quality of the latest dimpled golf ball, the

dizzying precision of a grocer's bacon slicer, and the convenience of Mr Kodak's wonderful box camera — I might have explored any one of several very different directions, when so kindly given the opportunity by the Editor to take responsibility for the latest *Vehicles of Progress* column.

Nevertheless, my choice of what I consider to be the most significant Vehicle of Progress in our time should not come as any great surprise, given my well-known interest in prudent financial management. I argue here — and passionately I might add — that few institutions of the modern world approach anywhere near the importance of *Banking* as a peerless vehicle for encouraging, instigating and preserving Progress of every important kind in the modern world.

If we look back a century or so, there was little in the way of organised banking to support the enterprise of hard-working manufacturers and traders. Informal procedures for securing essential loans, and obtaining good advice about their likely profitability, held sway: a firm handshake between men of honour was a simple and effective means of conducting business at one time, no doubt, but it could also on occasions give rise to unscrupulous or ill-informed dealings. There is no doubt that many invaluable labour and cost-saving inventions might have gone by the board without ever seeing the light of day had it not been for the courageous and far-sighted investment that only an experienced and well-informed banker can supply.

Very many of us who read and contribute to this excellent journal are descended from such stock: long distant generations of Cunliffes and Pickersgills once played a leading role in the development of the textile industry in the north of England, many of whom developed ingenious new techniques for the efficient manufacture of cloth. They knew hardship and disappointment, but through the formation of timely partnerships, succeeded in creating an industry that eventually grew into something of worldwide importance, bringing together the producers of cotton (and other raw materials such as sugar and tobacco) in India, the West Indies and, eventually, the southern States of America, with manufacturers back in England.

By this time, generations of Cunliffes had established major cotton mills in Lancashire, and generations of Pickersgills had begun to take on the responsibility for developing stable and responsive finance houses, that soon grew into international banks to fund business in the textile industry, expanding through the second half of the last century to include the related industries of shipping and the railways. Sometimes our banking ancestors were brave enough to take considerable risks in the investments they made, and in due course forged business relationships that bridged the Atlantic Ocean, to the benefit of the whole United Kingdom.

I write, of course, as someone whose own father was a leading figure in that very banking world, together with his brother, carrying forward the torch first lighted by their father and grandfather. All these men dedicated themselves to the selfless creation of prosperity – Cupidity has never been the motivating force of leading bankers, so much as social responsibility and a commitment to the welfare of those whose labour in some small way contributes to national prosperity. This is a justifiable source of immense pride in all of us who are their descendants, and constitutes what I believe to be an unassailable case for recognising *Banking and Bankers* as key vehicles of progress in our time.

23

At the end of 1913, Nell suddenly decided to go back home. *Suddenly* is what she told everyone, anyway; up until then she'd kept quiet about how much she'd hated being in England, because she couldn't afford to fall out with her family. But she'd begun to think about leaving again almost as soon as she arrived and the thought never went away; she wasn't made to feel as welcome as she'd imagined she would be. You couldn't put your finger on it, she told Tom in one of her many letters, because they always spoke nicely to her; but all the same she could see they didn't really want her there.

She did her best, for nearly two years, well aware that life in Baltimore wasn't going to be any easier now than when she'd left and she was in no hurry to cross that ocean one more time. But at least in Baltimore she had friends who cared for her and did not deal in hidden meanings, and she had Tom and his family. She knew that the day when she would move in with them for good was fast approaching. Whenever she stayed in the past it had always been easy and warm; they always made her welcome, gathering round her every evening to sing songs and laugh at her jokes. She hadn't really sung a song or made a joke since arriving in England and when she did try, once or twice at Frances and Basil's house, Frances always gave her a look so she didn't carry on.

And she was as poor in England as she had been in Baltimore, where at least she might retrieve the remains of her own inheritance when Manny died, which could happen any day judging by the state of him the last time she'd seen him. So all things considered, she definitely needed to go now. It surprised her greatly to find her sisters upset by the news of her decision, and her daughters too for that matter, as if they would never see her again. And indeed, who could say whether or not she'd ever return, but for now she was certain that she no longer had a home in England.

The evening before she left, after Frances had gone to bed, Nell asked Basil if she could discuss something with him and he couldn't help hoping that she was about to offer them a small financial helping hand; you never know. Instead, she opened her bag and pulled out a crumpled pile of old papers and envelopes tied up in a green ribbon. She clutched them in her lap.

"I want *you* to take charge of these, Basil," she said very quietly, looking at him with the kind of lingering stare people give you when they have something important to reveal, and want you to know the weight of it. Basil sat still. He was well used to people telling him they had important secrets and then staring at him in silence for a while. On no account show impatience.

She continued to clutch the papers and look at him, damp eyed.

"Charlie's old papers. Letters and the like," she said. "I'm so sorry I never managed to have a proper talk with Frances about her father. In the end I just couldn't bear to. Maybe these'll help. She might find them interesting. Letters from the Navy and things like that I imagine. But it's important that you look through it all first. Just to make sure everything is all right."

"All right?" he asked, cautiously.

"Oh, *you* know," she said, and nodded meaningfully. "Things men get up to. Just take a look and see if it's safe for Frances to see. Nothing distressing. Would you please check through it all, all of it?"

"And if there *is* anything of a, um, distressing nature?"

"Then destroy it, of course," she said. She shook her head. "Consign it to the deep."

Full fathom five thy father lies, thought Basil.

Nell was leaning forward urgently now, still clutching the letters hard. Then she subsided, and gave them to Basil.

"It'll be such a relief," she said. "Not to have to wonder what's in them any more."

It was surprisingly painful when she left. Painful because Nell was sad, and Frances was sad, as they both felt they were saying goodbye for ever, and there was a muddle of feelings and memories involved in that thought. The children cried, because they could feel sadness in the air, and they could see tears in their grandmother's eyes, which must have been because she was sad for them so they joined in and set each other off until there was quite a chorus of howling, which only stopped when their daddy clapped his hands and made them all cheerful again, and then drove their madly waving grinning grandmother away to the station in his new car. As they left, the children turned their attention to their mother, who was crying now, so they started up again.

A few evenings later, when the house was quiet and everyone else was asleep, Basil opened the pack of letters, took a deep mental breath, and looked to see what he might find there. Hopefully something of Charlie, some fading sense of the man.

Dating back as far as 1859 he found a short kindly note from Captain Hodgkinson, wishing his boy good fortune on *HMS*

Britannia and giving him important Royal Navy advice: keep your uniform clean and be smart at all times, always carry out orders instantly and be first in line whenever there's a difficult job to be done. Another from his father congratulating him on his promotion to sub-lieutenant before he was even 20, after his courageous service on the *Euryalus*. Then, little more than a year later, even more fulsome congratulations on his elevation to lieutenant. A long gap after that, until there was a very curt letter from the Admiralty confirming his retirement from the Navy, around the same as a most loving letter from his father, reminding Charlie of every ship he had sailed on and telling him he could be very proud of his excellent naval record. And finally, a shaky letter from his mother a few years later, informing him of his dear father's death, a brief three years before his own.

There were plenty of letters from Nell, a whole batch of them which Basil felt he shouldn't open, but in the end he began to skim through them to see if they might be suitable for his wife to read. There was nothing exceptionable in the first flurry of notes and instructions that she wrote around the time of their engagement in 1871, but her correspondence burst into life with a blistering warning she fired off at him when he was on the *Lord Clyde*, about rumours she had heard of him dancing with Maltese widows. It made Basil smile to think of Charlie reading it. Then there were some concerned letters directed to *S.S. Malta Hospital* urgently seeking further news of his health, and finally a passionate imagining of their future life together. In the interests of good taste, Basil did not finish that one, which turned out to be the last letter Nell ever sent him, because – as she mentioned numerous times – the day of the wedding was advancing fast and presumably they were never apart again after that. None of these told him much about the man himself.

There were a few others from Malta. One, also sent to the hospital around the same time, was from a Captain John Bythesea, warmly thanking Charlie for his outstanding service and dedication during the very difficult time they'd endured together; Bythesea (could that *really* be his name?) also sent his sincere best wishes for a rapid recovery from that wretched fever. Then nothing for several years, until a rather opaque communication from a lady called Elizabeth. It thanked him for his kind thoughts and congratulated him on the birth of his son, briefly recalling her fond memory of the time he had rowed her and her sister around Valetta Harbour, and wishing him the very best for the future. Given how few letters Charlie had actually kept, Basil found it noteworthy that he should hang on to something so anodyne. He searched for more from her, but found none. But then he found a letter from Charlie himself, that he must have written not long before he died, in 1885, which had been returned all the way from Malta with "Not known at this address" scrawled across the top. It was a pitiful thing.

My darling Lizzie

It is a long time since I have written to you, and even longer since you have replied to my letters. I hope you are all right.

I myself am not all right at all. I am in bad debt, I have three children who are hard to feed what with the farm not going well and me not being that well either. Another one died young some time ago and it's just the three now. Nellie is quite well but is not always so fond of me and I can hardly blame her.

This morning I lay in bed thinking of you, before I got up to go and work in the fields all day again. I thought of the times we spent together and can't believe it so long ago. The best days of my life I'd say, looking back now. Then I think, I will go and find her, and maybe when she sees me she'll just say hello Charlie, I knew you'd come back one day.

It's late night right now and I know I shouldn't write like this, you told me that enough times but I just have to, just this last time because I don't think my health is going too well at present. So not really ever coming to find you, I know that, but at least I can tell you one final time how I loved you better than anyone.

Your adoring sailor, Charlie

"Crikey," muttered Basil. "Crikey." Well, he thought, Nell really hadn't looked through all this stuff. He stared at the letter for a moment longer, imagined what would happen if Frances should ever be allowed to lay eyes upon it, and poked it straight into the glowing embers, watching intently until it was all burnt away.

There was just one final set of letters to read, written in a denser and more florid hand, all with the name of sender on the back: George King-Hall, Lieutenant at first, Commander later on. It was getting late, Basil's head was spinning, but he ploughed on.

24

Basil got to the Army and Navy stores in good time, but George King-Hall was already there waiting, seated by a window with his letter held up in the air as promised, to make him easy to recognise. As it turned out, retired admirals are remarkably easy to recognise anyway, even when not in uniform: Sir George was sitting stiff-backed, stern, perfectly turned out in a smart dark suit and gleaming shoes, with a distinguished officer's perfectly trimmed white beard, of the kind once sported by Captain Smith of the *Titanic*. Basil hurried over, pointing towards his own clerical collar with a cheery grin as he approached. Sir George jumped up out of his seat.

"Reverend Davies I presume?" he asked, giving him a firm weather-beaten shake of the hand.

"So kind of you to find the time to meet me, sir," said Basil.

"Oh I think I have plenty of that to spare," said King-Hall.

Basil had given no thought to trying to find George King-Hall, and then was amazed to come across a report of his return to England in *The Times* shortly before Christmas. He wrote to him care of the Admiralty early in the New Year, and miraculously got a most business-like reply from the man himself a few weeks later offering to meet the following Wednesday afternoon, three o'clock sharp, with precise instructions for identifying one another.

"You must be proud of all that you achieved in Australia, Sir George," he said, as he sat down opposite.

"Any success that I had there was only through God's grace," George assured him.

"And your next assignment, sir?" asked Basil.

"I'm calling it a day," said George. "Anything after my time in Australia will be a let-down I think. I am entirely reconciled to the prospect, I assure you."

Basil nodded, realising that this might be sensitive territory.

"So," he said, "I do appreciate the opportunity to talk to you about Charlie Hodgkinson. Anything that you can tell me would be greatly appreciated."

"May I ask why, exactly?"

This was quite a difficult question to answer. It was curiosity as much as anything, but that wouldn't do.

"I think it is sometimes tragic, the way that a person's life can come and go and leave no visible mark," said Basil. Sir George didn't look convinced. "I think my wife would profit from knowing more than she does about her father's life. Her mother and her aunts have always avoided talking about him, and I think that has had a deleterious effect upon her."

Sir George frowned. "Hodgkinson's career in the Navy came to an unfortunate end, and I can understand why your wife was not told about that."

"Yes of course," said Basil, backing off. "It's his earlier career in the Navy that really interests me. He seems to have done well enough for quite a while."

Sir George looked like he regretted being there. Basil tried another tack. "I just thought, from the letters you so kindly wrote to him, that he might have mentioned such things."

"Not his earlier life, no," said Sir George. "And I must say, anyway, that I do have serious reservations about you having chosen to read those letters, which were of course entirely private, and should more properly have been destroyed on his decease."

Pompous old bugger. "His widow gave them to me," Basil explained. "She couldn't bear to read them herself, but was keen that someone should. She didn't want him to disappear without trace when she was gone I think. I feel I owed that to her, but I am very sorry if I have offended you by doing so."

"No offence taken, of course," said Sir George. "I do think, nonetheless, that you will need to be cautious about what you share with your good wife."

Basil nodded. "Of course, sir," he said, as gravely as he could.

Now that he had said what he had felt he must say, King-Hall began to relax slightly. "Well, very good. Tell me a little about yourself, Reverend Davies, if you would. Where is your parish, if I may ask?"

Basil understood the need not to hurry this. It was important to build some degree of trust with the old chap if there was to be any prospect of learning anything worth learning. He talked about himself for a few minutes, told him how he'd once taught future naval cadets, worked with miners in the north-east and the unemployed in the midlands, and also how much his parish work meant to him. King-Hall nodded approvingly. "There are few professions more influential and necessary to the well-being of the nation than the Church, to my mind," he said. Having read his letters to Charlie, it came as no surprise to Basil that George King-Hall was a man with a strong inclination to piety.

"Well I'd say the Royal Navy comes a close second," Basil said. King-Hall looked momentarily shocked at the mere suggestion that anything on earth might be considered greater than the Navy, then saw Basil smiling and said well, first equal perhaps. Then he looked at his watch and told Basil that he could spare a further fifteen minutes or so, as he had an important meeting to attend at Caxton Hall, just around the corner.

Basil got on immediately with some questions about life in Malta back when he first knew Charlie, and it proved to be a productive tactic. It turned out that King-Hall, despite his show of stiffness and propriety, was quite a gossip.

He made it clear that he'd never spent very much time with Charlie in person, but their paths had indeed crossed during the time both of them spent in Malta in the early 70s, Charlie on the *Lord Clyde* and himself on the *Lord Warden*. Joint exercises, and so on. "And the dances," said King-Hall. "We used to have marvellous dances on our ships back then, great fun." He reminisced fondly about a superb one on the *Warden*, and then in quite a catty way about another on the *Lord Clyde* that had been a complete disaster. Clearly a story he'd told many, many times. "I can remember Charlie Hodgkinson at that dance, quite well," he said. It was noticed among the chaps that Charlie had made a bit of a conquest.

"But enough of that," said George, and Basil silently moaned. "Time to go I believe." He suggested that Basil might like to walk along with him, and he readily agreed. George held on to his elbow as they went down the stairs, then put his arm through Basil's as they headed up to Caxton Hall while he chattered on about his own boy who was about to be posted to his first ship. As they approached the Hall, Basil saw posters outside proclaiming "The National Temperance Federation – Open Meeting – February 11th 1914, 4.00 pm. Chairman Sir Thomas Whittaker MP PC" and decided their time together really was up. Sir George, though, squeezed his arm and asked him if he would care to join him for the meeting. Basil could think of nothing he could less wish to do, but said he would be delighted.

The meeting was as long and tedious as Basil had feared. Sir Thomas Whittaker gave an interminable speech relating his very many fruitless efforts to persuade his colleagues in Parliament to introduce licensing laws, with a relentless attention to detail that would, Basil was sure, have turned any man to drink. The meeting was then opened to the floor, some sorry tales of drunkenness were tearfully told, and fanciful plans for finally solving the problem proposed, the most unexpected being the suggestion of giving away free tickets to the Cinematograph to keep men out of the pubs. No-one really knew what to make of that and there was a moment of uneasy silence until Sir George raised his hand to speak. Receiving a friendly and knowing nod from Sir Thomas, he stood up to deliver his thoughts on a quite different topic.

"I am, as you well know sir," he said, "Admiral Sir George King-Hall, very recently retired from his Majesty's Royal Navy, and I must confess to everyone here that there have been times in my long and varied career when I have feared for the security of our island fortress, so harmful has been the burden of the cursed alcohol upon some of our Navy's brightest and best young men, from the ordinary rating up to the future admiral. The harshness of conditions on some of our ships in the long distant past no doubt suggested an argument of some kind, however specious, for doling out regular quantities of rum to the ordinary sailor, as one of the few indulgences possible on a long and harsh sea voyage. Given the speed and comfort of modern ships, there can be no further justification for sanctioned drunkenness within our nation's Navy, or indeed within any other of our essential institutions. I believe that we must raise our ideals to the very highest, and petition Parliament to take radical steps for freeing all our young men from the lure of alcohol, and especially those in the Navy and Military." Murmurs of agreement. "Thank you for your attention." Mild applause.

As they were leaving, finally, Basil able to think of little else but a pint of beer, Sir George grasped his arm once more and asked him if he had enjoyed the meeting.

"Oh yes Sir George," said Basil. "It was inspiring."

Sir George beamed. "I daresay I have put the cat among the pigeons there, but so be it. It had to be said." Basil congratulated him on his brave words, and Sir George beamed some more.

"Well my boy," he said. "We have lots more to talk about, do we not?" Basil said that he hoped that might be so – maybe they could possibly arrange a further meeting?

"No time like the present, I always say!" cried Sir George, in an ebullient mood now. "Why don't you come with me to my club, and we can have a good talk over dinner?" This was more like what Basil had hoped for in the first place, and he accepted immediately. It was just a short taxi ride up to Piccadilly, but time enough for Basil to wonder if he would be allowed just the smallest of brandies when he got there.

For most of the meal, Sir George regaled Basil with tales of his time in Australia, and the extraordinary outpouring of gratitude that the whole country had shown him on his departure. Basil bided his time until they'd finished their plates of beef swimming in gravy. Now, both of them contemplating a large spongy dessert covered in fruit and cream, he dared to bring the topic back to the Malta of the 1870s.

"Of course," said Sir George, "the most notable thing during that time, as far as Charlie Hodgkinson was concerned, was the unfortunate grounding of the *Clyde* some way to the north of Malta. The *Warden* was sent out to rescue it, which was a bit of a beastly business for the poor chaps on the *Clyde* but quite fun for all of us, I have to say. No blame accrued to Charlie, of course – indeed it is my strong recollection that he acquitted himself well throughout. A most promising young officer."

"So what went wrong?" Basil asked. "Did he get any blame for that? Was that why he left the Navy?"

"Oh no," King-Hall said. "That came a year or two later when he was in Sheerness. Shore-based appointment." King-Hall was warming to his central theme. "A far from uncommon occurrence, as I hope I made clear this afternoon at Caxton Hall," he said. "At least he had a father who fought his corner, and used his influence with the Admiralty to permit Charlie to retire."

"But what did he *do*?" asked Basil, feeling like he'd was never going to get there.

"Drunk on watch. All there is to it, but almost a hanging offence in the Navy. He was extremely fortunate not to be court martialled and dismissed out of hand." King-Hall shook his head. "But I did not blame him then, and nor would I ever now. I see drink as a disease, not a vice, and a disease that was long rife within the Navy."

"But how did such a responsible young officer end up like that?" asked Basil, searching for more.

Sir George said he had no idea, it could be any number of things that would do that to a man.

"I thought the letter you wrote to him at the time was very generous and kind," said Basil. Well that turned into be a somewhat longer correspondence than intended, George confessed. "Each time I thought we'd brought it to a blessed end, up he'd pop again with another problem, another crisis of some kind, until I heard that the poor chap had died. From an acquaintance of his brother Teddie Hodgkinson, as I recall. Now *he* was a very decent chap – lieutenant on the *Ajax* at the time. When I first learned of it, I thought, oh his poor widow. But knowing all the problems he had, I wonder, maybe it was for the best."

They moved over to the leather armchairs and coffee. Basil still harboured a faint hope that he'd be offered a brandy; a whisky would do just as well. But nothing doing. Still, the atmosphere was quite mellow by now, and he dared to return to the unfinished tale of Charlie's conquest.

"When you were talking about the dance on the *Lord Clyde*, you alluded to something about Charlie and a young lady. Might that have been someone by the name of Elizabeth Camilleri, by any chance?" he asked.

"Lizzie!" said King-Hall, "the very same!"

Did you know her at all? Basil asked. Not well, said King-Hall, but I did become friendly with her younger sister Annie. Annie Kingston, as she was then. The occasional dance or a dinner, the opera, riding sometimes, that kind of thing. Entirely platonic of course, he hastened to add.

"Did Miss Kingston ever talk to you about Charlie?" Basil asked.

"Not so far as I remember," Sir George said. "I can't think why she would have done really."

Basil tried another approach. "You returned to Malta many years later, did you not, at the beginning of the present century?"

Sir George gave a rather bitter laugh. "I did indeed," he said. "Not the most rewarding appointment of my career."

"Chief of Staff for Admiral Sir John Fisher, I believe?" asked Basil, who had done his homework.

"A fine man, of course, but not someone to work with. For. He wasn't in the least interested in hearing the advice or opinion of anyone other than himself, including his Chief of Staff. It was a great relief to me when I returned to England."

"And did you hear tell at all of Miss Kingston or Mrs Camilleri when you were there?" Basil asked, imagining the answer would be no.

There was a long pause. "Yes in fact," he said. "I received a note from Annie, inviting me to tea. I believe she'd seen a picture of me in the newspaper, alongside Fisher. I'd never have recognised her if I'd passed her in the street. She had two grown-up children, and looked nothing like the girl I remembered. We didn't have much to say to one another."

"And I suppose you didn't learn what had become of her sister?" Basil asked, suddenly hopeful.

"Oh but I did!" he said, leaning forward. "It seems that Mrs Camilleri had died many years before. She'd drowned whilst sailing around the coast with some chap. Caught in a storm. It'd clearly been a source of very great sorrow for Annie," he said. "But all in the past, all in the past."

Well, there's a story out of reach forever, thought Basil.

"I gather from his papers that Charlie was off in the far east for quite a while, as a young midshipman on the *Euryalus*," he said. "Some little war in Japan I believe. I must say, I'd never heard of such a thing."

"Was he indeed?" said Sir George. "That's most interesting."

At that moment a rather distinguished looking gentleman, whom Basil recognised but could not place, came over and put a friendly hand on Sir George's shoulder. He nodded at Basil. "How d'you do, Father?" he said.

"This is Reverend Basil Davies, John," said King-Hall, "Reverend Davies, permit me to introduce Admiral John Jellicoe."

Basil jumped up to shake his hand. "Oh good heavens," he said, grinning. "I've seen your face on cigarette cards!"

Jellicoe laughed appreciatively, and it dawned on Basil that in situations like this, amongst the top of the top brass, a poor clergyman such as he could take as many liberties as he liked. Jellicoe sat down with them, ordered a brandy from a passing servant, and nodded towards Basil to see if he wanted one too.

"Thank you very much, I would indeed," said Basil. "A fine way to end a magnificent dinner."

"John," said King-Hall, glancing at Basil with a brief look of regret, but saying nothing further. "I think you might know all about this. The Reverend here is interested to learn something about what went on in Japan, back in the 1860s, with the *Euryalus* and so forth. I believed you served with Arthur Coe – had he not been out there on the *Coquette* during all that?"

Jellicoe nodded vigorously. "Yes indeed! Arthur Coe! Good man, had a rare old time there as he told it. A pretty rum affair."

"I'd love to hear more," said Basil, as the brandies approached.

"Well now," Jellicoe began, entering full after-dinner mode, "it all started back in '62, I believe, in a single moment of madness …"

"Good Lord," said Basil, when he'd finally finished. "War's a strange business at times, isn't it?"

"Every time," said Jellicoe, standing up and reaching out to shake Basil's hand. "Pleasure to have met you."

The mention of war led to Sir George squashing Basil's spirits by telling him about Sir John Fisher's longstanding prediction that war with Germany was inevitable, sooner or later. Basil asked him if he really thought so, and King-Hall told him not to worry too much about it: Fisher got many things right, but just as many wrong. Basil thanked him for his kindness, and Sir George said, "Well, now you know as much as I do about it all. I can't tell you what part Charlie will have played in those events, but he must have been in the thick of it."

"I imagine it made a lasting impression on him," said Basil. "Being so very young at the time."

"It's the Navy," said Sir George. "Same for everyone. Anyway, you've got the picture I think. Doubtless you can imagine the rest."

They parted amicably, but Basil knew that their brief relationship had now expired, and he charged off to Euston to catch the last train back to Northampton. Sir George chose to spend the night at the club; he was due at the Admiralty the next day, to wrap up his career once and for all. As he lay his head down on the pillow he thought, well, I suppose that's what it's going to be like for me from now on. Reminiscing about past glories with tipsy vicars.

25

Basil admired and respected his wife's decency and determination, but over the years he had also come to dread those moments when, out of the blue, she'd been excessively upset by some small thing that to him seemed hardly worth noticing. He'd always supposed that it was something to do with her mother sending her over to her aunts in England at a tender age, a decision that none of them seemed inclined to explain. Possibly it all went back further than that, to the sadness of losing her father when much younger. Whatever the reasons, he had learnt to avoid such topics altogether, because it turned out that facing up to difficult problems was not always the best way of dealing with them after all.

So he'd been in no hurry to tell Frances about her father's letters, which he had secreted away in his study months ago. The proper moment to bring the subject up never seemed to arrive, and the longer he it put off the worse he imagined it would be when he did, for both of them. He'd almost convinced himself to forget the whole thing, but then he told himself, be a man, she won't kill you. So today was to be the day and, though he didn't wish to ruin the mood, he knew it would be far worse if he left it any longer.

It was their wedding anniversary, but Frances's current delicate condition and memories of the chastening conclusion to last year's high jinks, favoured a more restrained celebration this year. Basil pored over his maps during breakfast and suggested a trip to Buckingham, for an early lunch at the White Hart and perhaps a gentle walk around Stowe Park afterwards. They left the chicks in the nanny's capable hands, squeezed into their tiny motorcar, and were in Buckingham in good time for a bit of shopping before enjoying a nice roast at the hotel.

During a very ample luncheon they reminisced about their early secret outings together, the joy of journeys through the spring-time countryside and the stinking terrors of London traffic in winter. They recalled the testing times involved in gaining her family's approval. Basil admitted that he'd been shocked to discover that his vicar's collar and respectable education had not cut much ice with some of them at first.

"They're always like that," Frances said. "Just protecting their little darlings from unsuitable men. And they didn't seem to trust my judgement on such matters."

"You showed excellent judgement," her husband assured her. "In my opinion."

"Well they never seemed to think so. It felt to me like they were always waiting for me to get things wrong. They still do."

"A lot of people might envy you having so many people looking out for you."

Frances looked unconvinced. "Your family is so much easier," she said.

Basil nodded. "Yes, but not half so entertaining as your lot. I've grown quite fond of them all, over the years," he said.

"I find that hard to believe," she said, thinking of how he complained during Aunt Mary's interminable visits.

Basil patted his wife's hand and reminded her that he'd married her for better or for worse, and anyway he considered himself very lucky to have so many in-laws to choose from. She gave him a dubious look, and he wondered if the moment had not come for some fresh air and a serious conversation.

"Gosh," Frances said as they crested the hill of the Grand Avenue and looked along the ruler-straight road stretching ahead as far as you could see, all the way down to a distant monument.

"The Corinthian Arch," Basil explained, grandly. "And through the dead centre of it, you can see Stowe House."

"I can't," said Frances.

"Maybe a short walk then?" he suggested. "We can get closer to it."

"A short one," she allowed him.

They drove down to the arch, around the side of the estate and along a farm track, until the road came up by the grand house itself, with its manicured gardens and endless columns. He stopped the car on a grass verge just past the main drive. "We're not going any closer are we?" Frances asked. "I don't think I like big houses very much. The people who live in them always seem to be shouting."

He shook his head. "I don't think grand houses are really for us, are they? We can walk straight down to the church from here, if that's not too much for you."

Frances found it hard going, and was breathing heavily by the time they turned into the little graveyard, in the shadow of the massive mansion behind the trees. "I need to sit down," she muttered, pointing towards an old bench under a lime tree. They sat quietly together while Frances caught her breath. After a short while, she saw her husband blinking rapidly.

"Have you got something to tell me Basil?"

"Yes, dear. Something I should have mentioned a while ago," he paused, trying to gauge her likely reaction. She nodded sharply for him to carry on.

"Concerning when your mother returned to America," he continued. She waited, saying nothing. "Well it's nothing much really," he continued. "Or maybe you will think it is, but anyway the thing is ..." Frances sighed. "The thing is she left me a whole packet of letters and papers belonging to your father, that she asked me to read through, if I wished. And pass on to you, if I judged it appropriate to do so, I believe is what she said."

Frances made him wait in silence for a good while before she replied.

"I know all that," she said at last, very calmly.

"You *do?*" he cried.

"Mother told me all. She wrote me a long rambling letter confessing what she'd done."

"She did? When was this? Why on earth didn't you tell me?"

"No arguing today Basil, no cross words at all, remember?" He tried to take her hand but she waved him back, not unkindly. "I'd written to her in January," she told him. "For her birthday, to say how much I'd enjoyed having her stay with us. Which wasn't entirely true, but I didn't want to leave things badly between us and did my best to be affectionate. She replied immediately and was very pleased, and couldn't resist pouring out the whole story about giving you these things belonging to my father. She kept apologising and saying how she really regretted doing it the way she did, she should've given them to me at the time, obviously, she said. But she insisted that I shouldn't be cross with *you*, it wasn't *your* fault if you'd not told me about it already, which of course you hadn't but I forgive you."

"And you didn't mind?" he asked, dumbfounded.

"I did indeed," Frances said, a little grimly. "I believe I went slightly berserk, and quite possibly threw some china down the stairs. Poor Betty will confirm this. But fortunately you were away in London all day."

Basil groaned.

" – it's not important. The point is that it was hardly your fault that Mother trusted you with this. You're very trustable. Of course she should have given the letters to me but I suppose

251

that was meant kindly. When I'd calmed down a little I went into your study and it didn't take me very long to find them all, because you're really not very good at hiding things. Or maybe you wanted me to find them, I don't know. Anyway, I read the whole lot, every last one."

Basil waited for her to say more, but she seemed to have nothing more to say, just sitting silently, staring at the tombstones scattered over the little churchyard.

"How did they make you feel?" he asked, feeling he should break the silence. "The letters?"

She shook her head. "I felt sorry for him sometimes, the things Mother wrote to him. But I didn't like the letters from his Navy friend. George whoever – they all seemed to be about subjects that were very, I don't know, *personal*. Not things you talk about. And there was one from a woman in Malta that seemed a bit odd to my mind too. It seems to me that my father had secrets."

Basil nodded, and thanked God he'd burnt the one Charlie had written to Lizzie. "He was a decent bloke, you know," he said, very softly.

Frances was silent for a while, then she asked him what made him say that. He told her about his conversation with the very same George Whoever, now an ancient Admiral, and tales he was able to glean of Charlie as a young man out in Japan fifty years before, when he'd found himself in the heat of battle.

Tell me about them one day Basil, she said. But not this day if you don't mind.

"Oh you can read it all for yourself whenever you want. I wrote it all down as best I could, just for you. I tried to imagine what it had really been like, how it might have affected him. Just a young lad, no older than your cousin Jack."

It was not strictly true that he'd written this entirely for Frances. He'd briefly entertained the possibility of writing something for Mary Harriette to put in her newspaper. There didn't seem to be much room for the likes of poor Charlie in the official version of the Pickersgill-Cunliffe saga, even if he deserved to be remembered as much as anyone else. His story was a damned sight more interesting than most of the stuff that filled the pages of *The Family News* which, despite Basil's best efforts to liven it up a bit, was rapidly running out of steam now anyway.

But he knew really that she'd never accept it, the way it turned out in the end, and he didn't send it to her; more than anything, for fear of how angry he'd feel when she sent it back.

On their way home, Basil asked Frances what she'd done with the letters. She told him that she hid them all away until she'd read them enough times to absorb everything in them, and then she burnt them, every one until not a single word remained. She was determined that no-one else should ever see them, not even her sister and certainly not her sister's pompous husband.

"Actually, I was very surprised you never noticed they'd gone, to be honest, Basil," Frances said, over the squeaks and squawks of the little car's straining suspension. "You're not very good at secrets, are you? That's something nice about you I suppose." She felt moved to give him a peck on the cheek just then, but found herself too firmly wedged in her seat to get close enough.

"So do you think you'll ever want to read this thing I wrote?" Basil finally asked. She shrugged; she'd think about it. He suspected she would, eventually, and she'd probably destroy that as well. It's a good thing he'd made a carbon copy, he thought. It'll be all that's left of her poor father soon.

1. Bombardment of Kagoshima, Japan, August 1863

```
The   world   was   exploding   around   young   Charles
Hodgkinson, just eighteen and a midshipman on HMS
```

Euryalus. He stumbled and clambered over rope and boxes of armaments, shoving and shouting at the sailors in his way, battling back to the Captain to make his report. Cannon shells and roundshot were landing all about the ship, under fire with no prior warning from 37 guns in the Japanese forts along the shore.

The *Euryalus* was the flagship of a squadron of British Naval vessels – the *Pearl, Persueus, Argus, Coquette, Racehorse* and *Havock* – that had arrived two days earlier in the Bay of Kagoshima, to do whatever was necessary to achieve a final resolution to the Namamugi Incident, in which an English merchant had been hacked to pieces by some samurai he'd managed to offend. It was intended as a show of force, with no serious intention of spilling blood. On the morning of the 15th, after two days of futile diplomacy, Admiral Kuyper tried to move things forward with a relatively harmless demonstration of imperial power, capturing three of the Prince of Satsuma's ships moored in the bay. But far from caving in immediately, the Prince ordered the bombardment of the British squadron, out of range as yet on the edge of the bay. As soon as the shooting started, the Admiral responded by issuing an order to pillage then destroy the captured ships, whilst the British ships moved up the bay in order to fire back on the Satsuma's guns. The wind was by now beginning to blow like a typhoon, it was raining hard, and some ships experienced considerable difficulty getting into position on the line.

The *Euryalus* had inadvertently steered between fort no. 7 and a target that the Japanese gunners were in the regular habit of firing at for practice. She was broadside on to the shore, and the Japanese gunners had her range, just so. As he got nearer to the quarterdeck, Charlie could see Captain Josling talking into Commander Wilmot's ear, trying to make himself heard over the roaring wind. Suddenly, coming from the shore to his left, he glimpsed and then heard a round black object spinning through the air above the sea, heading straight towards the ship. He stopped and watched, transfixed, as it continued to rise over the water and then, without warning, suddenly dip down towards the quarterdeck. It looked for a moment like it might pass over the heads of the officers standing there and into the water beyond. But an instant later there was a ghastly explosion of cracking bone and splintered timber, anguished shouts and then stunned silence as a red cloud of dust and spray rose up and dispersed in the wind and rain.

He ran the rest of the way to see two bodies splayed across the deck, their officers' uniforms splattered with brain and blood, beside which knelt the British Chargé d'Affaires, who had been awaiting a chance to talk with the Captain just as the cannonball came through. He looked up at the surrounding horrified spectators who were, in turn, looking down at the remains of Captain Josling and Commander Wilmot. "It's taken off both their heads," he explained, and then began to shake his own head as if to clear his mind of what he had just seen. Hodgkinson also just stood and stared, until the bellowing voice of the Admiral, roaring at the gun crews to get their bloody guns firing, brought him back to his senses.

"Midshipman," the Admiral barked, and Charlie snapped to attention. "Get together a detail and collect these bodies rightaway." As Charlie turned to carry out the order, the Admiral grabbed his shoulder and added with furious emphasis "– with all due respect, do you understand? *ALL DUE RESPECT.*"

The sea was becoming even wilder and Charlie had to shout with all his strength to make himself heard. He pointed forcefully at three of the more experienced looking ratings in front of him who knew what to do without being told, and in short order they wrapped the bodies in sailcloth along with what remained of each man's head and carried them below to the Captain's cabin. Meanwhile Charlie grabbed a few others and with buckets of water they set about splashing the remaining bone, blood and brain off into the sea, and then began to scrub the deck clean. "SCRUB AND SCRUB AS HARD YOU CAN!" Charlie shouted over the storm, although the driving rain was doing the job for them now.

Before that was done with, the 110 pounder Armstrong gun on the forecastle violently exploded as the gun crew tried to fire it, throwing them all down onto the deck, stunned but not badly injured. Very soon after, a 10 inch shell came in from one of the Japanese batteries and exploded just by the muzzle of another gun, instantly killing seven members of that crew. By then, the brave *Euryalus* had begun to move out of harm's way and the whole squadron took its departure from the scene soon after.

That evening in the midshipman's quarters there was a great deal of confused and excited talk about the shocking day, and more than a few bad dreams during the night that followed. It was the first time Midshipman Hodgkinson had seen serious action, and he was proud to have survived it without showing fear. But deep inside his stomach a knotty sensation, not fear exactly but something foreboding, silently took shape.

2. Battle of Shimonoseki, Japan, September 1864

In the months after the Kagoshima Bombardment, the Prince of Satsuma developed excellent relations with the British Navy, declaring himself most impressed by the speed and manoeuvrability of its newest ships. He was keen to modernise his own Navy, and saw the wisdom of learning from European expertise. But tensions between the Japanese and foreign powers from Europe and America, whom many in the government viewed as barbarians, continued to boil. These tensions reached the next crisis in a battle one year after Kagoshima, when a force of sixteen ships representing Britain, France, the Netherlands and the United States came together to take control of the Straits of Shimonoseki, that were crucial to them for trade and international intercourse.

The fighting began in earnest on the 5th, the allied fleet firing throughout the day at the Japanese defences on land, the sailors on the *Euryalus* doing so with particular passion in revenge for what had happened at Kagoshima the year before. This went on all day, with no small degree of success for the allies, amidst brave and persistent resistance from the Japanese. Having made good progress, it was decided early on the morning of the 6th to send forces onto land to finish the business off. Charlie was in the thick of it again as a member of a party of 200 men from the *Euryalus*, under the command of Captain Armstrong. They joined another 1500 sailors and soldiers of various nationalities attacking targets all along the coast.

In a frenzy of shouting, whistles, and shouted commands, the force from *Euryalus* quickly set off up one side of a tall valley, with a battalion of British marines charging up the other side, all heading towards the Japanese stockade that stood at the top. There was considerable excitement among the men now, and they ran up the hill, still shouting and cheering, stopping sometimes to take aim at an enemy from behind the pine trees edging the road and then carry on. More excitement than discipline, in fact, with much ammunition wasted on imaginary foes on the hillside. Some men were wounded, and one sailor was killed by an arrow, but for the most part the British force, including Charlie, advanced up the hill without significant losses until the ground became less steep, and they could see the stockade a couple of hundred yards ahead of them. The shooting from the Japanese became more intense.

The sailors from the *Euryalus* and the battalion of British marines joined together there, and moved forward to storm the stockade. From where Charlie was placed in this force of five hundred or so men, he found it hard to see much of what was going on at the front, but the Queen's Colour was clearly visible ahead as the leading company began to attack the stockade. He and the men around him cheered and pushed forward, but then a volley of fire from the stockade brought down the Colour Sergeant, Thomas Pride, and the Queen's Colour dropped out of sight momentarily. There was a general moan from the men behind but then, to wild cheering, the flag quickly rose up again and moved forward many yards, musket balls flying everywhere.

The battle was quickly over after that, and the Japanese in the stockade soon surrendered or made their escape, unhindered, down the road inland. Towards the end of the day, the British sailors and soldiers all gathered high above the Straits, just standing around and sitting on the guns they'd taken, sharing stories of the day. There had been seventy-two killed or injured among the various allied forces, Captain Armstrong catching a bullet in his ankle. But the main topic of conversation was the pluck of seventeen year old middy D.G. Boyes, who had been alongside when Sergeant Pride was struck down by Japanese guns. Without a thought for his own safety, without pausing for thought of any kind, he had grabbed the Colour and lifted it up high, bullets whistling through the flag and some even through his uniform, and began to lead the charge once more. It was, as everybody who saw it and everyone else who heard of it agreed, a remarkable act of bravery from one so young.

Later that evening, in the midshipman's mess, Charlie came over and splashed another beer down in front of him. "You're a real hero Boysie," he said, as drunk as his comrade. "You saved the day man."

Boyes grinned, shook his head in disbelief at what he'd done, flushed and proud. "Drink up Hodge my boy," he said. "We've all earned it."

Charlie wondered whether he would have done the same, saved the day without a care for his own life; he liked to think he would but you never can tell. He was just glad to have come out of all that chaos still in one piece, and prouder than anything to be one of the boys. One of the men.

One year later, back in England at Southsea, Duncan Boyes was invested with the Victoria Cross for conspicuous gallantry, along with Colour Sergeant Pride and an American called Seeley. It was Boyes, though, who was the pride of the Navy that day, and a national hero for a short while.

But the same heedless headstrong behaviour that had won him such acclaim subsequently brought him down, rapidly and without mercy. Early in 1867 he

was court-martialled and dismissed from the Navy
for a drunken attempt to climb into the naval yard
in Bermuda, having lost his pass. It was rumoured
not to be his first clash with authority, and not
the first time drink had been involved either. But
the shame of it, the complete loss of the world's
respect and admiration, and the full-time drinking
that never really eased that loss, threw him into
a deep depression. He moved to New Zealand, to work
with his brothers on their sheep station, but did
not last there very long. In 1869 he jumped out of
an upstairs window in Dunedin, the death certificate
giving *delirium tremens* as cause of death.

When Charlie and his fellow officers in the
wardroom learnt of his sorry end, they heartily
sang Rule Britannia! Britannia Rules the Waves! in
memory of poor Boyes, before raising their glasses
to the Queen and then, it being a Friday, to *A
willing foe and sea-room,* words which never failed
to tighten harder the knot in the pit of Charlie's
stomach, a permanent malign presence at the core of
his being, for which the remedy could only ever be
another drink.

PART FIVE

1914-1916

26

It was birthday season in the Davies household: Helen (4) and Godfrey (3) on the 20th, Pauline (2) in a couple of weeks' time, to be followed by the arrival of number four (0) also in July some time, hopefully. Today, June 29th 1914, was the turn of Basil (34) and he had arranged to be home in time for birthday cake and candles with the children, which excited Helen very much, took Godfrey by surprise, and was an enjoyable mystery to large-eyed Pauline. Frances had instructed Harriet and Betty in no uncertain terms that on this particular evening they were not to admit *any* of the visitors that were always turning up at the house to see the Vicar. This was family time.

Frances was an excellent mother and Basil was a good father in his own excellent ways, which were not the same kind of ways in which Frances was excellent. He was seldom aware of what was going on with the children from one moment to the next, which as far as Frances was concerned was her job anyway but it did mean that he quite often had to improvise and understand at a moment's notice, when there hadn't been time to brief him. But he was fun and funny, quick-witted and usually able to get away with pretending that he did already know an important piece of child-news that he was very much expected to know. His presence always excited and slightly scared the children, but it wasn't as if their mother didn't quite often frighten them, and more than slightly when she wanted to.

They were allowed into the big front room, under the big old chandelier, and ran around the big oak table with a very big cake in the middle, with a lot of candles burning bright. When Basil came grandly in, pretending to look amazed and shocked by the sight of the flaming cake, the children rushed towards him and explained that it was his birthday. He told them he doubted it could be that, because he was too old to have birthdays any more which further surprised Godfrey, but Basil quickly laughed and thanked them all warmly for his lovely birthday tea and blew the candles out with a single puff, clutching his heart melodramatically as he did so. At which moment the children were allowed to give him the present they had crafted for him, with their mother's help, out of ribbons, a piece of wood with a face painted on, pipe cleaners, and parts of an old wooden toy car.

Later on, while Percy took Evensong at Holy Sepulchre Church, Basil accompanied Frances to the pictures at Vint's Palace. It was a lovely warm evening as they walked down through the town and many people were also out walking, the occasional one hurrying towards Basil with something they just had to mention to him. Frances saw each one off, Basil giving a cheery wave but not slowing his step for a moment.

The climate inside the cinema was sultry and the atmosphere quite raucous but that was how they enjoyed their cinema in Northampton. Vint's Palace was not some smart bioscope in the West End of London, just a long thin hall with a hundred seats, more or less; a place where the audience didn't hesitate to pass judgement on what was presented to them, and were more than ready to join in the action if stimulated to do so. As Basil and Frances found their way down to some empty seats near the front, their fellow spectators were talking to one another, calling out, eating, drinking, and in some cases snoring their way through the spectacle on the screen, whilst every now and then kids would start yelling and chasing one another up and down the aisle. Beneath the screen Vint's wife was plonking out an accompaniment, which few expected to have much relevance to the action on the screen. As they sat down to watch a grainy and scratchy newsreel of the recent arrest of Mrs Pankhurst and two hundred other suffragettes at Buckingham Palace, the melody of "Down at the Old Bull and Bush" rose up incomprehensibly from the piano.

Not that anyone heard much of that, as the plonking was immediately drowned out by loud jeering and worse from the audience which was to a man, and woman, unsympathetic to the suffragette movement and its posh leader. The noise briefly calmed down for the next film, a short wintry travelogue about trekking in the snowy peaks of the Swiss Alps, to the melody of "The Man Who Broke the Bank at Monte Carlo", that Basil acknowledged did at least have some connection with foreign travel. The audience was not entranced by the grainy views of distant mountains, but soon perked up when *Daisy Doodad's Dial* came on, the loudly appreciated tale of a young woman who gets arrested whilst practising for a face-pulling competition, to the accompaniment of "Two Lovely Black Eyes", a brief flash of genius from Mrs Vint.

This was followed by a second newsreel, as scratchy and jerky as the first one, involving the launching of large German warships. The pianist took a brief and barely unnoticed break during the six minutes of this little feature, but she was back on station for *Looping the Loop at Hendon*, in which two brave pilots set about demonstrating the extraordinary manoeuvrability of the latest aeroplanes, just managing not to die in the process.

Next came the first half of a split-reeler called *Olives and their Oil*, to which nobody paid the slightest attention. The second half of the reel, *Kid Auto Races*, followed immediately and Frances sighed quietly at the prospect of having to watch motor-racing, but remembered that this was her husband's birthday treat. It soon became apparent, though, that the racing cars – which she began to realise were indeed driven by children – merely served as background to some idiot from the crowd who insisted on putting himself in front of the camera whenever he could. It seemed to her that everyone in the cinema was being cheated somehow. Why on earth show a film that had been interrupted by a horrible little man with a stupid moustache who looked more like a tramp than anything? What was the world coming to?

Things improved, briefly, when the wretched tramp disappeared and they got to see some of the racing. Men were pushing boys in their wooden cars up a steep ramp and then sending them down as fast as they could, so that they went flying around the track like mad things. But just as it looked like they'd got rid of the awful little man, he came running out on to the track to pick up his hat, which he'd probably thrown there himself in the first place, just to get some more attention. It very nearly caused a horrible accident. "Oh for Heaven's sake!" she cried, and looked at Basil indignantly. He grinned back.

"Don't you know who that is?" he said, laughing, as the little man began to fight with the camera people and kept getting knocked over.

"What do you mean?" she said, more irritated than ever.

"Look harder," said Basil, encouragingly.

Now the little man was standing right in front of the camera that was meant to be filming the races still going on around him. The two men working the camera were clearly getting more and more impatient but even when they pushed him over they couldn't manage to get rid of him. Suddenly the little man went right up to their camera and pulled a rude face at it, and the film ended with a close-up of that. Everyone else laughed, and the film came to a sudden end.

Then she knew exactly who it was. As soon as she saw the horrible face he was making, she knew, despite the disguise. It was the same face she saw that time long ago when she tried to keep up with poor Hannah and her boy as he dragged her through the streets to the Infirmary. The face he showed her when he wanted her to leave him alone. Oh, she knew who it was all right. Basil said that his mother must be proud, to see him succeed so, and Frances muttered that she would not be pleased at all to see her son looking so poor and shabby in front of so many people.

This was followed by *The Rollicking Rajah*, featuring an English actor in dark make-up pretending to be a visiting maharajah and singing a cheerily obnoxious song before a group of under-rehearsed chorus girls. The film depended on the perfect synchronisation of a sound disc with the moving pictures, an innovative technical challenge that defeated Vint's projection skills, the sound running further and further ahead of the pictures as it went on. The audience helped things along by vigorously joining in the chorus, in time neither with the sound nor the pictures. "All the girls admire the Rollicking Rajah, the wonderful Rajah, he's a multi-millionaire. He stays in Rotten Row, he's riding a charger. ... the Rollicking Rajah, of Ranjipuuuurrr..." It received a big cheer at the end.

Then came "The Deadly Turning", Episode 4 of *The Perils of Pauline*, and the climax of the evening for most in the audience. Mrs Vint came back to the piano and proceeded to charge up and down the keyboard throughout, which seemed to meet the requirements of the film pretty well. In this episode, Pauline decides to enter an international motor race (for Heaven's sake!), so that she can win the big money prize and give it to the poor. A plan to kill her during the race, by throwing tacks in front of her car, goes badly wrong and the villains' car crashes instead, apparently killing them. For once, it seems, Pauline is not left hanging off a rocky crag or lying on railway tracks, which was a bit of a disappointment for the audience, despite the usual message at the end.

CONTINUED NEXT WEEK!
See the next exciting ep-
isode in this theater for
the further exciting ad-
ventures in
THE PERILS OF PAULINE

It was the last item in the programme, and when it finished the lights came on for a two minute break. Basil and Frances, having arrived just after the programme started, stayed on for what they'd missed.

"I suppose it's too soon to see a newsreel about yesterday's tragic events," he said.

"Yesterday's events?" asked Frances.

"The assassination of the Crown Prince of Austria and his wife," said Basil. "In Sarajevo."

"Where's that?" she asked. In Bosnia-Herzegovina, he said. Where's *that*, she asked. In the Balkans, he said. She sighed. They're always shooting each other there, he explained. Then the lights went back down, and *Mabel's Strange Predicament* began.

"Here's Charlie again!" cried Basil, delighted. Frances frowned her disapproval but couldn't take her eyes off him whenever he appeared on the screen. No-one could. This time he was part of a proper story, a convoluted and farcical bit of nonsense involving a young woman who gets locked out of her hotel room in her pyjamas, and hides under a bed. Charlie played a tipsy masher hanging around the hotel, and steals the show from start to finish. Frances couldn't resist laughing at the things he did, the way he moved and the looks he gave, but sincerely hoped that he would get rid of that awful costume.

When they got home, as Harriet was going off to fetch biscuits & cheese and the remains of the birthday cake for a light supper, she waved towards *The Times* lying on the dining table. "Reverend Percy came round and left that for you Vicar. Said you wanted to read about what happened yesterday, whatever that might be." Basil grabbed the paper and opened it immediately.

"Austrian Heir and his wife murdered," Basil read out. "A student's political crime. Bomb thrown earlier in the day. How awful."

"Did they have children?" Frances asked.

"Yes, I think so," said Basil looking through the paper. "Three I believe."

"How sad," she said.

"Listen to this," said Basil. "*On their way to the Town Hall the Archduke and his Consort had narrowly escaped death.* Some chap threw a bomb at their car, and the Archduke fended it off with his arm. It exploded behind his car, injuring a number of important people and some passers-by, apparently. But they carried on to a Reception at the Town Hall."

He read down the page, shook his head in amazement. "Apparently," he said, "when they got to the Town Hall the Archduke had quite a go at the Mayor: 'What is the good of your speeches?' he bellowed apparently. 'I come to Sarajevo on a visit, and I get bombs thrown at me. It is outrageous.' I imagine he was quite upset."

"Well you can't blame him," said Frances.

"I certainly cannot," said Basil. "Not surprisingly, a planned visit to a museum was immediately cancelled. But what's unbelievable is that they leave again in the same car and the

269

driver takes the wrong road, straight to where another assassin is waiting. Unbelievable. What a bloody farce!"

"Do NOT swear," said Frances.

"They go straight back to where they'd just been attacked," he continued, "and come across this other chap, Princip. He can't believe his luck, takes out his pistol and fires three times at them. End of Archduke and Consort."

"Basil. You must not make light of such a dreadful thing," said Frances severely.

"I'm not making light of it, and I know it isn't funny," he said, "But you must admit it's farcical. Assassins popping up all over the place."

The image flashed before his mind's eye, just for an instant, of the scruffy little tramp, running up like a demented clown, throwing a smoking bomb and charging off again with that crazy little run of his before anyone could stop him, to the cheers of an appreciative crowd.

"This is a little worrying, I must say," he said. "It says here 'No-one has attempted to gauge its possible effect on the stability of Europe, and the diplomatic world is almost stunned.' The stability of Europe for crying out loud!"

"Oh I trust not," said Frances, who'd clearly had enough by now.

"Come back next week for a further exciting episode," Basil murmured to himself.

"I'm rather tired now Basil," she said.

He put his arm around her. "Time for bed," he said, and she didn't argue. "It's been a tremendous birthday." He gave her a little peck on the cheek, Harriet was summoned to clear up, and he went to his study. He felt wide awake still, and thought he might finish the day by getting one or other of the several bits of writing he owed various publications out of the way. Time to get one final Vehicles of Progress article written, he decided, so that he could be done with that thankless task once and for all. A vague idea for it had been forming all evening.

The Cinema as Progress! He could tie it all up somehow, in a last clever little piece about how cinema was a breath of fresh air: educational, informative, entertaining, democratic – look at the tramp, with his chippy ways, standing up for the ordinary man. Rude, obnoxious, disrespectful and very funny. It was about time people got to laugh at their betters, see them knocked off their pedestals occasionally. This was progress for everyman, same as the railways, the bicycle, the motor cycle, the Brownie camera and, I don't know, Ivelcon bloody soup. Something along those lines.

By mid-July Frances was finding the last weeks of her pregnancy intolerable, and Basil couldn't hold off the growing fear that the two of them were bringing an innocent into a world that no longer had time for innocence. The thought of war made him feel increasingly bleak but he said nothing more about that to Frances, and could only pray that it would all come to nothing, which is what everyone else seemed to believe. He went to watch the latest newsreels as soon as each one came out, and saw solemn statesmen and generals of various nations proclaiming soundless platitudes and warnings, intercut with film of foreign soldiers marching or warships going to sea, and anxious faces crowding the streets of European capitals; more or less the same faces he met every day in his church, in the streets, in the pub and at his front door.

As July drew to a close, and the outside world filled with dread, Frances grew increasingly peaceful and content. Every day the children played happily for hours on end in the long vicarage garden, and she sat out there with them, absorbing the warm air of summertime. On the evening of the 28th Basil tried to finish his piece about the cinema for the *Family News* but quite soon abandoned the attempt, because for the life of him he could not come up with any satisfactory or optimistic conclusion. He resolved instead to tackle the present crisis head-on. "The wheels are coming off the Vehicles of Progress all around us," he wrote, "and it seems that the whole of Europe is tumbling pell-mell into the flames of conflict." He stared at what he had written in disbelief, then crumpled it up and threw it into the wastepaper basket. By the end of the day, Austria-Hungary had declared war on Serbia, and his wife had gone into labour.

27

from Mary Harriette's Diary

July 29th 1914

Cloudy but warm. No letters. War between Austria and Serbia – will it embroil all Europe? Gave orders for school treat. Telegram from Basil: "Margaret arrived last night".

July 30th

Letter from Basil; all well; baby 7lbs.

July 31st

Summer once more. Letter from Milicent. War clouds very bleak. Belgrade in flames.

August 1st

War clouds blacker than ever, and the general upset seems inevitable. ... Read "Scott's Last Expedition", till 1.0. ... Milicent writes that all foreign students have left Oxford in a hurry, and the evening paper tells that Germany has given Russia a warning to cease mobilizing, or else – !

August 2nd

At luncheon time we learnt that Germany has declared war on Russia, and all was excited talk about our own future. I did hope the European war would not come in my day, but Germany has been intending to do it for years. My Bible Class insisted on War Hymns, so I took occasion to exhort them to "walk warily in these dangerous days", not to get excited, but to do their duty extra well, and be very economical in everything. ... Evelyn, Gertrude and I had a little talk together over our personal duty in the household. Evelyn & I think we had better cash a cheque in the small notes to be issued, so that we may hoard the gold we have in hand. Heavy showers at intervals.

August 3rd

Germany has invaded France without notice, and also Luxembourg which is neutral. Fie! We are calling up naval reserves, for she will also pounce on us if it suits her.

August 4th

Banks closed till Friday. Germany threatens Belgium and King Albert appeals to King George, so we are mobilizing. Read much, and tried to be brave. ... went to Mother. Talked to her about loyalty of the Colonies, Kindliness of USA and amusing incidents in the London crowd, always returning to the power and goodness of God.

August 5th

Raining. Slipped down early and was soon joined by E. We declared war against Germany yesterday! Read papers, finished Scott and felt braver after reading his brave death, though I wept over it. ... The Blathwayts promised to give us any news they may get of Jack and Gerald. Letter from John, back in the Worc. Regt. Says he expects to be a Captain or a Corpse very soon. Also letter from Milicent. Usual evening.

August 6th

German reverse in Belgium. Lord Kitchener is war minister. Great joy! ... John has gone to Worcester and Gerald starts on the 14th. Margaret tries to be brave, the poor girl! Well! We all want our men to be in it!

August 9th

Nell very homesick and keen to return, but by now I expect she is glad to be in U.S.A. She still makes a great thing of her sadness over the death of the dreadful Dr Dent, whom nobody but her mourns. Frances writes that it is beyond her comprehension, that her mother should feel that way about a man she should never have married in the first place.

August 10th

We hear sundry tales of the silent disappearance of our troops at night and it is said that we have 150,000 in Belgium now.

August 13th

Kitchener is fortifying places all around London and over the kingdom. Harry came down in his Daimler soon after tea. Jack had left, and poor Harry was feeling it badly, but he only wanted silent sympathy which sisters know how to give. He does not sleep, and looks very worn. He says Winchester is already full of our wounded! But as Germany is not supposed to know we have left our shores, nothing is told in the papers.

August 17th

Rose Fell came, looking brown and well after a holiday at Bournemouth. Begged her to keep to her work and not to volunteer. Basil and Frances next arrived, he rather pensive, she very bright and well. They had been stopped several times on the way here by Scouts and police, and expected to be stopped again on the way back. Once Basil had paused for a smoke, and told the boy scout his was a German car, and the horn was a thing for strewing bombs. Some small boys who had gathered round, listened eagerly, till one said with a smile "But you ain't a German, all the same!"

***

"Your grandfather was a decent man," insisted Mrs Pickersgill Cunliffe. "I didn't want to marry him at first but mother said I must, and then she died as soon as we married and I never really forgave him for thinking he could replace her. But I came to respect him in the end."

"Of course Granny," said Frances, wishing she could leave.

"Sometimes I wake up in the night thinking that I am to have another child," her grandmother said, suddenly agitated. "I know it's my duty but I cannot do that again. I sometimes fear he isn't finished with all that."

Frances didn't know what to say, but her grandmother just as suddenly relaxed.

"You have a new baby, do you not, dear?" she said.

"Yes," said Frances, relieved. "Margaret."

Her grandmother thought about this.

"Margaret?" she asked. "Her husband has just gone to war, hasn't he?"

"Not that Margaret, Granny," said Frances very patiently. "I think you might mean cousin Margaret," Frances said, wincing.

"I know very well whom I mean," said grandmother. "I was talking about your cousin."

"Yes of course, Granny," Frances said. "I'm sorry."

She looked more carefully at Frances. "I know who you are, you know. You've just had a baby and she's called Margaret too."

Frances had a photo to show her grandmother, but this was brushed aside.

"Your husband hasn't gone to the war, though, has he?" Mrs Pickersgill-Cunliffe said, as if she'd been waiting all along to say this. "Is he too old? I don't believe he is. He's not as old as whatshisname."

"Gerald?"

"No you silly girl. Basil I mean. He's not as old as Gerald so why hasn't he joined the army yet?"

Frances blinked at her grandmother, unable to think of anything to say.

"Your mother married a hopeless man too," Mrs Pickersgill-Cunliffe continued. "My husband had his faults, but he didn't deserve to die like a dog, under the wheels of a train."

"I don't think that's quite what happened, Granny, was it?"

"I'll tell you a secret," her grandmother said, very confidentially. "Your grandfather had discovered that the thing he had always feared more than anything was about to happen, that's the long and the short of it. I will say no more."

"Sorry, Granny, what thing do you mean? Sorry," Frances said, doing her best.

"That he was about to go bankrupt, obviously," she said, more impatiently than strictly necessary, nodding her head vigorously at the same time, to fend off any kind of disagreement. "He spent the whole weekend going back and forth from our house to his brother's house and working in his study. He wouldn't talk about it but when he was gone I let myself into his study. There were contracts and insurance policies and notebooks covered in calculations all over his desk. It was clear that we were in trouble."

"Are you sure, Granny?" Frances asked, perhaps unwisely.

"Am I SURE?" her granny cried out. "Of course I'm sure. I know what happened. By the Monday morning your grandfather was grey with worry. Grey. He hadn't slept for days. After breakfast he just said he was going to London straightaway, and before anyone knew it he was found lying beside the railway tracks with his legs crushed, still clutching his newspaper. Apparently when the doctor came and tried to take it from him he refused at first to give it up. He wasn't dead."

She was weeping, as much in anger as in sadness, it seemed.

"He got it all wrong," she said, bitterly. "There was no need for any of it."

She stared at the ceiling and lay her head back.

"But he was a brave man," she said. "I'll give him that. It was brave of him, to do what he did."

Frances had never heard mention of such things, not in any of the versions she'd heard before, not even in the torrid account told her once by a pile of over-excited cousins as they all hid together in the woods behind the Hermitage.

Helen Dale Pickersgill-Cunliffe suddenly seemed to have had enough of these memories, and of her visitor too, and fell back into instant sleep. Frances tiptoed out, relieved. She hurried down to the library hoping to tell Rose what her grandmother had been saying, but everyone else was there too by now. Mary Harriette, Basil and Gertrude returned from their golf, Aunt Evelyn sitting to one side, looking distant and knowing as usual, and a Miss Gladys Nash, who had dropped in for tea, watching everyone like a well-mannered hawk.

"How was Granny, dear?" Mary Harriette asked.

"Quite confused I'm afraid, Aunt Mary," said Frances. Mary Harriette nodded sadly, and Aunt Evelyn pulled herself wearily up from her armchair to return to her thankless duty at her mother's bedside. As she was sitting down, Frances leaned over towards Rose. "Granny was saying the strangest things," she whispered.

"Rose dear," Mary Harriette said, not permitting anything in the way of private conversations during tea, "do tell us how things are going on in London presently."

"Well I thought I'd seen everything in my time as a nurse," said Rose, "but the last few weeks have taken even a cynical old stager like me by surprise." She'd only just returned to her district, now that the war had started, and it was even worse there now than she'd feared.

"There's hardly a house where there's not one or more gone to war. One of my mothers, her husband's gone off to the front, she's left looking after six children, another on the way. She had a leg off not long ago, and her good one isn't much good either, really. She really misses her husband. But she said her best friend was only too delighted to see her old man go. Hoped the German's would do 'im in.

"Another one I saw on that first day back said she reckoned the war was a good thing in some ways; some of the men being out such a long time, what with the lock-out and the strikes and all, the one-an-tuppence a day was better than nothing. Might as well be killed in the war as die of starvation at home. Lots of them are near to starving, you've no idea. Some of the poor dears haven't got any marriage lines to show the authorities, and just can't believe that the War Office won't lift a finger to help them."

Gladys Nash shook her head and looked sour, so Mary Harriette moved the conversation on before the old lady said something regrettable about the undeserving poor.

"How are things in Northampton, Basil?" she asked. "Do you see many troops there?"

"I certainly do," he said. "Large numbers of Royal Welsh Fusiliers who – "

"– tell me, Vicar," Miss Nash blithely interrupted. "Do you have expectations of going to the Front yourself?"

There was an uncomfortable silence.

"I'm sure that Basil is too modest to say that he has already attempted to volunteer, and been turned down on a matter of health," Mary Harriette quickly said.

Basil nodded, and confirmed that that was indeed the case, but assured her that he had every intention of serving in some capacity or other and, as he was attempting to explain, was currently Chaplain to the troops in Northampton.

"Oh I didn't mean to suggest –" the old lady protested.

" – of course not, Miss Nash," said Basil. "A perfectly reasonable question, and one that I am sure I will be asked many times more." Frances looked on in dismay, knowing only too well how sensitive Basil was about this.

"And I must say that I have the very deepest admiration for those from our families who are even now setting off to the Front," Basil continued. "Charming young Jack, brave John, sturdy Gerald, my own excellent brother Brom, who is bringing his considerable medical skills, just like our most admirable Nurse Fell intends to do!"

Everyone applauded and said Hear! Hear! "And we must constantly pray," said Mary Harriette, "that we see them all return home again by Christmas."

Gertrude wondered if things might indeed be over quickly, now that troops could be moved so fast with modern transport, and had all these modern weapons too. Aeroplanes even. Wouldn't modern warfare be a very different thing from the messy business of wars in the past? Everyone looked to Basil for confirmation of this reassuring possibility, but he just shook his head. Well, he said, I am afraid to say that Germany is somewhat ahead of us in that respect.

After tea Frances related her conversation with Granny to Rose, as the two of them walked round and round the fountain in front of the Hall.

"What was she suggesting, do you think?" Rose asked.

"I don't really know," Frances said. "Should I tell Aunt Mary about it?"

"Best not," said Rose. "See what Basil says when you get home."

Frances took her cousin's hand. "Rose, are you really going to volunteer? Go away to war? I couldn't bear anything happening to you."

Rose smiled. "Whatever I do, I know that I'll be fine, don't worry," she said. "I want to be part of it all. But it isn't easy – they don't seem to want to let women near the war. They'll take the saddest wretch of a man into the army, but us girls have to plead to be allowed to go and do something useful."

"You're much braver than me, you know. Every time I think of how you went and attacked that awful motorcar man, it makes me shiver. To think what they might have done to you."

Rose laughed. "Well I didn't actually hit him," she said, and gave Frances a little hug. "But if I can cope with someone as foul as him I'm sure I can cope with the German army."

"You can just tell them how disgusting they are," Frances whispered to her, as all the others came out for a stroll around the garden.

Basil announced that it was time to go – apparently there were children waiting for them at home, he said, working hard to appear more cheerful than he felt. Off they went laden with peaches and small treats for the children. As he drove away down the drive, Basil shook his head and muttered to himself, and Frances patted him on his knee.

"Basil?" she called, over the noise of the car and the road, "are you all right?"

He nodded, turned briefly and smiled back at her. "Of course I am!" he said, and took a deep breath to calm himself down. It was never easy to spend a day with all the Family at once, however nice they tried to be, and this particular visit had made him feel worse than ever about being so safe and comfortable, when most other men were facing such danger and privation.

"Granny said something very interesting today, Basil," Frances called, over the rumbling of the engine.

"Really?" he called back.

"Family news, you might call it," she said.

"Later perhaps," he said, as they were waved down once again by the very same Northwood policeman who'd stopped them on the way there, and had to go through the same rigmarole of identifying themselves, plus a quite a lengthy and tedious interrogation this time.

"And one more thing, Father," the policeman said finally, before letting them travel on. "No more making fun of scouts. Those lads represent the King you know. Next time you try that kind of thing on, you'll find yourselves arrested on a charge of sedition I daresay."

Basil drove away slightly shame-faced. "Sorry dear," he said. "I didn't mean to nearly get us hanged."

28

from Mary Harriette's Diary

August 29th

First naval success; small but brilliant. No letters. Mr Jeun came to tune the pianos. To Church with G. Collected clothes for the Belgian refugees at Folkestone. All are shocked at the burning of Louvain. Henceforth Germany is beyond the pale of humanity. The worst of it is that such conduct is contagious and I find myself hoping that Russia will repay her double for her cruelties. Our native troops are coming from India by their desire.

August 30th

We four sisters went to Church at 8.0. Prayed much for the Kaiser and his people: they are God's children, and our brethren and fellow servants.

September 2nd

Letter from Frances who has two subalterns in the house, and half expects their Major also, as he is envious of his juniors' pleasant quarters. The maids are evidently enjoying the society of their orderlies immensely.

September 18th

Harry arrived to luncheon, looking ill and old, but cheery about Jack, who had written. We had read Gerald B.'s letters to his mother yesterday, in which he said he had met Jack who told him he was "enjoying himself". Jack's Colonel had written high praise of Jack to his wife, who told Arlette; he is a grand boy. After tea, as we sat at our works, around a fire, a telegram was brought in. It was from Margaret, saying Gerald was killed in action. Later came a note from Isabel. How will she bear it? Poor things! Poor things! A very sad evening. Card from Frances of the Lion & Mane. Said the Commendatory Prayer at family prayers.

September 19th

Bright and frosty. Wrote Mrs Blathwayt before breakfast. Letter from Virginia, who wants her mother. Note from Harry to Evelyn: Jack killed in action, a glorious end to a blameless life, but oh! Our hearts are sore indeed. Wrote Mrs Spalding for mourning, Frances, Virginia, Abigail, Audrey, Margaret, Arlette, a stop press for F.N. Tea in billiard room. All went very well. After tea Kay and I knitted in library. Vicar came. He had heard about our Jack, so came to sympathize. He was plainly nervous, but our demeanour reassured him, and he stayed some time. Usual evening. F.N. proofs came. Evening paper fairly bright.

29

H arry told Basil he would be welcome to visit him, when they talked after Mrs Pickersgill-Cunliffe's funeral in Coulsdon, waiting at the very station where her husband had his accident over thirty years before. Harry had just performed his role as head of the family with great dignity, but did not manage to hide a sadness that had nothing to do with his mother's death. Basil asked him how he was faring. Badly, he said. Perhaps we could talk soon, Basil suggested, and Harry said he'd appreciate that.

It was less than an hour's ride to Staughton Manor. Basil rumbled through the flat and empty countryside, buffeted by the wind that blew the last leaves from the trees, clearing his thoughts for the ordeal ahead. The day was beginning to fade by the time he arrived, but a single light in the porch of Harry's grand house showed him the way up the drive. Harry came out as he chugged to a halt, and greeted him with a firm handshake. Let's go to my study, he said, and chat there over a cup of tea.

The walls, mantlepiece, and desk were all covered in pictures of his family, his wife, his girls, and his only son: Jack passing out of Sandhurst, Jack taking part in Trooping the Colour, Jack fishing, Jack riding, Jack as a schoolboy, Jack smiling, Jack the British Grenadier, Jack trying to look older than he was, the final picture taken of him as he prepared to leave for war. Harry watched Basil looking at the photos, which he did most carefully, glancing up at Harry from time to time.

"He was such a fine young man," Basil said.

"Far too young," said Harry. "Just nineteen."

"He looks proud of his uniform," said Basil.

"Immeasurably," said his proud father. "Proud to fight for his country."

Basil continued to look at the photos. "You were a soldier for some years, weren't you Harry? I suppose you remember that feeling?"

"I suppose I did," said Harry, uncertainly. "I never faced a real war, not like this one. No-one has, I imagine. No-one was prepared for a war like this. Not poor Jack, I am sure of that."

They sat down either side of Harry's desk. "It was just cruel Basil," he said. "It wasn't grand and heroic, he wasn't even granted the time to find out what it means to face a foe. He just discovered, for a few short and frightening minutes, what it means to feel confused, and fearful, and then be shot like a dog."

Basil waited for Harry to continue.

"He'd led the first wave of the advanced guard, straight up the steep hill over the River Aisne," Harry said. "It was his first real action."

"That would have taken tremendous courage," Basil said.

"The Germans first appeared to have given up or retreated, but when Jack and his men got to the top, at Coup de Soupir, there were tons of the buggers up there, shooting away. Jack ordered the men to take cover behind straw stacks, and would not take cover himself until he thought they were all safe. That's when he was first shot, and fell down in the road, injured but not too badly I believe. In a matter of moments they were overrun, and the Germans took all the surviving soldiers prisoner, including Jack, who could only lie there in the road and wait."

Harry stopped here. Basil dreaded to hear what he knew was coming next. Harry took a very deep breath, sighed, stared into the fire, and continued.

"He did not have long to wait, as it turned out," he said, his voice deep and very low. "Almost immediately, the rest of the advanced guard came into sight and the Germans decided to retreat. Rather than take an injured prisoner with him, the German officer in charge casually walked up to Jack where he lay, took out his revolver and shot him in the neck, killing him straightaway."

He was trembling now, his fists clenched and tears running down his face. He lifted up his eyes and looked in anguish at Basil, who found himself crying too, which he normally never did, whatever the sad story he was hearing. He reached out to touch Harry's hand, but only managed to do so briefly before Harry jumped up and walked over to the window.

"You know what happened next, presumably?" he asked, looking out into darkness.

"I believe so," said Basil.

"That the Germans were immediately captured soon after, and court martialled there and then for what they did to my son? The officer that shot Jack was sentenced first, and executed immediately. It was also decided to shoot every tenth German soldier, apparently, although I have no idea if that sentence was carried out."

"Do you wish that it was?" Basil asked.

Harry paused for a long time. "I would gladly have torn the officer's head off with my bare hands, and I've often imagined his screams while I did so," he said. "As for his men, no, it's not – there's no satisfaction in that, is there? Just boys like mine was."

They sat in silence for a while, then Basil asked, "All this runs through your head day and night, does it not?"

"Every minute."

"Far worse for you than for him," said Basil. "For him there wasn't even time to know fear. Just the briefest instant of uncertainty, and then blackness, nothingness, no pain, nothing at all. A life that was no less wonderful for being short, and a life that was blessed in many ways, with nothing but blessings really, until it just ended, without warning, like that, never to know anything of the sadness and decay of earthly life."

Harry moved uncomfortably, and Basil sent up a small prayer that saying these things, that he truly believed, might not sound hollow.

"Yes, I do know that," Harry said. "I am proud that he acted as he did, and if he had to die out there I know that it could have been very much worse." He stared at Basil, tears still falling. "But I can never accept that he had to die. Never."

Basil suspected Harry had probably had all the comfort he could bear just then. Nonetheless, he asked "Does prayer help?", in case Harry was waiting to be asked, but he shook his head and said it did not, not yet, thank you Basil. So they talked for a short while about the Battle of the Aisne. Basil trusted that the deadlock would be broken soon, and Harry told him that it didn't look very promising.

Arlette knocked on the door, and cautiously leaned in to say she'd had a light supper prepared for the two of them. Basil got up and clumsily hugged her. He didn't know her at all and Frances had told him little beyond saying that she was pleasant enough. She smiled and nodded slightly at him, then hurried away. The two men went to the dining room and ate some very decent cold roast pork, with quince jelly, and an excellent cheddar.

"You must certainly stay the night, Basil," said Harry. "You can't ride back in the dark."

"That's very kind of you," said Basil. "But it's amazingly light out there tonight so I'll probably ride straight back home." As they relaxed with a glass or two of madeira, Basil tentatively ventured to bring up a different topic.

"It concerns your late mother. Well, more your father really," Basil said, ready to abandon the topic instantly if need be.

"Do go on," Harry said. "I'm always trying to turn my mind to other matters."

Basil told him, as well as he could, what Mrs Pickersgill-Cunliffe had said to Frances back in August, concerning his father's agitated state in the days before his accident on the railway, and his possible financial worries. Basil said he realised that the old lady's mind had been wandering a good deal in her final months, but Frances felt it might be something important. She was worried now that she hadn't told anyone about it at the time; Mary Harriette at least. "I suggested it would be better if I raised it with you," Basil concluded, with an apologetic smile.

"Very sensible," Harry agreed.

"I'm sure there's nothing in it," Basil said. "But I did feel I should mention it."

Harry looked at his desk, the very one that had been in his father's study all those years before, and thought in silence for a minute or two. At last he said, "Well there may well be, actually, something in it. But Mother never told me any of what you say she told Frances. I'd always assumed she knew nothing of my father's financial dealings."

"Can you remember much about that time?" Basil asked. Harry said he remembered every moment of those days. He'd never talked about it until this day.

"I was away at school when the accident happened," he said, "and it caused quite a stir among the other boys, as you might imagine, to have the father of one their own number knocked down by a train.

"I'd been called into the housemaster's study on Monday after lunch to be told that my father had been badly hurt that morning, and during evening house prayers he made an announcement, and there was a prayer for my father's recovery. The chaps in my house seemed to be fascinated by the whole thing, and I resolved to give nothing away. And in truth, apart from the self-consciousness of being watched by everyone, I don't think I felt anything very much at first, I just knew that this might be something unimaginably big in my life and I should prepare myself. Just trust in the Lord, the Chaplain told me when he summoned me after lunch the next day. He made us pray together for a couple of minutes, but fortunately he soon hurried off to attend to other urgent business.

"Later on Tuesday Ellis, my older brother, came to see me straight from the hospital, and he assured me that things were going along quite well, and there was no great cause to worry. Similar brief bulletins of this nature arrived by post during the days that followed. Then on Friday or Saturday my housemaster called me in to tell me that my father had had his left leg amputated, below the knee. I asked the house master when that had been done. "Oh, just a couple of days ago I believe. He's making excellent progress though." I couldn't believe he'd known this all that time and not told me.

"Ellis came to see me again that day or the day after. Apparently our father's condition was still very serious, but he'd seemed very spry earlier that day, and everyone was hoping that it might not be necessary after all to remove his other leg. Things went extremely quiet over the following week, and I think I began to hope that it would not turn out badly after all. But the following Sunday before evening chapel, nearly two weeks after the accident, my housemaster invited me for tea and cake by the fire, and the Chaplain was there too. I thought they were going to tell me that Father had died, but they just said that he was very poorly. I couldn't understand what they meant by that. *Very* poorly, I'm afraid, the Chaplain said.

"I was called out of his Latin lesson in the middle of the next morning, Monday, and directed to the house master's study where Ellis was sitting in silence, looking at the floor. My housemaster solemnly told me that my father has passed away early that morning, and then he shook my hand. After all these years I still detest the man.

"I returned home with Ellis and by the time I got back to school some days later, I discovered that interest in my father's accident had grown considerably amongst my school-friends. At first they simply came up to me, shook my hand saying grown-up things like 'heartfelt condolences old chap' and 'deeply sorry to hear your news'. I kept noticing conversations being quickly curtailed whenever I appeared, and on Friday I walked into my best friend's study and found him with two other friends clustered around a newspaper on the desk, one of them reading out loud from it. They were horrified to see me there.

"I asked them what on earth they were doing and they told me that it was the report of my father's inquest. They said I should probably not read it and I told them that was for me to decide. I read it all through without a word, and then asked them what else they'd collected anything about the accident and very sheepishly they delivered up a considerable number of different newspaper reports and pieces cut out of magazines, a couple of which one of the boys admitted had been sent to him that very day by his father. They even gave me a copy of *The Times* for the 22nd, the day of the accident, which they'd stolen from the school library.

"I couldn't understand what on earth they wanted with that, and they told me it was what my father had been reading when he was crossing the tracks. The thought it might provide a clue as to what happened. I picked up all the papers they'd amassed, and went off with them slamming the door behind me. I've kept every bit of it ever since.

"I'd be happy to show it all to you, if you're interested," Harry suggested, and Basil said that he was, yes, very much.

Harry brought out the old box and turned a number of old and browning news clippings out onto the desk. Start with the shorter news reports first, Harry advised.

"I don't quite understand," Basil said immediately. "*Mr Cunliffe was head of the influential American banking firm John Pickersgill and Sons until its dissolution a few years back, when he retired, at a comparatively early age, with a large fortune.* So where was he going to that morning, in fact?"

"Who knows?" said Harry. "This was not a topic that my mother would ever discuss. She said she had no idea of his business dealings, and that quite rightly he never discussed such things with her. She said that as far as she knew he hadn't retired. My brother Ellis thought our father probably still kept up with his many contacts in London, and was probably involved in important deals, and so on. He did go up to London quite regularly, but who knows what for." He handed a longer clipping to Basil. "Here's the actual inquest report. It's the thing that goes into the greatest detail."

Basil read it through very carefully, and then went back to the start and tried again. "It's quite confusing about the trains and all that," he admitted. "Which was the up line and which the down?"

Harry drew a little sketch. The road from Hooley House, he reminded Basil, was to the west side of the railway, the side of the station ticket office and the up-platform for London. At the northern end of that platform there was a crossing for passengers going to the down-platform, and just north of that crossing a signal box, which obscured your view of the trains coming down from London if you were close to it.

As the inquest report made clear, there was a seat on the down-platform where his father liked to sit and read his paper in the mornings. Apparently he didn't usually take a train up to London when he first arrived at the station; he would cross the lines to read his paper on the station bench, and then presumably go back over for a London train later on. Do you follow? Harry asked, and Basil nodded.

The family clearly never read the inquest report properly, said Harry. "Perhaps that's understandable," Basil suggested. "Too painful."

"Maybe," said Harry, "but they tell it wrong, they always smooth over the inconsistencies in the story, or things they'd rather not know about. They never get the order of events correct, or where he was going at the time he was hit. My mother, or Mary Harriette, or Ellis even. It was always nonsense like 'he was crossing the line to catch the London train' and 'he was absorbed in his newspaper, and thrown along the platform'. Well, as you can see from the inquest report, he was crossing *away* from the platform for London, he could not have been thrown *along* the platform because he was *between* the tracks when the train hit him, and he was *holding* the newspaper in his right hand not *reading* it when he was hit. And they talk about him going to work as if he'd never retired." When Harry had tried to correct any of this at the time, they'd just shake their heads and tell him, well, no-one can know for sure what happened, and never will. And you certainly don't know better than everyone else (you're far too young).

Harry passed Basil the biggest item in the pile, *The Times* for the Monday morning of the accident. "Turn to page 5," said Harry, "and go to the bottom of the third column."

Basil saw it immediately: THE COMMERCIAL PANIC IN AMERICA and then *The pressure at the banks and the excitement in commercial circles are intense.* The *Times* seemed to be suggesting that a major crisis had threatened, and been averted, but Harry felt sure that the paper played it all down in order to avoid fomenting further panic. In reality, it turned out to have been a major financial disaster with serious long-term consequences. It had begun the previous Friday with the collapse of the revered counting house of Cooke and Co, which had made a fortune during the Civil War. As soon as this happened railroad shares and corporate bonds began to crash, and a panic ensued that threatened the American banks, and any banks associated with them. Such as Pickersgill and Sons."

"Did it suffer badly?" Basil asked.

"Ellis asked Uncle William about that, and he just said that it was his business and none of ours. After that Ellis couldn't bear to raise the subject again."

"But as far as you know," Basil said, "was your father right to be worried about his finances? Did anything emerge after his death?"

Harry shook his head. "No-one knows. He may have lost money at this time, or previously. I believe there may have been some disappointments in the will."

"So," Basil asked, finding himself suddenly intrigued, "what do you really think happened that morning? In the light of all these facts?"

"I think," said Harry, "that there are only two possible versions of what happened. Either dreadfully bad fortune or wilful self-destruction. The facts are as reported at the inquest, the only question is whether or not my father intended to die. My mother's recollection of that weekend merely confirms my opinion about this, really. My father was a man of excellent judgement, but on this occasion must have been severely distracted by his worries when he arrived at the station, a loss of concentration that was further aggravated by the approach of an unscheduled train. As a consequence, he made the fatal decision to cross at the very worst possible moment. Nothing deliberate about it whatsoever in my opinion."

Basil nodded agreement. "It could only be an accident. I can't see how one could manufacture such an occurrence, given the particular circumstances of that morning. Utterly implausible," he said with great conviction, at the same time wondering, but is it really?

"Exactly," said Harry. "I don't for one minute believe that he meant to throw himself in front of the engine. Which, I might say, is exactly what my school fellows liked to believe, as I know because I spotted some of them acting the very thing out on the playing fields, two of them playing the engine and another one my father."

"Really?" Basil asked, horrified. "School boys can be so very stupid. But I am quite sure you're right. Just an unfortunate combination of events, everything that could possibly go wrong did go wrong at exactly the worst moment. Poor man, poor man."

"He was immensely brave immediately after," said Harry. "Lying there and directing those around him to get him to on the next train to Guy's Hospital, get hold of his doctor, send messages to everyone. Incredible presence of mind, and telling everyone what to do, as ever."

It was around ten p.m. by this time and, despite Harry's further entreaties, Basil set off for home. He told Harry that he had an early service the next morning, but that wasn't true. He simply relished the prospect of this night-time ride. Admittedly, headlamps were not permitted now that it was war-time, but he was willing to risk turning his on if necessary on these deserted roads. And, as he had hoped it might, the wind had calmed and left clear skies under a brilliant full moon. Perfect conditions for a heavenly journey, and no other lighting needed at all.

The two men parted warmly, Basil risking a brief clasp of Harry's shoulder. As he moved off, though, he saw Harry standing still on the front door steps, looking bereft, thinking no doubt of other, less forgettable departures.

Rumbling serenely over deserted country roads, Basil pondered the truth of Mr Pickersgill-Cunliffe's encounter with the train. He let the known facts speak to him, and found himself conceiving the somewhat different story they might be trying to tell, his imagination fired by the brilliance of the moonlight. What if the poor chap *had* elected to kill himself and, knowing the penalties – legal, financial, reputational – that he would have to pay should he fail, made absolutely sure it would appear to have been an accident? The late Mr Pickersgill-Cunliffe was a successful man of business, with a renowned eye for detail and the power to direct people's attention and opinions where he wished. He would have done all he could to hide the fact that he meant to die.

When Basil finally reached his dark and silent house, everyone sleeping peacefully, he went straight to his study and typed all night like a demon, racing to keep up with a narrative that came to him from the strange and inaccessible part of his mind that always gave him his best ideas.

Dawn was approaching by the time Basil finally dragged himself up the stairs, to find his wife wide awake and waiting for him. He told her about his evening with her Uncle Harry.

"The poor man," she said. "There is nothing so terrible as losing a child. I know that for certain."

Basil agreed. "He is not at peace," he said. "And I can't see that he ever will be."

Each tried to contemplate the death of children, but could not.

"Harry was convinced that his father's death was nothing more than a sorry accident, to a man under considerable stress at the time," Basil said, changing the subject. "And he thought you were quite right in not talking to your aunt about it."

She was glad to hear it. "And is that what you think, Basil?" she asked. "That it was simply an accident?"

"I told him I thought so too," he said. "But the more I rode the more I began to think how it might have been otherwise. I wrote down my thoughts as soon as I got home. That's what I've been doing until now. Writing another family story for you."

"Saying what exactly?" she demanded to know.

"That it was not really an accident," he said.

"Why on earth would you want to write down such things?"

"Just see if it had the ring of truth," he said.

"And did it?"

"Not sure," he said.

"A night well spent then," she said. "And what will you do with it now?" He wasn't sure about that either. Would she like him to read it through to her? She said definitely not, and he felt relieved. "I think you should simply burn it," she said. She stared at him, waiting for his response. He seemed reluctant. "I mean it, Basil. You must burn it." He nodded at her, his eyes drooping with sudden tiredness. She clasped his wrist. "Come to bed now, dear."

On the afternoon of Christmas Day, they took the children for a walk up by the race-course to see the hundreds of soldiers camped there. Basil was their official chaplain, and would be holding a special service for them later on.

Frances rocked baby Margaret's pram slowly, and quietly watched the soldiers sitting outside their tents, talking, cooking, hanging up their washing, cleaning their guns, waiting. She thought of her father, and Basil's account of him at war. "They're so young," she said, after a while.

"Exactly," said Basil. "No idea about the ordeals ahead of them, just getting on with what they have to do."

They walked on, past the little terraced house where they'd begun their married life. "I'll miss this town, won't you?" he said.

"We'll be safer in Cornwall. Things feel so dangerous here now. We must keep the children safe from all the airships and battleships and bombs." There was a sudden loud crash of pans from the mess tent, and raucous laughter from the men nearby.

"Thank God you aren't going to war, Basil," Frances said, clutching his arm. The children came screaming past them, excited by the soldiers everywhere.

30

Torn from Mary Harriette's Diary. Addingham, Yorkshire, 1915

Words pour out of me, but there is no-one left to read them. My audience has departed, and needs me no more. My name is Prospero, I must break my staff and bury my book, and abjure my magic. Merrily shall I live now under the blossom that hangs on the bough. Now my charms are all o'erthrown, and what strength I have is most faint.

Once upon a time my sisters and I tried to bring harmony and understanding to the whole roaring family of Babylon but now God in His wisdom has scattered us far and wide, and confounded our language. We built our tower too high and now we are cast out.

Let me not dwell in this bare island by your spell. Let me go to Naples, to the warm south. Eastbourne! I have lost my dukedom, and now am Exiled to dark cold Viking lands.

I cannot talk to myself because the servants are listening. I cannot walk out into the woods and scream, because the old men there will hear me. I continue to write as I always have, but to no avail because no man or woman may read my words lest they think me mad! I am the mad tricoteuse of Yorkshire and I shall sail down through the Dardenelles to Gallipoli knitting shrouds for the

Turks and bed socks for our boys. I shall weave a righteous banner and raise it high in Constantinople.

When I was young I used to scream and scream until everyone left the room in terror. Now I write and write and nobody will ever read the words I write. I have knitted for so long that there is no-one left alive who has seen my hands at peace.

Call the chauffeur, I have a train to catch and I must have a corner seat. I am not well, I need apple pie, cream, brandy. Call the Bishop, and tell him I am lost. When the morning comes I am bound to be myself once more, although the longer we must wait for the morning to arrive, the less likely it is to ever come. To come ever. Ever to come.

Rose greeted her cheerily, when morning finally arrived, and asked her if she'd slept well.

"I did not, to be honest," said Mary Harriette.

Rose knew that. All night she heard her aunt shuffling around, going downstairs, coming back up again, her door slamming shut, things falling to the floor, the creak of the old bed as she tossed and turned. At one time Rose thought she might have even heard her shout something. It can't have been a happy night for her, and nor had it been a peaceful one for Rose.

"Are you feeling all right, Aunt Mary?" she asked, slipping into her nurse's mode.

"Yes of course dear," she said. "Still not used to living here, I think. The noises at night are not the same, the house makes its own sounds. Or maybe it's the silence that disturbs me, and I wake fearing that Mother has died."

Rose looked alarmed.

"I do know she is dead, dear," her aunt said, smiling. "But in the night, you don't know things in the same way, do you? Or even where you are sometimes."

Rose nodded. She was not a good sleeper herself, especially not now, feeling impatient all the time, waiting and waiting to get out of filthy London and go where she could do something useful. It was beyond her understanding that she still had not been given permission to go to the Front. What else did they need to know about her? There was nothing she couldn't do if she set her mind to it, but no-one would let her do this. She was asking for nothing, she wasn't afraid of the mud or the shells or the dreadful things she would see, and still her application stayed trapped in some bureaucratic purgatory.

She wanted her mother to persuade her father to help, now that he'd returned from America. He was no longer in the army but he knew influential generals and had once done something famous in the army himself, halted a riot without a shot being fired, although now he was a Christian Scientist and spent most of his time lecturing to Americans about the evils of medicine. Her mother did promise to ask him, but she also said, you know what he's like. It was Rose's only hope, time was running out, and the war would be over before she got there. To Rose it felt like the one chance she would have in her life to not be chained down because of her sex. She wanted to go to war because she was young, British and brave, and longed to be where a woman can do whatever she chose to do, whatever needs to be done. The Front was that place, she was sure of it.

She knew that Aunt Mary didn't want her to go, and would keep telling her, so she'd stopped talking to her about it. Her mother was coming over from Filey to pick her up later that morning, and Rose was impatient to hear what her father had said. Meanwhile they talked about everyone else but herself. About all the places where the other aunts were living now; how Frances was coping with her four children; Virginia's husband, happy killing Germans; Nell, who could not cross the Atlantic again until all this was over; poor Margaret, poor Harry and Arlette; and lovely John who was fully recovered from his injuries and back with his regiment in the Dardanelles. Aunt Mary said the papers were reporting that the Dardanelles campaign should soon bring an end to the war; hopes were high.

Rose started tidying up the breakfast things, just to keep busy, but Aunt Mary told her to leave that to the maid. "It's a beautiful day," she said. "Shall we take a picnic to Bolton Abbey when your mother arrives?"

Mary Harriette's sister Alice was the opposite of her in every possible way: practical, optimistic, confident, with a glow about her. Her husband was away as often as he was home, and that was fine as far as she was concerned. It allowed her to get on with all the things she liked doing: carpentry, designing buildings, building them herself sometimes. Living relatively nearby, she had been a tremendous help settling Mary Harriette into her home, which God knows the poor woman had needed at first.

When she left Northwood Hall at the end of March and moved up to Yorkshire, to one of the houses that had belonged to the Cunliffe family for several generations, Mary Harriette found herself in unfamiliar territory in every sort of way; rather more so than she'd anticipated. Not only a new landscape, and a harsher climate, but also a less certain status than she had previously experienced: whilst her name had deep roots in the town, she herself had none. She hadn't given it great thought when she arrived, but in her first weeks there a new awareness of her situation began to dawn on her.

It was a big thing to start having any kind of new awareness at this stage in her life; especially because so much else had filled her mind in the months since her mother died, and further back than that indeed, ever since the war had begun and dignified resolve seemed to get her nowhere. It had been nearly one year of almost unrelieved hell, which she had survived by doing what she had to do: mourn, oversee the dismantling of the family home, appear strong, make plans, worry about people, and say goodbye to *The Family News*, a greater grief than she could ever have imagined.

What kept her going was the grounding she had received from birth, in what it meant to be a member of her proud family. It had guided her throughout her life at all times and in every possible situation.

Moving up to Addingham had been the late Mrs Pickersgill-Cunliffe's intention for her senior unmarried daughter ever since her husband had inherited ownership way back in 1866, the outcome she'd skilfully engineered many years before as his young wife. When Mrs Pickersgill-Cunliffe died in November, Northwood Hall sold and its surviving inhabitants all dispersed, Mary Harriette had little choice but to move there. She accepted it as her destiny and tried to embrace Addingham with an open heart.

There had been prominent Cunliffes there since the 1750s. They built the mill down the road from where she now lived, and thereby accumulated great wealth and presence in the town. The locals welcomed the employment, but the management could never resist the latest cost-saving technologies, which led to riots, broken equipment, and the army. Presumably the work of disgruntled outsiders because the locals were always loyal and grateful, but there's still a risk in living too close to where you make your wealth. Not of course that that was any longer an issue by the time Mary Harriette took the family name back to Addingham but nonetheless, there was history in that town, and she could feel it rightaway.

The first time she went to a service at the church, knowing that the time had come to show her face, she found the experience surprisingly uncomfortable. She was acutely conscious of the eyes of the congregation upon on her, and tried to keep her own eyes away from the stone shields and stained glass windows and elaborate plaques all around the walls, all of them monuments to her own family: grandparents, great grandparents, great uncles, great everyone. There was even a window in honour of her poor father, who hadn't lived a day there in his life. Mary Harriette caught some of the congregation looking at her grimly, as if to say we know very well who you think you are.

But she wasn't about to be ashamed of her family, however determined she was not to succumb to the sin of pride, or any appearance of it. She *was* proud of them, the name did stand for something, even if she herself did not. She had no ambitions to be lord of the manor or lady bountiful, whatever the locals might imagine. Her own reality was more humble. The house needed repairs that she could barely afford, because she wasn't rich any more. The family money had been dispersed along with the family and was no longer what it once had been. On top of that, the servants needed more guidance. *She* needed more guidance. The garden needed sorting out, the damp needed drying out, she wanted a car – which her brother Harry thought a bad idea – and worst of all was that the lane on which the house stood was in a truly terrible state. This did not merely affect her own house but all the others along the lane, from the wealthy end nearer town to the small millworkers' houses just before the lane dropped down to the mill itself and came to an end. Its poor condition had been a big issue for a while now, and when Mary Harriette arrived she quickly picked up a feeling, expressed with varying degrees of subtlety, that she might wish to take the matter in hand herself.

There was a notable lack of healthy young men of the kind who would once have been easily persuaded to mend a road for a few shillings. Well there still were men, but most of them weren't much use, being too old to fight or fix roads. There was the usual smattering of those too cowardly and lacking in moral fibre to go to the Front, but they didn't deserve paid work. At least the older ones were determined to show that they could do younger men's work and took the responsibility of looking after things and the ladies very seriously indeed. Mary Harriette was particularly cheered when a pleasant elderly gentleman from up the road came over to meet her and tell her a few truths about the neighbourhood. A nice old chap, Mr Hall, of the middling order but well-enough educated and keen to help. And talk, which he happily did for nearly two hours.

He told her that he had already resolved to sort out the lane himself, and Mary Harriette did her best to encourage him with the offer of a substantial, but not excessive, contribution to the overall cost and some thoughts on his plan. They agreed on the next steps, which he promised to get on with, and that set him off about the various attempts to improve the town he had witnessed over his lifetime. She was struck, shaken really, by the way he kept revealing, unintentionally or maybe not, the part played by her ancestors in the story of every attempted improvement in the town. As he told it, at every turn it had always been "Well, the Cunliffes object", for one reason or another. But he told her how much he admired her house, and was very pleasant to her, so he probably meant nothing unkind by it.

Nonetheless, this was quite an eye-opener for Mary Harriette. It was the first time in her life, the very first time, that she had ever contemplated the thought that a family such as hers, well not just any family but *her* family in particular, could be viewed as anything other than a blessing to its neighbours. Her parents, her sisters, her brothers even, herself – all of them had always put the local community before their own interests. So strange that others might not see it that way.

Obviously this wasn't literally about her, her brothers and sisters, her parents; the people of Addingham knew nothing about any of them. But this was a message, a warning even, about what it means to be an important family anywhere; one that deserved to be taken seriously, because the world was changing terrifyingly fast now. It shook her to her very foundations and she reflected on it, alone by the fire, all evening long. Before going to bed, writing in her diary as she still did every day, she noted how this man had made her see that a dominant family might not be a Vehicle of Progress.

She told Alice and Rose about this, as they sat on a blanket by the river that ran below the haunting ruins of Bolton Abbey. She said that it shocked her to think that anyone might think of her as clinging to the past.

"Progress can look after itself," said Alice. "Mother used to drive us mad sometimes, did she not, with her unbending insistence on doing everything the way it had always been done? But maybe we need that right now. We look to you for that now, Mary."

"The world would fall apart if you ever changed, Aunt Mary," said Rose, squeezing her hand.

As they walked back to where Alice had left her car, Mary Harriette trailing behind them up the hill, Rose at last had a chance to ask her mother what her father had said about helping her application forward. Alice turned to her, and took her hand. "My darling," she said, "he absolutely refuses to do anything that would send his precious daughter anywhere near the war, with all those soldiers. He knows what they're like, soldiers. So maybe best to let the whole idea rest for now, don't you think?"

Rose was a bright girl, but the truth of what her father had done never even entered her head. What her mother knew, that she did not, was that he had already made it very clear to his old comrade in the War Office that his daughter sadly lacked the mental sturdiness to withstand the pressures of life at the Front, and whilst he wished it could be otherwise, strongly advised against her being accepted, however hard she pleaded. Alice thought it was a disgusting thing to do to the girl, but was hardly going to make him change his mind.

Not many nights later, Mary Harriette had a dream, from which she awoke in quite a state.

She found that she was inspecting the progress of the repairs to the lane alongside her house, and taking care where she stepped because the light was poor and the path was treacherous and wet. She could hear people in the dark, down the far end of the lane, and tried to reach them, to see how the scraping and digging was coming along. She saw the silhouette of a man trying to climb up out of a ditch in the distance; there was a thunderstorm in progress and when the lightning flashed she saw him slipping in the mud. She knew he was in trouble, and when she hurried closer she saw that it was John, blood running down his face from a wound in the side of his head. He struggled to his feet and then with a brave smile cried "on you go boys!" before falling back into the earth.

She had been certain for a long time that she would never see him again. When the news of John's death reached them a week or so later it brought Mary Harriette the comfort of knowing, at least, that her constant fears for him were ended now.

31

The summer solstice 1916, the war a familiar fact of life by now. Frances and her four children waved madly at the disappearing Basil, proudly kitted out in his splendid RAF uniform, as he chugged off down the lane on his special lightweight military motorcycle.

"Has Father gone away to War?" Godfrey asked, as the sound of his father's motorbike drifted off into the distance.

"No, you stupid boy," said his older sister. "Just to Falmouth."

"Falmouth? Must he go on a *ship*?" Godfrey continued, even more worried.

"Yes," said Helen, scenting an opportunity. "Just like Lord Kitchener."

"Is Daddy Lord *Kitchener*?" moaned Godfrey.

"Stop it Helen!" Frances said, firmly, "don't tease your brother." She crouched down to a distraught Godfrey. "No, darling," she said. "He's just Daddy, and he's only gone to join a nice friendly camp in Falmouth for a few days, and then he'll be home again. Safe and sound."

The postman came up the lane with letter from her mother, postmarked Piney Point, Maryland, USA. She'd finally left the Baltimore hospital where she'd spent many unhappy weeks, things going steadily from bad to worse with the discovery of gangrene in her foot, and a diagnosis of diabetes. Her life had hung in the balance several times, the condition of her heart causing considerable alarm, which in turn had delayed a much needed leg amputation. Frances asked her doctor in Truro about the prospects for someone in such a condition: not good, he was sorry to tell her, not good at all; it could only be a matter of time. Since then Frances had come to dread each fresh bulletin from across the ocean. She knew she would never see her in this world again; the time for home-truths had clearly passed by for ever, and she preferred to think as fondly as she could manage of her doomed mother.

The jaunty tone of today's letter came as a pleasant surprise. "I'm very happily ensconced in your brother's house," she wrote, "recovering from the journey and looking forward to spending a few days at the county hospital very soon, and be done with my poor old leg at last." There was no reason, Tom had apparently told her, why she might not enjoy some good years after that, in the bosom of his little family. Frances was far from convinced of the wisdom in making such rash promises, but was glad nonetheless that her mother felt hopeful after so many weeks of despair.

"What extraordinary news about Lord Kitchener!" Nell had scrawled. "A great man! and dying a hero's death, which he would have wished I am sure. But I couldn't help think of your father as I read of it." She told Frances, for the first time, how Charlie had seen things in the Navy he could never talk about, things that came back to him in his dreams sometimes and made him cry out in his sleep. "He was a brave man too," she wrote. "I know that for a fact."

Then, squeezed into the last tiny patch of space on the page, Frances deciphered a small afterthought that brought a tear to her eye. "I'm reminded of the silly little stories I used to tell the three of you, about your father's adventures at sea," her mother wrote. "You loved those, didn't you?" Frances certainly did, though she'd not thought of them as silly or little at the time. They were unforgettable, these stories that she and Tom and Virginia longed to hear in the bleak evenings after their father had disappeared from their lives without warning.

It was late in the day, sunlight still breaking in through heavy curtains, and children not much inclined to sleep. Frances had sent the little ones to bed, but allowed Helen and Godfrey to stay up with her as a special treat, on account of it having been their birthdays yesterday, and on her own account too. They were seated together on the big old vicarage sofa, Frances in the middle with a wide-eyed child either side of her.

"Once upon a time, when your grandfather was a very young man," she began, and the two children giggled in excitement. Not a squeak, she warned, if you want to hear the story of your brave grandfather *all* the way to the end.

"Once upon a time, when your grandfather, my daddy, was a young sailor, there was a big battle at sea," she began again. "This was long long ago, of course, when the ships of the Royal Navy were grand and tall and made of wood, with great high masts that the sailors had to climb, and large white sails." Godfrey started to ask if his grandfather ever climbed the mast, but she put a shushing finger to her lips.

"The ordinary sailors were called tars, and wore wide flapping trousers and striped shirts and big blue caps, and often ran barefoot around the decks, which were shiny and wet and slippery when the sea was rough. Your grandfather, whom everyone called Midshipman Charlie, was sailing all the way to the other side of the world for the first time in his life on Her Majesty Queen Victoria's Ship the *Euryalis*, which was the most important ship in the whole fleet because the Admiral, who was also very important, sailed on it too.

"A midshipman like your grandfather had to work hard day and night, taking orders from the Admiral and the

Captain, doing jobs all over the ship as fast and as bravely as he possibly could. He had to make sure the decks were washed and the door handles polished and the big ropes coiled up and the great heavy cannon balls carried up all the way from the bottom of the ship to where the big guns were, in case they had to fight off pirates and bad people like that.

"It must have been terribly exciting, don't you think? To sail all the way around the world looking out for pirates and bad people like that, and stop them from doing the bad things they liked to do all the time, and I'm sure Charlie and the rest of them had all sorts of adventures on the way, in faraway oceans filled with whales and turtles and giant octopuses. They probably stopped off in strange foreign countries to give gifts to the natives and buy food for the next stage of their journey, food like no-one had even eaten before, like flying fish pie and hippopotamus stew. Midshipman Charlie worked hard all day long, but he didn't mind because he loved adventure and couldn't wait to fight the pirates whenever they might have the good luck of finding some.

"And one day they certainly did find them, or rather the pirates found them first, because the air was suddenly full of bangs and crashes and great big splashes coming out of the ocean. A black galleon full of pirates had seen them coming, and was now firing off cannon balls at them without a word of warning. And that's when the big battle began."

Both Helen and Godfrey were staring wide-eyed at their mother, mouths hanging open, hardly daring to hear what happened next, nor daring to interrupt her in case she might not tell them.

"Midshipman Charlie had to duck his head whenever he saw a cannonball coming over, and he kept shouting at the other sailors to watch out and do the same. A few of the sailors did get hit on the head by cannonballs and one or two poor lads fell down dead, but the sailors mostly dodged them and the worst they got was a soaking from the big splashes that the cannonballs made.

"Midshipman Charlie was much too fast on his feet to get hit, and he ran all around the ship making sure the gun-men knew where to fire their own cannonballs back at the pirates. Suddenly he heard a shout from the other side of the ship, and turned to see several rough and ugly pirates climbing up ropes on the side of the ship with sharp shiny cutlasses clutched in their teeth, which they meant to use for killing British Navy men. Midshipman Charlie grabbed a big long sword and ran across the deck, jumping over ropes and cannons and hatches as he went, towards the biggest ugliest pirate of the lot, their leader the Pirate King, who was already on the deck by now, waving a giant cutlass around and making for the Admiral.

"'Not so fast my man!' your brave grandfather shouted, and grabbed a rope hanging from the mast to swing himself in the air right over to where the Pirate King swaggered. He let go of the rope at the last moment so that he landed right on top of him, with a great crash. The big ugly pirate pushed him off onto the deck, and came roaring at him, meaning to cut him in two with a single swipe of his cutlass. Midshipman Charlie jumped straight back onto his feet though, and the two of them had a sword fight that went on for ages and ages, up and down the deck whilst all the sailors cheered Midshipman Charlie on, until he finally had the roaring bully pushed back against the side of the ship, and made him drop his cutlass into the sea. In terror, the Pirate King tried to throw Grandfather off him and send him over the side into the raging sea, but Grandfather was too strong, and he grabbed a big long chain that was fixed to one of the cannons, and wrapped it several times round him before he could get away, so that he could only scream in helpless fury.

"When the other pirates saw what had happened to their king, they immediately turned and tried to run away, but they were much too slow. The British sailors grabbed them and tied them all up with rope, and promised them that it would be the plank for them soon enough me hearties, and no mistake.

"And then it was all over, and your Grandfather, Midshipman Charlie, found himself being cheered and lifted up high by all the other sailors, who set him down right in front of the Admiral. The Admiral shook his hand over and over, and thanked him for saving his life. 'You'll get a medal for this you know, LIEUTENANT Charlie,' he said, and everyone cheered and cheered, and Grandfather Charlie, who was a proper officer now and not a midshipman any more, blushed and modestly said, 'oh it was nothing sir, I was just doing my duty.'"

When he knew for sure that the story was ended, Godfrey asked his mother if all that had *really* happened.

"Well yes of course," said Frances, thinking of how her mother always used to answer that very question. "Exactly as I told it."

"I'm sure Grandfather must have been a most handsome sailor," Helen said, nodding solemnly to herself.

Once she finally had the children in bed, Frances decided to see if she might find a photo of her father as a young midshipman, to show the children. She thought she remembered seeing such a thing as a little girl, back in America. The only one she had herself was of a much older and wearier looking man, nothing like the dashing hero she'd told her children about, and imagined for herself. She decided to look in Basil's box of bits and pieces where he'd stored the letters her mother had given him. Perhaps there were mementos still in there that he'd forgotten to pass on to her, or decided to keep from her for her own good.

Sadly though, she found nothing more of her father there, no other letters, no pictures, nothing. There were just a few abandoned fragments of the writing that very occasionally Basil did for pleasure rather than just to pay the bills. Nothing much: just a couple of first drafts of the pieces he'd done for the Family News, an attempt at a humourous poem about a disastrous outing with a girl on a motorcycle with Punch? scrawled on top, and a long carefully typed piece called *A Fateful Decision*, which she'd never seen.

She looked more carefully at this, because it was beautifully typed out, and not full of scrawlings and crossings-out like the other pieces there. Gradually it dawned on her that this must be the thing he'd told her about ages ago, his account of her grandfather's railway accident that she hadn't wanted to read, that she'd told him to burn straightaway. She read it now, all the same.

32

A Fateful Decision

Mr C knew this railway better than most, certainly
better than any other passenger who travelled from
that Station. He knew which trains came through,
and when, and how quickly; he knew how far away
they were when you first saw them, how long it would
take for them to arrive, the noise they made as they
approached and the noise they made as they went
past.

The Junction was rather a dreary station, if
truth be told. There was not even the smallest of
buffets or a warm room to shelter in, only a single
bench on the down platform which was empty most of
the time. Mr C had never thought of sitting upon
it when he was still an active man of business, but
since his retirement he had had to forge purposeful
procedures for running a life that was now largely
devoid of purpose. He was certainly not yet ready to
stay at home during the working week, and incur the
disrespect of his wife and servants. He continued
to travel to London, where he sometimes conducted
certain items of business, had lunch in his club,
perhaps stayed overnight in the London home, and
spent the evening at the theatre or the opera.

But he was never in a hurry to take the London train, preferring to start the day, having left home at the time he had always left for work, sitting on the station bench, reading The Times and watching the world go by.

Watching trains go by, that is — the ones that stopped at the station, the ones that went thundering through and occasionally ones that were not on any timetable and appeared without warning. He had been using that station for a good fifteen years now but had never until his retirement given thought to the mechanics, one might even say the science, of the comings and goings of the trains.

A science upon which, most importantly, the safety of the railway's passengers depended, given the fact that they had to walk across the lines every day, boards filling the spaces between the metals, located at the northern end of the platform just short of the signal box. Mr C. knew the dangers of over-familiarity and the necessity of paying attention every single time one went over but he had never really known the moment at which it was no longer safe to cross when a train was due, nor how one was to make such a judgement in the first place.

Now that he had all the time in the world, he set himself the challenge of finding the answers to such questions and, being the man he was, he approached the problem scientifically, first of all amassing the necessary data. From the window of the trains he travelled on, he located the quarter-mile distance markers, placed all along railway track from London down to Brighton, that were closest to the Station in both directions. He identified points of reference relating to those markers that could be seen from the Station in each direction — a tree, an old hut by the track, telegraph poles – and one morning very early, walked a little way alongside the track, pacing the distances carefully, in order to locate additional markers for both an eighth and a sixteenth of a mile from the station in each direction, in the interests of precise calculation.

His tools were a notebook, his hunter watch, and his analytical mind. His point of reference at the Station was the edge of the passenger crossing nearest the approaching train. If the front wheels of the engine of an express train approaching from the north passed the three quarters of a mile marker, and the one quarter mile mark 45 seconds after, he knew first of all that it was travelling at 40 miles per hour, and secondly that it would therefore arrive at the level crossing in 22½ seconds, in which case he could amble across when it was just a quarter of a mile away.

If he dallied longer, until the engine reached the 220 yard marker, then there would now be just eleven and a half seconds remaining in which to make a safe crossing, which was feasible if he walked briskly but hardly prudent, given the risk of stumbling, or attracting the unwelcome attention of the station master.

He set about verifying his calculations most rigorously, just standing by the rails and <u>imagining</u> crossing at a particular moment before an approaching train's arrival, to see if he would have survived the attempt by counting out the seconds in his head. He soon found himself having become so adept at these visual estimates and imagined crossings, that he was increasingly able to rely on the intuitive judgement to which his mathematical efforts had given birth, rather than try to do actual calculations as a train chuffed and clattered towards him. Rack of eye, not algebra, became his primary means of measurement and guarantee of safety. Satisfied with the extent of his rigorous testing, he knew that he had his crossing times down pat, and would calmly wander across to the far side whilst others hovered nervously at the side just because they could see a train approaching in the distance.

Not that he actually ventured any really close shaves, much as he was tempted to, because he detested the thought of being reprimanded by anyone, anyone: stationmaster, porter or elderly passenger. The pleasure he derived from all this, really, came from the mental peace that settled over him when he concentrated on the trains, from the love he had come to feel for them: for their engineering, their relentless power, their magnificence. He could feel the comings and goings of all of them in his bones by now.

On Saturday September 20th, a messenger boy brought a note to him from his brother W., directly to the greenhouse where he had been working diligently all morning, tending his exotic plants and listening to the passing trains, whose weekend schedule was a mystery to him.

The note read Major financial crisis in NY, come immediately, W. His brother (not a man of many words) lived a short carriage ride away, in a somewhat grander house than Mr C.'s, on account of being the older brother. When Mr C. arrived, W. wasted little time on pleasantries and outlined the events that had taken place in New York the previous evening, the information having come through to London via the transatlantic telegraph during the night.

"We are ruined," Mr C moaned, when he could at last find his voice.

"Well, old chap," said his brother, "I'm sorry to say that it looks particularly bad for you. I think, as a consequence of my efforts at diversifying my assets in recent years, that I myself might manage to slip through this difficulty relatively unharmed, to be honest."

Mr C. could only nod, stunned and disorientated.

"It does look," continued his brother, "as if the bonds that you had taken out recently against your debtors' default are themselves forfeited. It could well be that you will yourself soon incur debts that will swallow up what remains of your income."

"Everything?" whispered Mr C.

"I regret to say, yes," said his brother. "Apart, that is, from your very substantial life insurances, which obviously count for nothing whilst you live."

Mr C. stared at his brother in disbelief. What was he saying? Surely not.

"Is this all certain?" he croaked.

"There are obviously circumstances in which your own liability within the situation would be discontinued immediately, thus protecting your existing assets even though you lose all other income."

"Circumstances?" he gasped at his brother, who nodded slowly and silently at him.

"Should the worst occur, you understand," W. then said. "Should the worst occur. But perhaps there is no need for that. I will of course do all I can to assist you and your family through the most difficult period. You will certainly be forced to sell both your houses rightaway, I am afraid, but perhaps you will be permitted to retain one of your Yorkshire properties. Life could go on and I will ensure you all a respectable income though not,

obviously, anything commensurate with what you are
currently accustomed to."

Thank you, said Mr C, that is good to know.

Mr C returned home, determined to find a solution to
problems that his brother may well have presented
in terms more pessimistic than strictly necessary,
an approach that he had himself always favoured
until now, seeing the clear articulation of the
worst possible outcomes as the absolute sine qua
non of responsible banking. On this occasion,
though, he was rather more inclined to look for
any sign whatsoever of a silver lining to these
newly gathered clouds of doom. Without more than
a discouraging grunt to his wife, he hurried to
his study, and began to explore the state of all
his assets, including, crucially, the ones he had
always kept hidden from his brother.

He worked through the night without sleeping,
unable even to contemplate sleep, studying every
contract, policy and bond certificate he possessed
and looking for a less desolate interpretation of
the current situation. He returned to his brother's
house early on Sunday afternoon, and outlined the
reasons he had found for a small degree of optimism,
in the hope that these would encourage his brother
to contemplate the mortgaging of his own bank's
assets in order to shore up his debt, should things
come to the worst. "I am not," he repeated one more
time, "entirely devoid of assets, and see no reason
why I should not come through this, if you would be
willing to stand guarantor in the short-term."

W., expecting no less of his brother, had
prepared his reply carefully. "I must speak as an
honourable banker at this stage," he said, "and not
as your loving brother." Mr C. gave a deep sad sigh.

"And as an honourable banker, my answer must be no, to my eternal regret as your brother."

He went home not knowing what he would do, but clear about the fact that if action of any kind was to be taken, it must be taken quickly. He slept for a short while in his armchair, until his wife came in and demanded to know what was happening. It seemed to him, in fact, that she already had some idea, and had probably been into his study in his absence. "Mind your own damned business," he growled.

"Mind your own damned language," she said, and slammed out the room.

He finally accepted defeat around two a.m., his whole body aching, his neck in burning pain and his head intolerably throbbing. The one thing he knew above all else was that this must be done before the panic in New York infected the London Stock Exchange on Monday morning. He could think of a thousand reasons not to go through with such a desperate plan but, try as he might, it was a prospect less dreadful than that of his family being thrown out into the world without any of the benefits that he had struggled to provide them throughout his life. 54 was hardly old age, but a decent span to have attained nonetheless and he had thought on occasions that taking control of one's own end was a manly and honourable deed.

He had read once in The Times that the act of suicide was known to favour certain conditions, and thrived on the following three in particular: a) a melancholic and pessimistic disposition; b) financial difficulties, chronic, acute, or both; c) the wherewithal to commit the act effectively. Whilst he personally would have argued with the suggestion that he in any way qualified for the first one of these, he had to acknowledge that the other two obtained in abundance at this particular moment. Especially the final one, in that it was essential, if life insurances policies were to be honoured, that there could be no suggestion whatsoever that suicide was involved.

If there was one respect, at least, in which he was still in a strong position to exercise control over his own destiny, it was this. He had made an entirely rational decision, he was sure of that, as he was sure also that he knew enough to do the thing properly. Maybe his desire to understand everything about the speed at which trains roared over the passenger crossing concealed a perverse attraction to the idea of sudden violent death, but if that was the case, it was too deeply concealed for him to be aware of it.

"I did this for you and for the good of our family, you know," he said to his wife, who had sat beside his hospital bed for several days by now. "I could not tolerate the thought of you all being made destitute. I was clear in my mind. There is no need to be sad."

Mrs C. grunted, and dismissed this remark with a flick of her hand. "Your mind is wandering, dearest," she said. "It was an accident. If you had meant to die, I am sure you would not have failed as you did."

He would have liked to tell her about the change to his plans that had been forced upon him at the very last minute, but he did not have the energy to explain that he had only been afforded a split second in which to make a judgement, and it turned out to be the wrong one.

It was hardly his fault. Just as he was calmly walking towards the level crossing, watching out for

322

the scheduled Hastings train on the down line, he suddenly heard the whistle of an unexpected train coming up from behind, on its way to London. It was not going fast, and for a moment Mr C. wondered, recklessly, if he might modify his plan and throw himself in front of that but then he asked himself, what if it stopped at the station? He had the ghastly vision of himself crouched on the level crossing in front of the wheels of a stationary engine, before a crowd of jeering passengers.

He consulted his watch. Rapid mental arithmetic told him that the approaching train, whatever it was, would have gone all the way through before the Hastings express came too near. What's more, it would appear to be indisputably the case that he had simply been overwhelmed by trains coming at him from every direction at once. It was a Godsend, a sign that confirmed the correctness of what he was about to do.

Except, of course, that in the event he did not get it quite right. The plan that he had fashioned so meticulously during the night required him to start walking slowly and deliberately, eyes fixed on the ground, at the moment the Hastings express passed the 110 yard mark. He knew exactly the speed at which he should walk in order to place himself in front of the engine with hardly a second or so to spare, just time enough perhaps to turn towards the driver in a vivid dumb-show of surprise.

But he had never practised these timings in the perceptual wake of another train passing so unexpectedly and so closely a moment earlier, and he failed to afford himself sufficient time to locate and focus clearly upon the 110 yard marker before the express, which was on schedule and approaching fast, passed it. He blinked hard twice, to clear his sight, and it was that second blink that ruined his plan. Unsure whether he was too soon or too late, he then set off at the intended pace but just a moment later was horrified to realise that the train had already arrived. He tried to spin round and retreat, almost made it indeed, but didn't manage to get far enough away from the engine to avoid the impact of the driver's step.

He looked at his wife, appealing silently for her understanding, wearily letting out his breath for a moment and lying quite still. She reached out and stroked his forehead. "Whatever your intentions, my dear," she told him, "I know that they were honourable. But we cannot choose our own fate. It is all God's will, our lives are in His hands and not our own." He did not know as yet if he was to live or die but on balance, given the way things were going, remained confident of the latter outcome.

Frances read the whole piece through a second time, trembling slightly to think that something so fanciful could possibly be true, and knowing that she must burn it straightaway, whether or not it was. Nobody – no-one in her family – would be able to forgive someone from outside the family, not even Basil, for desecrating the memory of the very first Pickersgill-Cunliffe in such a way. She could not possibly risk it ever being found even if the more she thought about it, the more she believed every word. What a clever man that husband of mine is, but what a fool as well, she thought, as she put the thing in the grate and struck a match.

For the avoidance of unpleasantness, as much as anything.

EPILOGUE

Family Items – Ghost News

♦ Lieutenant Jack Reynolds Pickersgill-Cunliffe, whose death at the Battle of Aisne was reported in the issue of October 1914, continues to wander the fields of Northern France in the company of fifty thousand other souls, trying to comprehend the end that came without warning to an unfulfilled life.

♦ Miss Abigail Adams, who had the honour of acting as tutor to Mrs Basil Davies when first arrived in England long ago, is blissfully immaterial now and for ever in the misty peaks of Academe.

♦ Captain John Cunliffe Pickersgill-Cunliffe, whose leadership to his men at Gallipoli proved to be such an inspiration, is currently at large in boundless jungles, seeking new challenges and fresh game.

♦ Mrs Helen Dale Pickersgill-Cunliffe is reputedly in Heaven, and has found very little there to disappoint her certain hope of eternal bliss.

♦ Mr John Cunliffe Pickersgill-Cunliffe, the eminent banker, butterfly collector and horticulturalist, passes eternity in the restful solitude of his extensive greenhouses that flank the railway in a spectral dimension of southern England. He appears to have found quiet contentment in the cultivation of heavenly plants, although the faint whistling of distant trains, that he once so loved to hear, no longer affords him joy.

+ Mrs Elizabeth Camilleri, late of Valetta and once most kind to one of our number, continues to haunt the dreams of sailors there with laughter and unaccountable longing.

+ Lieutenant Charles Hodgkinson (RN Retired), friendless and becalmed on the dark ocean of eternity, has out of the blue heard the siren voice of his brave widow Nell and, wafted by a favouring gale, flies over the waves towards her. We are not shy, she beautifully sings to her one true love, We're very wide awake, the Moon and I!

ACKNOWLEDGEMENTS
AND SOURCES

I am immensely grateful to the following for reading the book at different stages, and for their very generous encouragement and criticism: Tara Stubbs, Emma Huxter, Rebecca Eynon, Alison Gomm, Charles Crook, Lisbeth and Eivind Brevik, and Vincent Strudwick. Also to Kathy Davies several times over, for reading each stage as soon as it was finished; not to mention putting up with me writing the thing all the time.

Very special thanks are due to Mair Doyle and Jon Doyle for contributing to the design of the cover with their skilful choice and arrangement of the beautiful lettering.

I owe my cousin Nicky Donker immense thanks for introducing me to our shared ancestors, upon whom the book is based, and to the diaries of Mary Harriette Pickersgill Cunliffe covering the years from 1872 – 1935, an extraordinary record of the times. I also drew on the archive of *The Family News*, held in the British Library, and an unpublished memoir of the Pickersgill Cunliffe family compiled by Michael Godfrey Bell (2011). I made considerable use of as well as Dave Masters' excellent *The Fiery Wheel* (2014) and the published writings of its subject, the motorcycle journalist Ixion, my grandfather Basil Davies. This book isn't a family history but it would be nothing without access to that history and the surprises it contained.

The following were also very helpful: *Vibrant with Words: the Letters of Ursula Bethell*, edited by Peter Whiteford (2005), books about Charlie Chaplin, including the one he wrote about himself (1964) and those by David Robinson (2001) and Peter Ackroyd (2014), Vera Brittain's *The Women of Oxford* (1960), Peter Hartley (1973) *Bikes at Brooklands in the Pioneer Years*, Gates & Tatar's *Annotated African American Folktales* (2018), *Transatlantic Speculations* (2018) by Hannah Catherine Davies (no relation) and the doctoral research by Christophe Nitschke on the same topic.

I discovered Ernest Satow's fascinating *A Diplomat in Japan* (1921) on the Internet, along with George King-Hall's diaries and a great deal more besides, far too much to mention here. Finally, there is a devastating article about Lord Nuffield, the veracity of which cannot be proved but which I do firmly believe, that tells a story far worse than the one in this book; one that cannot be ignored – https://tinyurl.com/y5egbkas

Matador